WICKED SHADOWS

A. D. JUSTICE

STEELE SECURITY SERIES

WICKED *Shadows*

Steele Security, Book 5

A.D. Justice

PROLOGUE

Twenty-One Years Prior

Elle Moore crouched low to the ground, darting from her hiding spot behind a shrub to a new position behind a tree. Her best friend and partner-in-crime, Beth Condra, followed her, staying close on her heels until she joined Elle behind the huge oak tree. Elle covered her lips with her index finger, indicating for her cohort to remain silent before she pointed toward the driveway they were casing.

"He's standing beside Jeff's car," Elle whispered and dropped to her knees on the ground. "Peek around the tree, but don't let them see you."

Beth slowly knelt, keeping her eyes locked on Elle's. "What if they see me? What should I do?"

"Just do it real slow." Elle emphasized the words with an emphatic pump of her arms, her fingers spread wide and her palms down.

"Okay." Beth put one hand on the ground to steady herself and peered around the tree, her movements painstakingly measured. "I see him. He's with Jeff. And he's not wearing a shirt!"

"What? Let me see!"

Elle jerked Beth back and quickly assumed her partner's vantage point. She was mesmerized by the black-haired, muscular young man with her brother. "Oh my gosh," she gasped. "Is he supposed to do that out here? He's almost naked. What if someone calls the cops on him?"

His athletic shorts sat low on his waist, revealing all of his upper body, from his broad shoulders to his narrow, muscular waist. Elle blatantly stared, completely enraptured by his presence, and wished there were a tree closer to the driveway so she could get a closer look at him, her hero.

"I don't know why we're even doing this. I mean, he's *old*, Elle. He's, like, in high school or something," Beth complained, suddenly bored with their mission. "Why don't you just go out with Scott? He likes you a lot. He keeps asking you to be his girlfriend."

Elle shook her head from side to side but kept her eyes trained on her singular focus. "Scott's all right, I guess. But no one else will ever compare to Devon Kane. I'm gonna marry him one day, Beth. You just wait. Besides, the house down the street is for sale. Maybe we can live there."

"Yeah, that's a good idea. Then you'll still be close to home," Beth agreed, with all of her youthful wisdom. "It's too hot for this, Elle. Let's go swimming already. You promised we'd get in your pool today."

"In a minute." Elle automatically dismissed her friend's demand. "They're washing Jeff's car. They don't know we're here."

Unable to tear her eyes away, embarrassment and panic grew wild when Devon turned his gaze and met hers. His dazzling smile made her blush just before he raised his hand beside his face and gave her a small, knowing wave of his fingers. Her jaw dropped, her eyes flew open wide, and her muscles froze in place.

She was so busted.

Jeff was leaned over, washing the side of his Mustang GT when Devon's movement caught his eye. Jeff followed Devon's line of sight, and anger hit him as soon as he spotted the girls hiding behind the tree.

"Elle Marie Moore, get over here right now!" Jeff yelled across the front yard and threw his soapy mitt in the bucket.

"He used your whole name," Beth whispered, her tone rife with fear. "That's not good."

Elle considered her options. She could pretend she didn't hear him and run like the wind to the backyard, or accept the consequences and get it all over with at once by doing what he said. Resigned to the fact that there was no other choice but to live in the same house with her brother for the next few years, Elle decided to go with the latter rather than the former. Her eyes downcast, her bottom lip quivered as she maintained a death grip on her best friend's hand. The pair of seven-year-old, towheaded girls marched across the grass toward Jeff and Devon. Each step brought more dread than the last and made Elle's feet feel like they were weighted down with cement blocks.

She chanced a glance at Jeff but quickly dropped her eyes again when she saw his arms folded over his chest and an irritated expression boring straight through her. She'd been caught spying on them in the past, but that had been many spy missions before this one. She thought she'd improved her technique since then, but apparently, she was too sloppy. Future excursions would require more stealth, more craftiness, and much better hiding places.

"Elle, what have I told you about spying on us?" Jeff demanded.

"Not to," she mumbled.

"Why do you keep doing it? It's weird. You're creeping me out."

"Because she's in lov—" Beth almost told on Elle, but Elle jerked her arm down hard and cut her eyes at her friend.

"Shut up, Beth," she hissed. Glancing up at her brother, she continued. Her voice quivered almost as much as her legs shook. "We're playing a game. It's not a big deal, Jeff."

"Would it be a big deal if I tell Mom to ground you from the pool all summer?" Jeff taunted.

Tears filled her eyes and spilled over her lower lids then slid down her cheeks before they dropped onto the concrete below. "No, Jeff," she pleaded. "I didn't do anything to you."

Two large hands slid under her arms and hoisted her up in the air. Before she knew what was happening, she was held by protective, muscular arms against a warm, bare chest. "Leave her alone, man." Devon's tone held a strict warning. "She's just a little kid having fun playing outside. Quit being so damn mean to her all the time."

Elle looked up at Devon, devotion shining in her big, gorgeous, hazel eyes. He wiped the lingering tears from her cheeks and talked to her with the kindest timbre in his voice. "Hey, it's okay, Elle. Don't cry, sweetheart. You're my girl, aren't you?"

Unable to speak, she nodded her head enthusiastically.

"Then you should know I'll take care of you. I'll kick Jeff's ass if he's mean to you again. No more crying. Okay?"

That elicited a small smile from her, and shyness took over, forcing her to avert her eyes. "Okay."

"Whatever game y'all are playing isn't bothering us. Go have fun, darlin'."

"Okay, we will."

Devon put her down, and Elle stood rooted to her spot for a few seconds before she tilted her head back to look up at him again. Even at sixteen years old, Devon was taller and thicker than any of Jeff's other friends, but he never once made her feel like she was a nuisance to him. A small smile played on his lips while he waited for her to say what was on her mind.

"You're my hero, Devon."

"And you'll always be my girl, Elle. You remember that when you get to be my age and all those boys are hitting on you." Devon winked at her, causing the butterflies in her stomach to flutter and turn somersaults in her belly.

"Let's go swim already," Beth complained.

With her heart full and a smile permanently affixed to her face, Elle wordlessly grabbed Beth's hand. The two rushed to the backyard to join Elle's mom in the pool.

The scorching Georgia sun didn't faze Elle at all that day as she and Beth jumped into the lukewarm pool water. Devon's words kept ringing in her ears. *You're my girl, aren't you?*

"What the hell was that about?" Jeff's tone was accusatory when he turned to Devon.

"She wasn't doing anything but watching us, man. You're way too mean to her. We did a lot worse when we were her age. In case you haven't noticed, your little sister is already pretty for her age. She's going to be a knockout when she gets older. And she's smart as a whip.

"If you don't quit being such a dick to her, she won't come to you later when she needs your help. And believe me, she'll have guys all over her when she hits our age. She'll need you, and you'd better be there for her, or I'll kick your ass then, too. You should be glad you have a little sister who even wants to be around you."

"I fucking hate it when you're right," Jeff huffed.

"Then I guess you're always hating on me, huh?" Devon laughed, lightening the mood.

"Hey, you weren't right about that algebra test. I almost had to go to summer school over that."

"No, my answers were right. You weren't wearing your glasses and wrote down the wrong thing."

The two best friends finished washing their cars before they joined the rest of Jeff's family in the pool. Jeff's parents, Danny and Tanya, best friends and long-time neighbors of Devon's parents, were like a second mom and dad to Devon. Mark, Jeff's younger brother and the middle child, worshiped the older boys almost as much as Elle did.

Watching the interactions between the close-knit family was bittersweet for Devon. The shadows of memories from his childhood were always on the fringe of his happiness, waiting to bring him down.

∽

"You're doing *what*?" Tracey asked. Her hands dropped to her side, and she leaned toward her son.

"I'm joining the CIA. They offered me the perfect job, so I can't very well turn it down."

"You didn't say it was just a CIA job. You said you were joining the black ops team. That means you'll be a spy, doesn't it?"

"Among other things. Yes."

"Why are you doing this, Devon? You just got out of the Army. How many tours did you do in the Middle East? I lost count! Now you'll be permanently undercover, and I'll have no way of knowing if you're dead or alive. I'm your mother—I need more of a reason than it's 'the perfect job.' You have to help me out here."

He pulled a chair out and sat, joining his father Phil at the table. His fingers traced invisible patterns on the table while he avoided their heavy stares. His voice was uncharacteristically low when he spoke. "When Ava disappeared, I was supposed to be watching her. But I got distracted—I don't even know for how long. When I looked up, she was gone. The whole time we searched for her, I wanted to tell you it was all my fault but I couldn't bring myself to say it. I figured when we found her, you'd be too happy to punish me for not watching her. But we never found her. And I've never forgiven myself. This is my way of helping other people, even if they never know I've helped them."

Phil cleared his throat nervously, fighting the emotions welling up in his throat and constricting his ability to breathe. Tears flowed across Tracey's cheeks as she rushed to her son's side. She stroked his hair before holding his face in her hands, forcing him to look at her when she spoke.

"Devon, you were only nine years old. You were not responsible for watching your little sister. You were not responsible for Ava's abduction, and you couldn't have stopped it even if you tried. A grown man took her, and he could've taken you too. There isn't a day that goes by your father and I don't thank God to have you. You don't have to do this to make amends for Ava. We love you. Ava worshiped you. We've never blamed you for what happened, and we never will."

"I need to do this, Mom. It's important to me. I'll be okay—I'm a big boy, and I can take care of myself now." He gave her a small, reassuring smile before standing and pulling her into his arms. "I love you both. Don't worry."

"Devon, I'm your mother. It's my job to worry about you."

"If I find the man who took Ava, we'll never have to worry about him taking another child again."

Tracey sank into his arms a little farther, half in hope and half in fear he'd do just that.

1

———

CHAPTER ONE

Current Day

"Miss Sinclair, they're ready for you." One of the many runners announced through the closed door, letting her know the production crew had finished lighting the set for the next scene.

"I'll be right there," Elle called back.

So many other actresses would kill to be in her position. Her long, perfectly coiffed hair fell straight against her shoulders, the highlights and lowlights accentuating her facial features. Professionally applied makeup hid any minor skin imperfections that would've been magnified a hundred times on the big screen. She stared at her reflection in the mirror, barely remembering who she'd been before the madness of her life as a celebrity began. The one goal she'd worked so hard to attain had become the very thing she wanted to run away from most.

A second knock on the door meant the crew grew more impatient, ready to finish the scene so they could go home, only to start it all again early the next morning. Like a robot, Elle rose from her seat and plastered a smile on her face as she rejoined the cast and crew.

She hid her irritation when she realized the set had been opened to a select group of entertainment news reporters to help create early buzz for the movie.

Even on lower-budget films she'd starred in, she normally insisted on a closed set to keep the paparazzi out—and anyone else hoping to capture the perfect shot to twist and misconstrue into sensationalized lies for headlines. Such was the life of a movie star, even one classified as an on-the-cusp A-lister like Elle. She'd already experienced the backlash of the vicious rumors that ran rampant through the entertainment circuit. The general public apparently believed every word printed in big, bold letters, even without one shred of credible evidence.

Sex sells, but so do lies, she thought as she took her place beside her costar.

In front of the cameras, Jax Hart was charming and charismatic. His commanding presence on-screen filled the theater seats around the world and produced record-breaking opening weekends with each new release. Cast opposite him in any role was the absolute dream of every single actress, a sure bet to thrust her into the stratosphere of fame and fortune.

Off-screen, Jax Hart was actually Jason Hartman, and he was a far cry from the dashing and daring hero he pretended to be. Elle's agent, Ray Burke, often reminded her how hard he worked to land her the leading role, rather than a brief cameo appearance so many other models-turned-actresses would find themselves cast in. But she'd been in the entertainment business long enough to know exactly what Ray *wasn't* saying.

He was getting something out of the deal.

A trade-off had been made to benefit him. Otherwise, Ray would've pushed one of his established A-list clients instead. Judging by Jax's daily diva-worthy demands, she couldn't help but think somehow, she'd drawn the short straw in Ray's under-the-table deal. Regardless, if all the stars aligned, and the directors and editors worked their magic on this movie, she'd be able to pick and choose her future roles *and* possibly have a say regarding who the studio cast as her leading man.

With everyone in place, Elle switched gears in her mind and fully immersed herself into character. They'd reached another sex scene in the romantic drama storyline, and thankfully, it would be the last shot of the night. While Elle wanted nothing more than to get it over with and get away from her costar, she had to be convincing when she portrayed her character's desperate love for Jax's alter ego. As with every other scene, the only way she could even remotely do *that* was to lose herself in the memories of another man.

When Jax cupped her cheek with his hand, it wasn't his palm that radiated the heat through her body. Jax's lips brushed against hers, but her lips remembered the feel of another's instead. Every touch, every sound, and every scent pushed her further into the dream world she'd created and used as an escape from her unpleasant reality. Even though she was fully clothed, the flesh-colored suit gave the illusion of nudity while it added to the ambiance of the scene. In her mind, there were no barriers between her and the man of her dreams, their bodies completely intertwined in an erotic dance.

"Cut!" Vince, the director, yelled. "Holy shit, that was so fucking hot. If I didn't know better, I'd swear you two have been practicing that scene quite a few times in private."

Elle was abruptly pulled from her fantasy when Jax rolled off, leaving her feeling exposed and self-conscious, despite the fact that the bodysuit covered her completely. The smirk on Jax's face after Vince's comment said it all. He thought her performance was because she wanted *him*. Nothing could be further from the truth, but Elle couldn't tell him that and risk the repercussions.

"I guess it was okay," Jax replied with a dismissive shrug. "I'll know better when we review the film."

"You won't be reviewing the film, Jax. That's my job. Elle, you keep that up, and you'll have to prepare an acceptance speech before you know it." Vince clapped his hands and rubbed them together vigorously. "Hopefully, so will I."

Elle responded with her best smile, putting her acting skills to the test again. "Thanks, Vince. That would be a dream come true for us both, wouldn't it?"

Vince's response didn't register in Elle's mind, because Jax jumped into the conversation concerning awards and statues, showing no humility in his quest for validation of being loved for his abilities and not just his face. Annoyed, Elle walked toward her dressing room to change, lost in the make-believe world with the man she missed more every day. She silently mused over how he'd invaded all of her senses yet again, when he wasn't anywhere near her.

It'd be another long night of tossing and turning, dreaming of him and what they couldn't have. No amount of cold water could douse the fire he'd lit in her long ago.

"It's been a long day," Beth grumbled, echoing Elle's thoughts when Elle stepped into the trailer. "I'm beyond ready to crawl into bed and zone out in front of the TV until I pass out from exhaustion."

"That sounds perfect. We're out of here as soon as I throw my clothes on."

Elle grabbed her shorts and T-shirt off the clothes rack and quickly changed while Beth gathered their belongings. When they walked out, Elle heard Vince's and Jax's voices carrying across the lot. "Let's go the other way. I don't want them to see us and start another conversation. I've had all I can stand of Jax for one day."

"That guy is a serious jerk. He propositioned me again while I was doing his makeup today. I've only told him 'no' about a hundred times now." Beth shuddered at the thought.

"Yes, he's a complete ass. This movie can't wrap soon enough. But I'm so glad we're on the same set. After I accept my award, my first diva-demand will be to have you as my personal makeup artist for every movie."

"Hey, getting assigned as your personal makeup artist for life is my dream job. Don't tease me."

The forty-five-minute drive to their shared apartment in West-wood seemed to fly by, and they were home in no time. Beth would no doubt assume Elle's long day of filming wore her out, but the truth was she felt like she was revved up on a triple-shot of espresso. Her thoughts stayed on her dream man, reliving every moment of every encounter, remembering every word spoken, and wishing circumstances were different.

True to her word, Beth retreated to her bedroom and was soon sound asleep in her bed. The TV volume was high enough to drown out any other noise, and the light from the screen cast a soft blue hue over her room, changing with an occasional flicker. Elle paced in the living room, close to wearing a path in the rug with her back-and-forth marching. She gripped her phone, sorely tempted to dial the number she'd memorized by heart years before.

She couldn't bring herself to do it, though it tore her to shreds inside to deny herself the pure pleasure. She desperately wanted to hear his voice, but she knew once she did, it wouldn't be enough. Frustrated, she walked into her bathroom, started the shower, and washed away any remnant of Jax's scent from her. No amount of water could remove the other man from her thoughts, her fantasies.

When she dragged her soapy washcloth between her legs, her sex clenched from the slightest friction. The intensity of the sensation nearly brought her to her knees. Need for a release mixed with her desire for him, and it rippled through her, heightening all of her nerve endings. She removed the handheld shower head from its cradle to rinse the soap from her body and then let it linger at the apex of her thighs. She closed her eyes, dropped her head back, and pictured him there in the shower with her.

Frustration transformed into exasperation when the jet stream of water did nothing to bring relief. Elle quickly dried off then climbed into bed. As soon as she closed her eyes, the image of him was there again, mocking and teasing her from afar. Her hand slid down, finding the silky wetness between her legs. Since he refused to leave her memories, she stopped resisting and allowed them to run rampant through her mind. With his name on her lips, she climaxed while she envisioned her initial rendezvous with him eight years earlier.

Though, it still felt like just yesterday.

Lying in bed alone after a long day on the set, eight years after their first night together, she could feel his touch on her skin. She smelled the masculine scent of his cologne. Wood, amber, and earthy spices mixed with the heady aroma that made up his signature scent. She rolled over in bed, pulled the extra pillow close to her in a lonely hug, and let the tears fall wherever they landed. She missed him so much. At twenty-eight, she was fatigued and burned-out from modeling since age twelve, and she found she wished for a simpler life. With him.

What would her life be like if she'd stayed with him all those years ago? That question had played on a constant loop in her mind since the day she told him she had to leave. When he asked her not to go. When she'd decided her career was more important.

As she slipped into a restless slumber, words from her youth returned and taunted her with what she couldn't have.

No one else will ever compare to Devon Kane.

THE SUN HADN'T EVEN MADE A HINT OF AN APPEARANCE WHEN THE alarm went off. With her eyes still closed, she smacked the clock to stop the irritating noise that dared to pull her from one of the best dreams she'd had in months. The scene in her mind was more real-istic than any movie set she'd been on. Cool wind blew on her face, sending her long locks flying in every direction, as she strode hand in hand with Devon through the grassy clearing on the mountaintop. The weight of the world was lifted from her shoulders, and she was without a care in the world for the first time since she entered the modeling contest. Her demure smile was genuine and conveyed the contentment she felt inside—her life with Devon was simple. Easy. Stress-free.

"Elle, time to get up," Beth said from the doorway. "We have an early morning scene to shoot, so we have to get you into hair and makeup before Jax gets there. He primps longer than any woman I've ever seen."

With the grace and elegance of a zombie, Elle slid out of bed and walked straight to the shower. The spray of hot water helped her to peel her eyes open and face the long day ahead of her. She was thankful for one advantage of being on a movie set—her hair, makeup, and clothes would be done for her, sparing her the time and energy it would take otherwise. After she towel-dried her hair and threw on comfortable clothes, she and Beth left together for the studio.

The lot was eerily quiet that early in the morning, when it was still dark and most of the cast and crew on the other sets hadn't yet arrived. Security patrolled the area in golf carts, their serious expressions daring anyone out of place to step foot inside the gates. Still, when Elle and Beth stepped out of the car, a troubled chill surged up Elle's spine, and she looked around the darkened lot nervously.

"Everything all right, Miss Sinclair?" a deep voice asked from behind her.

She quickly turned and immediately recognized the familiar face of one of the foot patrol security guards. "Yes. Just spooked myself, I guess."

"I'll escort you ladies to the makeup trailer to make sure you get there safely."

Elle smiled and nodded, relieved they weren't alone, and turned with Beth to cover the short distance to shelter.

"Will Mr. Hart be joining you this morning?" the guard asked.

Elle stifled a laugh, knowing all too well why he asked about Jax's presence. The reputation of diva-like demands from some stars preceded them. With Jax, however, his outrageous demands made him the ire of most lower-level cast and crew members who'd had the misfortune of working with him. One of Jax's main rules was no crew member was allowed by contract to make direct eye contact with him —including security.

"Mr. Hart will be here early this morning, but I'm not sure what time. We arrived earlier than usual," Elle explained.

Elle had vowed early in her movie career she'd never be known as one of those actors—the ones like Jax who distanced themselves from everyone who supported their work. Keeping her down-to-earth personality had benefited her more than once. She'd found out first-hand that the people who were paid to cater to her needs were much more willing to make her time on the set easier just because she was kind to them.

When they'd stepped inside the trailer, Elle turned to the guard and gave him her sincerest smile. "Thank you for walking with us, Roy."

"Yes, thank you so much. Same time tomorrow morning?" Beth flirted.

Roy's smile spread across his face. "My pleasure, ladies. Have a good day."

Elle closed and locked the door, the uneasy feeling still lingering in her chest. Beth watched her movements closely as she prepared her makeup supplies. "What's wrong, Elle?"

"I just have a bad feeling, Beth. Nothing's happened, but it just feels like we're being watched."

"It's probably all the rumors that have been flying around the studio lots the last few weeks," Beth replied offhandedly.

"What rumors?"

"You know," she insisted. "About the actress who was reported missing from one of the other stages."

"I have no idea what you're talking about, Beth."

"Have a seat. We need to get started," Beth replied. She continued talking while applying Elle's on-screen makeup. "It's been almost two weeks ago now, but one of the actresses on another movie set was rumored to be missing. She didn't show up for work after they'd already filmed several scenes with her, so production is on hold until she shows up or they find a replacement."

"What do they think happened to her?"

"Some say she's in rehab somewhere and the studio execs are keeping it secret for her. But when a couple of the makeup artists said that wasn't true and something bad happened to her, they got in a lot of trouble. They may not be able to work on the lot again."

"That's really scary, Beth."

"Why? Maybe the stress got to her, and she's in the hospital some-where. You know how delicate all these actresses are."

"I beg your pardon," Elle replied jokingly, her Southern accent making a rare appearance in her tone.

Beth laughed at Elle's reply. "The first time you can't take a joke from me, I'll drag you out of this town and whip your ass."

"You've threatened me with that for years. Maybe I should try it and see if you'll really do it. I'd love to take a long vacation some-where far away from here."

"You know, there's a way you can do that. Pick up the phone, have your assistant make the arrangements, then text your agent and tell him you're leaving after you're already gone."

Elle inhaled deeply and released her breath on a long, wistful sigh. "I wish I could."

"Why can't you?"

"Oh, no reason, other than the little obstacle called a contract obligation that says I have to finish filming this movie."

"Minor details. You could always check in to a spa, otherwise known as a mental hospital, and take a nice long break."

"At this point, I'd even take that. But that reminds me what I was going to say before you sidetracked me. A while back, before this movie started filming, I heard about another actress dropping off the face of the earth during production. Why isn't any of this on the news?"

"Probably because she isn't well-known enough, Elle. I hate to say it, but it's true. Unless you're the female equivalent of Jax Hart, you're replaceable in this town. As soon as they find someone who fits the wardrobe they already have, the latest gone girl will be forgotten."

Throughout the day, Beth's words stayed with Elle, weighing heavily on her shoulders while she did her best to pretend she was someone else. The best part about the day was none of her scenes included Jax. Even though every scene required multiple retakes from different angles, the time seemed more productive without his pretentious presence on the stage.

When she and two of her costars left the sound stage building during a set break, raised voices immediately caught their attention. The trio of women stopped and gawked at the awkward scene unfolding in front of them. The normally bustling area between the stages was subdued, with the crew members using any excuse to avoid leaving the area and missing the conclusion.

"If you ever, and I mean *ever in your entire miserable life*, touch me again, your junk will be stuffed and mounted as a trophy over my fireplace. I don't give a shit what kind of badass you play on the screen, you're not man enough to handle me."

Katrina Fox stood in Jax's personal space, as close to his face as she could get without actually touching him, and her shouts carried across the lot, echoing off the many buildings and returning to the onlookers like an instant replay.

"Calm your tits, babe," Jax replied, his tone patronizing and his expression one of disdain. "If you're not into men, you should still give me a try. I guarantee you'll be back for more."

Katrina's hands curled into fists as her anger reached a tipping point. "Don't you dare try to downplay what you did or pass it off as my fault. I am happily married, and I've put up with your bullshit long enough. If I bring my husband on the set, he will kick your chickenshit ass. Keep your fucking hands off me, Jax. Or, so help me God, you will regret it."

Unwilling to accept her refusal of his overt advances, Jax's temper flared, revealing his true self. "No, Katrina, *you'll* regret it if you don't shut your fucking mouth and take it. You're nobody. You really think the execs will side with you over *me*? I'm their golden cash cow, baby. I get what I want, when I want, and from whomever I want. Your only job is to say '*Yes, sir, may I have another*' when I come for you. Keep causing a scene like this, and you'll be gone with a snap of my fingers. All those fat, old men you had to fuck to get here will mean nothing."

Katrina's arm swung back as she prepared to power through his face with her fist. Elle caught Katrina's elbow just in time and stopped her from following through with it. Katrina's head whirled around, fire shooting from her eyes, and a deep shade of red covered her face.

"Don't, Katrina. The trouble this will cause you isn't worth it. Take care of it through the appropriate channels," Elle urged her.

"You know as well as I do the studio talking heads will just look the other way for him," Katrina countered. Jax's smug expression made Elle want to finish what Katrina had started.

"Not if you handle it the *right* way."

Understanding lit in Katrina's eyes, and she nodded at Elle. "You're right. Thank you, Elle."

Jax's arrogant air instantly deflated when Katrina's fiery gaze swung back to him. Katrina stormed back through the door to her assigned sound stage, and Jax glared at Elle.

"You shouldn't have done that."

"No, Jax. *You* shouldn't have done that."

2

CHAPTER TWO

The next morning on the set, Elle's bottom jaw dropped to her chest when she reviewed the updated call sheet outlining the scenes that would be filmed. The last-minute notice aside, the number of set changes required ensured everyone would be on set until the wee hours of the morning.

"Can they do this?" Beth whispered as she gawked at her call sheet. "With our union contracts, can they legally get away with this?"

"Maybe not legally," Elle whispered back. "But they have a long arm, Beth. Don't get blacklisted."

Throughout the tedious hours of filming, Elle had to endure scene after scene with Jax, not only pretending she didn't despise him, but that she was in love with him. On more than one occasion, she mused about that golden statue and how it would be hers if she could only convey to the world her true feelings for her costar. Since everything was filmed as the set was needed, rather than in order of the script, her numerous scenes had thankfully been short ones. Her longest scene was scheduled at the end of the day, and she knew it would be her hardest scene to date.

"Get Elle and Jax set up for the next scene," Vince instructed. "We need to get as many finished today as possible. We're already behind schedule, and we can't get another extension on the time we have this stage."

While the crew scurried about, quickly correcting last-minute set details, the second assistant director left to fetch the main stars. Their workday had already been longer than the updated call sheets indicated, causing every crew member to inwardly grumble about the extra hours. While several whispered threats of calling their union representative the next morning, none dared to show their displeasure with the working conditions. Getting called back to work on another movie in the near future was more important than going home at the scheduled time.

"Elle, sweetheart, you're being such a trooper today," Vince praised her as she walked to her mark.

"My job isn't as physically demanding as our crew's jobs. As long as they're working, the least I can do is keep going, too."

Several nearby crew members looked up and gave her small, appreciative smiles as she sat in the side-stage makeup chair. When their smiles faded, Elle knew exactly who had entered the sound stage from the door behind her without even turning around. Beth approached her to freshen her makeup before the cameras started rolling again.

"How are you holding up?" Beth murmured while she worked.

"Okay, other than wanting to shave Jax's head and tattoo a pile of shit on it so everyone knows what a shithead he is."

Beth barked out a laugh and quickly covered it with a mock coughing fit.

"If you're sick, you need to leave. We can't have Elle catching a cold right now," Vince snapped.

"I'm not sick, sir," Beth replied without elaborating, knowing Vince wouldn't want to hear it from her anyway. Lowering her voice, she glared at Elle. "You can take the girl out of the South, but you can't take the South out of the girl."

"You would know as well as I do," Elle whispered back with a smirk.

Beth stepped back and admired her work. "There. You're perfect. Go break a leg."

"That's for theater work," Elle disputed.

"Then go break Jax's leg."

"Now you're talking," Elle replied with a chuckle.

"What'd the jackass do this time?"

"He barged into my trailer, without knocking, while I was changing clothes. I know he does that shit on purpose. Anyway, he offered his services to make me the best-paid female actress, if I'd service him on my knees right then and there. My hands were shaking from being so mad.

"Beth, I didn't even think about what would happen before I picked up the vase of flowers from the table and threw it at his head. He ducked, and it hit the wall behind him. Shattered glass flew everywhere. He spewed some vague threats at me and stormed off, back to his trailer.

"Of course, the noise was loud, and a few of the crew members came running. It was so sweet how concerned they were for me. The cleaning team rushed in and cleaned up the mess before anyone else realized what had happened. I'm surprised he didn't go running to Vince about me."

"It's too late in the process to replace you now. Production will wrap in a couple of days if we keep going at the filming pace we have today. Besides, the scuttlebutt around the crew is Vince is covering up something major, something that could be a career-ender. Most bets are it has to do with Jax harassing actresses and other women on the set, that he's crossed the line with the wrong woman."

"If that were true, Jax wouldn't have propositioned me. Vince would've made sure he had Jax under control, especially if it's something serious enough to affect their careers. It has to be something else."

"Hide that worried look on your face, Elle. Here come Vince and Jax. Time to put your acting skills to the test," Beth whispered while pretending to style a strand of Elle's hair.

"Elle, we're shooting the last scene you and Jax have together next. It's the breakup scene, so I need to see some real tears, real emotions, real heartache. Take a few moments to be alone and do whatever it takes to get into your character's frame of mind. We need you in top form so we can get this in as few takes as possible," Vince explained.

"You got it." Elle gave the reply he expected to hear, but inwardly, all she could think about was how thrilled she'd be to break up with Jax at the end of filming. Then she'd just have to make it through the months of press junkets with him, with all the fake articles about how their love was what made the scenes so authentic rather than their acting expertise. "I'm going to wardrobe to change into my costume now. Then we can wrap up this scene as soon as I'm all sad and depressed."

"I should hit wardrobe, too," Jax replied.

Elle narrowed her eyes at him and gritted her teeth. She opened her mouth to reply, but Vince beat her to it.

"You can wait on changing clothes. You have other things to do first. Besides, with all the set changes the grips are working on for the next scene, the wardrobe room is the only quiet place left for Elle to get into character. You stay away from that room as long as she's in it, or you'll deal with me, Jax Hart."

After she changed, Elle made herself comfortable on the small sofa in the back of the room, closed her eyes, and transported herself to another place and time. She drew on the memories she kept locked inside her, the ones she both wanted to forget and wanted to relive every day. Emotions welled up inside her chest when she released the first scene and allowed every second, every feeling, and every sensation to flood her mind. Once she started reminiscing, she couldn't stop the onslaught of sorrow that followed.

When she reached the point of no return, she rose from the couch and walked directly to the stage. For Elle, the emotional scenes were the rare times she wouldn't speak to anyone who wasn't written into the script. To remain in character and give the best performance she could muster, she immersed herself in the role and became the character. The character's pain and hers became a singular state of mind, and she poured her broken heart and soul into her performance.

When the final take was finished, and she'd recited her lines a dozen times with more heartrending emotion each time, Vince yelled "Cut." Elle blinked repeatedly, seemingly waking from a trance, and her gaze swung around the room. The familiar sound of sniffles floated on the air as others rubbed their eyes while discreetly whisking away the moisture gathered in them.

"You're done for the day, Elle," Vince said softly. "You can go ahead and change."

Elle nodded and briskly walked back to the wardrobe room. Getting into character was fairly easy, but leaving it behind was another matter in itself. She was unable to speak to anyone with her pent-up feelings still entirely too raw and barely under control. She was thankful that scene was the last shot of the day. She'd need the rest of the night to put the beast back in its cage so she'd be ready to work again the following day.

On the way back to their apartment, she stared silently out the window while Beth drove. Her thoughts took her thousands of miles away, a year into the past, and reminded her of how carefree she'd once felt.

"You've had a pretty rough day. Are you all right?" Beth asked, her voice soft but full of concern.

"I miss him, Beth. I can't keep living like this. It's been a year. Either I have to contact him, or I have to let him go." Saying those words out loud marked the first time she'd admitted to her best friend what had been weighing heavily on her heart.

"Have you tried calling and talking to him about it, Elle? I really think you should before you make any decisions. You've held on to him for a long time."

"I've thought about calling him more times than I can count, Beth. But I come to the same conclusion every time. If I meant as much to him as he does to me, I'd already know it. I wouldn't have to ask or wonder. So, I'm sure as hell not calling him to hear him confirm it."

Beth stretched her arm out and squeezed Elle's hand, offering what little support and solace she could. Elle's gaze stayed trained on the window, not seeing anything in the blur rushing by outside. The tears she shed on the set were real, but they were for her character's situation. The tears sliding down her cheeks in the darkness of the car were all for herself. For what she wanted more than anything. For what she'd never have.

Beth's ringing cell phone pulled her attention away from Elle. After a quick glance at the screen, Beth's eyebrows drew downward and an ominous feeling settled in her chest. "It's Analise, one of the makeup artists on the lot," she told Elle before accepting the call through the car's Bluetooth.

"Hey, Analise, you're on speaker."

"Beth?" came the tearful reply.

"What's wrong?" Beth asked, gripping the steering wheel.

"Katrina is missing. They think they can explain this away and make me shut up, but I know better than the lies they're spreading about her."

"Analise, I have no idea what you're talking about. What do you mean she's missing? What lies? Who's trying to shut you up?" Beth asked.

"She didn't make it home last night, and she didn't show up for work today. The studio executive assigned to our movie released a statement to our crew. It was more like a gag order, really. His statement said Katrina was going through a rough patch with her husband and had to leave town so she can pull herself together. The movie has been put on hold until she regains her composure because it would cost too much to redo all her scenes. He also said if we told anyone about this, we'd never work on a movie lot again," Analise explained.

Beth and Elle exchanged concerned glances.

"From a financial standpoint, that would make sense, Analise. From what I've heard, Katrina was in more scenes than not. If the movie's almost wrapped, that would be a lot of wasted money." Beth tried to calm Analise's fears with rational reasons why a production hiatus would make sense.

"That's true, Beth," Analise agreed. "Except, Kat wasn't having marital problems. They're crazy in love with each other. They're even actively trying to get pregnant. I talked to her husband Jay late last night and several times today. We've been looking for Kat everywhere. Now I can't reach Jay."

"Analise," Beth faltered. "I don't even know what to say. I didn't know you were so close to her."

"We've been close for many years. I don't advertise it because it just invites more trouble than it's worth. But Kat is one of my best friends, and our husbands even hang out together a lot. Beth, I know we're being fed lies. I know something bad has happened to her and now maybe to Jay. She would've called me by now. I'm scared, Beth, for her, for Jay, and now for my husband and myself."

"Are you working tomorrow, Analise?" Beth asked.

"No, the first assistant director told the entire crew to stay home for the time being. The executive and the director have a meeting with the investors to explain what's happening. I'm going out to look for Kat and Jay everywhere I can think to look."

"Don't do that," Beth warned. "I don't know what's going on with Kat and Jay, but I can tell you're honestly terrified. If you believe something bad happened to them, you have to stay as far away from it as possible. Go to your mother's house and stay in Oregon until they call you back to work or you hear from Katrina."

"But, Kat—"

"There's nothing more you can do now, Analise. Protect yourself and your family." Beth disconnected the call after Analise promised to leave the state and remain at her mother's indefinitely.

"Katrina was fighting with Jax when I left the stage last night. She said he'd put his hands on her, and she threatened to have her husband kick his ass," Elle said quietly.

"You saw it yourself? You didn't tell me about this."

"I saw them fighting. Katrina was about to punch him, and I stopped her because I knew he'd have her blackballed, or at least make her life hell for as long as possible. I told her to handle him the right way instead, so he couldn't fight back. What if my advice backfired on her somehow and they fired her?"

"What's the right way?"

"Release proof to the press if the studio execs won't put a stop to his harassment, then start legal proceedings against all of them. The bad publicity from the scores of women who would come forward would be too much for even their public relations team to bury."

"Just promise me you'll be careful. I don't know what's going on or where Katrina and Jay are. But you're a witness, and I don't want them coming after you. Just finish your scenes and get away from the lot. It has bad juju all around it," Beth replied, uneasiness filling her tone.

"No argument here. My scenes will be wrapped up in a couple of days, and I'll be free of Jax Hart until the promotional tour begins."

The rest of the drive back to their shared apartment was made in silence. Concern for their friend on top of an overly long and draining day left them both too exhausted to carry on a conversation. An hour later, thanks to interstate construction slowing traffic, they arrived at their apartment and retreated to their separate bedrooms. After Elle finished washing before going to bed, the events of the day caught up with her, took over her mind, and kept her awake past the point of fatigue.

She rolled over and grabbed her cell phone from the nightstand. She stared at the list of her favorite contacts for a few seconds before selecting her brother, Jeff. She let it ring a couple of times before realizing how late it was on the East Coast. He answered just before she ended the call.

"Elle? What's wrong? Are you okay?" Jeff answered, his voice thick with both sleep and concern.

"I'm okay, Jeff. I'm sorry—I forgot how late it was there, or I guess, how early. Go back to sleep."

"I don't think so, little sis. You don't call me for no reason, especially not this late even on Pacific Time. So go ahead and tell your big brother what's bothering you."

"Something strange is happening on the lot, Jeff. This will sound crazy, and I know it's big and there are multiple movies filming at once, and—"

"Spit it out already. You can explain it away after you tell me."

"Over the past few months, more than a couple of women have disappeared from the lot. The last one has me rattled, though. I just talked to Kat yesterday. Kat's best friend, Analise, called Beth tonight on the way home. She said the studio execs are lying about Kat's whereabouts. Analise was terrified something bad has happened to her friend. And..." She paused, afraid to speak the words. "I've had the eerie feeling someone was watching me a few times after I left the sound stage."

"Elle, if there's even the slightest chance something is off, you need to have a bodyguard with you at all times. Don't take any chances."

"I'm sure I'm overreacting."

"And don't dismiss your gut feelings. I'd rather you have a huge entourage of security guards and be safe than put it off and be sorry later."

"Okay, Jeff, you're right. I'll have Ray contact a couple of bodyguards first thing in the morning."

"I'm coming out there. I don't trust your agent to do what he's supposed to do. Do whatever you have to do to get me full access to the studio lot. You're not leaving my sight." Jeff was suddenly wide awake, his unease over the situation at maximum capacity.

"Jeff, you can't just leave your job to come babysit me because I have the heebie-jeebies. I'm not even sure I can get a full-access pass for you. I'll make sure Ray does his job, and there are always security guards on the lot," Elle argued.

"Elle, there may be guards, but that place is huge. There's no way they can be everywhere at once."

"I'm sure it's nothing but my overactive imagination."

"Your imagination has never been overactive like this before, so stop trying to get rid of me. Do I need to call Mark and have him come down from Paso Robles? He can leave right now and be there in a few hours to keep an eye on you until I get there."

"No, don't bother him, or Mom and Dad. I shouldn't have called you with this. With all the sound stages, there are hundreds of crew members on the lot at any given time. I'll get a personal bodyguard, and it'll be fine. I'm sorry I worried you. Go back to sleep, and I'll call you at a decent hour tomorrow."

"Okay," Jeff replied reluctantly. "If I don't hear from you early in the morning, I'm calling Mark, and I'm booking my flight to LAX."

Elle laughed softly, glad she had two brothers who would do anything for her. "Fine. I'll call you twice tomorrow." Lowering her voice, she added, "Thank you. Good night, Jeff."

"Good night, Elle."

CHAPTER THREE

"It's your favorite sister, calling to report in as ordered by her older and demanding brother," Elle announced when Jeff answered his phone.

"Smartass little sister," he laughed. "Have you called Ray Burke, the worst agent in Hollywood yet?"

"I call him that every day," she joked.

"Very funny. You know what I mean. My mouse is hovered over the 'purchase' button for my plane ticket so I can kick your ass before I protect it myself."

"I've talked to Ray, and two bodyguards will be waiting outside my apartment first thing tomorrow morning."

"Why do you still live in an apartment, Elle? You've made more than enough money to buy an outrageously big house in Bel Air or Malibu with a security system to rival Tony Stark's."

"I have commitment issues. This way, I only have to agree to a year-long lease, and I can pay my way out of it if I need to break it. Plus, the threat of finding a new roommate is the only way I can guilt Beth into never leaving me."

"Have you told Mom, Dad, or Mark about this yet?" Jeff asked, suddenly serious again.

"No, there's no need to alarm them. I don't even know for sure anything's wrong. I could be overreacting to nothing at all."

"So, you only wanted to alarm me because I'm the one who's clear across the country from you? The one who'd get to you last if anything did happen?"

"Exactly!" She burst out laughing. "No, Jeff, because you're the level-headed one. You were supposed to tell me I was imagining things and I needed to get over myself. You broke the rules when you agreed with me."

"I could tell you were scared, and you don't get scared for no reason. Elle, I did some research this morning on what you told me about that missing girl. Do me a favor, and don't walk anywhere without an armed escort, even around the lot. Those bodyguards need to be there with you today. Since you haven't called Mark to get him to come down and stay with you, I'll call and talk to Ray myself if I have to. But those guards need to be there today."

"What did you find out, Jeff?" Elle asked slowly, clearly not actually wanting the answer.

"Let's just say the entire story has already been all neatly tied up with a pretty pink bow on top. Pictures are posted that any idiot with a smidgeon of technical savvy can tell have been doctored. Quotes from unnamed sources that draw sympathy for her circumstances without giving any details or verifiable information are plastered everywhere. The director wishes her well and has promised to be patient while she deals with what life has handed her."

"What's the story?"

"The articles claim Katrina and her costar Oliver fell in love on the set and took off to Cabo for an extended lovers' vacation. Both spouses were left at home, reeling from Katrina and Oliver's deceitful actions. The articles say both soon-to-be-former spouses left town, headed for undisclosed locations, so they can grieve without the prying eye of the media watching them."

"It's all a cover-up, from the highest level down," Elle replied in disbelief.

"No doubt about it."

"Okay, I'll call Ray back and insist he have two armed bodyguards waiting for me on the lot today."

"I'd rather you not go to the sound stage at all until they're with you," Jeff urged.

"Jeff, I don't have enough clout yet not to show up for work and have the director be okay with that. Today will be a long day. There's no break in the schedule until early afternoon, so I'll be inside the sound stage at least until then. I'll be fine."

Jeff released a heavy sigh, conveying his annoyance without words. "You are so hardheaded, you know that?"

"I love you, too. Thanks for looking out for me."

They disconnected with Elle promising to call Jeff immediately if her agent gave her any trouble over when her protection would be onsite. She repeated the conversation to Beth before calling Ray.

"Someone is lying, Elle. Katrina wouldn't have done that. Jeff needs to have someone check the pictures and verify the dates. I'd bet my entire year's salary none of them is recent," Beth objected.

"I agree, Beth. I'm calling Ray right now. Whatever is going on will not happen to us."

She scrolled through her contacts and hit the number for her agent. She held her breath, dread filling her with each ring that passed without an answer.

"Elle, my darling, it's not often I'm graced with two phone calls from you in one morning. What can I do for you?"

"Ray, I need those two armed bodyguards waiting for me at the sound stage by the time I leave today. Tomorrow is too late."

"Did something happen? Do I need to call the police right now?"

"No, nothing has happened yet, but I don't want to wait and leave anything to chance. Text me back with their names and pictures so I know who they are when I see them."

"Of course, of course. Consider it done, my love. Hey, aren't you due on the set in about twenty minutes?"

"Yes, I'm pulling into the lot right now. Don't worry, I have the best hair and makeup artists in the world to make sure I'm camera-ready on time."

"You're a natural beauty. You don't need makeup like everyone else does," Ray schmoozed. "Now, I'm off to ensure you feel safe and sound at all times. You'll hear back from me soon."

The busy schedule and moving to the various sets kept her busy throughout the day and well into the night. After the director yelled the final "Cut," she was exhausted and could no longer hide it.

"Vince, I need a break. I've been going nonstop since I got here this morning."

"I know, Elle. We're behind, and the studio can't extend our time with the sound stage. We'll call it a wrap for the night and start back tomorrow morning," Vince replied.

"Miss Sinclair? I have this message for you." A short, young girl smiled shyly as she passed the handwritten note to Elle.

"Thank you." Elle smiled warmly, despite her irritation with her situation. The young girl's smile brightened. She was clearly content with just being acknowledged by one of the main stars. Watching the girl walk away with an added spring in her step reminded Elle why she'd always been cognizant of how she treated the crew. Her positive thoughts changed immediately when she read the message. "You son of a bitch!"

"What's wrong, sailor?" Beth asked with a smirk.

"Listen to this. *'Elle, darling, your bodyguards will be on the set first thing in the morning, as you requested. —Ray'* They were supposed to be here *tonight* to escort us home. I need to find a better agent."

"Go change and let's go home. Your clothes are in your trailer. We'll deal with firing Ray and finding a competent agent in the morning. I'll meet you at the car and be your bodyguard for the night."

"I feel safer already," Elle replied with a sardonic chuckle. "I'll be right there."

When she stepped out of the sound stage door, she was surprised to see how busy the lot was so late. Crew members darted from one place to the other, various teams hustling to finish their work for the night. Once inside her trailer, she checked her phone for messages, chatted with her mother via text, then changed into her regular clothes. When she opened the door of her

trailer and stepped out, the unnatural silence that met her frightened her.

Her skin prickled with cold chills in the warm Southern California air. The feeling of being watched hadn't left her for several
days, but the shudders flowing over her in waves were stronger than
they'd ever been. Someone was out there, watching and waiting. She
knew it beyond a shadow of a doubt.

She rushed toward the car lot where they'd parked, wielding her
apartment key like a weapon, ready to stab someone in the eye if
necessary. Her thumb slid up the side of the key, holding it firmly in
her grasp. The car was mere steps away—the safety and security of
the interior were her homing beacon, and her feet instinctively
carried her to it. A fleeting thought of having words with Vince about
keeping security on the lot until everyone had cleared out crossed her
mind as she reached the car. She extended her arm and grasped the
handle, relief flooding her because she'd made it safely.

"Miss Sinclair."

Startled, she jumped and whirled around at the sound of a man
behind her. Before her brain could register what her eyes witnessed,
everything around her went completely black.

STRANGE NOISES ROUSED ELLE FROM HER DEEP SLUMBER. SHE FOUGHT
against her own muscles to force her eyes to open. Sleep felt so good
to her overexhausted mind and body, and she hadn't had a decent
night's sleep in so long. But if Beth already had company over, then
she'd apparently slept later than she realized. She rolled over in the
bed and fought the grogginess that had overtaken her, covering her
like a heavy blanket. After sitting up, she rubbed her eyes and realized when she felt the thick, stiff mascara still caked on her eyelashes
she didn't wash her makeup off the night before.

That was her first red flag. As a model and actress, she never went
to bed without completing her nighttime beauty regimen, no matter
how late she'd returned home. The second red flag immediately

followed the first when she realized how hard she'd slept. Running on fumes and a few hours of sleep every night had become her normal. She peeled her eyelids open, and a full-blown panic attack ensued. Her eyes traveled around the room, taking in the décor and furnishings. Reality and facts clashed with denial and self-preservation.

She wasn't in her bed.

She wasn't in her room.

She wasn't in her apartment.

She had no idea where she was.

The plush bedroom was as large as the entire apartment she shared with Beth. The furniture was all one-of-a-kind pieces from exclusive, appointment-only boutiques in Beverly Hills. The paintings adorning the walls were multimillion-dollar originals, not available for purchase to the average citizen. Vases of fresh flowers filled the room with their sweet fragrance. Floor-to-ceiling windows made up an entire wall, with what was sure to be a spectacular view when it wasn't still pitch-black outside.

She slid out of bed and panic nearly incapacitated her when she realized she wore a strange gown rather than her own clothes, but she had no memory of how she got in it. Determined to figure out where she was and why she was there, she began opening drawers to search for any clues. Every drawer only served to increase her anxiety, yielding nothing except more plain cotton nightgowns like the one she wore, mingled with various feminine toiletry items.

She rushed through the room, checking the expansive closets and the bathroom but finding nothing of use. Nothing that revealed any information and nothing that gave a single hint of where she was being held. Her chest heaved with heavy breaths, and her mind raced as she tried to recall what last happened to her and how she got there.

She moved to the door and quietly turned the knob, opening it slowly to peek into the hallway. When she found it was empty, she tiptoed out of the bedroom and ran barefoot toward the front of the house. The long hall was just one indication of how large the house was. The number of doors that lined the hallway was the other. Her anxiety ratcheted up another notch as she tried to formulate an escape plan in her jumbled thoughts. From whom she had to escape and why they'd taken her to start with were beyond her capacity to analyze at the time. All she could think about was finding the door that led outside, then when she was far enough away, she'd focus on who and why.

The end of the hall opened into an expansive family room, taking away the relative cover the smaller space had offered. A quick perusal around the room revealed much of what she already knew—she was held in a multimillion-dollar house. That fact frightened her more than if she'd awakened in a derelict house. With more resources came more security, more privacy, and less chance of anyone hearing her cries for help.

The large, wooden door to freedom came into view and propelled her body forward. Her feet smacked against the marble floor of the foyer, and her heart hammered against the inside of her chest. It was so close now—all she had to do was reach out and grab the door handle, then she'd be outside, one step closer to freedom.

She flung the door open, letting it slam against the wall when she released it. Across the spacious front porch, down the steps, into the thick, manicured grass of the sprawling front lawn, and toward the brick wall that encased the estate, she ran as hard as she could. The adrenaline coursing through her veins blocked the burning in her thighs and the pain from the lack of oxygen in her lungs.

Her sole focus was how she'd scale the brick wall that stood between her and the open road. A few more feet to go. A few more feet and she'd find help, learn what had happened to her, and stop long enough to cry her eyes out. But first things first—the wall.

Her legs carried her so fast, her body bent in half from the forward momentum when a strong, muscled arm grasped her around the waist. All the air was knocked out of her from the sudden stop, leaving her gasping for breath and nearly incapable of fighting back. The muscular arm easily lifted her off the ground and turned to face the house, carrying her away from freedom with every step.

From the outside, it was a gorgeous mansion she ordinarily would've admired. Palm trees lined the circular cobblestone driveway. Tall, white columns framed the archways along the entire front of the house and the matching detached garage. Ornate statues were evenly spaced along the drive. The stark white elegant marble figures were accentuated by the deep green privacy hedge.

The heavy thud of boots and clink of metal pulled her eye from the house and onto an approaching man. Dressed all in black and wearing a leather vest, he smirked as he strode toward her. His lewd smile made her skin crawl, and her breath hitched in her chest.

"Look who we have here, running around the yard like she owns the place," he said as his fingers slid down her cheek. "You woke up sooner than I thought you would. So, where were you going?"

Fear seized her from the inside out, stealing her ability to speak or think rationally. She shook her head from side to side, though she didn't know what it was she tried to convey. She only wanted to get away from both men. Seized by fear, all she could think was how she wanted to wake up from the nightmare that had become her life,

"You were trying to run from us. Don't lie to me now," he snarled. "You were trying to get out of here and call the police on us."

He waited for her to reply, but her vocal cords were paralyzed with fright.

"I'll tell you a secret, sweetheart. You would've been better off calling them from inside the house instead of trying to get over that high fence. But, we won't make the mistake of underestimating you again."

He raised his other hand to her face and gave a small spray bottle two swift pumps, sending the droplets directly into her nose and mouth. Within seconds, she was knocked out, her muscles as limp as a rag doll, and theirs to do with as they pleased.

CHAPTER FOUR

"Would you look at her? I wish I had her hair. And her eyes. And her face. And her body," Brianna mused as she watched TV. "She's perfect in every way."

"All of the tabloids are reporting she's dating Jax Hart. I bet that'll make for some interesting love scenes in their upcoming movie. The book they based it on is a scorcher." Chaise fanned herself.

"Was the book based on our sex life?" Bull questioned.

"Uh, no."

"Then it wasn't hot enough." He smirked with confidence.

"Do you believe the stories about them in those magazines are real?" Brianna probed, ignoring Bull.

"No," Shadow interjected. "They're not."

"You sound pretty sure. Has the CIA sanctioned stalking movie stars or something?" Brianna teased.

"Anything I do is sanctioned." His smile lit up his deep blue eyes and his handsome face.

"Because of tenure and all that jazz, huh?"

"Something like that." Shadow winked at Brianna before his gaze floated back to the TV and the beautiful woman's face filling the screen.

"Apparently, they want to make up their own happily-ever-after ending for the hottest silver screen costars," Chaise replied to Brianna, ignoring Shadow's interruption into their conversation.

"They can make up any ending they want," Shadow grumbled. "Her happily ever after won't be with that jackass."

Chaise and Bull casually laughed at Shadow's offhanded comment but otherwise continued the conversation about the movie still in production. Brianna, however, wasn't as easily fooled by Shadow's aloofness. She locked her gaze on him, sensing she was finally in a position to use his tactics against him. Her inherent curiosity and journalistic instincts kicked into overdrive when he became unable to hide his discomfort with being under her scrutinizing gaze.

The muscles in the corners of her eyes squeezed together, narrowing in suspicion as she tilted her head to the side. He shifted positions in his seat and stared a little too hard at the TV, not allowing his eyes to move from the single spot. For a man who noticed everything about his surroundings, his choice to ignore the way she saw straight through him spoke volumes of what he'd never willingly verbalize.

"Shadow," Brianna gently chastised the giant of a man she loved like a brother, convinced he'd spook and run away from her otherwise. "You have to look at me at some point."

"Sunny," he replied with her nickname. "You are my little sister, and I love you. You know that, right?"

"I do. Without a doubt." She leaned over and put her hand on his arm. "And you know I love you. You're my brother, by love if not by blood."

"You realize some things are better left unsaid, right? Some questions don't need to be asked and answered."

"You literally saved my life, Shadow. If there's anything I can do to help you, I'll do it in a heartbeat. But if you don't want to talk, I'll respect that, too."

He nodded, deep in thought, and then lifted his eyes to hers. "Fine. Let's take a walk outside."

"I'd love to." She squeezed his arm in silent reassurance. "Noah, my love. Keep an eye on Amelia, Emery, and Gray, please. We'll be back in a little while."

"You're trusting me alone with all three of the kids at once?" Noah's grin lit up his face and made Brianna groan.

"I know that look. Don't force me to hide all the chocolate before I leave, Noah Steele," she warned in her stern, motherly voice.

"Yes, ma'am." He saluted her but couldn't hide his mischievous smile. "Whatever you say, princess." Noah turned his gaze to Shadow and issued his own directive. "Take care of my wife on your walk, Shadow."

"With my life, Reap."

"We're not even leaving the grounds, Noah," Brianna chuckled.

"You've been known to get into trouble a time or two without even leaving the house," Noah deadpanned.

"Fair enough. Ready to go, Shadow?"

"I know I'm going to regret this," Shadow mumbled under his breath. "Let's get it over with."

"You sound like you're about to be tortured." Bull didn't bother to hide his amusement at Shadow's discomfort. "Should I get the buckets of water ready?"

"I'd take waterboarding over talking about my *feelings* any day." Shadow shook his head and opened the door for Brianna to walk through first. Once she'd cleared the threshold, Shadow turned to Bull and whisper-shouted, "Come find me in five minutes. Save me!"

The door latched closed with the sound of roaring laughter on one side and complete silence on his side when he met Brianna's narrowed stare. His chest expanded with his deep breath, and he slid his sunglasses on his face. "Looks like I'm all yours now, Sunny."

"Uh-huh." She turned and began walking across the manicured lawn of the estate she shared with Noah, forcing Shadow to step quickly to keep up with her.

When they reached the terrace close to the pool, Brianna pulled out a chair and took a seat. Shadow followed suit, his sunglasses shading his eyes from the bright Florida sun, but his long face expressed his inner turmoil. He inhaled a deep breath and waited for the questions to begin.

"You know Elle Sinclair."

It wasn't a question. It was a direct statement, and she expected confirmation.

"I know Elle *Moore*," he corrected. "Sinclair is a stage name. But yes, I know her. I've known her most of her life, actually."

"Ah, finally. A look into the elusive Shadow's life." Brianna teased him to make it seem less formal and put him more at ease.

"Yeah, yeah, okay. I know her very well. We first started seeing each other about eight years ago, but it's been very..." He paused to search for the right word. "...sporadic."

"What do you mean by that? Why do I feel like there's more to the story?"

"I mean, for the first several years, we saw each other as much as we could. Between our jobs getting in the way. Sometimes, it was weeks apart. Sometimes, it was months apart."

The outer corner of her eyebrow lifted, arching in a silent question. Shadow shrugged one shoulder and continued.

"I'd show up out of the blue and surprise her. We'd spend a couple of weeks or more together, have the best time of my life, and then I'd leave again for the next job. I wouldn't see her again until the next time I had a break in the case or between assignments."

She studied his face, analyzed his words, and considered what he *wasn't* saying. "You're in love with her. Aren't you?"

"I can neither confirm nor deny your assumption."

"You just confirmed it. Why not just give it an honest try, stay together and see what you can have?"

"We already have too many strikes against us." He shook his head and dropped his shielded gaze to the ground.

"She's a good bit younger than you, isn't she?"

The humorless scoff before he replied confirmed her suspicion. "Yeah, that's actually the first strike against us."

"You're what? Thirty-five, close to thirty-six?"

Shadow nodded, and his full lips disappeared into a thin line.

"I think I read she's around twenty-eight now. That's honestly not a big deal, Shadow."

"Not now, no. But considering Elle's older brother was one of my best friends when we were growing up, the age gap doesn't help."

"I see." Brianna nodded slowly, realization settling in her mind. "You knew her as a little kid."

"When she was around seven, she developed a major crush on me. She'd follow Jeff and me around, spying on us from behind trees. It didn't matter what we were doing. She just wanted to be close to us. At the time, she was just my buddy's kid sister. You know? I never even considered..." His voice trailed off, leaving his thoughts unspoken, but there was no need to say it.

"You never considered anything would be kindled between you two, many years later, now that you're both adults," Brianna surmised.

With a heavy sigh, Shadow relented and decided to lay it all out for her, knowing she'd tell him the truth, regardless if he wanted to hear it or not. "Strike one, she's my buddy's little sister. That's just an unspoken rule every guy knows not to break."

"Wrong." Brianna shook her head vehemently and stopped his confession with her firm tone.

"What?" Shadow recoiled, jerking his head back as he openly gaped at her. "What do you mean 'wrong'?"

"Chaise is Noah's little sister, and she's happily married to one of his best friends. Do you think Noah would want anything less for her? Bull is his brother by choice, but now, also by marriage. Noah wouldn't change that for anything, no matter how much he enjoys giving Bull a hard time about it."

"Hmm," Shadow reflected. "You may have a point there."

"Of course I do. Please continue."

"I'm kind of afraid to now. Strike two, we've already covered. Elle's so much younger than I am. Believe me when I say I see the beautiful woman she's grown into. But I can't help but think, sometimes, that it's just wrong because of that little girl I remember."

His suspicion of Brianna's reaction was unmasked as he waited for the tongue-lashing he knew would come. His argument was weak, even he knew that. But his self-induced illusion had adequately sustained him for the past eight years. Somehow, he knew, deep down, Brianna would obliterate his delusion and smack him in the face with a dose of reality.

She tried to hide her mirth but failed magnificently. Her beautiful smile didn't last long, though, before it turned into a full belly laugh. Tears pooled in her eyes as she pointed at him, attempted to speak, but couldn't form the words over her outbursts of laughter. He crossed his arms over his chest, leaned back in the chair, forcefully blew out his breath, and refused to look at her.

"Okay." She finally managed to speak and wiped the tears from her eyes. "Let me catch my breath."

The thin line that formed his lips disappeared completely, and he attempted to project boredom with the entire conversation. It took all of Brianna's restraint not to start laughing again.

"Shadow, this is *me* you're talking to here. You know better than to say something stupid like that to me. She's not that little girl anymore, and you're not that young teenager anymore. Eight years' difference in age is nothing after you're both legal adults. The only reason you even mentioned knowing her as a child is because you're still hung up on her being the 'little' sister of your friend. She's his *younger* sister, but she's not *little* anymore. And you, my friend, are reaching, but you're only fooling yourself.

"Now, let's hear strike three."

"Strike three is a little harder to get around. Even you won't be able to argue with it," Shadow replied with confidence.

"Try me."

"She started modeling when she was twelve and moved to California with her parents after Jeff and I had already left home for college. When I first saw her in commercials, ads, and magazines, I was so proud of her. Kind of like a big brother would be. The older she got, the prettier she became. Then almost overnight, she was fucking drop-dead gorgeous. Even then, I only admired her from afar.

"While I was with the CIA, I was on assignment here in Miami, and she was sent here by the modeling agency. She called me when she landed, and our first three-week escapade began. When she first called me, I thought it was nothing more than a rekindled friendship. Getting to know each other again after so many years apart, mostly catching up on her life since I couldn't very well share the majority of mine.

"But the attraction was there from the beginning, and it was intense. Somehow, in those three weeks, I fell hard for her. The last night she was here, I knew I should just walk away and let it be her summer fling, but I couldn't. We'd spent every night together up until then, and I wanted that last night with her. I drove her to the airport early the next morning for her flight, and she shocked the hell out of me. She asked me to move to LA with her."

"What did you say?"

He removed his sunglasses and rubbed his eyes, stalling for as long as possible. He lifted his gaze, and Brianna was surprised at the sadness she recognized in them. "I asked her to stay here with me. Of course, she couldn't. But what shocked me even more than when she asked me to go with her was I honestly meant it when I asked her to stay here with me."

"But she couldn't. Her work was in LA, and she had to go back to it."

"Right, she had to go back to the bright lights and camera flashes that lit up everything around her. My job, my whole world, is in the darkness. In the shadows. Covert operations and instantly recognizable supermodels aren't exactly good bedfellows."

"Did you ever tell her you were with the CIA?"

"No. I couldn't tell her because I was still classified as an active covert agent."

Shadow turned to fully face Brianna before he continued. His expression became smug when he knew he had her dead to rights. She couldn't argue with his logic about their jobs. The odds of being a model who was also a household name were minuscule. The ability to conduct undercover governmental operations with invisibility was vital to national security and his very life. No way could she call him out on that.

"Strike three is our chosen professions. Neither of us can give up what we've worked so hard to attain, what we've invested so many years in perfecting."

"Bullshit."

"Huh?"

"I. Call. Bullshit." She emphasized each word and leaned toward him as she spoke. "That may have been true at first, but you've been out of the CIA for a while now. You've been with Steele Security for the last few years, not in some hostile, third-world country on a clandestine operation. If you hadn't been so stubborn this whole time, you could've rekindled this relationship long ago."

"Rekindled? Who says we've burned out?"

"Fine. You've had years to legitimize it, then. You've had plenty of opportunities to come out of the darkness and the shadows and walk with Elle in the light. But you haven't. Because you're scared."

"You think I'm scared?"

"I know you are." She smirked.

"Of what? I can't wait to hear this."

"You're a career bachelor, Shadow. You come and go as you please. Even in her life—you said you just show up out of the blue with no warning when it's convenient for you. She drops everything for you every time you appear, doesn't she? Gives up her plans without hesitation. Devotes every waking moment to you."

"Yeah." He drew out the one-syllable word, hesitant to hear the rest of Brianna's scolding.

"Hmm."

He didn't like that sound. Nothing good ever came from that sound. "What?"

"Just wondering. In the last eight years of this so-called relationship, what exactly have you given up for Elle?"

Her words hit him like a sledgehammer to his stomach, stealing his breath and rendering him speechless. He was unable to argue with her logic, because she'd been correct in everything she'd said to that point. He'd only fooled himself into believing his pathetic excuses. There were some events from the past year he couldn't bring himself to tell Brianna, though. Truths he had difficulties dealing with in his own mind, much less verbalizing. The most frightening unanswered questions popped into his mind without Brianna even addressing them first.

How long ago did Elle figure me out?

Are the rumors about her and Jax truths instead?

Has she given up on me and moved on to him?

"Yeah, that's what I thought. Shadow, only you can decide what you really want. You've been alone for a long time, and maybe you like it that way. But if she's the one you love, and you can't stand to think of her with someone else, you need to do something about this situation soon. That news about her and Jax could be complete hyperbole. But is that a chance you think you should take?"

"Thanks for the talk, Sunny. As usual, you've given me a lot to think about."

SHADOW STRODE INTO HIS TWELFTH-FLOOR CONDO AND WALKED straight out onto the balcony overlooking the ocean. His thoughts had stayed on Elle since he left Noah's house, but his conversation with Brianna struck a sensitive chord he didn't even know he had. With his forearms resting on the railing, he stared off into the night, second-guessing his every decision and revisiting his every mistake.

His mind soon drifted back to their first night together eight years earlier.

He could still feel her quivering under his touch. She tried so hard to hide her apprehension, but he could be blind and deaf and still feel it rolling off her like the waves crashing on the shore. The rapid rise and fall of her chest, the pink tinge of her cheeks, and the dilation of her pupils were all telltale signs. Signs he was trained to identify.

But he couldn't deny her desire for him.

The ringing of his personal cell phone pulled him from his ruminations, giving him a welcome reprieve.

Until he saw the caller's name.

CHAPTER FIVE

"Devon, I need your help."

Jeff's frantic tone made the hair on the back of Shadow's neck stand at attention and salute. There was only one reason why Jeff would react with such strong emotion.

"Tell me."

"Elle is missing. She called me a couple of nights ago. It was late and she was scared. She said she thought someone was watching her. I should've listened to my gut and flew out there the minute we hung up. She convinced me she was just being paranoid. If anything has happened to her, I'll never forgive myself."

Jeff's agitated state had him spewing information at Shadow in half thoughts and out of sequence events. Shadow couldn't make sense of Jeff's ramblings, though he understood why he reacted so forcefully. The mere mention that Elle was missing was enough to push Shadow over the edge. But his friend called for a reason—for his expertise in high-pressure situations. He'd need all his wits about him, and all the details he could uncover, to get through it himself.

"Calm down and start over. This time, start from the beginning and walk me through everything. Every word she said. Don't leave anything out, no matter how small you think it is."

Shadow listened intently as Jeff took a deep breath, released it slowly, then recounted the entire conversation. He told Shadow about Elle calling late Pacific Time when she'd returned home from the lot, about the missing girls and fake press stories, and how she felt so uncomfortable she was at the point where she wanted armed bodyguards with her at all times.

"I'm kicking my own ass right now for staying here instead of flying out there to be with her. She said she'd call Mom, Dad, and Mark to alert them. Mark could've stayed with her until I got there." The guilt infused in Jeff's tone was palpable, thinking he'd let his little sister down when she needed him the most. "She never calls me that late, Devon. That should've been the first clue to slap me upside the head and make me see something was seriously wrong."

Shadow listened to his friend, soaked in every word and every detail, then tried to soothe him as best he could.

"Hey. Quit beating yourself up. That's my job. How long do you usually go without calling to check on her? Despite the number of times I've told you to stay close to her so you can protect her every second of every day."

"You're not helping. And I talk to my sister every few days. Our schedules aren't always conducive to multiple conversations per day. But this is different—she called me and she was scared. Now I can't reach her or Beth. Mark is on his way down there now, but he runs the winery for our parents. He doesn't have a clue where to start looking for her.

"I need your help, Devon. Elle needs you. I feel it—something bad has happened to her."

"I'm on the next flight to LAX. I'll find her no matter what it takes. You said you can't reach Beth either. Do you know if they were together on the set?"

"Yes, Elle said Beth is her makeup artist. They've been riding back and forth to work together, especially since they both work such long hours. It just makes sense since they live together. It's not a good sign that they're both missing, is it?"

"Jeff, I know you're on the verge of doing something really stupid.

I can hear the panic in your voice. The more you obsess over what you should've, could've, would've done, the more likely you are to make a rash decision. Swear to me you'll give me time to do some digging around before you go off half-cocked and make things worse." Shadow's request more closely resembled an order.

"You have my word. I know you work for a security firm, but I didn't know who else to call. I'm sorry for dragging you into this."

"Don't be. I wouldn't have it any other way. I'll call you when I get to LA. But if you hear anything else before then, don't wait to contact me."

Shadow and Jeff hung up with the promise to keep each other updated on any new developments. Shadow retrieved a phone from a hidden safe in the wall. He stared at it longer than necessary, hating the fact that he was forced to use it at all. But she was worth it. He would do whatever it took to ensure she was safe and sound, even if that meant he'd be indebted to the CIA again.

With the phone powered on, he hit the send button and made the call. After two rings, the call connected and Shadow squeezed his eyes shut while he waited for the coded answer.

"Luigi's Pizza Delivery. What type of crust would you like?"

"Deep dish, extra garlic, extra cheese."

"Shadow," came the surprised response. "It's been a long time, my man. Must be something important for you to call in. What can I do for you?"

"Hey, Steadman. Good to hear your voice again. You know I need your help."

"Whatever you need. Lay it on me."

"What have you heard about actresses disappearing lately?"

"You sure you want to go there, Shadow? You're cleared to be read in, but once I do, there's no turning back," Steadman warned.

With his thumb and index finger firmly pinching the bridge of his nose, Shadow considered his options.

"If Elle Sinclair is involved, then read me in."

"Just remember you asked for it after you hear all the classified details. Don't show up in my apartment in the middle of the night and kill me," Steadman replied with a chuckle.

"You don't live in an apartment. Are you testing me, or did you really think you could hide from me?"

With a nervous clearing of his throat, Steadman gave Shadow the case details. Every point relayed made Shadow's heart move up into his throat a little bit more. By the time Steadman finished reading him in on the classified file, Shadow knew his involvement in the case was Elle's only chance.

"Create my new identity and backstory. Make it as bad as you can, then transfer the files to me. This won't be easy, but I need inside as of yesterday," Shadow commanded.

"There is another undercover agent who has embedded himself with the group. Maybe he can help you get inducted on a fast track. He may not agree to it, though. He's spent two years undercover, working his way up the chain, gathering intel. It could look too suspicious for him to bring you in now."

"Who is he?"

"Nick Tucker. DEA."

"I know him. Get a hold of his handler and get word to him that I'm coming in. You'll have to show me as an ex-con, recently paroled, and coming back home to California from a federal penitentiary. Don't leave anything out, Steadman, or you'll get us both killed."

"Have I ever gotten you killed before?" Steadman asked, taken aback at Shadow's lack of confidence in his abilities.

"Maybe you should transfer me to another analyst to handle my background cover."

"Come on, Shadow. You know I'm joking. It'll be flawless. Trust me."

"I'm CIA, Steadman, I don't trust anyone. But you can trust me when I say it better be the best backstory and fake identification you've ever created, or it'll be the last one you ever create."

"It'll be so good, even other analysts and operatives won't know it's fake. Guaranteed."

"Always a pleasure working with you, Steadman."

While he waited for his new identity and criminal record to be created, he called Jeff, knowing he couldn't share any information, but he had to warn Jeff and the rest of the family off the case. They couldn't actively search for her while Shadow was undercover, especially against the forces he'd be facing.

"Devon, have you already heard the news?" Jeff asked as soon as he answered the phone.

"What news?"

"Mark said a local news channel reported Elle and Jax eloped and took off on a secret honeymoon. They sent messages through their agents saying they're sorry for any concern they created for their well-being, but they're just so happy and so in love, they couldn't wait one more day.

"Devon, that is the biggest pile of horseshit I've ever heard. Elle can't stand Jax Hart. She sure as shit wouldn't run off and marry him. I'm looking for a privately chartered flight to get me out to California immediately."

"Jeff. Stop." Shadow's stern tone and terse words stopped Jeff's concerned tirade.

"What? Your turn to tell me," Jeff replied.

"You have to follow my instructions to the letter. You can't allow your feelings to overrule anything I'm about to tell you, regardless of how dire the situation seems. This is life or death, Jeff."

"I've always been amazed by your ability to find out things no one else could. That only became greater once you left the Army. So, I won't question you, Devon. I called you for a reason. Tell me what to do."

"You, Mark, Danny, and Tanya need to go to LA. Stay at her apartment and keep the media pressure up. Get in front of every camera you can and claim that story is a lie. Ask why the sheriff's department isn't taking you seriously. Whatever you have to do to keep her picture front and center in the news.

"Look for her in every trendy place a movie star would want to be seen. But Jeff, do not mention me. Do not look for me. Do not attempt to contact me in any way. You have to trust me on this. There's no other way. If you have any doubts, I need to know now."

"No doubts at all."

"You won't hear from me for long stretches of time. You, your parents, your brother—none of you can go getting all antsy on me. Let me do my job."

"I got it, Devon. I'll make sure Mom, Dad, and Mark get the message, too."

"You say that now. But when you're worried about her and don't hear from me, your mind will play tricks on you. You can't fall into that trap. When you start feeling despondent, remember this conversation."

"Thanks, Devon. I appreciate it more than you know. I trust you— no matter how bad the circumstances appear."

"If I send word instructing you to leave town, do not waste time. Leave immediately. No packing, no questions, just get to your parents' house and wait for me."

"Got it. Even though you're scaring the shit out of me. I know you won't tell me anything more."

"No, I won't. But for your own safety. Have a good flight. I'll be in touch as soon as I can."

The next call he needed to make was to Noah. A commercial flight wouldn't get him to LA fast enough from Miami. From what Steadman told him, time was definitely of the essence. Even telling Jeff what he'd told him was taking a huge risk, but keeping Elle's face and family in the news would hopefully buy more time. He only hoped his plan didn't backfire on him.

"Steele," Noah answered.

"Reaper, I need a favor—and I need it right now."

"Of course. Whatever you need. Name it."

"I need the private jet for a ride to LA."

"No problem. You need the team to go with you for backup or anything?"

"Not this time. I have to go this one alone."

"Understood. If anything changes, you know we're more than willing to jump into the fire with you," Noah replied, recognizing the code phrase they'd already established to identify Shadow's CIA missions.

"I know, Noah. If I don't make it back from this one, I want you and the guys to know how much I've relied on and valued your friendship."

"You know we feel the same way, Shadow. But I have to tell you, I'm more than a little worried about you, talking like this. You've never been hesitant to walk into a mission before."

"This one is different, Reap. This is a high-stakes poker round, and the dealer holds all the best cards. I'm going in on a long-shot gamble that I can pull it off successfully. But I can't and won't take you, Bull, and Rebel down with me if and when this mission goes wrong."

"We'll be in LA as soon as the plane returns and can take us out there. At least we'll be close if you need to pull us in."

"Actually, it would be helpful to have you there to cover a few people for me. They'll be making waves and could unknowingly draw the wrong attention to themselves. I'd feel better knowing you're there to watch their backs."

"Done. Fill me in on what they're doing."

Shadow packed while he recounted his conversations with Jeff and what he'd instructed Elle's family to do. After the time they'd spent together and all the missions they'd completed, Noah understood perfectly what Shadow hoped to achieve. With Noah's experience on highly classified operations, Shadow had no doubt he'd already deduced what the mission entailed, at least partially.

But the devil was in the details.

CHAPTER SIX

Eight Years Earlier

"I'm so glad you're here with me." Elle wrapped her arm around Beth's shoulders and squeezed as they walked along the shore, the water lapping at their feet.

Elle's parents, Danny and Tanya, moved her and Mark from their small town in Georgia to sunny Southern California a few years after Jeff and Devon went off to college. A modeling agency signed Elle at twelve years old after her mother submitted headshots in a competition Elle had read about in a fashion magazine. As thrilled as she'd been with the possibility of having her dream career, she knew what she'd miss most about Georgia were Devon and Beth. But her parents had concluded the once-in-a-lifetime chance was too good of an opportunity for their natural beauty to pass up.

Elle's thick, long blond hair was naturally wavy, and it perfectly framed her big hazel eyes, high cheekbones, and symmetrical facial features. Her teen years had ticked by with Elle gaining more and more popularity. Requests for magazine covers, cameo spots on established television sitcoms, and contracts to be the face of major name-brand designers poured in from her agent. By the time she'd turned twenty, her name was instantly recognized across the entertainment industry.

"What do you want now?" Beth asked, arching her eyebrow with a sideways glance at Elle. "I've been here with you for two years."

"I just found out I have to go to Miami for three weeks," Elle began explaining.

"Yes, I can see how that would be a hardship on you. Such a difficult and terrible life you live. Three weeks in Miami Beach. Photoshoots, bikinis, sun, sand, and salt water. Yes, I feel your pain."

"You're about to feel pain, all right," Elle laughed. "You're such a smartass. Before you so rudely interrupted me, I was going to ask if you can go with me. Now, I'm just not sure I want such negativity to taint my trip."

"Believe me, if I could get away to South Beach for three weeks, I would definitely taint your trip. I would taint the shit out of it. But the agency just contacted me about a small production that begins next week. You are looking at the newest member of the hair and makeup specialist team!"

"Congratulations, Beth! I'm so happy for you. Not that I ever had a doubt. I just know how hard it is to get in."

"Well, doing your hair and makeup and using those pictures in my portfolio didn't hurt my chances. With you being a hotshot supermodel and all."

"Supermodel. That's so funny, like I wear a mask and cape, parading around the city to fight crime. Maybe they'll create a comic book character based on me," Elle joked.

"I'm so glad fame never went to your head," Beth replied, her tone rife with sincerity. "You've never adopted the diva mentality no matter how much success you've achieved."

"You've never let me. You always remind me where I came from, and that you'd kick my ass all the way back to that small town in Georgia if my head got too big," Elle laughed.

"So, you could say I'm your brain trust. Your driving power behind the scenes."

"Let's not get carried away, Beth."

"Seriously, I wish I could go with you. What's the trip for and why will you be there so long?"

"I've just been selected as the new face of Kylie Rae Romano. Her new clothing line will be revealed soon, and they want me there for it. So over the next three weeks, they'll fit me, shoot me, and use me to help promote it. All while they use *her* status to promote *me*."

"Sounds like a lot of work." Beth scrunched up her nose in disagreement. "All work and no play."

"Beth..." Elle hesitated, capturing Beth's undivided attention. "Devon is in Miami. Jeff mentioned to Mom he'd talked to Devon the other day. I'm going to call him while I'm there."

"Elle, you've always had a crush on him. You know I'm all for having a good time, and hell if you don't need to let your hair down and have fun for once. You've worked since you got that first contract when you were twelve. But I know you. A fling with Devon wouldn't just be a fling to you."

"You're getting a few miles too far ahead of yourself, aren't you? How does seeing him again after all these years mean I'll have a fling with him?"

Beth stopped walking and turned to face her friend. Concern masked her face and burned in her eyes. "You didn't have the typical high school experience, Elle. You were homeschooled while you shuffled from one photoshoot to another. From LA to New York and everywhere else in between. Your parents sheltered you, as they should have in this industry. You're twenty, riding high on your modeling career, but you've never really dated and had that whole experience of heartbreak, letdowns, and the occasional orgasm that makes up for it all."

Elle's cheeks flared red. After years of being on one set or another, with everyone looking at her with a critical eye, very few things embarrassed her at that point in her life. Her sex life, or lack of one, was one of those things that mortified her more than anything.

"I just haven't seen him in a long time, and this is the first chance I've had. He's been in the Army or something—and stationed all over the world. How can I not see him when we're finally in the same city?" Elle argued her point.

Beth smiled sadly, knowing she couldn't dissuade Elle from her course. "Just be careful. You're my best friend, Elle. I know you—I just don't want to see you hurt. So, when do you leave?"

"Saturday—three days away. Kylie Rae is a huge name in fashion. This will open so many doors for me—even small parts in more television shows and movies."

Elle's excitement was contagious, and soon, dreams of the movie parts were in both their eyes. "That would be so amazing, Elle. To see you on the silver screen and announce to the world, 'That's my best friend!' I wish I could be in Miami with you when this new era of your career kicks off. You can bet your ass I'll be on the set with you when you do your first major show—TV or movie."

The pair continued their trek along the shore, watching the waves and enjoying the warmth of the sunny day. They chatted about the upcoming possibilities and how life could drastically change in the very near future. But Elle's thoughts kept returning to her imminent trip to Miami—and the potential of seeing Devon again.

Perhaps it was the schoolgirl crush she'd had on him since the day she'd met him driving her need to contact him. Maybe Beth was right in her assessment, especially since Elle didn't have anyone else to compare to him. She still believed the impression she'd formed as a child.

No one compared to Devon Kane.

By the time the wheels touched down in Miami, her excitement couldn't be contained. As much as she couldn't wait to start a new venture in modeling, her thoughts were tied to Devon. The first second she had alone, she planned to call him. She'd managed to wrangle his cell number from Jeff, despite his protests and questions.

"Okay, ladies. You have today to rest and hydrate before we start shooting the swimsuit shots tomorrow morning. Call me if you need anything. Otherwise, I'll see you bright and early." Leslie, the photographer, and his crew left the dozen models assigned to the shoot to find their own way to the hotel.

Elle grabbed her suitcase off the conveyor belt and hit send on her phone before she changed her mind or lost her nerve. After two rings, the sexiest masculine voice answered.

"Kane."

"Hi, Devon. This is Elle Sin— Elle Moore. How have you been?"

"Is this *the* Elle Sinclair, model extraordinaire, calling me?" Devon teased, though his tone revealed he was thrilled to hear her voice. "I must've died and gone to heaven."

"Knock it off," she laughed. "I'm in Miami for the next few weeks. I just landed, actually. Jeff mentioned you're in town too. It's been a long time, but I'd hoped we could have dinner one night and catch up."

"I'd love to. I can't wait to see you. Do you have to work today?"

"No, there's nothing planned for today at all."

"I'm coming to pick you up right now, then. You need to get out and have some fun while you're here. Where are you staying?"

She gave him the name of her hotel, with the caveat to give her enough time to get out of the airport first. With his signature laugh, he agreed to wait a couple of hours before meeting her in the lobby. With the time set, she kept reminding herself to stop thinking of it as a date. They were simply two old friends who had a chance to become reacquainted as adults.

Of course, that didn't stop her from rushing to her room, showering, and dressing as if she had a date. It didn't stop the butterflies that danced in her stomach or her heart from racing with excitement. It didn't calm her jittery nerves from wondering what he looked like after all these years apart, or if she'd even recognize him when she went down to the lobby.

When she stepped out of the elevator, she saw heads turn and heard whispers as people recognized her. But his eyes were the only ones she felt. His stare was the only one she couldn't tear her eyes away from. His face was the only one that registered out of all the people milling about. Any concern of not knowing him faded into nothing when his dark blue eyes connected with hers.

The years apart had done nothing to diminish her feelings for

Devon. Seeing him again after all the years made her heart turn flips in her chest. He'd always been an athletic, muscular young man, but the fully-grown man in front of her was even more impressive. Cut, defined muscles bulged under his shirt. From his wide, thick shoulders down to his tapered waist, the man was a specimen to behold. His jeans sat low on his hips. The snug-fitting denim gave a tantalizing hint at the muscular legs underneath.

"Elle, you're even more beautiful in person than on all those magazine covers," Devon said when he pulled her into his arms.

She slid her arms around his neck and returned his embrace. "You don't look so bad yourself, Devon. It's so good to see you again."

He kissed her cheek and flashed his dazzling smile. "I'll be the envy of every man in the world today. I get you all to myself. Are you ready for a day away from all the bright lights of the camera flashes?"

"You have no idea. In fact, you can even get us completely lost for a while, and you won't hear a single complaint from me."

"No chance of getting lost, but you'll feel like you're in another world. Let's blow this joint."

Devon extended his arm, and Elle wrapped her hand around it. The young, handsome boy she remembered had grown into a head-turning, gorgeous man with rippling muscles everywhere. He could give any male model a run for his money. The strength he naturally projected made her feel protected and safe. Even at her model height, he still stood taller than her. Their conversation flowed with a natural ease while they waited for the valet to bring his car around.

When a shiny red convertible Corvette stopped in front of them, Elle cut her eyes to him. "This is how you're whisking me away to anonymity? In a convertible Corvette that screams 'Look at me'?"

"Yep," he confirmed. "They can't snap pictures of you if you're flying by them in a blur."

Devon opened the passenger door and helped her into the car before his confident swagger carried him to the driver's side. On the interstate heading south with the top down, she felt carefree for the first time in what seemed like forever.

"Where are you taking me?"

"To a small but nice place in the Keys a friend owns. He rarely uses the house, and it's set on a private beach. It's a good place to go and not be seen or recognized by anyone. There are small, family-owned restaurants nearby."

"Sounds great. I should've brought my bathing suit, though, if we're going to the beach."

"Clothing is completely optional, so you don't even need one."

Her gasp followed by her chin hitting her chest made him laugh out loud. He couldn't keep up the façade even if he tried. Not with her.

"Have you lost your mind since the last time I saw you?"

"That's entirely possible, darlin'. But I'm only kidding about this. Partially anyway. If you twisted my arm really hard, I'd relent and let you skinny dip. Otherwise, we'll just walk around the small shops and find a tiny shred of cloth you can pretend is a bikini."

"I can already tell this outing will be memorable. Did you bring your loincloth or will you be going commando in the water?"

"One thing about me, darlin'. I'm always commando."

Heat filled her face, and she was infinitely appreciative of her sunglasses and the already hot South Florida temperature. The combination gave her the illusion of not being affected by him. She chose to ignore the deep rumble of his chuckle.

The small, unassuming beachfront home was surrounded by palm trees, giving the yard much-needed shade from the punishing rays of the sun. Devon strolled to the front door and unlocked it, pushing the door open for Elle to enter first.

"This is home for the day. It's not much, but it'll do for my plans."

"What are your plans?" Elle asked as she walked through the small beach cottage, trying to hide her nerves behind a quick perusal of the house. "What's on the agenda first?"

"First, I'll feed you. Then we'll grab a bathing suit, and we'll take my boat out for a spin. You still like to swim, don't you?"

"Are you kidding? I love it!"

"Let's go, then. You can leave your purse here. Everything is within walking distance from here. Today is all my treat."

"No. I called you, Devon," she protested. "You're not treating me when I proposed it."

"The hell I'm not. My momma raised me to be a Southern gentleman. You should already know that." With his hands firmly planted on her shoulders, he steered her toward the door, slipped her purse from her shoulder, and dropped it on the couch. "Now, let's go."

"You're such a stubborn man." She shook her head and rolled her eyes.

"You have no idea. I'll get my way no matter what I have to do." The smile in his voice only amplified his charm.

A quick stroll through the quaint streets led them to a small restaurant. If Devon hadn't pointed it out, Elle would've completely missed it. Though she was used to the attention from swarms of other people, it felt different coming from him. Opening doors, pulling out chairs, choosing the day's events, and taking care of her without being paid to do it made every gesture feel spontaneous and genuine. That was the exact opposite of how everyone else except Beth reacted to her celebrity status—being cordial because of what they could gain from her in return.

He ordered their lunches and turned his full attention to her. "You've grown up on me, Elle. I remember the little seven-year-old girl who followed me around all the time. Sneaking around cars, hiding behind trees, or using the corner of the house as cover to spy."

She smiled, remembering her favorite game of spying on Devon and Jeff. "I didn't know you were aware of all that at the time. I really thought I was being sly and that you didn't know you had a shadow."

An odd look flashed over his face, but it was gone as quickly as it had appeared. Unsure of what caused his discomfort, Elle kept talking, reminiscing over her childhood. "There was another time I'll never forget," she began, and she searched his eyes for a clue of his thoughts. "I never told you, I guess because I was so young and enamored of you. But you were always my hero. You made me feel welcome when Jeff tried to make me leave you two alone. You were always kind to me when he was my pain-in-the-ass older brother.

Then you saved my life and put yours in jeopardy at the same time. I've never forgotten that, Devon. I never will."

"I was just in the right place at the right time. That doesn't make me a hero."

"You ran out in front of that speeding car and grabbed me, Devon. You almost got hit while saving me. That does make you a hero. I wouldn't be here right now if it weren't for you. I never thanked you. I was so shaken up at first, then an embarrassed nine-year-old afterward. So, thank you. You're still my hero."

"Enough about me. We're here to talk about you. What are you doing in Miami?"

"I just signed on as the model for Kylie Rae Romano's newest fashion line. Over the next three weeks, I have multiple photoshoots in different locations around Miami. I'm here with eleven other models for the swimsuit shoot, too."

"Such an exciting life. You're always in front of the camera. Your face has been on the cover of every major magazine. There's hardly anyone in the free world who doesn't know your name. That's so impressive, Elle. Your whole life is in the spotlight."

"It's surreal. Some days, it's more than I ever thought it could be. Other days, it's more than I can take. I guess it all equals out in the end, though."

"You'll get movie deals before you know it. With your innate beauty, they won't be able to resist you."

"I'm actually starting acting classes soon, so I'll be ready to break in to that market next."

Devon nodded, understanding her life was on a fast track to more stardom, more notoriety, and more spotlights. "Well, while I have you all to myself, let's go grab that bathing suit and take the boat out. There's a great reef we can snorkel about three miles offshore. You need a day away from your adoring fans every now and then, don't you?"

"That sounds like heaven on earth. You have no idea how ready I am for this."

7

CHAPTER SEVEN

They strode together in comfortable companionship to an island-themed boutique a few stores down from the restaurant. The locals were sheltered in their island lives, content to live in their own paradise and not invite the pressures of the mainland in. Elle's presence wasn't noticed any more than Devon's was. With a new bathing suit in hand, they walked to the marina and boarded his boat.

While he maneuvered out of the marina and the no-wake zone, Elle retreated below deck to the small cabin to change into her new bikini. She grabbed the bottle of sunblock on her way back to the deck and stopped in her tracks when she cleared the doorway. A shirtless Devon stood at the helm, navigating the boat away from the island. Behind his mirrored shades was the man she'd idolized for years from a distance. But he was suddenly very close.

She slid her sunglasses over her eyes and walked toward him. "Sunscreen?" She managed to utter the single-word question.

One corner of his lips twitched, but he kept his tone neutral. "Sure."

She stepped behind him and shook a dollop of lotion onto her hand then began rubbing it on his broad shoulders. Mesmerized by the ripples and ridges of his muscles, her movements slowed as her fingers memorized every inch of him. With deliberate concentration, she committed every sensation to memory so she could relive the moment repeatedly. She squeezed more from the bottle and continued exploring his arms and coated his lower back, taking her time since she'd run out of excuses to keep putting her hands on him. With reluctance and disappointment filling her, she took a step back and began coating herself.

"You missed a spot," he said casually.

She looked up at him, but his back still faced her. "Where?"

"You didn't get my chest or my ears. Do you want me to fry out here on the water in the harsh Florida sun?"

She grinned to herself, thrilled he'd challenged her the way he did. If it had been left up to her, she wouldn't have had the courage to do it on her own. But with him all but daring her to continue, she was more than happy to oblige.

Firm strokes of her fingers glided across the smooth skin of his chest. Though his eyes were hidden, she felt them moving over her face as if he'd physically touched her. His muscled body was firm and strong under her touch. At first, she hadn't noticed how rigid he'd become. The more she massaged the lotion into his skin, the faster his chest rose and fell with his breaths. His lips parted, and his eyebrows disappeared completely behind the rim of his sunglasses. Even with her inexperience, she loved knowing her touch affected him as much as his presence affected her, and even more so when he couldn't hide it as well as he thought.

Intentionally adding long, smooth strokes, she increased the pressure, massaging the thick striations of his muscles more than rubbing the lotion. Relishing in his masculine quality. Allowing her fingers to roam over the hard ridges of his defined stomach muscles. From the corner of her eye, she noticed his hand gripped the boat's steering wheel tighter, his knuckles turned white, and he became as stiff as a board.

Rising up on her toes, she brushed her breasts across his chest when she reached for his ears. She gingerly stroked over the lobes and the upper rim, drawing in the powerful scent of his cologne with every inhale.

"Have I missed anywhere else?" she asked breathily.

He silently raised one eyebrow, the arch appearing over the top of his sunglasses. One side of his mouth lifted in a slow smile, then the other side followed, revealing his white teeth against his tanned skin. "That's a dangerous question to ask me, Elle. I already have to keep reminding myself you're Jeff's little sister. That little towheaded girl still lives behind your eyes."

Being doused with a cold bucket of ice water would've felt better than the way his words dashed her hopes that something more than friendship could develop between them. His words, though they weren't meant to hurt her, left a sting in her chest that momentarily clogged her throat. The emotions welled up inside with the realization he didn't look at her at all the way she saw him.

Beth's warning reverberated in her mind, confirming she'd gotten her hopes raised for something that would never be reality. She'd misread cues and put too much emphasis on her own feelings, projecting them onto him and seeing what she wanted to see. But his reminder that she was simply his friend's sister brought her feet back to the ground and her head out of the clouds.

She snapped the lid of the sunscreen bottle closed with more force than necessary before stepping out of his personal space. "I haven't been known as 'Jeff's little sister' since you two graduated high school. Where are the masks, snorkels, and fins? I'll get them ready while you steer the boat."

"They're in the storage compartment under the bench seat in the back of the boat." He kept one hand on the wheel as he turned to watch her walk away. His head was leaned to the side, his eyebrows drawn together, and his gaze fixed.

Knowing he scrutinized her every move, she pushed her disappointment aside while preparing the snorkeling gear. After he'd planned an excursion to give her a reprieve from prying eyes, the last thing she wanted was to seem ungrateful. Feeling hurt was her own fault, she reasoned, for setting such unrealistic expectations. At least she had the answer she needed and could stop holding out for the one she couldn't have.

Lost in her thoughts as she knelt in front of the storage area, she was startled when she felt strong hands grip her arms from behind and lift her to stand. She was whirled around with no effort, instantly facing him. His sunglasses were pushed up on his head, and she saw the questions swimming in the depths of his blue eyes. Without changing his gaze, he removed her sunglasses and stared deep into her eyes.

"What's wrong, Elle?" He held her face in his hands, keeping their connection intact, refusing to let her look away from him.

Her lips parted to speak, but a reply wouldn't come. How could she explain how foolish she'd been? If she spilled her true feelings to him, the rest of their day together would be awkward. Uncomfortable. Ruined.

"Nothing's wrong." Her voice was intentionally more upbeat. She forced happiness into her eyes. Whatever it took to avoid being mortified by the truth.

He narrowed his eyes, crinkling them at the corners, and lowered his brows in a demanding gesture. "For the record, I know you're lying to me. You didn't even feel the boat come to a stop or hear me walk up behind you. What was on your mind just now?"

"Just the things I need to do." She was intentionally vague while stating the truth at the same time.

"Giving me a version of the truth isn't a loophole I'll let you get away with for long. Just remember that."

"Are we already at the reef?"

Her abrupt change of subject didn't go unnoticed, but he decided against challenging it for the time being.

"Yeah, we're here. Do you know how to snorkel?"

"Of course. Last one in the water buys dinner tonight." She grabbed her gear, climbed over the bench seat, and jumped off the boat's platform into the shallow water around the sandbar. "You're too late. Looks like you lose, Devon," she taunted.

"If 'losing' means I get more time with you tonight, I'll take 'losing' any day." With a flying leap, he jumped into the water next to her.

She squealed with laughter when the wall of water splashed her. It turned to playful laughter when his hand wrapped around her ankle, and she knew he was about to pull her underneath the water with him. Without a second to spare, she drew in a deep breath, and her head disappeared under the water. He wrapped his strong arms around her waist and resurfaced with her attached to him.

Water dripped off their faces, and the slight waves lapped around them while he kept a tight hold on her. "Now that you're at my mercy —" he smirked "—don't lie to me again. I can tell—I can *always* tell. You became upset with me when I said you're Jeff's little sister. Why?"

Resigned to being caught dead to rights, she decided to come clean with him. It was time to spill the secret she'd harbored for as long as she could remember. "I wanted you to see me as more than some little girl from your hometown. More than your friend's little sister. But apparently, our roles are set. I was just disappointed. That's all. It's fine—don't worry about it.

He nodded slowly, studying her face and her eyes. "You think the way I look at you is simply as my friend's little sister? I don't think you heard exactly what I said. I have to *remind* myself of it constantly, because that's not at all what I see when I look at you now.

"You're gorgeous, without a doubt. You're strong and fearless and smart and determined. You are kind, genuine, loving, and funny. I couldn't have made a more perfect woman if I'd made you myself. You're fucking sexy as hell, every inch of you, every part of you, inside and out. Before you get it in your head that I don't want you, think again."

He watched with rapt attention as a droplet of water rolled down her cheek and onto her lips. In a rare lapse of self-control, he couldn't resist licking the water from her lips. With a light swipe of his tongue across the part in her lips, he sampled her unique flavor and was immediately addicted. One taste only made him want more.

He took every bit of what she willingly offered. With his head tilted to the side, he slanted his mouth over hers and drove his tongue inside.

His tongue slid against hers, and she gripped his hair tightly. Every silky-smooth pass of her tongue on his pushed him closer to the edge of losing all restraint. Low moans emanated from her chest when she wrapped her legs around his waist, crushing her thinly covered chest to his bare one. His hips surged upward involuntarily, brushing against her clit through her barely there bikini bottoms.

He gripped the hair on the back of her head and pulled lightly, separating them and ending their sensual hold. His voice deepened, and his intent gaze pierced her soul. "Don't ever think I don't want you. It takes all my willpower to think of anything other than the things I want to do to you. With you. Things I want to watch you do."

"Maybe you should reserve your willpower for more important things."

"You'll be the death of me yet." With a surrendering groan, he crushed his lips to hers for one more taste. "Now swim over to the sandbar and get your gear on so we can snorkel while we're out here. Before I change my mind and choose more interesting activities." He lowered his head and licked up her neck, sending chill bumps across her skin.

He reluctantly released her as they made their way to the shallow water. Once they were both ready, he led the way to the reef. They explored the underwater sanctuary like two overgrown kids who'd found sunken treasure. Minutes turned to hours, and by the time they climbed back aboard Devon's boat, Elle's energy had been depleted.

With the gear stowed, she plopped down on the bench seat and lay back, her arm bent across her face to shield her eyes. "I just remembered something. I was supposed to rest and hydrate today so I'd be ready for the lights and cameras tomorrow. Guess I completely messed that one up, huh?"

"Yeah, you really did. Maybe they'll fire you, then I'll have you all to myself for even longer." He stood over her holding a cold bottle of water, letting the small pieces of ice and water droplets fall on her bare skin.

When the ice hit her stomach, she jerked up with a start and came face-to-face with the bottled water. "I heard you need to hydrate."

"So thoughtful of you."

"It's good of you to notice. I do try."

When they returned to land, it was late afternoon, and Devon found he wasn't ready to let Elle leave. "You're tired, aren't you, darlin'? It's been a long day. Flying across the country late last night, shopping, snorkeling, trying to have your way with me. You've been very busy."

"Trying to have my *what*?" she laughed, playfully punching him in the arm.

"Why don't you go take a hot shower, curl up in the bed for a nap, and I'll wake you when it's time to eat? We're only about an hour from your hotel, so I can still have you home before your curfew."

She eyed him suspiciously for a few seconds, then relented. She didn't want their time together to end, and she decided taking him up on his offer was the best all-around solution. "I can't turn that offer down. Don't let me sleep too long, or I'll be up all night tonight."

"That's not much of an incentive for me to wake you up soon."

"You are going to be the death of me," she quipped, throwing his earlier words back at him.

That odd expression quickly passed over his face then disappeared again. She watched him closer this time, waiting to see if he revealed anything else. His eyes softened, but his face gave nothing else away. She raised up on her toes and placed a light kiss on his full lips. He returned it and cupped her face with his hands. He continued holding her face when she broke off the kiss. "What was that for?"

"You said you can tell when I'm lying. Well, I can tell when you're hiding something. For whatever reason, you don't want to tell me what it is. But I want you to know, I'm here when you're ready to talk about it."

She left him alone to mull over her offer while she showered, changed back into her clothes, and crawled into the bed. Once her head hit the pillow, she was fast asleep with dreams of Devon replaying the day's events. His words. Their kiss. The feel of her body crushed to his. How protected she felt in his arms. Every superb sensation brilliantly repeated in her mind's eye, where she felt loved, desired, and sheltered.

The scent of food cooking pulled her from the best sleep she'd had in weeks—and the best dream she'd ever had, period. She rolled off the side of the bed and walked into the kitchen. Finding Devon shirtless, in his form-fitting jeans, and barefoot would've been enough to ignite any woman's libido. When she realized he was cooking dinner, her heart melted. When he turned and saw her standing in the doorway, he smiled and pitched the hand towel over his bare shoulder. Her gaze traveled down his chest, over his stomach, taking in the happy trail and sexy V, and landed on his unbuttoned jeans.

Her mouth opened, and she sucked in a surprised breath. Her tongue darted out, reflexively wetting her lips as she continued to stare. When she met his knowing gaze, she didn't have enough wits about her to be embarrassed. She was too busy enjoying the view.

"See something you like?" He pushed off the counter and stalked toward her with slow and deliberate steps. "Elle, if you keep staring like you'd rather have *me* for dinner than this food, I'll make sure you're fed all night long."

Caged between his arms with her back against the wall, she watched as he fought his desire for her. The war between what he wanted to do and what he should do played out in his blue depths, and she wanted it to be the last time the thought of hesitation ever crossed his mind. She reached up and gently touched his lips, lightly gliding her fingertip over them. Over his chin. Down his neck, over his Adam's apple, to the hollow dip at the base of his throat. She lifted her eyes to meet his when her fingers continued their journey. She splayed her hand flat against his chest and raised her other hand to match.

The uncertainty in his expression changed to a raging inferno before her. He leaned in closer. His lips barely hovered over hers, grazing with the lightest touch when he spoke.

"Don't think I don't know what you're doing. Fuck if it isn't working, though. You seem damned and determined to have this your way. Be careful what you wish for, Elle. In this case, you may get more than you can handle."

Shocked by his words and the way he saw through her, she stood rooted to the floor and drank in his closeness, his masculinity, his commanding presence. The words she wanted to say wouldn't come. Not that she'd blurt them out even if she could speak, though she doubted her feelings were a secret from him. He seemed to be a mind reader, and she was apparently an open book.

"For tonight, I'll keep my gentlemanly reputation intact and save you from yourself. If you look at me like that tomorrow night, I won't be responsible for my actions."

"Tomorrow night?" Her voice was low and unsure, a complete contradiction to the confident persona she projected in her pictures.

"You're here for three weeks, right?"

"Right."

"Then you're mine every spare minute for the next three weeks. I may have to disappear for work now and then, but I won't leave you for very long. So, before you test my resolve again, let's eat and then I'll take you back to your hotel."

"You're not staying with me tonight?"

He narrowed his eyes at her, gauging the motive behind her question. Satisfied it was legitimate, he placed a warm kiss on her cheek before replying. "I'd love to stay with you tonight, but I have work to do. It'll be late before I finish, and I know you start work early tomorrow. If there were any way I could get out of it, I would. Believe me."

"Stop. I just showed up and called you out of the blue. I don't expect you to drop your whole life for me." She cut her eyes playfully to the side. "I only expect you to drop all your other girlfriends for me. That's all."

His brilliant smile lit up his gorgeous face, amusement sparkling in his eyes. "Done. I don't have any girlfriends, so that's not a problem."

He retreated to the stove to serve their dinner, his demeanor unchanged from his usual cheerful self. Though, she couldn't help but notice he didn't make the same request of her.

8

——————

CHAPTER EIGHT

"**Y**ou look like you've been up all night. What did you do? I said to rest and hydrate." Leslie glared at Elle from around his camera.

"I tried to rest last night, Leslie. The room above mine apparently pulled an all-nighter. They'd stop the music and noise long enough for the manager to threaten to kick them out, then they started up again." She struck a pose and moved slowly through the constantly clicking of the shutter.

"You should've called me. I'll take care of it right now, though." He put the camera down and snapped his fingers. On cue, his assistant appeared at his side. "Meechelle, Miss Sinclair needs a new room, with silence and tranquility on all sides. Not around loud revelers."

A few minutes later, Meechelle reappeared, apprehension covering her face. "Leslie, the hotel is sold out. There are no rooms to move her into."

"Must I handle everything?" he sighed. "As soon as the shoot is over, you'll have a new room, Elle."

She didn't have the heart to tell him she had no intentions of sleeping that night either. Devon promised he'd stay with her all night. She had twenty days with him, and she planned to make the most of every opportunity she was given. "Maybe the partiers will check out today," she offered.

"Meechelle, take her to the spa for a couple of hours while I shoot the others. Come back to me when she looks rested and photogenic again."

Two hours later, Elle emerged from the spa, refreshed and renewed. Leslie and Elle focused on the various moods he needed for the project, directing her into poses and sexy pouts to complete his overall vision.

She felt the change in the air and heard the low murmurs of whispers around the outdoor set. Without visual verification, she knew what had everyone buzzing—or rather, *who* had everyone's attention. Devon stepped into her direct line of sight, and their eyes met in an instant.

"That! Yes! That look!" Leslie yelped and moved in for a closeup shot.

Devon watched Elle, ignoring the obvious stares and questioning eyes all around him. In truth, he'd been watching her since she walked out of the spa. His training made him stealthy. Deadly. Invisible, when he wanted to be. He'd been invisible long enough at that point—he wanted her to see him. He wanted to see her reaction, to gauge her response, to read her body language when she was surprised by his presence.

What he got wasn't at all what he expected.

The look she gave him was more lethal than any he'd encountered. It was deadly to his way of life. The way it struck his core was detrimental to the plans he'd made. The fact that he liked it more than he should warned him to run while he still could.

But he knew it was already too late for that plan to work in his favor. Three weeks. He could handle three short weeks of being exclusive with a beautiful cover model.

Even if she was the younger sister of his friend.

Even if she'd celebrate her twenty-first birthday during their time together, further accentuating the age difference between them.

Even if it meant he had to give up the cover of shadows temporarily and live in her limelight.

"The spa must've been exactly what you needed. I've never seen you look more beautiful, my dear." Leslie stepped to the side, the camera all but glued to his face, while another man held Elle's singular focus. "Oh, honey, I love the fierce look, too. You're giving me so much to work with today, it'll be hard to choose just one."

The smirk covering Devon's face confirmed he'd heard Leslie, and he knew exactly what prompted the change in her expression. It was bad enough when the buxom sable-haired beauty in the string bikini approached him, but when the overtly flirtatious intruder put her hand on his arm, Elle became irrationally jealous and possessive.

Relief flooded her senses instantly when his response included a gesture toward Elle. The bikini-girl looked over her shoulder, immediately recognized Elle, and scurried away from Devon. Pride over witnessing the small victory swept over her, and Devon's smirk transformed into a beaming smile.

Smooth, Moore. Real smooth, she thought.

"And that's a wrap for you, my love. Rest. Hydrate. Come back to me even more gorgeous tomorrow." Leslie kissed the air on either side of her face and dismissed her when he called the next model into range of his viewfinder.

"I didn't expect to see you here today." Elle approached Devon, delighting in the sensation of his eyes heavy on her barely clad skin.

"Where the fuck was that bathing suit when we were on the boat yesterday? It's probably a good thing you weren't wearing it. You'd still be held in a secure, remote location where no one except me could find you."

"Promises, promises."

He wrapped his arm around her bare waist and pulled her to him. "I've warned you about that." He leaned down and captured her mouth with his, not caring that dozens of cell phone cameras captured their every move. "Let's go. I have more plans for you today. Do you get to keep the bikini?"

With a chuckle, she shook her head. "Not this time. Are we going back to the boat?"

"That's not what I had planned, but I'm game if that's what you want to do."

"Honestly, I don't care if we go play Skee-Ball for six straight hours. Just take me with you."

"Who told you my plans?"

"I'll never tell. Let me change, and I'll be ready to get out of here."

"Shorts. T-shirt. Bikini. Then dress for dinner and dancing tonight."

She stopped walking, waiting for him to give the punch line of his joke, but none came. "You're serious?"

"Of course. You're mine today. Remember? Move that fine ass. You're wasting daylight." He playfully smacked her on the ass, making her jump and squeal with laughter at the same time.

"Come on up. I'll have to pack a bag with all my makeup, hair stuff, shoes, clothes, jewelry—"

"Fine. Start with a bikini, T-shirt, and shorts. We'll come back here for the rest later. I'm still coming up to your room with you right now, though."

Devon roamed around her room, making himself at home and checking every nook and cranny of the space while she changed clothes. When she emerged from the bathroom, she found him standing on a chair, checking the smoke detector.

"Everything okay?"

"Absolutely. Just can't be too careful." He stepped down from the chair and raked his eyes up and down her. "You could wear a black plastic garbage bag and make it look sexy as hell."

"Such a sweet talker." She patted him on the cheek with her palm, accepting any excuse to touch him.

"We need to go now. Or we won't leave this room at all for a very long time. Then we'll miss our reservations."

"By all means, lead the way. I'm curious to see what you have planned for me today."

"A day you'll never forget." He laced their fingers together, picked up her bag, and pulled her into his side after they were through the hotel doorway.

"It'll be extremely hard for you to top today. That was so amazing! If we do that every day for the next three weeks, it'd never get old."

"Hmph." Devon had sulked since they left the research center.

"Are you still pouting?"

"Yes. Yes, I am." He crossed his arms over his chest.

"You're not even going to hold my hand now?" She managed not to laugh, but hiding her smile was impossible.

"Nope."

"He was just so amazing, Devon. I couldn't help but fall in love with him."

He cut his eyes sideways at her, his mouth gaped open in shock, and his eyes narrowed in disbelief. "You're still defending your actions? Unbelievable."

"But I'll probably never see him again," she argued.

The elevator doors opened, and they stepped in together. Devon punched the button for the seventeenth floor and waited for the doors to slide shut. As soon as they were alone, he pinned her to the wall with his body and kept his eyes trained on hers. "For the record, you're not allowed to have any other boyfriends. Ever. Not when I'm not around. And especially not when I'm there to witness it."

"But I've always loved dolphins...and you're the one who took me to see him."

"He got more kisses than I did. That's not acceptable by any stretch of the imagination. He knew it, too. Did you see how he smirked at me?"

"I saw the smile all dolphins appear to have on their faces. But I don't think that was a malicious smirk toward you."

"It's an alpha-male thing. You wouldn't understand," Devon countered.

"Ah, I see. Well, I'll make it up to you. Just tell me, in alpha-male code, how to do that."

"I'd much rather show you." He covered her mouth with his and gently licked across the part in her lips. "After dinner. You're making us late again, distracting me, and wreaking havoc on my plans. Go shower and get ready, woman. I'll be back in an hour to pick you up. You'd better be ready, or you'll be in even more trouble."

"Yes, sir." She saluted him in a joking fashion and slid out of his embrace. "Whatever you say."

Elle rushed to dress for a night of dinner, dancing, and more with the man she'd never been able to get out of her mind. Giddy with excitement, she hurried through her hotel room, threw on a dress and heels, and perfected her hair and makeup. She was putting the last earring in when the knock on her door came. One hour, on the dot. After peeking through the peephole, she flung the door open and grabbed her clutch from the table.

"I'm ready. On time, even."

Devon quirked one eyebrow upward. "Damn. I was looking forward to your punishment for making me wait."

Their date night would forever be etched in her memory. Beth was correct when she said Elle's professional life didn't leave her much time for a personal life. After their dinner over candlelight, Devon took her to a loud, packed club to dance. Approaching the bouncer, she was seized by fear at the thought of being turned away for being underage. Devon shook hands with the enormous man guarding the roped entrance, leaned in to his ear to whisper something, and stepped back to give the bouncer room to unhook the velvet barrier.

"Come on in, Shadow. It's been a long time, brother."

"Thanks, man. Good to see you."

"Your private room on the third floor is ready when you are. Enjoy."

Devon tipped his head at the bouncer, put his hand on the small of Elle's back, and led her through the crowded nightclub with ease. Whether it was his size or his dark expression, she wasn't sure, but the sea of people seemed to part willingly to move out of his path. The curved staircase leading to the private rooms gave the hopping club an air of glamour and class. They made their way to the third floor, and he led her to their exclusive corner room.

"Shadow?" she asked when he'd closed the door behind them.

"It was my nickname when I was in the service. The bouncer is an old Army buddy of mine."

A rapid knock on the door was immediately followed by several waitresses entering with trays of drinks and hors d'oeuvres. They placed them on the private bar and left as quickly as they appeared.

"You've thought of everything. I was worried they wouldn't let me in and I'd be mortified after being turned away in front of the crowd outside," Elle confessed.

"I'd never let anyone do that to you." He brushed a strand of hair away from her face, his fingers grazing across her skin and heating her from the inside out.

She stepped into him, held his face in her hands, then raised up on her tiptoes to initiate a kiss. When their lips connected, his reaction was tentative at first, but she was undeterred. Swiping the part of his lips with her tongue, she moved in when his mouth opened to her.

At first, she thought she was in control of their encounter. But he quickly proved her wrong. His fingers weaved through her hair, gripping at the roots, and he angled her head where he wanted it. The urgency and demanding nature of his tongue's caress overwhelmed her senses with a feeling of sheer perfection. When he broke the kiss, she was afraid he would pull away from her altogether, tell her he thought it was a bad idea, and then disappear from her life.

"Let's have a drink," he suggested then moved to the trays. He returned with two glasses—a beer mug for him and a glass of Moscato d'Asti for her. "We need a poignant toast."

They held up their glasses, and she waited for him to continue.

"To old friends reuniting, creating new memories, and never regretting a single moment."

"To us," she added.

"Ready to go dance?" he asked after they'd finished their drinks.

"Absolutely. You don't have two left feet, do you?"

"You just want to insult me again, don't you? After repeatedly kissing Sammy right in front of me."

"Sammy. The dolphin," she clarified.

"Come on." He chuckled under his breath as he took her hand. "Let's go dance so I can pretend to accidentally grope you on purpose while we're on the dance floor."

"Mr. Kane, if you keep talking like that, you will absolutely sweep me off my feet. You are such a romantic."

On the dance floor, in the middle of the throngs of bodies writhing to the music, Devon and Elle moved to their own beat. He held her close to him, bumping and grinding, rubbing and caressing, blocking out every other person in the room. A few hours later, the alcohol had been consumed, the food was eaten, and neither could deny where their course would take them next.

"I heard Leslie say you're supposed to rest and hydrate tonight. I seemed to have single-handedly screwed that up for you. Maybe we should head back to the hotel now."

"Absolutely," she agreed. But sleep was the last thing she wanted.

The ride back to the hotel was quiet, each lost in their own thoughts of how the night would end. Or wouldn't end. When he turned into the hotel drive, the lines separating the valet parking from self-parking loomed before them.

"Valet." Her single-word instruction was enough to convince him.

They exited the car, and he escorted her into the lobby. With the bank of elevators in sight, she sensed his second thoughts were getting the better of him. She took his hand in hers and faked confidence she in no way felt.

"Come upstairs with me, Devon. Stay with me tonight."

Without waiting for a reply, she pulled him toward the bank of elevators and pushed the call button. His hesitation had lasted a split second before they stepped onto the elevator. But once he relented after the doors closed, he gave her hope and reinforced her confidence. He wanted her as much as she wanted him, and there was no way in hell she'd let him back out on her after they stepped out of the elevator.

Holding his hand, she opened the door to her room and mentally noted how he hadn't even attempted to release hers. With the door closed and locked behind them, she turned to face him, meeting his heated stare.

"You're sure about this?" he asked, though she knew he still unsure.

"I've never been more positive of anything else in my life, Devon."

With a slight shake of his head, he stepped into her and took complete control of her body. "Then I should warn you first. This is my domain, and when we're in the bedroom, I'm in complete command."

Her lips parted with her sudden inhale, her cheeks flushed, and her eyes grew wider at his declaration. Waves of shock and excitement rolled through her. "Okay." Her reply came out as a raspy whisper.

His blue eyes darkened to nearly black when he leaned in closer to her, a glint of realization sparkling before he masked it. "Have you ever done this before?"

She shook her head. "No."

Devon hid his shock.

He remained her hero. After all the years apart, he couldn't help but look out for her best interests. "I warned your brother to keep the guys away from you. I never thought I'd be one of those guys I warned him about. I'm not sure how he'd feel about this."

"I guess this is where I should confess something to you." She watched his expression for any subtle changes. "I always knew you'd be—" she air-quoted his words "—'one of those guys.'" Elle searched his face and witnessed his expression soften before she spoke next. "And I don't care what my brother thinks about it. This is my life."

"Elle." Her name on his lips signaled his surrender and issued a warning.

"Devon."

A sudden passionate embrace had her in his arms, and their

bodies melded together in perfect harmony. Their clothes disappeared, strewn in various places around the hotel room. She barely registered the sound of the condom package ripping open before he deftly rolled it onto his impressive length. He lifted her in his arms and carried her to the bed, then placed her in the center before he covered her body with his own.

His deep, searing kisses branded her with a brush of his tongue, leaving his invisible mark and claiming her as his and only his. He rolled her onto her side and slid his finger along her slit, stroking the sensitive skin and dragging the moisture from her sex around her clit in a deliciously teasing movement. Her gasps filled the air as his murmurs filled her ears when his fingers filled her body. Her pleasure coated his hand when her body could no longer contain the intense sensations building from within.

His powerfully strong muscles expanded and contracted when he rolled back on top of her. His hips pushed forward, delightfully teasing her limits. She arched her back as he slid his manhood across her drenched opening. He hovered above her, waiting for her consent while he maintained eye contact. She nodded. Her gaze never left his; her certainty never faltered. Slowly, his long, thick cock slid into her, and he became acutely aware that he was her first. The twinge of pain she undoubtedly felt would soon get replaced with waves of pleasure. He'd make sure of that. Sweat-covered skin slid across sweat-covered skin, heating each other almost to the point of spontaneous combustion.

Their eyes remained locked as he surged into her, over and over, and a deeper connection passed between them. The knowledge they'd never be as they once were, along with the realization they both wanted more settled between them. He gripped her legs and drove into her until she screamed his name in ultimate bliss, and her body shook from the intensity.

When he asked if she'd ever done that before, he had referred to being submissive to another man in the bedroom. She'd answered truthfully, and that excited him more than he'd allow himself to show. But the moment he realized she'd never been with another man in any way, he knew he was in over his head. The way her body wrapped around his cock, tight and wet, snug and soft, feeling as if she was custom made to fit him.

She'd fallen asleep after their first time, but he couldn't sleep even if his life had depended on it. She lay beside him with the sheet pushed down to her waist and the moonlight streaming across her breasts. He watched her sleep for the first hour, holding on to his last shred of willpower to avoid waking her and taking her again. The cool breeze from the air conditioner drifted over her, causing her nipples to pebble.

That was the exact moment his resolve broke.

He leaned over and covered one of her firm peaks with his mouth, instantly warming her cold skin. One taste of her wasn't enough, and his careful ministrations turned to voracious feasting. He slid his hand down her stomach as her fingers weaved through his hair. His fingers crawled over her slit slowly at first, testing the tenderness of her sensitive tissues before delving deeply inside her.

She slid her other hand down and covered his. His immediate thought was she was stopping him because she was too sore. But she surprised him when she spread her legs and pushed his fingers inside her wetness. Her hips bucked involuntarily, and she moaned with pleasure.

"Mmm, that's my girl," he murmured in her ear. "You like that, don't you?" He thrust two fingers into her while rubbing her clit with the callused pad of his thumb.

Her fingers gripped his hair as she rode his hand, the waves of ecstasy rippling through her body. He slid down and settled between her legs. His mouth teased her clit with more pleasure than she'd ever known. When his warm tongue laved her from bottom to top, the pleasure dragged her over the edge, past the point of no return, and her body shook from the intensity of it.

After lapping up every last bit of her essence, he crawled up her body until his cock was poised at her still wet entrance. "Are you ready for me, Elle?"

"I'm more than ready for you, Devon," she purred. "I must have died and gone to heaven. I've never felt anything like this before."

His hips surged forward, driving into the hilt with one forceful lunge. In one hand, he held Elle's hands above her head. The other hand reached behind her knee and pulled her thigh toward her chest, changing his angle and deepening his penetration. Her screams of pleasure echoed off the walls, and his name rang in the air. It was a sound he wasn't likely ever to forget.

Over their three weeks together, every spare minute she had away from modeling was spent with him. They took long strolls on the beach, they talked, they shared, they laughed, they played, and they inevitably grew closer. Their three weeks together felt like both the longest and shortest period of her life.

Her last night in Miami, he'd suggested they meet for dinner at the restaurant in her hotel's lobby, knowing she had an early-morning flight out the following day. She dreaded the moment when their dinner was over, and he stood to leave the restaurant. Something stopped him, though, and their eyes locked in a heated but silent debate.

He stayed with her the rest of the night, making love to her twice more while he demonstrated a few of his other masterful bedroom skills before she had to leave for California. He insisted on driving her to the airport early that next morning for her flight, though the other models planned to ride together. Part of her wanted to deny his request, knowing it would be hard enough to say goodbye. But, a bigger part of her heart needed to know how he'd react to her departure.

Would it affect him in the way she knew it would her?

He parked in the unloading zone and left the car running. Without saying a word, she reached for the door handle, but he grabbed her other hand in his and stilled her movements. "Elle, don't leave here thinking this was just a long one-night stand. It's not, by a long shot."

"Then, what is it?"

"It's more complicated than that."

"Come to LA with me." She blurted out the words before she realized what she was asking, what she hoped, what she begged of him.

"Stay in Miami with me." His eyes were sincere, his voice held no humor.

She tried hard to fight back the tears before she replied, "I can't."

He nodded, and disappointment flashed in his eyes. "I understand."

With heavy hearts, they exited the car. He grabbed her bags from the trunk and checked them with the curbside valet. A tender kiss was their only goodbye before she watched him drive away from inside the terminal.

CHAPTER NINE

Five Years Earlier

"Elle, you know how much I love you, right?"

"I know you love me when you want something. What is it this time? My shoes? My brand-new gray ostrich leather Hermes purse that I haven't even used yet? Spill it."

Beth's devilish grin made Elle stop dead in her tracks. "Dear God. What have you done? I'll be forced to kill you any minute now, won't I?"

Beth dismissed the threat with a shrug of her shoulder and the broadening of her smile. "I may have let it slip to Bruce and Josh that you're single. Josh may have expressed considerable interest in changing your relationship status. Bruce may have suggested we go out on a double date this weekend so you can give Josh a chance. Josh and Bruce may have already made plans for the four of us."

"No." The firm tone of Elle's rebuttal contradicted her normal demeanor, catching Beth off guard even after years of being at her best friend's side. "Beth, you know better than to set me up on a date with anyone. I'm not interested, and I won't go out just for the sake of going and then have our pictures splashed across the front page of every rag magazine. You know how vicious they can be. I can't believe you'd do that to me."

Elle's hands shook, her voice quavered, and her heart raced. She was angry with Beth and her boyfriend of the month, Bruce, for being so presumptuous and cavalier with her career. But she didn't want to face the deeper underlying reasons fanning the flames of her anger. At that moment, she found it was easier—safer—to place the brunt of it squarely on Beth's shoulders.

"I'm sorry, Elle. You know I'd never hurt you. It hurts me to see you pining your life away for a man who obviously doesn't feel the same about you. It's been three years since you started this insane relationship with him in Miami. It's not even a relationship." Beth search for the right word, and her agitation grew with each passing second. "It's an *arrangement* to benefit him! He just happens to show up out of the blue, and you drop everything to spend a few weeks with him. Then he leaves again, and you don't hear from him for several months.

"Think about it, Elle. Who's here to pick up the pieces of your shattered heart when he kills every hope and dream you have? Me. I'm the one who loves you and shows you every single day. How could you even think for a second I'd do anything to hurt you?"

The verbal slap from Beth's words didn't sting nearly as much as knowing she was right did. A vision of all the times Beth had stayed up all night, whispered comforting words, and kept her arm wrapped around Elle until they'd both fallen asleep from sheer exhaustion flashed through Elle's mind. Beth had been her best friend for more years than not, had been with her through the best and worst moments of her life, and had only ever shown loyalty.

"Beth, I—"

"You know what? Save it. Bruce and I have a date tonight, but I think I'll just go to his place instead of him coming here. Don't wait up for me."

With that, Beth stormed out of the apartment and slammed the door behind her. Elle sank down onto the couch, bent at the waist, and rested her face in her hands. As usual, Beth called it like she saw it—no holds barred, no sugarcoating, and no excuses. Almost every other time Beth had interjected, her frankness had been Elle's saving grace. The exception to the rule was when the discussion involved anything remotely related to Devon.

"Beth, I'm sorry. You're absolutely right," she confessed to the empty apartment. "Everything in my life fades to background noise when Devon shows up. It's not even a conscious choice that I make. Every time there's a knock at the door, my heart races and thumps like a bass drum because I hope he's there. I look for him everywhere I go, hoping he'll appear out of thin air.

"And you know what else? I wouldn't even question it if he did. I'd just be *so fucking happy* that he was beside me, the reason why wouldn't matter. I guess that creates another question, doesn't it? I'm so in love with him. I'm so happy to get a few weeks with him now and then, I don't ever question why that's all I get. Why do I settle for less than I want or deserve?"

Even though she couldn't say the words to Beth, she believed getting the thoughts out of her head and into the open was a step in the right direction. She looked up, dried her tears with her fingers, and released an exasperated breath. A rap on the door caused her to jump, then her eyes dropped to the side table where Beth's keys laid. She'd stomped out of the apartment in such a huff, she didn't grab her keys first.

"I'm glad you forgot your keys," Elle called out through the closed door. She swung the door open wide and held the forgotten keys out in the palm of her hand.

"You haven't given me any keys," Devon replied with a sexy smirk. His eyes traveled up and down her body, drinking in every inch, branding her without a single touch. "But whatever you're offering, I certainly won't refuse."

She squeezed her fist around the keys. The sharp metal tips bit into her skin, but all she felt was complete exhilaration that he was there. The initial ardent expression in his gaze, the sexy timbre of his voice, and the confident air he projected create the ultimate lady-killer package. But the way he looked at her when his eyes softened said he never wanted to leave her. When his arms snaked around her waist and held her tightly against him, he revealed he'd missed her every bit as much as she'd missed him. The way he buried his face in her hair and deeply inhaled her scent exposed his vulnerable side, the one that wanted to hide away with her and never be found.

This is why I can never refuse him, she reflected. *This is what keeps me coming back for more. Every. Single. Time.*

Still holding her in their intimate embrace, he gently pushed her backward until they'd walked into the apartment and locked the door behind them. Time passed while they clung to one another, but neither was prepared—or capable—of letting go. He returned with a different demeanor each time. Just as she never knew when to expect him to show up, she also had no idea what kind of mood he'd be in.

When he returned sullen and quiet, she automatically knew his only solace was found in her touch. For the first few days, while he worked through whatever weighed on his mind, she'd learned not to move out of his reach. Though she had no idea what drove his need, she knew he needed the closeness their physical contact provided.

On the rare occasions when he was agitated and easily annoyed upon his reappearance, he took his dominance in the bedroom to a stratospheric level. His commands were direct and without mirth. He expected and accepted nothing less than full submission from her. She complied with his instructions the moment they were spoken, offered more than he requested, and bit her tongue. Once he'd worked through what bothered him, he became more like himself again, albeit a more subdued version.

As she stood there in his embrace, she tried to assess his frame of mind. His sexy, playful remark when she opened the door more resembled his usual demeanor. But the way he held her signaled something was different. Something had happened that affected him deeply.

"What are you thinking about, Devon? What's bothering you?" Her tone urged him to talk to her, to share a part of his life she knew nothing about.

His arms tightened around her in response.

"You have to let me in. I *want* to be part of your life."

"Darlin', believe me when I say, you're the *best* part of my life." Though his voice was partially muffled, the sincerity of his words flowed through her, filling her with hope. He lifted her with ease, held her tightly against his chest, and she wrapped her legs around his waist. He sat on the couch and adjusted her position without releasing his hold. He raised his head, met her questioning eyes, and felt compelled to share what he could.

"You know I spent time in the Army, in Special Forces. There's a lot of bad shit going on with a buddy from my old unit. He's more than a friend—he's part of my family. He's the brother I never had. His whole world has just been turned upside down. I have no doubt he can take care of himself. But he doesn't know the people he's mixed up with like he thinks he does—or what they can do to him."

"But you know they're corrupt. Why haven't you told him?"

"Because I can't—not yet anyway."

"I don't understand, Devon. If he's your brother, how can you not warn him about these people? Are you part of them—or in business with them?"

"It's a little more complicated than that, darlin'."

The suspicion in her eyes and the difference in how she looked at him were the very reasons he'd avoided discussing anything to do with the cases he worked. In their three years together, she'd accepted his ambiguous reasons for not calling regularly and the months he wasn't accessible at all. When he explained the classified nature of the missions he carried out in the Army, he implied his current work had the same conditions. But that was the extent of how much he divulged about his job and the activities it required of him.

After hearing he was aware of and involved with shady people, Elle naturally had more questions about his job, about his friends, and even about him. Questions he couldn't answer. Answers he couldn't give. Secrets he couldn't share. His undercover missions lasted months on end at times. But when the assignment concluded, he'd always made his way back to her. There were times his investigations brought him to LA, and though it went against his better judgment, those nights were spent in her bed.

He'd agonized over those decisions. Had he been careful enough not to be seen? Had he inadvertently made her a target? Too many times to count, he'd considered what he'd do if anyone hurt her, especially if he was the reason why. There was no hole deep enough, no island remote enough, and no place too far away for that man to escape the wrath of Shadow's blade. Any shred of information she had about his operations put her in more danger than she could imagine. He'd already crossed a line by sharing what little he'd said.

The hero light she'd always cast over him had begun to dim. The doubts about him started taking root in her mind. She had no idea of the dark, dangerous, and deadly exploits he'd carried out. She was utterly unaware of the horrible acts he was capable of doing—and frequently performed in the line of duty. While he had no qualms about doing whatever the job called for, there were facts about him he never wanted *her* to know.

Yet, he witnessed the skepticism and wariness mix with her feelings for him. He felt her body stiffen ever so slightly when the anger rolled through her, though she tried to hide it. Her eyes narrowed faintly as she pondered her next question—how to ask, and if she genuinely wanted the answer.

"Do you still talk to Jeff?"

"Occasionally."

"Have you told him about us?"

"No, I haven't."

The corners of her eyes squeezed together perceptibly. "Why not?"

"Because I don't feel the need to announce and advertise my private life to anyone."

"Wow." She pushed off his lap to stand in front of him. She ran her fingers through her hair in frustration as she began to pace. "I don't know which statement to be offended by first. That I'm lumped into the 'anyone' category. That you shut me out of your public and private life. Or that there are underhanded people who don't deserve your allegiance, but they seem to know more about you than I do. Beth was right."

And there's the resentment, he thought.

"What was Beth right about?"

"She and I had an argument right before you showed up. About you."

I know. I heard the entire conversation, then disappeared before she walked out. He kept his face impassive, concealing his true thoughts and feelings. "What about me?"

"What are we doing, Devon? What is really happening between us? Are we simply friends with benefits, or do you genuinely have feelings for me?"

Unshed tears glistened in her eyes as she fought with all her might to keep the fears at bay. He watched her chin quiver, her chest rise and fall with the deep breaths she took to calm herself, and the way she squared her shoulders to prepare for his response. She was the most beautiful woman he'd ever seen, inside and out. She deserved so much better than him, so much more than he could give her. But he'd be damned if he could do the gallant thing and walk away to let her move on without him.

"After three years together, you're asking this now? You're asking me if I have feelings for you? Of course I do, Elle. Strong feelings. But my job isn't a conventional nine-to-five, home-for-dinner type of work. There have been so many times I've wanted to tell you everything, but it's because of my feelings for you that I don't share the details of it—for your benefit."

"It doesn't feel like I'm important to you."

"You are not just *anyone* to me, Elle. The only other people who get a glimpse of the real me are the men from my unit. We worked in life-and-death situations twenty-four-seven, so we knew everything there was to know about each other. We were all well-trained for our roles and never let each other down. But even they don't get the side of me I give you.

"Don't think I haven't recognized all the ways you help me when I show up here. You were trying to determine what state my mind was in as soon as I walked in here. The weeks and months I'm away, I miss you every bit as much as you miss me, if not more. I tried to explain to you early on in this relationship how I'd be in and out of town, unreachable at times, but I'd always be back for you."

"You're right. You did tell me that, but I didn't realize it would always be this way."

"What are you saying, Elle? Just spit it out. Lay it on the line so there's no confusion."

"I'm saying I want more than this. I want more than you showing up occasionally, then leaving for extended periods again. I love you, Devon. I've loved you for so long. But if you're telling me we'll never have a full life together, that I'll never know more about you than I do right now...I'm saying I don't know if I can do this anymore."

He stood and walked to her, his once-hidden emotions instantly palpable in his eyes. "Elle, I don't want to lose you. If you're giving me an ultimatum of choosing between you and my job, at this moment, there's no way I can choose. Not tonight anyway. There's too much at stake to walk away now—from you or the job. It's a no-win situation for me. If you love me, give me more time to see this through."

"Give me a time frame. How much more time do you mean? Days? Weeks? Months? Years?"

"At the rate it's going now, it'll only take a couple more weeks to wrap it up once I go back. Of course, anything can happen between now and then."

"Go back where?"

He smiled, knowing she was testing him. "Miami."

"When are you going back?"

"In a couple of days."

"You flew all the way across the country to stay here for a couple of days?"

"I'd fly here from anywhere in the world if it means I'll have a couple of days with you."

Tears spilled over her bottom lashes, and Devon gently wiped them away with the pad of his thumb while he waited for her decision. "Well, that sweet-talking just earned you two weeks. You'd better finish whatever it is you're doing and get back here to me two weeks from the day you leave me. *Two. Weeks. Devon.*"

"Yes, ma'am."

They spent the following forty-eight hours in Elle's bed, only leaving her bedroom to restock their supply of food and drinks. Devon alternated between being dominant and possessive, gentle and affectionate, employing his full arsenal of moves and maneuvers to help remind her how much she missed him when he was away.

He waited until she'd passed out from exhaustion the first night, then raised up on one elbow to watch her sleep. Thoroughly relaxed, she wore a peaceful and contented expression—he'd even dare to say she was truly happy. She'd confessed her true feelings to him when she said those magic words. Naturally, he already knew she was in love with him and had been since their first encounter. No doubt she'd waited for him to confess his undying love first, then decided she couldn't wait any longer when she issued her ultimatum.

"Here's something you don't know about me," he said, his whisper barely audible. "I love you, Elle. You captured my heart that first day in Miami. The first time we made love, I knew I never wanted it back. But you can't know any of this. If the day ever comes that I let you go, believing I don't love you is the only way to make sure you'll stay far away from me."

Neither of them slept the second night. Devon had an early flight out of LA to get back to Miami and finish the job. The hours of driving into her core, slow and deep, didn't quench his desire. It only caused him to crave her more. The taste of her skin, the aroma of her arousal, the sound of her moans and screams were the equivalent of throwing gasoline on a raging fire. Hour after hour, their sweat-slick bodies remained joined as one, drawing out their pleasure and delaying their separation as long as possible.

Just before daylight broke, Devon begrudgingly left her bed to head to the airport, with the promise of returning two weeks later. He settled into the private jet and waited for the pilot and crew to finish their preflight check. The taste of her wet, salty goodbye kiss lingered in his memory. He wasn't likely to forget the feeling of releasing her from his arms either. Every time he had to leave her was harder than the last. That realization drove him to make a decision right then and there.

Once this case was over, he'd resign from the CIA and only work for Steele Security. With the way Noah's company had grown since its inception and continued to thrive, a bicoastal security firm was most definitely in the cards. Ideas formed one after the other, visions of how his life would change created excitement for the future. He spent the flight working up a full plan of attack for their new life together once his current assignment ended.

Wheels down in Miami, his undercover cell immediately began ringing.

"Shadow, our business associates are lined up and ready to move forward with our joint venture. I hope you've kept your promise to me."

"Of course, Richard. Have I ever let you down before?"

"Our meeting with the board of directors is in one week. I need you to be there with me. They want to meet you in person," Richard demanded.

"Let me know where and what time. I'll be there," Shadow replied.

"One of my men will contact you the day of the meeting with the exact location. It's been a pleasure doing business with you."

Richard Hollingsworth had been in the Army with Shadow and his brothers. He was missing for three years, presumed dead, after an illegal arms deal went south on him. He'd recently been released by his captors in the Middle East and was back in the States, in the market for a dirty CIA operative who could reestablish his supply chain without questions. Part of Shadow's covert operation was to be the middle man and take down all the players financing Richard's treasonous acts at once.

"My plans are already falling into place," Shadow said to himself as he jogged down the plane's steps to the tarmac.

After switching to his secure cell, he called Steadman. "Hi, Uncle Steadman. Just wanted to let you know the order for the birthday cake is being placed. They'll call me back later to give me a time to pick it up."

"I hope you ordered the chocolate cake. You know it's my favorite," Steadman replied with a chuckle.

"Is there any other kind? I'll call back later when I have more information. Get the family ready for our big dinner celebration next week. This cake has several layers."

Over the following week, Shadow gave his all to his assignment. He ensured every T was crossed and every I was dotted. The stars seemed to align when the cache of weapons arrived on time, cementing his cover and ensuring the deal would go through as planned. Once the money was exchanged and they took possession of the illegal arms, every federal agency identified by initials would swarm the spot and take them all in.

Then his undercover life would come to an eventful end.

He knew something was wrong when his secure cell began ringing. Those calls were normally one-way only. For Steadman to call him meant there was a major new development in the intelligence community.

"Uncle Steadman, I'm surprised to hear from you. Did you change your mind on the flavor of cake?"

"Shadow," Steadman replied with all seriousness. "He has Reaper's girlfriend, Brianna. He's going to kill her." He rattled off the address of the abandoned warehouse where Richard held Brianna captive.

Shadow glanced at his watch as he sprinted to his car, calculating how long it would take him to reach her. He loved Brianna like a sister and was almost as close to her as he was to Noah. Her only hope of survival was if he intervened, and he knew her death would be more than Noah could endure. His tires slid to a halt behind the warehouse, and he chambered a round in his gun as he ran toward the back door, praying he wasn't too late to stop a cold-blooded murder.

~

When the plane landed at LAX, Devon walked unhurriedly toward the baggage claim area. He'd lost the spring in his step and the gleam in his eye.

He was in LA to get them both back, along with the love of his life.

After dropping his suitcase off at his hotel room, he drove to her apartment and parked on the street outside. He already knew she wasn't home, but he'd wait until she showed up. If it meant getting down on his knees and begging, then so be it. One way or another, she had to talk to him and hear him out. He was ready to tell her everything.

When a couple of hours had passed and she still hadn't shown up, he turned on the radio to help pass the time. The local station's disc jockey was reporting a celebrity sighting at a trendy new restaurant.

"I just heard the one and only Miss Elle Sinclair is about to roll up in a long, black limousine. I can't even tell you how jealous I am of the guy she's with tonight. She is even hotter in person than she is in the pictures, if you can imagine that. And believe me, I can imagine a lot with her."

The car's engine roared to life, and his foot stomped on the gas pedal, pulling out of his space with peeling tires. The car deftly weaved through traffic, and he ignored blaring horns and angry shouts as he passed the other cars. Luckily, he found an empty parking spot a block away from the restaurant, not caring he'd illegally parked in someone's reserved spot. When he was as close as the throngs of people and photographers would allow him to get, he spotted her exiting the limo.

The man she was with extended his tuxedo-clad arm toward her, and she wrapped her dainty one around it with a beaming smile on her beautiful face. Dressed to kill in a short black dress that clung to her curves and showed off all her best assets, she stopped several times for pictures as the paparazzi yelled one question after another at her.

"Elle, who's your date?"

"Is he an actor?"

"Is he a model?"

"Where did you two meet?"

"Is this a serious relationship?"

"Are you off the market now? Are you exclusive?"

Lightbulbs flashed. People elbowed each other out of the way, vying for the perfect spot to snap the best picture. Young girls screamed Elle's name, yelling they loved her and wanted to be her.

It was the first time he'd seen in person how crazy her fans were over her. He knew she was famous, had hordes of fans, and was sought after for modeling gigs and movie parts. Living in the limelight was a foreign concept that he thought he was ready for and had a handle on. But that was before he watched that scene unfold. He realized even if he left the CIA, he couldn't be recognizable to that degree and still be effective as a security team member.

Their lives were just too different. Regardless of how much they tried to make it work, it was still as if they were attempting to fit a square peg in a round hole. It would never be as good as it should be. And he couldn't hold her back from happiness anymore. She'd moved on, though he'd never had the chance to explain that he was two weeks late because he'd saved Brianna from being shot, but her condition had been touch and go for a while. He couldn't leave Brianna, Noah, or his assignment until all the loose ends were tied up. He'd called repeatedly and left messages, but Elle wouldn't accept them.

Seeing how happy she was with her new date seemed to explain why he couldn't reach her. It was time to let her go, so she could have her career and the type of relationship she wanted. With a heavy heart, he drove back to his hotel, considering what his next move would be. Leaving the life of a spy was a definite. He'd had enough of that world to last a lifetime.

"To what do I owe the pleasure?" Steadman asked as a way of a greeting. "You're not on a sanctioned assignment."

"I'm calling in my 10-42."

"That's not funny, Shadow."

"No, it's not. This is my official end tour of duty notice. I'm not accepting missions as of now."

"Shadow," a stern voice replaced Steadman's. "What the hell is this?"

"This is my official resignation. I don't know where the confusion is. I quit."

"Your leave is approved. No one quits the CIA. We'll be in touch when we need you. Keep the phone. Don't make us have to find you."

The line went dead, and he chuckled a humorless laugh. "Well, that went better than I expected."

After finding there were no flights available until the following afternoon, he lay on his back on the bed, staring at the ceiling. The pictures in magazines and on television of Elle with other men over the prior three years had been bad enough, even though he knew she was his. But seeing her earlier was different. It wasn't a movie promotion or a platonic date to a premiere. She'd moved on without him, and as much as he wanted to wait at her apartment for her, he knew himself too well.

His personal cell woke him from a restless sleep. At first, he thought he'd let it roll to voice mail, but a glance at the name on the screen made him scramble to answer it instead.

"Hello."

"Devon? I swore I wouldn't do this when you didn't show up, but I can't move on without having this talk with you. Tell me it's over. Tell me you don't want me. Tell me I don't mean anything to you," Elle demanded through slightly slurred words.

His mind yelled at him to tell her what she wanted so she'd finally be happy without him. But his heart was selfish and couldn't lie to her. Wouldn't lie to her. "I can't tell you any of those things, Elle."

Her watery reply drove a searing hot knife through his heart. "You don't want me, but you don't want anyone else to have me either. Is that it?"

"No, that's not it at all. In fact, if you're finished with your date for the night, why don't you come on over to my hotel room and I'll show you how much I don't want you."

"How did you know about my date?"

"Because I'm fucking here and watched you walk into the restaurant on the arm of another man." His teeth were clenched together as he spoke, and the muscles in his jaw jumped in anger. "And I have called you, repeatedly, but you haven't answered any of them."

"Why were you late?"

"Because my friend's fiancée was in the hospital, fighting for her life, and I couldn't just leave them. Wrapping up the job took a little longer than I thought it would, but then I told you that was a possibility when I was here last time."

"My phone was mysteriously misplaced when I woke up on day fifteen. My assistant ordered a new phone, with a new number, and none of my existing contacts would download to my new phone for some odd reason. I tore Beth's room apart tonight until I found my old phone. Where are you?"

"Already on my way to you."

10

CHAPTER TEN

Three Years Earlier

One button at a time, he moved down the front of her blouse. His eyes stayed locked on hers, establishing his dominance and enjoying every second of it. Her arms hung loosely at her sides as he'd instructed, submissive regardless of how badly she wanted to speed things along. They'd been apart for too long and she was dying to touch him, but he loved how making her wait only increased her eagerness for him.

"I can almost hear your thoughts, Elle," Devon chided gently. "Are you trying to will me to go faster with your mind?"

"I would never, Devon. That would rob you of your favorite part —building the anticipation of what you're planning to do to me."

One eyebrow lifted in amusement, along with one side of his lips. She'd repeated his words from another time together back to him almost verbatim. "To be honest, that's not my favorite part. But it does rank fairly high on the list."

"You do have more self-control than anyone I've ever met. You'll have to share some of that with me one day."

"What I want to share with you has nothing to do with my self-control. You can have all you want."

He pushed her shirt off her shoulders and let it fall to the floor. Her bra quickly followed, leaving her standing completely bare to him. Exactly the way he wanted her. He bent his head and sucked her nipple into his mouth. The warmth of his tongue laved it, tasting and teasing with each pass. Her peak hardened and his teeth grazed over it, eliciting a moan of pleasure from deep inside her chest.

"Touch me," he instructed, and she readily complied. Her fingers wrapped around his girth and stroked back and forth along his length. "That's my girl. You don't know how many times I've had to do this myself, while thinking of you."

Her knees suddenly buckled when his fingers found her wet center. When he plunged them inside her without warning, the intensity of the welcome intrusion stole her breath. As he pumped his fingers deep inside her, his mouth continued to work magic on her breasts, giving ample and equal attention to both. One of her hands kept stroking him while the other gripped his shoulder tightly as his ministrations brought her closer to the edge of her climax.

"Oh my God, Devon!"

Before her body had recovered, he was on his knees in front of her, pushing her legs farther apart. "That was one. You'll give me several more tonight."

Before she could reply, his mouth covered her core. His warm tongue circled her clit, deliberately avoiding making direct contract with the most sensitive spot on her body. He leisurely trailed his finger along her slit with just enough pressure to let her know he was there. Waiting for him to take his attentions to the next level was sweet torture, but she knew he'd make her wait longer if she asked for it.

Patience, my girl. Have I ever left you anything but completely satisfied? He'd asked that the first few times she'd tried to rush him, before she learned her lesson and let him have his way with her in the bedroom. Or the living room. Or outside, depending on where they were when they'd reunited.

She watched with rapt attention as he pulled her leg over his shoulder. He smirked up at her, his smile smug and knowing, and she couldn't contain her smile.

"You're trying to rush me again. For the record, I'm not making you wait because of how badly I want to taste you. But you'll have to be punished for that later."

"I didn't say a word," she replied through a giggle. "I've been a good girl."

"It's the thought that counts," he countered, his smug smile still in place.

She knew better than to argue any further, so she let him believe he'd won that round. While he enjoyed being the dominant one, the aggressor, he certainly didn't mind when she took charge to please him. She'd easily learned how to distract him, and in doing so, she'd enjoyed even more pleasure at his hand...and mouth...and enormous cock. While her mind momentarily wandered to their other escapades, he effectively brought her back to the present with a swift move.

Simultaneously, he sucked hard on her clit and thrust two fingers deep into her channel. Her inner muscles clamped around his fingers while her essence soaked his hand. His tongue licked and lapped her, and he pulled her closer to him until she straddled his face. She grasped his hair, tugging with abandon as each wave rolled through her. Her hips moved of their own accord, riding out the force of her orgasm, and she threw her head back when she screamed in pleasure.

"Mmm," he hummed against her. "That's number two."

One strong arm circled her, lifted her, and carried her to the bedroom. He lay on his back, his erection standing tall and proud, and he waggled his eyebrows at her. "Ready to go for a wild and wet ride?"

While taking in the perfect male form stretched out on her bed, she licked her lips instinctively. "I'm more than ready."

"Do that again."

She met his gaze with confusion. "Do what again, love?"

"Lick your lips like you're dying to take every inch of my cock down your throat."

"Now that you mention it," she purred seductively and crawled up his body. Poised over his thick cock, she repeated licking her lips in an exaggerated manner and watched his eyes darken with desire. With his recent torture of her in mind, she took her time exploring him. She ran her tongue lightly around the rim of his head, reveling in the way all his muscles tightened with her slightest touch.

When his eyes were squeezed shut, she opened her mouth widely and took him in fully, the tip hitting the back of her throat. Each time he drew in a harsh breath, the air barely passing over his gritted teeth, she increased her pressure and tempo. His hips bucked, rising to meet her movements, and his hands gripped her hair. "Fuck, darlin'. This kills me to say, but you have to stop."

"Oh? And why would I do that?"

"Because as much as I love the feel of your soft, warm mouth wrapped around me, it's been too damn long since I've been inside that sweet little pussy of yours. I plan on wearing it out tonight. And tomorrow night. Hell, every night I'm here with you. So, what are you waiting for? Climb on board."

With her sly smile in place, she straddled his lap and hovered over him. Her hand wrapped around his cock firmly and guided him to her waiting entrance. The slight burn of her body stretching to accept his size only increased her yearning for him. She slid down his length and stilled for a second when he was fully seated inside her. Her hips began rocking back and forth, then side to side. His fingers gripped her hips just before he began thrusting upward. She leaned back slightly, throwing her head back and focusing on the pleasure, when his thumb found her clit.

The mixture of erotic stimulation caused stars to ignite into fireworks behind her closed eyes. As she pushed down, he plunged upward. The erotic connection in the middle hit the spot every time, with each pulse building into an overpowering culmination before they reached the summit and tumbled over together. Elle fell forward, lying on his chest, as they fought to catch their breath and slow their speeding hearts.

"That was amazing," she said groggily, her energy spent. "I don't have the strength to move now, so I'm sleeping right here all night."

"Sounds like a wonderful idea to me. When I wake up in the middle of the night, you'll be in the perfect position to start all over again."

"Devon, I could sleep cocooned inside a mummy sleeping bag, and you'd say I was in the perfect position."

"Well, you are very fuckable no matter what position you're in. I'll give you that one."

Wrapped in his arms, warmed by the natural heat of his body, she fell into a deep sleep with her cheek resting on his chest. Hours later, she was pulled from a beautiful dream by a noise that seemed far away at first. When she gained her bearings, she realized the noises were coming from Devon.

He was talking in his sleep. Unintelligible words at first. Nothing she could make out to understand what he dreamed about. Then the next words, spoken with a more forceful tone, caught her full attention.

"Ava? Ava, no! Don't leave me. Stay with me, Ava. Stay with me."

～

"Are you ready, superstar?" Devon asked playfully. "Have you penciled me in for the weekend on your appointment calendar?"

"No, I most certainly have not penciled you in," Elle replied, mock offense rife in her tone. "That's my assistant's job. Those menial tasks are beneath me."

"My knee is the only thing that'll be beneath you. When I turn you over it and spank that ass for being so sassy with me."

"You love it when I'm sassy, and you know it."

"I can't deny it. I do love that sassy mouth of yours."

A flash of disappointment passed over her eyes for a split second before she tamped it down. "Okay, I'm packed and ready to go. I can't believe you're actually taking a whole weekend off from your six different cell phones."

"It's kind of hard not to take the weekend off when we're going to your parents and they live in the middle of nowhere. One of the last places on Earth that doesn't have cell reception." He shook his head in disgust and picked up their suitcases. "Move that fine ass. We have a three-hour drive ahead of us. Six if I have to pull over on the side of the road and have my wicked way with you."

"We are not stopping on the side of the road to have sex before we go spend the weekend with my parents and brothers." She put her hands on her hips and dared him to argue with her stern expression.

"Spoilsport," he muttered on his way out the door.

In the car on their way north to the vineyard country, they chatted mindlessly about anything and everything. When she could no longer take not knowing, she prepared herself to ask him about Ava. They'd never verbally agreed to an exclusive relationship, but that had always been Elle's expectation. From Devon's reaction to her going on a meaningless date with another man, she believed he'd felt the same.

"What's on your mind? Let's have it." Devon cut his eyes over to her.

"How do you always know?"

"It's my job to know, darlin'. What's bothering you?"

"Something you said in your sleep last night," she admitted.

He turned his head toward her, waiting to see the laughter in her eyes. But she was dead serious. "I talked in my sleep? What did I say?"

"You asked Ava not to leave you," she replied quietly. "Who is Ava?"

"Not who you think she is, darlin'. I know it bothers you, but I need you to trust me. I want to tell you about her, but not right now—not in the car. She's not an old flame by any stretch of the imagination, if that helps calm your mind."

From the way his naturally bronzed skin paled at the mention of Ava's name, Elle believed he spoke the truth. The innate happiness that was usually clear in his eyes had dimmed, leaving a sadness she'd never seen in them before that moment. Whoever Ava was, and whatever made her leave him, left a profound impact on him. Elle was confident he'd tell her everything when the time was right. As far as she was concerned, he'd always been true to his word.

"Okay, Devon. You can tell me later, when you're ready. I'll be here."

He gripped her hand in his, pulled it to his mouth, and pressed his lips to the back of it tenderly. "You have no idea how much that means to me, Elle. Knowing you're here for me. Some days, it's all I have."

"When are you going to tell me what your work involves? What you do. Where you go. Why you only show up for a few weeks or days at a time, then leave again. Even after all this time, there's still so much I don't know about you. But you know everything there is to know about me."

"It's not fair, I know, and I'm truly sorry it has to be this way. My occupation is dangerous, to say the least, and has always demanded unquestionable loyalty. My path hasn't been as well-lit as yours. When you step outside, hundreds of bright lights from cameras flash from every direction to capture a glimpse of you. My world has been in the shadows, where I'm invisible."

"That's why you refuse to be photographed with me? Because of your job?"

A mixture of pain and relief permeated her tone, instinctively prompting him to jerk his gaze to hers. "I'm such a fucking idiot. Darlin', I never realized I'd hurt you over that. My...activities... mandate I stay out of the public eye. I've gone to great lengths to keep my fugly mug out of the papers. If I could, I'd be in every picture with you. The world would know without a doubt you're mine."

"Does your world know you're mine?" She dared to ask, taking a gamble with her heart in a new way.

"To protect you, my world doesn't know you're associated with me in any way. But I think what you're really asking me is if the other ladies of the world know I'm yours. The answer is no, they don't know anything about you. Or me, for that matter." He paused and looked at her again. "But *I* know who has my heart, Elle. That's all that matters."

Devon turned onto a long, winding driveway lined with sycamore trees and followed it through the rolling hills covered with rows upon rows of grapevines. Danny and Tanya Moore had bought the one-hundred-thirty-acre property soon after they'd migrated west and transformed it into a family business. Their son Mark had success-fully managed and built the winery operations, establishing a lucra-tive vintner's private reserve with a long waiting list.

"Look who beat us here," Elle remarked, inclining her head toward the car parked outside the garage.

Devon's disbelief over what sat directly before his eyes prevented his keen eyes from identifying it first.

"What are my parents doing here?"

Elle laughed out loud, leaned forward in her seat, and fixed her eyes on his shocked expression. "I can't believe I actually pulled it off. You've always known when I've tried to hide anything from you. Not this time, though. My acting skills are definitely improving."

"You're an incredibly bad distraction, because there's no way I'm losing my touch. I'll just have to watch you closer and use different tactics in the future. Now, seriously, what are they doing here?"

"They're vacationing at my parents' house for a couple of weeks. They don't get to see each other as often as they'd like. Or you, from what they've told me." Elle pierced him with her perceptive stare.

"Sometimes I have to choose between going to visit them in Georgia or you in California. The odds of me picking *anyone* over you are slim to none, darlin'."

"You're going to blame me when we get inside, aren't you?"

"Abso-fucking-lutely." He grinned, and the mischief sparkled in his eyes.

Ready to face both families and get the questions out of the way, they exited the car and walked to the front door hand in hand. Elle glanced over her shoulder at Devon when she crossed the threshold into the sprawling home. "Are you ready for this?"

"As ready as I'll ever be."

A concurrence of laughter and voices engaged in multiple conversations at once echoed off the walls, emanating from the kitchen. Elle was greeted by a moment of silence when the families realized she'd arrived. Then the entire group jumped to their feet and rushed to Elle and Devon upon seeing them together. Hugs, handshakes, and squeals of delight filled the home—along with love.

"Devon, what are you doing here?" Tracey, his mom, asked as she wrapped her arms around him.

"Do you want me to leave?" he asked playfully and started moving toward the door.

"No!" She laughed and shook her head. "You know what I meant. How did you even know we were here?"

"He didn't have a clue until we were already here and I told him," Elle bragged. "I was finally able to keep a secret from him after all these years we've been seeing each other."

Devon shut his eyes tight and winced, waiting for the onslaught of questions to begin.

"Years?" Tracey's whirled back to Devon. "You've been seeing each other for *years,* and I'm just now hearing about it?"

Without even looking at Elle, he felt the heartache radiating off her from his mother's innocent declaration. Elle turned on her heel and started to walk away, but he caught her before she could get away. One muscled arm circled around her waist and pulled her back to his front, holding her firmly against his chest. His other arm wrapped around her, securing his hold. With his chin resting lightly on her shoulder, he kissed her sweetly on the cheek.

"That's right, Mom. Elle and I have been together since just before her twenty-first birthday. She came to Miami while I was working there, and we've been together ever since."

"You never tell me anything, Devon," Tracey accused, her finger pointed at him and her other hand on her hip. "I hope you don't keep everything a secret from Elle like you do from me."

"Tracey, stop harassing our son. We haven't seen him in months, and now it'll be months before he comes home again." Phil, Devon's father, affectionately pulled his wife into his arms. "How long are you staying?"

"However long Elle says we're staying." He squeezed her gently, attempting to elicit a response.

"Unfortunately, with the tight production schedule, we can only stay a few days. I'll have to get back to review the script changes, meet with the other cast members, and get my costumes fitted."

"You're here now, so let's make the most of it. We were just about to have dinner, so you got here just in time." Tanya led the group back to the table and grabbed extra place settings for Elle and Devon while the others began filling their plates.

"That was a subtle change of plans," Devon murmured under his breath.

"Yeah, well, that was a blatant slap in the face that Tracey didn't know about me after four years," she retorted.

Tracey and Tanya carried on a separate conversation that quickly silenced all the other sidebars. With all eyes and ears on them, they continued talking, unaware they held the room's engrossed attention.

"Mom and I had to have 'the talk' the other day. I think that was the hardest conversation I've ever had in my life," Tracey said.

"What do you mean 'the talk'?" Devon asked.

She met Devon's inquisitive gaze with a heavy heart. "She's declining quickly, son. We had to talk about her end-of-life wishes before it's too late. I needed to know exactly what she wants so we can respect her needs. She already has the burial plot beside Dad, but she didn't have an advance directive for medical procedures. We completed one together and sent it to all her doctors. Afterward, we hugged and cried for a solid fifteen minutes."

"I want to be cremated when I die," Devon announced definitively and impassively. Tracey and Elle both gaped at him over his announcement. "What?"

"You're too young. Don't even joke about that." Tracey shuddered, the mere thought too much to bear.

"I'm serious. Any of us could go at any time. If you needed to know Grandma's wishes, you need to know mine, too. I want to be cremated—it's important to me. I've left specific instructions that will be delivered to you, but I also want you to hear it from me."

The conversation continued, taking natural twists and turns, until they had covered a broad spectrum of topics. While Elle joined in, listening to their parents share amusing and embarrassing stories from both her and Devon's childhoods and laughing along with them, she mentally pieced together the brief glimpses she'd gained into his secret life. The sum of each individual part added up to one disturbing conclusion.

His work is dangerous.

He lives in the shadows.

He avoids photographs.

He hides me from his world to protect me.

He has "in case of death" instructions.

Who is Devon Kane? Do I even know him?

11

CHAPTER ELEVEN

One Year Earlier

"Elle Sinclair, best known for her supermodel days, had her big break on the big screen with minor, but memorable, secondary characters. Confidential sources have told us that's all about to change. One of Hollywood's most influential leading men, Matt Lane himself, has specifically requested Elle be his leading lady in the highly anticipated romantic comedy.

"Filming is scheduled to begin late next month, but the beautiful pair has been spotted together several times already. Is it too early to hope this pairing is more than just great casting? We may be looking at Hollywood royalty in the making. We'll keep our eyes on this couple and bring you more updates as they become available."

Watching television normally bored Shadow to tears, but seeing Elle cozied up to Hollywood's "good guy" on the nightly entertainment news certainly caught his attention. With his eyes glued to the screen, his hands curled into fists, and his nostrils flaring from agitation, he watched Matt put his arm around Elle's waist and pull her into his side. When she curled into Matt willingly, Shadow's blood began to boil. But when Matt placed a lingering kiss on Elle's cheek, Shadow finally moved.

"Hey, Reap. Just wanted to let you know I'll be away for a couple of weeks. I'll call you when I get back."

"No problem. Everything okay?"

"Yeah. Just a few things I need to take care of."

After he finished talking to Noah, he called Steadman.

"Shadow, my man. What do you have for me today?"

"I'll be off the grid for a couple of weeks. Don't send anything my way because I won't be checking in at all."

After a few clicks on his laptop, his ticket to LAX was booked. Then he started planning the ultimate destination—and that place didn't include *Matt Lane*. With his surprise plans securely in place, he threw his clothes into a suitcase and hurried to the airport. Every element of his actions went against the grain of his personality.

He didn't make rash decisions. He always carefully planned every move he made.

He only appeared to be spontaneous. Every move and counter-move were considered ahead of time.

Logic ruled his mind, heart, and actions. He wasn't a slave to his emotions. Rational thinking, sound decision-making skills, and careful analysis of every possible outcome had kept him alive in some of the worst places in the world.

All the years of extensive training and having the rules of working undercover drilled into his subconscious evaporated where Elle was concerned. No risk was too great, no stakes were too high, no matter what the cost to himself would be. She was worth it. She was more than worth it—she was the only light he could see at the end of his tunnel.

It appeared the only thing he couldn't do for her was the very thing she'd asked of him. He couldn't stay away from her and give her the time apart like she'd requested. He'd stayed away for as long as he could stand, and seeing her happy with another man was the tipping point. There was no doubt he'd pay the price of her wrath when he showed up out of the blue, demanding she see him. Even more so when he sprang the tickets to Jade Mountain in St. Lucia. For two. For two weeks of total seclusion.

His life of secrecy and disappearing with no word for weeks on end had taken an adverse toll on their relationship. Questions gave way to suspicions. The silence between them became deafening. He couldn't say the words she needed to hear, and she couldn't accept the way their lives had to be.

"Devon." She'd begun tentatively, and he read the signs of what was to come next. "There's still so much I don't know about you. Where you go. What you do. I feel like an outsider in your life, when I want nothing more than to know everything about you."

"I know you do, Elle. I don't know what to say to make you feel better about us."

She wrung her hands, and tears shimmered in her eyes. "This isn't working for me, Devon. As much as I want it to, as much as I love you, this isn't the life I want. We need some time apart to reevaluate our relationship and what we want out of it."

Devon nodded slowly. Not agreeing with her, but giving himself an extra moment to rein in his feelings before he spoke. "Time apart to reevaluate our relationship," he repeated. "How much time will that take? How much more time do you need apart from me than you already have?"

"I don't want you to come back until I call you. I don't know how long it'll take, but I can't constantly watch for you to show up and live my life at the same time. The longest we've been apart is four months—"

"That only happened once, and it couldn't be helped. I explained that to you."

"You did—you said it couldn't be helped. That's the only explanation you gave. Knowing how I felt at the end of those four months, I'm guessing I should know one way or another after six months apart."

"You want me to stay away for six months while you decide if you want me to come back at all?" The timbre of his voice lowered while the volume raised. He ran his fingers through his hair and clasped his hands behind his neck before releasing a forced exhale.

The tears spilled over her lower lids and slid down her cheeks. One quickly followed the previous, soaking her cheeks and leaving her eyes red and swollen. "Yes. But I understand if you'd rather end it now."

She's testing me, he thought. *Will I wait for her like she's waited for me so many times? Yes, Elle, I will wait for you however long it takes to prove my love for you.*

"Six months it is, then. I'll stay away until you call. When I hear from you, I'll run back to your side."

Unable to walk away without one more taste, he pressed his lips to hers, skimmed his tongue along the part in her mouth, and plunged inside when she gave him the slightest opportunity. Salty tears mixed with the heady flavor that belonged solely to Elle.

With a step backward serving as the foreboding symbol of their relationship, he left her apartment and her life, giving her the time and space she needed. He gave her what she asked of him to prove his love was real. He was willing to do for her what she'd always done for him—wait, and welcome her back with open arms when she was ready.

But seeing her with Matt Lane made him realize that proving he loved her hadn't been her plan at all. He'd misread her intentions completely. The time of separation was her chance to move on without him, to forget what they'd had, and to leave all the memories of their time together in the past. Moving on would be easier with someone new to occupy her time and her mind.

And her bed.

Then, Matt Lane would be a dead man.

Hours later, the plane landed at LAX, and he made a mad dash to Elle's apartment. His heavy fist beat on the door, demanding entrance.

"Let me in, or I'll break the door down and come in anyway. I know you're in there."

The deadbolt turned, unlocking the door, and she slowly opened it. "What are you doing here, Devon? I haven't called you."

"That's exactly why I'm here. You've tried to forget me, but it won't work. You love me, Elle. You've loved me too long to stop, and I won't let you just walk away from me without putting up one hell of a fight for you. I tried to give you space and time to come to this conclusion on your own. But you're too stubborn and headstrong. So if I have to camp out here in the hallway outside your door until you come to your senses, so be it."

She sighed deeply. "Come on in."

"Good call," he replied and stepped into the room. "Now, go pack. We're going away for two weeks. You won't need many clothes."

"Have you lost your mind? I'm not going away with you. I haven't seen or talked to you in months."

"That was your idea, not mine. You wanted that, I didn't."

"I needed it for my own sanity."

"Are you happy without me?" He crossed his arms over his chest and dared her to lie.

"No. I'm not any happier at all. I'm miserable, and I'm driving Beth crazy."

"Beth needs a break from you for two uninterrupted weeks. Come away with me."

"Bikinis, sand, and surf?" She knew him too well. His idea of uninterrupted paradise would be somewhere warm, with tropical breezes, the bare minimum of clothes, and no cell or internet access.

"You know it, darlin'."

Elle questioned her sanity while packing her suitcase. He just showed up after more than four months apart, and she was right back in the same position as if they'd never been apart. She couldn't resist him—didn't even want to. There was a certain romantic element to the way he insisted they couldn't remain apart. She wanted to believe him. More than anything she'd ever wanted in her life, she wanted to believe what he'd said. Her heart was convinced, but her mind still had serious doubts their lives would ever progress past the rut they'd been stuck in for ages.

"You won't regret it," he said from behind her.

She turned to face him. His hip was leaned against the door-frame, his eyes drinking her in from top to bottom, obviously delighted to see her again. His self-control was at all all-time high. From his heated gaze and darkened eyes, she knew he wanted nothing more than to entangle his body with hers so thoroughly they'd never be separate again. But he was still giving her time and space—in his own way.

"Reading my mind again?" She kept her voice low and quiet. Uncertainty clouded her mind and her judgment.

His thoughtful expression gave her an unusual insight into his thoughts and feelings. "Something like that. I know you, Elle, and while you think you don't know me, nothing could be further from the truth. You know I always find my way back to you. Even if you question everything else, you know there's nothing I wouldn't do for you."

"Where are we going?" She knew his words were meant to help heal—but they only seemed to cut deeper. She turned back to packing her clothes, anything to avoid his scrutiny.

Before she even felt his presence or his hands on her arms, he'd whirled her around to face him. He held her firmly in his grasp, as if he thought she'd try to escape from him. So many times, he'd almost told her what kept him away. That was one of those times when he wanted to blurt it all out. The covert missions. The classified details. The undercover assignments. He wanted to tell her everything. Would she even believe him? Some of the details of his life and what he'd encountered were beyond belief in the normal realm of civilian existence.

When he'd turned in his resignation to Steadman through the end of watch code, he had hope they'd allow him simply to walk away. No more clandestine missions, infiltrating areas angels feared to tread. No more eluding questions from family and friends. He'd be home for every holiday and special occasion.

He'd had high hopes for a normal life.

The CIA had other plans for him. A highly trained, seasoned

assassin who'd had access to every secret the country had, along with those of several other countries, was not someone they were prepared to just let go. When he'd first joined, many members had given him the same dire warning. "You can never really quit the CIA." He soon realized what they meant: "You can quit when you die." Since he wasn't ready for that extreme measure, he answered when they called.

The two weeks away with Elle had been taken without negotiation. He'd learned the best way to avoid having his plans interrupted was not to share them until the very last second. By the time they were in the air, he would be completely unreachable, and all his attention would be hers. Until then, he knew he had to give her more reason to go away with him before she changed her mind. She was on the cusp of walking away from him forever.

"We're going to spend two weeks away from everyone and everything else in the world. We're going to discover and rediscover everything about each other all over again. We're going to remember why we're together, why we first got together, why we've stayed together, and why we'll always be together. After the next two weeks, if you still want me to leave, I'll stay away and you'll never see me again. I guarantee it."

"Remembering how much I love you and why I do isn't the problem, Devon. But you have two weeks." *You have two weeks to convince me you love me.*

"We have two weeks." He bent his knees to put them both at eye level. "I can't wait to steal you away."

"You picked the perfect time. Filming starts soon on the movie with Matt Lane. When that starts, I won't be able to get away for several months."

His eyebrows twitched ever so slightly, but she caught the movement nonetheless. That small gesture gave his thoughts away completely.

"That's why you're here. You believed all the rumors about Matt and me being a couple. Unbelievable." She twisted out of his grip and stepped away. "This is about you claiming what you think belongs to you, isn't it?"

"No. It's really very simple. I don't want to lose you. This isn't what I want at all—I don't want us to be apart. And I sure as hell don't want you to be with another man. But if you're with me, I want it to be because that's what you want, too."

She exhaled sharply, releasing her exasperation as she gripped the suitcase. Her thoughts vacillated between telling him to leave and giving him the two weeks, for no other reason than she'd never have to wonder "what if." She dropped her chin to her chest and shook her head. "Okay, Devon. Two weeks it is. When do we leave?"

"Tomorrow morning."

"Not wasting any time, are you?"

"Not one minute."

The following morning came both too soon and not fast enough. Devon kept his arm draped over Elle all night, his front to her back. Though, he didn't sleep much, with his desire for her trying to take control of his willpower. But the last idea he wanted to reinforce in her mind was the assumption he only wanted to claim his property. Much more was at stake than his ego or pride. Their two weeks in a private island retreat would provide ample time to show her how he felt about her.

Before the sun rose, Devon was up and showered, ready to depart on their early-morning flight. Elle soon joined him in the living room, the tension between them still thick with uncertainty for the future.

"You still haven't told me exactly where we're going." Elle broke the heavy silence between them by focusing on the positive aspect of the situation.

"It's a secret. I can't tell you until we get there." He winked at her and smiled broadly, clearly pleased with himself.

Elle fought to tamp down the mistrust and stabbing pain in her heart from having one more secret between them. Even one she should appreciate—like a two-week exotic vacation.

"There are people who need to know where I am and when I'll return, Devon. There are contract clauses I'm required to honor, last-minute engagements that may come up, and someone will need to provide a statement for my absence. Even if I wanted to escape from everyone and everything, I wouldn't shirk my responsibilities and just disappear off the face of the earth. Other people depend on me to uphold my commitments."

The more she talked, the angrier she became that she even had to explain those simple facts to him. Facts that anyone else who had spent time in her life would already know about her. Yet the very man she'd devoted years to loving didn't give a second thought to the career she'd worked hard to build.

"We're going to St. Lucia. We're staying at Jade Mountain. Do you need to leave the number to the hotel with anyone? Beth, or your parents?" He gave her a card he retrieved from his shirt pocket. It contained all the information anyone would need to know about their location. Flight numbers, times, phone numbers, and the dates they'd be away.

"You knew I'd ask for this."

"Of course. You don't think I'd need to leave the same information with others, too?"

"I'm sorry. I obviously wasn't thinking straight. This is all happening so fast, and I still don't know what to make of it."

"We'll slow down to island time when we get there. Can we call a truce for now? When we land and you see it for yourself, you can decide if you want to be trapped in a tropical paradise with me for two weeks."

"Truce."

Island time sounded perfect to Elle. She slowed her racing thoughts long enough to study Devon intentionally for the first time in many months. She memorized every feature and expression that crossed his face. She began to realize his outward actions didn't always reflect what his eyes revealed to her. An odd thought popped into her mind from nowhere.

He is actually a very skilled actor. The only people he can't fool are those who know him best.

She suspected those people were few and far between, and she questioned if even she fell into that category.

I suppose I'll know for sure two weeks from today.

She rose and left a note for Beth on the kitchen counter, instructing her to share Elle's whereabouts with her assistant and her agent. Devon waited at the door until she'd finished, then carried their bags down to the waiting taxi.

Once they were in the air, she expressed her delight over flying first class. "You keep spoiling me like this, I'll start to expect it all the time."

"This is nothing compared to what awaits you, darlin'. You'll never want to leave once you see it."

"You know, it just occurred to me you flew across the country to my apartment, only to fly east again to the island. That's a lot of time in the air."

"You're worth every second of it. I've already told you there's nothing I wouldn't do for you. All you have to do is say the word."

"That's it? Just say the word, and it's mine?"

"Absolutely."

"What is the secret word that unlocks this magical treasure trove?"

"It's no secret, Elle. You own my heart. Whatever you need from me is yours, whenever you need it."

There, in his eyes, was the truth that matched his words. He'd never actually said the words "I love you," but she couldn't deny she'd always loved him. And she always would. Time and distance hadn't diminished her feelings in the least. She leaned over and placed a long kiss on his lips, savoring the moment of truth and the time they had to spend together.

12

———

CHAPTER TWELVE

The resort was more magnificent than she could've imagined in her most luxurious dreams. The sweeping mountainside suites featured a wall completely open to the elements and provided a stunning view of the twin volcanic peaks and the Caribbean Sea. At the edge of the open-air suite sanctuary was a private infinity pool, providing the guests an incredible sense of floating out into nature.

When Elle entered their expansive suite, she was instantly awestruck. One room flowed directly into another, so the panoramic view was never obscured. Entering that room felt as if she were entering an entirely new world. The sparkling water, the lush green trees, and the steep peaks of the mountains transported her to a place where stress and worries couldn't exist.

"Devon, this is...beyond words. There's no way I'll want to leave after being here for two weeks. I don't want to leave after being here for two seconds. Can we get lost in the jungle and stay here forever?"

"The *rain forest* is amazing. Forget the real world exists. Erase any memory of responsibilities waiting for us back home. Spend every day right here on this amazing island, exploring every inch of it and each other. Making love at all hours of the day and night. Having you all to myself and never sharing you with anyone else."

"The same goes for you," she retorted. "No more disappearing on me. By my side every day and night."

"You'd get tired of me real fast."

She looked over her shoulder, meeting his gaze. "Never."

They reached for each other at the same time. Arms encircled, lips clashed, and tongues demanded entrance. Hands moved with fluid precision, shedding clothes with no regard to where they landed. The urgency to have, hold, and feel each other commanded them, demanding their submission.

His arms slid down her back, and his hands cupped her ass and lifted her off the floor. She wrapped her legs around his waist and held on to him, their mouths fused together in an erotic union while he moved to the wall. With her back pushed against it and her legs tight around him, he freed one hand and reached down between her legs. His fingers, long and deft, found her wet center and gently pushed inside. The whimper that escaped her throat urged him on until her soft moans became cries of ardent passion.

"I love the fucking sexy sounds you make when you come. They're music to my ears, and this song will be on repeat all night."

He moved to the bed and set her down on the edge. On his knees in front of her, he buried his face between her legs. His warm, wet tongue licked up her slit before pushing inside to taste her fully. On cue, her eyes closed and her head dropped back. He wrapped his arms around her legs, his fingers gripped her thighs, and he pushed them up and farther apart. Her arms folded, and she gently fell backward until she lay flat on the bed.

His tongue circled and tantalized her clit while one hand traced her entrance, teasing her pussy until she'd coated his fingers with her desire. When he forcefully sucked her clit into his mouth, he thrust his fingers deep inside her waiting channel. She gripped his hair tightly, instinctively drawing him closer to her. He increased the tempo and pressure of his dual assault until her screams filled the air.

When he'd lapped up every bit of her ecstasy, he raised his eyes and met hers.

A slow, sexy smile spread across his handsome face. His eyes were so dark blue, they looked almost black. Knowing he'd only begun and had so many more plans for ravaging her body made the butterflies in her stomach turn somersaults.

"Fuck, that is the best sound in the world. I need to record that and listen to it while we have phone sex."

"As long as no one else hears it."

"My thoughts exactly. I'd kill a man for less than that."

His words should've given her pause, but when he lowered his head and began again, all logical thought and reasoning left her faculties. The feel of his mouth on her, so intimate yet so intense, rendered her speechless and incoherent. The orgasm built in increasing levels until it ripped through her with an unstoppable ferocity. The swirling and thrusting of his tongue mixed with the filling and stretching sensation of his fingers was too much to handle. The addictive part was that every time with Devon was equally as thrilling and pleasing. Every time, her body was left spent and satisfied. Every time was better than the last.

"Mmm, you taste so good." His lips brushed against her pussy as he spoke. His deep voice reverberated against her thighs, sending chills up her spine.

"You've set my body on fire. I don't think I can bear for you to touch me right now." Her words came out in a breathy staccato. "That was intense."

"I'm just getting warmed up. That was my appetizer."

"Now it's time for mine," she replied. She tugged on his hand lightly, and he let her pull him onto the bed beside her. She moved down his muscular chest and rippled stomach, leaving a wet, open mouthed swath of kisses until she reached his cock. It was standing at attention, hard and proud, when she wrapped her fingers around it. She slid her hand up and down the shaft while circling the head with her tongue, simultaneously teasing and pleasing.

Without warning, she took him deep into her mouth. The tip of his cock hit the back of her throat repeatedly while she worked him into a frenzy. Her head bobbed up and down, matching the speed of her hand. His fingers threaded through her hair, holding on while her soft, wet mouth worked wonders on his control.

"Elle, if you keep doing that, I'm going to come."

His warning was an aphrodisiac to her. Being the one who made him give up his control and give in to her ministrations made her feel emboldened, empowered. His release came soon after she increased her fervor, intent to see it through to the end. When she'd taken the very last drop, she swallowed it down and looked up at him through her lashes.

"You know, the noises you make when I make you come are pretty damn sexy too."

He smirked in reply, his smug smile sexy as sin on his handsome face. Then he reached under her arms and pulled her back up beside him. In one swift move, he rolled over on top of her and thrust his thick cock inside her to the hilt. She cried out in pleasure. The sweet burn of his cock stretching her only added to the intense pleasure. He pushed forward and arched back over and over again. His mouth covered the beaded tip of her nipple, laving her skin with his wet tongue. Each thrust became harder. Every sensation became stronger.

"You are mine, Elle," he stated definitively. "No matter how hard you try, you'll never be free of me."

"I don't want to be. I've never wanted that."

He stopped abruptly and stood beside the bed. Then he positioned her in front of him, bent over with her chest on the mattress. "I want you in every way imaginable." He ran his finger down the ridge of her spine, along the crack of her ass, and brushed against the puckered rosebud of her virgin ass. "This, one day soon, will be mine. There's no part of you I'd share with another man, Elle. Your every first will be with me."

"Yes." A one-word reply was all she could manage. Yes—to everything he wanted, anything he wanted.

He held his cock in his hand and rubbed it up and down her

center, coating the head with the wetness pooled between her legs. He suddenly pushed inside her, his fingers gripped her hips, and he drove relentlessly until neither of them could wait another second. When she screamed his name, her body locked down around him and forced his tumble over the edge in concert with hers.

After they'd cleaned up, they slipped into their private infinity pool. The healing touch of the cool water soothed her delicate skin. Wrapped in each other's embrace, they shared no less intimacy while talking about their hopes and dreams for the future than while in the throes of passion just moments before. Elle felt as if she'd met a new side of Devon. For the first time in several years, she thought they might actually have a shot at a happily-ever-after story of their own.

"Are you ready to go explore the island?" he asked.

"Yes, I can't wait to see everything this place has to offer."

They changed into shorts and sandals before leaving the suite, and the tension and doubts that hung between them only hours before had disappeared. Hand in hand, they strode through the hill-side terraces of the resort, excited about the plentiful activities their vacation destination would provide.

The luxurious spa and raving reviews over the couple's massage caught Elle's attention immediately. Devon insisted on booking the zip line tour of the rain forest for them both. Just off the beach at the bottom of the multilevel terraces and winding staircase was a shallow coral reef where they could relive their first date. They wound down the sweeping steps until they reached the beach below.

"We can't miss the tour of the volcanoes while we're here." Elle bounced on her toes in excitement while taking in the grandeur around her.

"If we have time in between our indoor activities," Devon teased. "We may not have time to put clothes on again after today."

"Then we'll go naked and really cause a stir around here." The spark of defiance in her eyes made Devon narrow his in return.

"If you think I'd let another man see you naked, you've got another thing coming."

"You know it turns me on when you go all Neanderthal man on

me. Just no pissing on my leg to mark your territory. I have to draw the line there."

His steps were casual, but his gaze held a playful warning. His advance toward Elle was slow but calculated, forcing her to back up in an automatic, self-preservation response. "Elle, you're the only person who's gotten away with mocking me more than once. The bodies of the other unfortunate people will never be found. Don't make me have to take you and hide you away, too."

"That depends. Where would you hide me? Is it as beautiful a place as this island? If so, I'll be sure to mock you again so we can stay. You'd have to stay with me to make sure I don't escape, of course." She smiled from ear to ear while she attempted to see how far she could push his ultra-controlled demeanor before he revealed more of his true self to her.

"It's not punishment if you like it and want it. I'm afraid you're not leaving me much choice."

Her watchful eyes never left him, waiting for him to made a sudden move on her, but she didn't see him move until she was already in his grasp. His speed was unbelievable, putting him on top of her before her brain even comprehended he'd made a move. She was in his arms and tossed over his shoulder in the blink of an eye.

He charged toward the water and dove in, turning on his back and positioning her on top of him at the last moment. Submerged in the aqua blue waters of the Caribbean, he pushed up and they surfaced with sputtering and hysterical laughter.

"You were getting a little hotheaded. I thought you could use some cooling off," he explained.

"Is that so?" She laughed as she wrapped her arms around his neck and her legs around his waist. He supported her in the water with his strong, muscular arms. "Always looking out for my well-being, aren't you?"

"Always have. Always will."

The following day, he woke her early for their zip line tour of the rain forest. High in the canopy of the lush green trees, she stood on a platform with nothing but a harness and a line stretched through the trees to keep her from plunging to her death on the forest floor.

"I think I'm going to be sick." She peered over the edge of the platform and quickly retreated when she saw the dizzying height.

He wrapped his arms around her from behind to make her feel more secure. "When the fear is too much and you feel like it's overtaking you, close your eyes. Feel me with you. Remember how this feels in my arms and let it calm you. I'm your shadow, Elle. I'm always with you."

"Next," the tour guide called out.

Elle opened her eyes and stepped out of Devon's embrace, her courage renewed. The guide connected her harness to the line and gave her a reminder demonstration of what to do.

"Now, just sit down in your harness, and simply let go. Soar through the trees and have the time of your life. There's nothing to fear."

She did as he said, keeping Devon's encouragement close to her heart. In an instant, she was zipping through the canopy. Amazing sights and beauty she'd never seen before quickly made her forget about her fears. The tree height became her friend, introducing her to new and wonderful experiences she never would've risked on her own. Her squeals of delight rang through the trees, quickly followed by Devon's laughter.

"I'm so glad you made me do this!" She jumped into his arms as soon as he landed on the next stop. "This is so much fun. Makes me wish I had a video camera on my helmet so I could watch it over and over again."

When they'd finished flying through the trees, Devon pulled her into his arms and kissed her on the tip of her nose. "I'm proud of you. Even though you were scared out of your mind, you handled it like a pro."

"I did what you told me to do. When I felt your arms around me, I felt safe and protected. You didn't seem to have any problem jumping off that platform at all."

He shrugged. "That wasn't high. I had to jump out of planes in the

Army, so being able to see the ground while attached to a line was a walk in the park."

"You never talk about what you did in the service. I never knew you had to skydive."

He grinned at her reference. "I went to Jump School to become a *paratrooper*. But that was a long time ago. Nothing to talk about now." He quickly dismissed the subject, regretting bringing it up, while also wishing he could tell her everything about his life so she'd better understand his position.

"What's on the agenda for tonight?"

"I thought we'd spend some time enjoying the privacy of our suite before our dinner reservations. Then maybe a romantic walk on the beach, find a quiet spot, enjoy more privacy, and start all over again tomorrow."

"Enjoy the privacy, huh?"

"Yep, and by that, I mean we'll explore every inch of each other's body. I can't wait to strip you down and taste you all over again."

"Maybe we should skip the dinner reservations completely and just eat in tonight."

"Don't think the thought hasn't crossed my mind a dozen or so times. But, with only having two weeks and so much I want to experience with you, it's best we go out. Besides, I want to show you off without the paparazzi around us."

"Fair enough. But only because I'd hate to deprive you of showing me off tonight." She tried to keep a straight face while teasing him, but she was unable to hold the expression when he stared at her suspiciously. "Especially considering you won't even be seen with me any other time."

"That's it. I'm spanking that ass tonight." His sly grin covered his face, the mirth of his words gleaming in his expression. "Keep talking to me like that. I'll come up with more punishment that's exciting to dole out."

"Promises, promises." She stepped out of his arms but held on to his hand. "Let's head back to the privacy of our room and begin that thorough exploration you mentioned."

Hours later, they emerged from the suite for dinner.

"I love how you have that just-thoroughly-fucked glow. I love even more that I'm the only one who knows what it looks like. It makes me want to take you back to the room and start all over again."

"You can after you feed me."

"Oh, I'll feed you all right."

"I need actual food for energy to keep up with you." She walked faster toward the restaurant before he changed her mind. Again. "We're already almost late. If they give our table away..." Her words trailed off, but the warning had been appropriately issued.

His responding chuckle left no doubt of how scared he was in the face of her threat. The deep timbre of his laugh rumbled through his chest, reverberating through her body and leaving tingling chills from the sexy undertones of it. She was forced to acknowledge part of her attraction to him was his dangerous and mysterious air. It only added to his appeal and her inability to resist him.

The open-air restaurant overlooked the mountains and ocean, giving them an incredible view of the moon shimmering off the surface of the calm water. The exclusive resort attracted the type of traveler who preferred privacy and offered it to others. Elle's presence didn't cause the slightest stir, giving them at least the illusion of anonymity during their meal.

"Today has been perfect," Elle gushed. "I've loved every minute of it. We should've done this long ago."

"I agree, so we'll have to make it a standing date. A yearly escape to a remote location."

"Absolutely."

"Great. Then you agree to let me kidnap you and take you away whenever I want."

"Well, I won't object, but my director may if I'm filming at the time you decide to kidnap me."

"Technically," he quipped, "I can find ways around that inconvenience."

"You have so many talents, I can't say I doubt that at all."

"To us." He raised his wineglass. "And to our lifelong commitment of standing dates in hidden locations."

"To never having to worry that a date with you will be boring or awkward." Elle raised her goblet and giggled during the clinking of glasses.

After dinner, they took a stroll along the shore, the gentle waves lapping at their feet. The ocean breeze kept them cool in the tropical heat, though Elle could've sworn she saw sparks arc from the heated glances Devon shot her.

"We're all alone out here," he whispered. "I can do anything I want to you, and no one would be the wiser. It's so very tempting."

"That goes both ways, actually."

His dark blue eyes flashed with a mixture of desire, admiration, and amusement. "Just when I think I have you figured out." He pulled her into his side, his big arm wrapped securely around her, and they walked back to their room with their bodies stuck together.

Their remaining time on the island was spent in much the same manner. By day, their exciting excursions took her to places she never would've dared or dreamed of going without Devon. Perilous journeys to volcanic peaks. Dizzying heights of rock climbing expeditions. Day-long hikes deep inside the rain forest. Underwater excursions to a beautiful coral reef.

Nights were spent in their open-air suite with room service delivering their meals more times than not. The in-suite infinity pool provided all the privacy they needed while allowing them to enjoy the moonlit views. Wrapped in a sensual embrace, they made love nightly, with one waking the other for a second round at some point before the morning sun lit up their room. The closer they were to the end of their two-week escape, the more desperate they both became for one more touch, one more embrace, one more kiss.

13

CHAPTER THIRTEEN

The morning before they were scheduled to leave, Devon snuck out of the room while Elle showered. He had a special surprise planned for her and didn't want to risk her hearing him on the phone arranging it.

"Hello, sir. How can I help you?" The suites had butlers assigned to cater to the guests' every need. Though they hadn't needed his services before, Devon knew he didn't have long before Elle would notice his absence, so he provided the basics and left the man to finalize the details.

"I need to arrange a spa package for my companion—after we return from a helicopter sight-seeing tour." Devon gave the butler his specific instructions, speaking low and looking over his shoulder frequently to make sure she hadn't overheard him.

"I'll be glad to arrange every aspect of it." With a few keystrokes, Devon and Elle were booked on the morning helicopter tour, and her complete spa package would begin immediately afterward.

"Thank you," Devon replied and turned to walk away after the butler handed him the itinerary.

"Sir?" the butler called to him. "This was left for you late last night. We don't allow unscheduled visitors in the suite area after the resort doors are locked. The gentleman was adamant you were to receive this first thing this morning."

He handed Devon a large manila envelope, and Devon's heart sank. No one knew precisely where he was or exactly when he'd return, so there was only one explanation for the unscheduled visitor. The fact that someone had tried to access the room he shared with Elle enraged him. Had that man been successful, his body would've been shark food, never to be found again—company man or not. The agent in him suddenly cringed at the room he'd chosen for their escape.

On paper, the idea was perfect. Secluded. Romantic. Private. Tropical.

In practice, he'd given whoever had followed him to the island a full-frontal view of every move they'd made. The unobstructed view looking out on the island was equally as open looking in with high-powered binoculars or a scope. His lapse in judgment and following of security protocol could've cost both his and Elle's lives.

He thanked the butler absently before rushing back to the room to check on Elle. His paranoia was engaged with a renewed ferocity. He'd been so busy living the carefree life, his guard had been down completely. He hadn't even sensed eyes on him or footsteps following him. With all his time and attention devoted to Elle, he'd unknowingly put them both at risk. He berated himself over his own stupidity as he stomped back to their door.

Elle stepped out of the bathroom just as Devon entered the suite. "Where have you been?"

He was relieved to see her wearing the short robe, though the belt was loosely tied and the fabric gaped open at her chest. "Just making sure our last day here is off the charts unforgettable."

"Care to share what awaits me today?"

"Nope. I don't want to share at all. I want every second to be a surprise. But do me one favor—get dressed in the bathroom. I overheard one of the butlers say they've caught people with binoculars trying to get a peep show before."

Elle laughed incredulously. "We've been parading around here naked and having sex on every surface in every position imaginable for the last thirteen nights. One more won't hurt now."

"You're probably right," he conceded. He decided there was no need to alarm her unnecessarily. If anyone from the company had seen them, he'd find out. If it had been someone with the press, the pictures would've already been all over the web.

He stole into the bathroom, locked the door for privacy, and silently opened the manila envelope. With the contents in his hands, he squeezed his eyes shut and shook his head. The death stipulation for leaving the CIA had suddenly become more appealing.

After memorizing the details, he put the documents under hot water and watched as they completely disintegrated. Though he couldn't deny that handy little trick was better than eating them to erase all traces, the fact that he was activated on his vacation didn't escape him. It was a clear message sent from high up the chain.

We can find you wherever you are.

The helicopter tour of the island was better than Elle ever expected. Though she'd seen many of the sights up close and personal, the morning tour bundled all the memories they'd made into a neat package and tied them together with a pretty bow on top. Thirteen days of perfection and bonding with the man of her dreams, the man she loved and had always loved. It had been the best time of her life, hands down.

"You've been quiet today. Are you ready to get rid of me? Run out of things to talk about with me?" She teased Devon, knowing he dreaded the end of their escapade as much as she did. She had simply decided to reserve her quiet suffering for the flight home the next morning.

"You know better than that. I wish I could keep you with me always."

"Don't go back," she pleaded. She'd decided long before never to ask him to choose between his job and her. Truth be told, she'd been laser-focused on her own career, and she took advantage of the mostly out-of-town-boyfriend to avoid splitting her own time and attention. But her career was no longer the most important aspect of her life. She wanted more—with Devon. "Stay with me. Quit your job, whatever it is that takes you away from me."

His eyes searched hers, but his expression was unreadable.

"Or take me with you, and I'll quit my job. Either way you want it —I don't care which. It's just too hard to let you go again now."

"I feel the same way, Elle. But I can't let you quit what you've worked so hard to attain. I also can't quit my job, even though I can't explain why. And I certainly can't take you with me. You are far too valuable to me to do that."

Her crestfallen face tore at his heart, though he hid his deep disappointment behind his passive façade. "Don't worry, darlin'. One day, we'll be together without all these obstacles between us. I'm working on it."

She snuggled into his side and swallowed the tears that threatened to fall. Crying wouldn't help and would rob them of the time they had left together. That also reminded her. "Hey, you said you had another surprise for me after the helicopter tour. I can't imagine anything could top this. So, what's next after we land?"

"It's two-fold, actually. First, you're going to the spa for a lot of pampering and girly stuff. After that is a surprise I refuse to spoil, so you'll just have to wait and see."

"You're not going to the spa with me? For a couple's massage?"

"No, I'm not letting some guy put his hands all over me—or you. I booked the only lady masseuse who was open for you, and I'll just wait patiently until you're finished."

"You could've booked the guy for me, you know."

"Hell, no, I couldn't have either."

Elle snorted with laughter at his refusal. "You know the studio brings in massage therapists for us, and sometimes they're male. It's okay. Just because he's a man doesn't mean it's wrong or bad."

"It is wrong for another man to have his hands on you, and it will be bad when my hands are on him."

"What about when I have to film a nude scene or a sex scene with another actor? How wrong or bad will that be?"

"Deadly. It'll be deadly wrong all the way around."

"You'd better hurry with that plan for us to be together all the time, then. That scenario will arise if I stay in movies long enough. Not that you have anything to worry about because there's nothing romantic about the scene itself. But the camera and editing magic can definitely fool you."

His responding growl conveyed his displeasure with her answer.

"And we're back at the heliport. I hope you've both enjoyed your flight," the pilot said into their headphones.

Elle and Devon cut their eyes to each other at the same time. They'd become so comfortable with their privacy that they'd forgotten the pilot could hear their entire conversation. She chuckled lightly and dropped her head in her hands, shielding her face in embarrassment.

"Yes, we loved it. Sorry you had to suffer through our whole conversation. I'm afraid you've spoiled us here with a sheltered vacation, and we've enjoyed the seclusion a little too much."

"Not to worry, miss. This radio has a convenient button that mutes your conversation for the pilot. When I have it muted, I just watch to see if you're speaking to me or not. Usually, the passengers talk amongst themselves and relive their stay. It's all part of the appeal of this resort."

When they exited the helicopter, Devon walked Elle to the spa and left her at the front desk. "Enjoy your Princess Elle package."

"Thank you. I'm sure I will." She rose up on her toes and kissed him before he got away.

Once outside the spa, he walked to the railing of the terrace and waited. Within minutes, he felt the weight of eyes on him and sensed the presence of someone too close to be a coincidence.

"Just a suggestion, but if you value your eyes and limbs where they are, I suggest you get out here now." Shadow spoke to the air, letting his voice carry to his watcher.

"I've heard your skills were incredible. But the stories could never match the real-life action."

"Rogers. You son of a bitch. If I find out you've been lurking outside my room and getting your rocks off watching my girl and me, I'll force-feed those rocks to you before I snap your fucking neck."

"I'm not that stupid. Besides, I just got here late last night. They wouldn't let me anywhere near your room. The target just arrived yesterday, and this is the only chance we've had to take him out of play. He's preparing to move a shipment of children. We're sanctioned to neutralize him. The syringe is taped under the bench beside you.

"Older man, completely white hair, naturally bronze skin. He has lunch reservations on the veranda in fifteen minutes. Table for one. He likes to eat alone. His table will be in a secluded spot. Handle this, and go enjoy the rest of your vacation. You picked a hell of a spot."

"Why don't you handle it and save us both the trouble?"

"He's above my pay grade. Should something go wrong, we'll need your unique skill set to handle it."

"It's past time for you to upgrade, then. Stop depending on me when you're afraid to get your hands dirty. Or when you're simply afraid."

"I'm not supposed to tell you, but the analysts think he could be connected to Ava's abduction. They didn't give me concrete intel, but for them to even mention it tells me they're at least one thousand percent certain."

"Oh, he's definitely a fucking dead man then."

Shadow reached under the bench seat beside him and retrieved the syringe. He knew it well—he'd helped perfect the current design. Small and easy to conceal in the palm of his hand, a simple push of a button released the needle and the contents in quick succession. He could be in and out of the area before the effects of the medication took hold.

The emergency team that would pick up the victim during his medical crisis were prearranged personnel from the company. Their only task was to help him along to the light and complete the mission. The medical examiner, also on the payroll, would rule his death as natural causes, the mixture of his blood pressure medication in combination with the elevated levels of potassium chloride in his blood would appear to be no more than he ingested too much table salt and didn't get enough exercise. In short—he ate and drank too much while not caring for his overall health.

It was easy to make the report say what was necessary to carry out orders when it was all orchestrated well in advance. Even the autopsy report with an official cause of death had already been completed, leaving only a few standard fill-in-the-blanks, and his death wouldn't be questioned by anyone who could do anything about it.

With the device in hand, Shadow strode casually to the area where his target sat alone, reading a paper and occasionally looking out at the spectacular view. Just beyond the unfortunate target was another terrace overlooking the trees and ocean below. With his sights set on the vacant terrace, Shadow wound his way through the tables and chairs, passing the man as he returned his glass to the table.

Shadow waited a few seconds on the terrace behind his target before he continued moving down more stairs to other areas of the sprawling resort. Each step took him farther from the man who'd grabbed his chest in pain. His request for a table away from everyone else would aid in his demise. The resort staff was busy serving larger parties at busier clusters of tables, oblivious to his emergent situation and his inability to cry out for help.

In his peripheral vision, Shadow saw the man's body go limp, and he knew the mission was complete. He kept moving down the side of the mountain, away from the commotion that would no doubt ensue within minutes. He planned to be as far away as possible when that happened.

"MY APPOINTMENT DIDN'T SHOW UP," THE LOVELY MASSAGE THERAPIST grumbled.

"Was it for right now?" Elle asked, an idea already quickly forming.

"Yes. He was adamant about booking this time then didn't even show up. Now I can't find him on the guest roster at all." Her brows furrowed in confusion. "That's so odd."

"Is there any chance I can grab his spot for my boyfriend? He won't let a man touch him, but we could do a couple's massage with two female therapists." Elle's excitement over the possibility was contagious.

"I'd be glad to do that for you. I'm Layla, by the way. Go grab your boyfriend, and I'll get the room set up for two."

Elle rushed out of the spa, thinking she'd find Devon just outside the door since he'd left her only minutes before. Another man stood at the rail instead. When he turned and met her gaze, Elle's blood ran cold. He didn't appear to belong in such an exclusive, high-end resort.

His hair was long and unkempt, even pulled back in the messy ponytail he wore. Faded black tattoos covered his arms, chest, and neck. Not the colorful, sexy tattoos that every man-candy with six-pack abs seemed to sport. These were decidedly prison tattoos—an ex-convict who'd been inked with a makeshift method while incarcerated. The letters across his fingers were distinguishable, even from where she stood.

EVILONES

As if she were propelled by some invisible force, her feet moved on their own to carry her away from him. His horrifying smile slowly crept across his haggard face, revealing missing and rotten teeth, but deeper than that, his evil nature. She moved quicker, her eyes scanning the area for Devon and the safety his presence inherently provided. She spotted him walking with his casual swagger across one of the private terraces where a guest sat alone, reading the paper and sipping on his drink.

Devon passed behind him just as the man put his glass down. She opened her mouth to yell his name when she saw something that couldn't have been. Even in the far reaches of her mind, she wouldn't accept what her eyes insisted she'd seen.

Devon's arm swung loosely at his side when he passed the guest, then made a quick stabbing motion before Devon had moved past the man. Elle's feet halted at the action, her mouth hung open, and her heart raced at breakneck speed. Consciously willing her feet to move again, she dismissed it and assumed she'd misjudged the entire scene.

Then the man slumped in his chair, and Devon rapidly descended the stairs, disappearing from her sight. By the time she reached him, she knew he was dead and wouldn't be revived by the time medical crews arrived. She wanted to help him, but she'd never learned CPR. The frothy spittle just inside his still open lips convinced her to alert the waiter so others who were more qualified could help him instead.

She ran back up the stairs, yelling for help as she ascended. She was met by two waiters, their faces panic-stricken as she described the man's condition.

"Call an ambulance. I think he may already be dead." Tears welled up in her eyes, and panic rose in her chest. "Do you know how to perform CPR?" she asked one of the men on their way back down the stairs.

"No," he replied while staring blankly at the dead man. He finally snapped out of his trance and began instructing the other waiter. "I'll go call the first responder team. You get an ambulance." They hurried away from the scene, calling for others to help, and left Elle alone with the dead man again.

Was I seeing things?

She didn't want an answer—but she needed one. She had to satisfy her overactive imagination. She had *not* just seen Devon jab something into the back of the man's neck moments before he slouched in his seat. Devon did *not* palm some sort of device before sliding his hand down into his pocket. The *only* logical explanation was that she had hallucinated all of it.

With painfully slow steps, she moved toward the dead man's back with her eyes glued to his neck and her breaths frozen in her chest. She didn't know what she'd find there, and she didn't know what she'd do with whatever she did find.

How can I report Devon?

How can I not report Devon?

Will I be implicated and investigated, too?

Will I go to prison for being his accomplice?

How can I believe he had any part to play in this stranger's death?

She knew him—the best side of him he didn't show anyone else. She felt she'd betrayed him for allowing her thoughts to stray as far as they had. He'd done nothing but love and care for her for the last several years.

Still.

One more step, and any doubt would be erased—one way or another.

She moved directly behind him, and her eyes searched the skin on the back of his neck. The way his head dropped to the side created folds of skin that obscured part of her view. A half step closer and her upper body slightly bent over to get a better look, she steeled her nerves and looked again.

"Excuse me, miss," a frantic man bellowed from beside her.

"Elle, what are you doing?" The familiar voice spoke in her other ear at the same time, causing her to jump backward. Devon lifted her up and away from the dead man as the medical crews began to move him.

There, in the folds of his skin, appeared to be something out of place. Something that didn't belong. Something so small, it would've been missed had she not specifically looked for it. A pinprick that could've just as easily been a bug bite. *In fact, it's more likely to be a bug bite than what caused his death,* she thought.

Who returns to the scene of a murder?

Cold chills ran over her body in the tropical heat of the afternoon at her next thought.

The murderer does, that's who.

Devon carried her up the stairs, giving the medical team room to work on the hotel guest. He pulled her into his arms, and she willingly buried her face in his chest.

"What are you doing out here alone? You were supposed to be getting pampered for our date tonight."

"I was looking for you," she stuttered, her teeth chattering.

"Darlin', even at this resort, you have to be careful. You're a celebrity. People know your face—and this is a small island. Word travels fast when famous people arrive." He pulled her closer, tightening his arms around her. "If anything happened to you, I'd never forgive myself for not being there to protect you."

Guilt further consumed her. How could she think so lowly of someone who obviously cared so much for her? What did that say about her character? These thoughts and feelings flew through her mind, mixing with flashes of what she thought she'd seen. Then he'd adjust his embrace and remind her how much she loved him all over again.

"Let's get you out of here. You don't need to see this," he murmured against her temple and placed a reassuring kiss there.

When they reached the top of the terrace, the sinister-looking ex-convict was still standing in the same spot. His cold stare drifted between Devon and Elle with no attempt to hide his interest in them. He kept his eyes trained on Devon for a second longer than normal, then cut his eyes to Elle again. That same unnerving smile covered his face, enhancing the evil and ugliness inside him.

For the first time in a very long time, Elle felt genuinely frightened and didn't know which way to turn. Her rock was beside her, and he was also the one she questioned. The scary-looking man didn't belong there, but he seemed to recognize them both. The dead man had rattled her beyond belief—but the events leading up to it caused her to question everything about Devon and herself.

And their relationship.

CHAPTER FOURTEEN

"You're treating me like I'm a fragile doll you're convinced will shatter any second now." The curt undertone in Elle's voice left no room for doubt regarding her frustration.

"For a while there, I thought you might." Devon watched her cautiously, unconvinced she was as "fine" as she professed.

"Who was that man standing outside the spa? Did you know him?" Her eyes held a challenge he hadn't seen before. She was asking more than her words conveyed, though she didn't want to admit it, even to herself.

"What man? Why would you think I know anyone here?"

"Don't think I haven't noticed how you answer with a question and keep everything as vague as possible." She moved from the dresser to the bed, packing her clothes for the flight home.

Devon could only watch with his heart in his throat. She'd only sampled a small taste of his life—and he'd even tried to keep her out of that, as easy as it had been. She wasn't cut out for the life of a spy, or a spy's wife. She was too well-known. She'd be used against him. She was truly his weakness—his Achilles' heel.

A simple mission had all but ruined his last night on the island with her. His last night ever. The events of the day revealed what he'd known all along. But like Elle, he didn't want to face or accept the truth he already knew. He had to let her go, once and for all. For both of their sakes, he had to sever their ties and allow her to live her life in the light of the stars, while he remained in the shadows where he belonged.

She folded a shirt and placed it in her suitcase. When she moved to the closet to get the next one, he stood and moved into her path, stopping her with his sheer size.

"Elle, it's our last night together," he began. His words struck a chord in her, forcing her eyes to fly up and meet his. "Our last night of vacation on this gorgeous island, with the incredible suite and warm infinity pool. I don't want to spend it fighting or being distant. Today was upsetting for you, I know. But do you think we can enjoy what little time we have left?"

Her expression softened, and she smiled lovingly up at him. "I would love that, Devon. I'd love to pretend this afternoon never happened and move back into our bubble of happiness where nothing bad can touch us. Care to pretend with me?"

"I'd love nothing more than to pretend all night with you." He leaned down and captured her mouth with his.

She expected his usual dominant side to emerge and start giving her orders. Not that she'd ever minded his take-charge attitude or his ability to make her feel like a rag doll by the time she'd snuggled beside him to sleep. But his gentleness surprised her. He took his time undressing her and laid her on the bed. He quickly shed his clothes and joined her.

His fingers glided over her skin as if they had a singular purpose of memorizing every inch of her body. Heated eyes followed their path, but his self-control kept his urges in check. Soft lips placed numerous kisses all over her, worshiping her body with palpable reverence and devotion. The intensity of his emotions streamed out of him without a single word to convey his thoughts. Every articulation he couldn't voice was clearly pronounced in the way he made love to her soul by simply caressing her body.

His nose skimmed along her stomach, and he inhaled deeply, drawing in her scent. The first splinter in her heart appeared.

His tongue blazed a trail over the sensitive skin between her breasts, greedily ingesting her flavor like a man starved. The splinter in her heart became a fissure.

He nibbled on the delicate skin along the side of her neck and watched with rapt attention as the cold chills flared out across her skin. One side of his mouth lifted slightly in amusement, but the smile never reached his eyes.

The fissure became a fracture.

Positioned between her legs, he straightened his arms to hover over her. He pushed forward, his cock brushing against her pussy before he nudged his way inside. Her eyes closed automatically when she moaned, relishing the sensation of him rocking into her. He stopped abruptly and waited for her to look at him again. With her eyes opened and locked on his, he began surging into her again with full, controlled movements. With bent arms, he framed her face and continued, never moving his eyes from hers. When he reached around to wrap his arms under her knees, his gaze never strayed— and he didn't allow hers to move from him. His message and intentions were clear.

Their connection was more than physical. In any other circumstance, long periods of direct eye contact would've been uncomfortable. But not that night—not with him. The feelings they conveyed to each other with only a slight shift of expressions communicated much more than words could.

When she thought he couldn't extract one more scream from her, he proved her wrong. When her skin became slick with sweat and her breaths became labored from exertions, he seemed to gain his second wind. When she didn't think her body could take his sensual form of torture one more second, he slowed his efforts to let her recover but didn't break their union.

When his body forced his release, a moment of grave sadness flashed across his face, deepening his already dark blue eyes further. She searched his face wordlessly, questioning him without verbalizing the fears inside. Everything about their encounter was different than every other time. Part of her tried to rationalize it was symbolic of the two weeks coming to an end and knowing they'd be apart for weeks on end again. But a dire warning registered, and she knew that wasn't the reason behind their profound lovemaking experience.

He dipped his head and brushed his lips across hers—lightly at first, then more firmly until a rift in his self-control revealed an instant of desperation in his caress.

Her heart shattered in her chest.

After rolling onto his side, he pulled her flush against him and clung to her as if she were his only lifeline in the sea raging out of control in a storm. Even after his exhaustive actions during their carnal union, tension streamed from him with full blunt force. She eventually drifted off into a fitful sleep in his arms.

One advantage a predawn flight held was no one actually wanted to speak to anyone else unless it was absolutely necessary. Elle was thankful for that, and for Devon packing the rest of their clothes while she showered, trying to wake up after their late-night endeavors. When she emerged from the bathroom, the butler had already taken their luggage down to the waiting taxi.

Devon closed his hand around hers, threw her carry-on bag over his other shoulder, and led her out of the room. The door clicked shut behind them, automatically locking them out of the room without giving them a chance for one final glance back.

When their plane reached cruising altitude, she yawned repeatedly while attempting to fight back the sleep that tried relentlessly to overtake her. He reached over to press the button to recline her seat then covered her with both her and his blankets.

"Rest," he commanded softly.

Her lips parted, ready to protest sleeping through more of their time together than absolutely necessary, but he stopped her.

"I enjoy watching you sleep. You're tired. Take a nap. I'll still be right here when you wake."

"Not sure I can sleep now, knowing you'll be watching me." A hint of melancholy bled through her attempt at levity.

Devon responded by covering her hand with his warm one. In the dimly lit first-class cabin, Elle ached to confess to every thought, feeling, and desire in her mind and heart. She wanted to tell him all her fears about their future, about her career, about him. She needed him to acknowledge and accept they were a vital part of each other's lives. More than anything else, she longed for him to explain what she'd witnessed the day before.

He squeezed her hand and inclined his head ever so slightly, urging her to close her eyes. She clasped her other hand on top of his as she rolled to her side and faced him. With the words on the tip of her tongue, the fatigue and weariness won when her heavy eyes closed and she slipped off to sleep.

When she opened her eyes, the flight attendant was passing out meals to the other passengers. Her tray and drink sat in front of her, already prepared for her to eat.

"Did you fix this for me?"

"Yes. We didn't make it to the special date I had planned last night, so this is my pathetic replacement."

"Thank you for doing that. Did you get any sleep?"

"No. But I watched you sleep, and that always relaxes me." He picked up her fork and handed it to her.

"Very subtle clue that you want me to eat, Devon." Her teasing sounded good to his ears. She sounded more like his Elle—the one who still thought he hung the moon and stars.

She chatted about the plot of the upcoming production in between bites of her in-flight meal. Devon pretended he listened to her every word, but mostly, he found himself staring at her to memorize small details no one else would notice. Like the small flecks of green and gray in her hazel eyes. How she couldn't enjoy her food unless she had at least two napkins. The way she loved tomatoes, but not on her sandwiches. She always ate them separately. But mostly he pictured his life without her in it and what that would mean for both of them.

He tried to remember what filled his time before he jetted off to LA every chance he had to see her. What did he do to occupy his days? How would he cope with all of that after having Elle in his life and his heart for so long?

For her sake, he had to let her go. He'd selfishly held on to her for far too long—and she'd allowed it to happen because she loved him. But it was time to show her how much he loved her—by doing the right thing, even if it was also the hardest pill to swallow.

"That was actually pretty good for airline food," Elle remarked, pulling him from his internal thoughts. "You've been quiet, listened to me blabber on nonstop, and stared at me while I ate. What's on your mind?"

The words were right there—waiting to be said.

"Just thinking about how busy you'll be with production and promotion. You'll have me pushed out of the picture in no time."

If he made it seem like it was her idea, his absence would be easier for her to accept. He wanted to give her that much peace about it.

"You really think I'd choose any role over you?"

"You'd have to, Elle. You're bound by contract. If you ever want to work on another movie, you can't worry about me."

Her eyes lit with fiery anger, though she contained her voice. "I know exactly what you're doing, Devon Kane, and it won't fucking work on me."

Her change in demeanor was unexpected. He immediately realized his reverse psychology tactic would fail miserably on her, and he needed to contain the situation.

"Elle—"

"Don't Elle me. I offered to quit and go with you wherever you go. That's how much you mean to me and how little acting means compared to you. Yes, I love it, but I've achieved it. I don't need more and more of it to feed my self-worth. I need you, more than anything or anyone.

"I've allowed this long-distance romance because it was convenient and what we both needed at the time. But that's not how I want the rest of my life to be, and I don't believe you do either."

He couldn't argue—and she was on a roll and wouldn't let him get a word in anyway.

"Whatever happened that made you so closed off has to be dealt with in some way. Talk to me about it, talk to a therapist, decide to let it all go and move on—whatever works for you. But I didn't get this far by being a shrinking violet who's afraid to speak up for what I want. And I'm no one's doormat. You've had time to come to this conclusion on your own, but you haven't. Not fully committed anyway. So I'm calling your bluff. What was it you and Jeff used to say? Oh, yeah—shit or get off the pot."

Fuck, you have no idea how much I love you, he thought.

The flight attendant returned to pick up their items before the captain announced they were arriving at LAX. Though she was disappointed they hadn't finished their conversation, she had every intention of resuming it as soon as they were locked away in her bedroom. And she wouldn't let Devon out until he'd given his word and a solid commitment for their future.

Before she'd fallen asleep on the plane, her mind and heart were heavy with turmoil and pain. All those awful thoughts about Devon had taken a serious toll on her ability to be rational. The sight of the dead man, Devon's proximity to him, the evil man who kept smiling at her—it all crashed down on her at once, compounded by the end of the best two weeks she'd ever had.

When she'd opened her eyes after her nap, Devon was the first person she saw. His proximity was the protective and calming presence she needed. There was never a time when he didn't hold a special place in her heart, in one way or another. And there wasn't a day she wanted to pass without him in it. The clarity she had was refreshing; the vision she had of their future was bright.

She knew who she wanted, needed, and loved. It was time for Devon to admit the same.

The cab ride back to her apartment was a stark contrast from the laid-back atmosphere of the island. Despite how long she'd lived in LA, she was amazed at how easily she adapted to St. Lucia and the privacy it afforded. The packed LA interstates, with all the angry drivers and crowded lanes, assaulted the island tranquility she brought home with her.

Devon carried her bags up to the apartment, walking behind her as she fished her keys from her purse. She breezed in, quickly reacclimating to the four walls with city-street-view accommodations she called home.

"Beth, we're back. Are you here?" Elle moved through the small living space, looking for but not finding her best friend. "Looks like we have the place to ourselves."

Devon gave her a small smile and set her suitcases down beside where he stood. It was then she realized he didn't have his own bags in his hands. She began shaking her head from side to side, fighting back the lump in her throat and the tears in her eyes.

Unsuccessfully.

In a couple of steps, he stood directly in front of her and began his prepared speech. He kept reminding himself his decision was best for her. He'd put her in enough danger. He'd risked her safety too many times. He'd wasted enough of her time.

His big hand cupped her cheek, and she leaned into it. The tears spilled over her bottom lids and covered her face. She didn't bother to wipe them away—they wouldn't stop anytime soon.

"Elle, I should've told you this a long time ago, but I couldn't. I've selfishly tried to hold on to you, and to keep you holding on to me. You deserve better—you deserve to have everything you've ever wanted."

His other hand covered her other cheek and held her gaze directly on his face. He leaned in and kissed her sweetly, longingly, hauntingly. When he pulled back, he finally muttered the words that would release her. She'd finally know the truth.

"I love you, Elle. More than my life. More than anyone or anything. I'll love you and only you, all my life. You're my girl —forever."

Her heart disintegrated.

He released his hold on her and backed away. With his hand on the doorknob, he pulled it shut as he backed into the corridor. The symbolic wall separated them. The door had literally been shut. She no longer questioned his feelings for her or how much he loved her. But he had to walk away. He had to give her her life back, no matter how much it killed him to live without her, without the anticipation of seeing her again, without the thrill of making love to her again.

He slid into the back seat of the waiting taxi and rode back to LAX. To the gate with the Miami-bound flight. To the only life he'd ever really known.

To a quiet condo.

With an ocean view that reminded him of Elle.

To a cold, empty bed that only taunted him with a chance to sleep but not exactly delivering on that promise.

And to a life of loneliness and emptiness in the wicked shadows of what once might have been.

~

THE DOOR CLOSED BETWEEN THEM WITH ELLE FROZEN WHERE SHE stood. Though she'd known and felt a major shift in his demeanor, she ignored her instincts, all the red flags her heart tried to warn her about. Unable to move, she waited where he left her standing, hoping he'd return on his own.

She had no idea how much time had passed when the door finally began to swing open. Hope sprang up in her chest, ratcheting her heart rate up as excitement and anticipation grew. She waited to see his handsome face, read his thoughts behind his dark blue eyes, and lose herself when his muscular arms wrapped her in the safety of his embrace.

"Elle? What's wrong? What happened?" The questions rushed from Beth the moment she saw the despondent expression on her friend's face. The tears flowed freely down Elle's cheeks, leaving tracks in her makeup.

Afraid to tear her eyes from Elle in her current condition, Beth made a quick glance around the apartment and spotted the suitcases still sitting beside Elle. Then she knew whatever had caused the current dilemma, it revolved around Devon.

Beth's heart hurt for her friend, knowing only time would lessen the pain, while never fully eliminating it. She locked the door, took Elle by the hand, and led her to the bathtub. She ran a hot bath and tossed in a lavender bath bomb.

"Undress and get in, love. I'll make us both some chamomile tea, and you can fill me in on what happened. Or, you can just lay your head in my lap and cry while I pet your hair. Whatever you need."

Elle nodded mindlessly, the blank expression she wore showed her thoughts were a million miles away. But she did as Beth instructed and sank further into the steaming water. Relief was nowhere to be found, however, because everything around her was tied to a memory of him.

When the water cooled, she wrapped a thick robe around her and joined Beth in the living room.

"Want me to reheat your tea?"

Elle shook her head and stretched out on the couch. With her head in Beth's lap, she let her hot tears flow. Beth stroked her hair and tried to comfort her as best she could, but the end of a dream left a hole in Elle's heart that couldn't be filled with promises of a better day to come.

Her only consoling thought before she fell asleep on Beth was how she'd lived through other heartbreaking and difficult situations. She'd come through this one stronger and wiser.

But first, she would hurt.

15
____

CHAPTER FIFTEEN

Current Day

On the private jet to LAX, Shadow planned his every move and how he'd infiltrate a well-known and dangerous motorcycle club past the probie level. Hell, even a probie was a step up from where he'd normally have to prove his worth. But he didn't have enough time to go through the standard process.

Elle and Beth didn't have enough time.

Over the past year, he'd kept his distance from her and let her live her life. He'd watched with a mixture of extreme pride and sorrowful regret how her career skyrocketed when she put all her energies into it. She was frequently sought out for leading roles, and the most popular strutting peacocks vied for her attention.

"Fuckers," he mumbled to himself. "Why couldn't it be those dickheads disappearing instead of Elle?"

The prior twelve months were the hardest Shadow could remember enduring since he was a kid. His trips to LA had not lessened. He still visited Elle, checked on her well-being, watched her work—though she never knew he was there. He wanted her to forget him and have the life he couldn't give her.

Only he couldn't let her go, and he didn't want a life that didn't include her.

"Maybe this is my ticket away from the CIA operations. If they knew how fucking crazy messed up I am, they wouldn't send me out anymore."

He glanced around the cabin of the luxurious Steele Security jet, thankful the flight attendant was out of earshot. While he wouldn't mind the company directors thinking he was crazy, he didn't want to share his instability with anyone else.

"That wouldn't work anyway," he realized. "They'd just send me to even worse places."

For the time being, his focus had to be solely on Elle and Beth if he was to have any chance of saving them. From the intelligence Steadman had shared, there was little hope of rescuing one of them, much less both. If two were missing, there were bound to be more.

Fortifying his mind and steeling his resolve, he cracked open the dossier on the outlaw motorcycle club he'd soon pledge to as a new member.

The Devil's Dominion Motorcycle Club.

He leaned back in his seat and began memorizing all the details and planning his offensive. Every word solidified his belief the chance of success was low and the risk of death was high. The Devil's Dominion was not known to suffer fools—or traitors.

Based out of LA, the motorcycle gang had spread to multiple states through smaller gangs brought into the fold—either by their request or via a hostile takeover and violent orientation. With the additions to their ranks, their total member count was estimated to be close to two thousand men.

An enterprise that size would have considerable resources at their beck and call. It would also need a mixture of criminal activities to fund it. With more than 150 chapters, their reach was far and wide. He had no doubt the case would require all his skill to pull off. On paper, they were a formidable opponent. Reality would be much worse.

Little information was known about their initiation process.

Those who had endured it were either still part of the club and didn't talk about it, or had been killed trying to leave the gang. His inside man, Nick Tucker, gave a detailed report two years prior, but he stressed the leaders of the group created new scenarios frequently. Each new round of probies endured more humiliating and sinister acts than the last. The harsh induction helped ensure they maintained their cruel nature as full-fledged members.

The highest concentration of members was in the LA chapter. With nearly 300 members, it was by far the most dangerous and least predictable. Fortunately, it was also the chapter Nick had infiltrated and worked his way up the chain during his two years undercover. As the current club treasurer, he was trusted implicitly and had proven his commitment.

According to Nick's handler, the two years with the gang had taken a significant toll on him. Shadow could only imagine what Nick had been forced to do to show his allegiance and gain their trust. For any criminal organization to accept an outsider, they would require the probationary member to commit a heinous crime—to prove his mettle and to have leverage to hold over his head.

The leader of all the chapters was an ex-convict by the name of Bobby Blalock, but his club nickname was Headbanger. He required every member to be a convicted felon, adding to the notoriety of the club overall. Every new member was assigned a nickname when they joined unless they already had one from an associated gang—but the club officers were the most notorious.

Using his secure phone, Shadow contacted Nick's handler, Jack Collins, to get the information directly from those closest to the action. "Jack, I'm on my way to LA. Tell me everything is ready for me."

"Steadman and I have been working on your background. It's airtight. They'll hire a private investigator to check you out. They've become very careful about any new members."

"Recently?"

"Fairly. In the last several months. Headbanger, the club president, has been extremely paranoid lately. His vice president,

Nutcrusher, personally oversees every new pledge, comparing their formal application to whatever the PI digs up."

"Headbanger and Nutcrusher. I'm sure there's a joke in there somewhere."

Jack chuckled darkly. "Not one they'd find funny. Nick joined at the most opportune time, before they became so suspicious of everyone. We built his arrest record and background around what he'd already told them."

"What is Nick's club name?"

"Renegade. He's the club treasurer, so they trust him with all the money. He and their sergeant at arms, Bonebreaker, convinced Headbanger to allow officers to nominate new members at the probie stage, so you'll skip the pledge stage. They still won't trust you until you've proven yourself, though."

"I've been reading up on their initiation process. It's fairly grueling but nothing I haven't been through before."

"Don't expect it'll be anything you've read about. They pride themselves on new and improved torture tactics. They have been known to order probies to kill someone for them, too."

Jack and Shadow discussed how he'd get in touch with Nick once he was ready to ride with the club. The only part of the agreement Shadow was leery over was waiting two to three weeks to allow changes to his features to occur naturally. His normally kempt hair needed to be longer and shaggy. His beard must be full and scraggly. Tattoos would be strategically placed to show his prison allegiance and felon status.

His motorcycle and leathers would be waiting for him at his rundown, sparsely furnished apartment, complete with dust and road grime to portray his recent ride across the country after his prison release. His photographic memory and training taught him how to blend in with any type of element and gave him a decided advantage, but earning the trust of a group of very suspicious criminals wouldn't be easy. He used the rest of the flight to pore over every detail of their known hangouts.

By the time he landed at a private airstrip in LA County, he'd moved past concerned and straight to murderous rage. Jack waited outside the fence in a beat-up truck. He looked the part of a retired lifetime club member in case he was ever spotted near Nick Tucker. In Shadow's case, Jack would lend credence to his cover story if anyone saw them pull up to the apartment together.

"Good flight?" Jack asked when Shadow had settled in the passenger seat.

"As good as can be under the circumstances. Have you talked to Nick directly?"

Jack chuckled. "Not since we last talked a couple of hours ago. We go weeks without speaking. But I got a message to him, and he'll meet us tonight at your place. Your cover story will be enough to explain how the three of us know each other if anyone questions it. Or, I should say, *when* someone questions it. Bonebreaker will suspect you immediately. He spent twelve years in prison because of a snitch who turned out to be an undercover agent. He suspected Nick, too, so don't take it personally."

"As long as he doesn't take it personally when I serve his cock and balls to him chilled before I finish killing him."

Jack arched one brow as he looked over his shoulder at Shadow. "Angry much?"

"Jack, I'm more than angry after reading that file. What they're most likely doing with Elle makes my blood boil. I'm already a deadly man, but I could wipe out every single one of them and not lose a wink of sleep at night."

"Your director at the CIA warned me about turning you loose on this club."

"Yeah? What was his warning?"

"He said I may not have anyone left to arrest if they pissed you off. Apparently, you have a reputation in the company for taking care of business, no matter how messy the situation may be."

"You've been warned correctly. Think of all the money we'll save the taxpayers in the long run." His tone held no mirth or indication Jack shouldn't take his words at full face value.

"Just remember there's always more to the story. Someone else behind the scenes, calling the plays, directing the activities, reading the field. We need to take that person down, too. So we need them alive to flush out who's financing the big ventures."

"The money isn't coming from their drug operations? I read they're in league with the Mexican cartels and pulling in major dollars from street-level dealers all the way up the chain to the manufacturers."

"They are, no doubt. But their new business is much more expensive—at least, initially. The number of people we think they're paying off leads to a staggering amount of money. We'll get into that more with Nick when he drops by later."

Jack pulled alongside the curb in front of an old, dilapidated building that probably should've been condemned decades before. The sparsely remaining paint was peeling, the overhangs were rotten, and the gutters had long ago fallen away.

"Charming place. You didn't have anything a little less pretentious? I'm not sure I can afford a room here," Shadow deadpanned.

"Sorry. Everywhere else was full," Jack retorted. "Come on in, and I'll show you around."

He unlocked the door and stepped inside. With his arm extended, he smiled at Shadow. "Here's your apartment. Try not to get lost."

Shadow stepped through the doorway and did a full 360-degree turn. "The janitor's closet at my old high school was bigger than this apartment. It's a good thing I'm not claustrophobic."

The only privacy in the small room was behind the bathroom door that would undoubtedly fall off the hinges at any time. It was barely hanging on as it was, but the slightest breeze or softest tremor would surely separate it from the hinges completely.

"No chance of getting lost in here. Bright side," Jack laughed and closed the door. "We've already stocked your fridge and cupboard. Here are your keys—one to the door, one to the garage, and one to the bike. That's the best thing about this place. The small garage next door is yours too. Your bike is parked over there."

"Let's go check out the garage, then." Shadow left the apartment with a quickness in his step that made Jack chuckle under his breath when he fell into step behind him. Shadow rounded the corner of the building and stopped in his tracks. "I'm sleeping in the garage, Jack."

The garage was formerly a service station, abandoned at least a decade before. The gas pump had been removed, weeds grew in the huge cracks in the concrete, and some of the upper windows had been busted out. The single roll-up door was all metal, shielding the inside from prying eyes.

Shadow unlocked the door to the small office area and turned to Jack. "It smells better in here than over there. Does this bathroom work?"

"Yeah. We actually just had it redone last year. You could open this place up and take in small jobs. Get your name and face known in the area to help draw them in to you."

"Good idea. I think I may just do that, with a back-office business of my own to make extra money. Make myself indispensable to the club before they even know what hit them."

"You are dangerous. Maybe you should quit the CIA and come to the DEA."

"No one ever quits the CIA, Jack. Haven't you heard?"

"I've heard stories. Never knew if they were true or not. So you can only quit when you die?"

"Only if you give a two-week notice first."

"Got it. Well, we'll do our best to avoid the notice and the death stipulation while you're here. Don't want you tarnishing my good record."

Jack and Shadow busied themselves with moving the small bed from the apartment over to the office behind the front counter, then the refrigerator and all the food. After they'd straightened up the tools left behind by the last tenant, Shadow inspected his new abode.

"I can't believe you were going to put me over in that little shithole instead of this nice, roomy garage."

"Honestly, I'm surprised no one before you thought of doing this. I'm going to take this as a good sign for things to come. Maybe you're just what we need to wrap this case up. Two years undercover is changing Nick. This group is merciless and ice-cold."

"Jack, I'll do what I can to help close the case against them and shut down their operations for good. But my primary objective is to find Elle and Beth before it's too late."

The low, mean rumble of a motorcycle engine grew louder until it stopped just outside the garage. Jack and Shadow exchanged glances and moved to the office area where they could see outside. A tall, muscular man swung his leg over the Harley and slid his skullcap off his head.

"Well, if it isn't Renegade himself." Shadow walked toward him, no expression on his face to give away his thoughts. He felt eyes on him, searing his skin and heightening his senses.

"Shadow," Nick replied, keeping his voice level and glancing up and down the street. "You all moved in?"

"Yeah. What little I have anyway."

"Well," Nick paused. "There goes the fucking neighborhood."

With raucous laughter and manly hugs, the two men greeted each other like long-lost friends. Appearances weren't a far cry from reality. They'd worked a couple of cases together—one before Nick joined the DEA and one afterward. They hadn't seen each other in quite a while, but they'd initially established a close working relationship while protecting Dominic Powers that carried forward to that very day.

"What's up with this hairstyle and manscaped beard? You turn into a pussy in prison or what?"

"You're still so fucking funny. I've been in admin-seg for the last year. One of my punishments was to cut my hair and beard."

"Administrative segregation. Why'd they put you in time-out for so long?"

"For killing another convict after he called me a pussy."

Nick threw his head back and roared with laughter. "Fair enough, brother. I brought you a housewarming gift. Maybe that'll keep you from killing me."

"Depends on what you brought."

Nick opened his saddlebag and withdrew two six-packs of beer.

"Guessing it's been a while since you've had one of these if you've been on lockdown for the past year."

"You're forgiven. Come on in and pop a top with us. Jack is here too."

With the door closed, the three men sat in the office and talked. To anyone outside, they were laughing and becoming reacquainted after a prolonged absence. Cans of beer were tossed, fingers were pointed as smiles turned to laughter, and hands moved wildly through the air in animated displays.

Every move and gesture were carefully orchestrated to maintain the façade they'd created. While they shared pertinent, detailed information in private, their secret spectator would be none the wiser. Looks could be very deceiving, and assumptions were downright deadly. Their ruse was perfected over time and with intense training. It was as ingrained in them as riding a bike.

"Who's watching us?" Shadow asked.

"Not sure. It's not Bonebreaker. I just left him with his ole lady. Not saying he didn't send someone to watch Jack or me, though." Nick took a swig of his beer.

"Are you any closer to cracking the case and finding out who's funding the change in their MO?" Jack asked.

"Not who's funding it, but I did find an interesting puzzle piece today. Large sums of money are being transferred from the club's accounts, routed through several dummy corporations, and finally deposited into an offshore account. Someone is already checking the dummy corporations' names and officers for me."

"What if no one is funding their newest venture? It could be the exact opposite," Shadow contemplated. "Maybe we've been too focused on it being one way to see other possibilities."

"Let's go over what we know, then. Lay it all out on the table." Jack stood and walked into the service bay area. "Come in here so we can quit playing those damn charades."

Nick and Shadow rose, laughing over Jack's description of their actions, and followed him into the garage.

"Jack tell you this place is kept clean by a perpetual de-bugger device?" Nick asked.

"No, but it's good to hear y'all are using that technology now. I'm having some of my own installed as we speak. I'll let them know to work around it."

"So, what do we know? Start from the beginning."

"Devil's Dominion has been involved in the usual illegal trades—drugs, prostitution, and weapons. Their main drug supplier is the Mexican cartel. They make regular runs to the border and meet their contacts. Then they come back, disperse their product to the satellite clubs for distribution, and collect the money from them weekly."

"The same guys travel to the border and back? No one left behind at the meeting?" Shadow clarified.

"No one left behind. Same set of guys because the cartel members know them. They rotate schedules randomly to avoid overeager DEA agents. But nothing other than drugs and money is exchanged."

"Same with weapons?"

"Yeah. Certain guys are tagged to gain weapons. They use their own ole lady, or some of the better-looking sheep they keep around the clubhouse, to lure guys from the local military bases. Once they get the supply chain established, all transactions are kept way under the radar. There's way too much press coverage on this to be tied to the weapons deals."

"That leaves the prostitution ring," Jack surmised.

Shadow crushed the beer can between his palms until it was as flat as a pancake.

"Calm down. Let's talk it through before you go all rogue on us," Jack said.

"Jack's right. The prostitution ring is fairly straightforward. They use the same sheep they keep around the club—or new girls they pick up hitchhiking. But as far as I know, they always bring them back to the clubhouse for the members to pass around."

"As far as you know. So there could be a deviation from the norm going on." Shadow stood and began pacing. "I'm reading you both in on a highly classified piece of intel we have."

"Highly classified piece of intel means it was obtained illegally." Nick raised his eyebrows at Shadow. "Blurring lines?"

"I have no lines where Elle is concerned. If I had to storm the gates of hell itself to bring her back, that's exactly what I'd do. If I have to kill every single member of the Devil's Dominion with my bare hands to get her out of their clutches, it won't bother me one bit.

"So, one of our analysts was combing through all the data and chatter from the time surrounding the disappearances and found something interesting. Katrina Fox was the first actress I'd heard about going off the grid, but she actually wasn't the first. A girl by the name of Carrie Snow was the first one.

"A similar story was given—she quit the film industry and settled down somewhere in suburbia. There were rumors of drug and alcohol addiction that plagued her. While our analyst was checking for anything related to Elle, Carrie's name came up. He marked it to research it later and called me on the flight today. Seems Carrie's name is hot on the chatter wheel these days."

"So your analyst hacked into the NSA's program and has been monitoring cell phone conversations for you across Southern California?" Nick was barely holding on to his sense of right and wrong after being a full-fledged officer in an outlaw motorcycle club for two years. He needed his friends outside the club to be his moral compass when his own was askew.

"You're completely missing the point. That's three missing actresses and a makeup artist who happened to be with Elle when she disappeared. The first one was weeks before Katrina—but her name is still active in the chatter. The goods haven't been delivered yet. Not with the intel he gave me.

"Where would they hide the girls they're not using yet? We've checked the known properties, and nothing jumps out as an obvious hideaway."

"Nowhere. The club has nowhere to hide girls like that. You're talking high-profile, instantly recognizable, the-whole-world-look-ing-for-them actresses. Our sheep are taken out in broad daylight and paraded in front of men on the street. They're openly offered to potential Johns on the sidewalks downtown.

"Most of these boys don't have a pot to piss in on their own. Your apartment over there would be a palace to more than half of our local chapter members. Did your analyst come across any other names that would be helpful in our search?"

"No, but he's still doing his analysis. He picked up on her name and searched every hit on that match first. It'll take him a little while longer to sort through the rest."

"And that doesn't bother you? Eavesdropping illegally?"

"Not a bit. It's not for my monetary gain. It's to save the lives of four young women and to prevent more from being taken. We know it was Devil's Dominion members who took Elle and Beth. That was confirmed by the patches on their vests. He followed them with local cameras as far as he could. The truck disappeared in an alley and never came back out."

"And you've already had the buildings scanned by satellites." Nick wasn't even asking at that point.

"Of course. One of the buildings is a parking garage. Too many large vehicles went in and out to identify one to home in on. Plus, they could've separated Elle and Beth and taken them on different routes. An incursion at one location could mean death to the others. I can't take that risk—I need absolutes in this case."

"Then I guess your friend needs to perform more illegal searches and find a connection to the money." Nick didn't try to hide his sarcasm or his disapproval.

"It's not illegal when they're suspected of domestic terrorism and treason." Shadow shot his words back at Nick, not hiding his disgust with the turn in the conversation.

"Domestic terrorism? By kidnapping a starlet and depriving America of their ninety-minute worship time?"

"You don't honestly believe their end game is to kidnap three beautiful, well-known stars and use them for a local prostitution ring, do you? They're going to trade them—desirable human slaves in exchange for weapons from a Middle Eastern country known for using biological weapons on their own people, Chinese syndicates who sell them into slavery in exchange for large amounts of laundered money, or anything else in between.

"Think like a DEA agent, Nick. Not like a low-level thug who only does what 'big boss Headbanger' tells him to do. Your biker gang is attempting to break in to the big leagues for a reason. Whether they want to use the weapons themselves or sell them to others for a shit-load of money doesn't matter."

CHAPTER SIXTEEN

Elle's parents, Danny and Tanya, and her brothers, Jeff and Mark, arrived at her apartment and frantically searched for any sign of her return. A small clue that confirmed she was fine, just avoiding the world. But none of her close personal belongings were there—purse, cell phone, or wallet. Beth's parents were scheduled to arrive later that evening, and Jeff had shared Devon's strict instructions with them.

"Mr. and Mrs. Moore?" The deep, authoritative voice boomed from the doorway. "I'm Noah 'Reaper' Steele. I believe you're expecting my team and me."

"Yes, though I've only heard Devon call you Reaper. He told us all about you. Please come in." Tanya urged him into the apartment, her eyes growing wider with each man who followed him.

"This is the rest of my team. Colton 'Bull' Lanier and Braxton 'Rebel' Reed. We'll be watching your backs at all times. I wanted to make sure you met us first. You won't see us unless we want you to know we're there, but when that happens, it'll be for a specific reason."

"Do you think we're in danger?" Danny glanced around the room at his family, his concern for their safety etched in his features. They were all anxious to start hounding anyone and everyone over his daughter's whereabouts, but he had to consider the safety of the rest of his family as well.

"There's nothing to indicate that," Rebel replied. "But there's also no reason to take chances."

"Right. Our information shows you own a lucrative winery. If this is a ransom case, the more leverage they have, the harder it'll be for us to gain traction. We'd rather be more cautious than necessary." Bull explained the situation in his usual straightforward manner.

"So let's get started. We'll take shifts and follow you when you leave. No one goes anywhere alone for any reason—even if that's their only demand. This is not up for discussion." Noah had the family sit and memorize the coverage schedule and how to contact them in case of an emergency. "First stop will be the studio office. You need to demand to speak with the executive in charge of production on Elle's movie. He'll refuse. Leave, and go back with a reporter and camera. Then don't take no for an answer."

"I can do that," Tanya replied. "If I need to pitch a tent and sleep in their office, I can do that too."

"Let's hope it doesn't come to that." The admiration on Bull's face contradicted his words.

Early the next morning, the Moore family arrived at the executive offices, their sights set on forcing the hand of the one responsible for releasing lies about Elle's disappearance. The secretary looked up, confused and concerned, when she heard the commotion behind the double doors that separated the executive suite. Tanya burst through the opening, threats and promises of relieving the security guard of everything that made him a man if he touched her again.

"Barry Jacobson," she yelled down the long hallway of executive offices. "We demand to speak with you this instant."

With Danny, Jeff, and Mark running interference with the guards, Tanya walked briskly down the corridor, calling his name loudly. "If I'm forced to leave without speaking to you, it will be much worse when I return."

A door swung open, and a graying man in his midfifties stepped out. "What can I do for you, Ms.—?" His voice trailed off as he searched her face for recognition. She knew the moment he realized who she was. "You must be Elle Sinclair's mother because she is the spitting image of you."

"That's right. Elle Moore is my daughter, and I want to know where she is right now."

He tried to hide his shock, but the way the color drained from his face couldn't be denied. "You haven't heard from her yet?"

"Would I be here if I had?"

"I'm sure she and Jax are still enjoying their honeymoon on some remote island. No need to worry."

"She's not with Jax on some remote island or anywhere else. We both know that is a lie, and I'll make sure the entire world knows it, too. You'll answer for why no police report has been filed, no questions asked, no searches performed. What are you hiding?"

"Ma'am, you need to leave the premises immediately before we call the police and have you arrested for trespassing." The security guard had finally gotten around the Moore men and approached Tanya.

"Tell you what," she replied calmly when she rounded on him. "You go ahead and call the police and have them wait right here for me. Because when I come back, the whole world will see it."

"Mrs. Moore—wait. Let's talk about this. Elle and Jax are perfectly fine."

"You have one hour to produce her," she replied to Barry. To the guard, she continued, "And you have one hour to get the LAPD here to protect you. We'll be back."

Once outside the building, Tanya's phone began ringing. With shaky hands, she dug it out of her purse.

"Very nice work," Reaper chuckled darkly. "You need a job with my team?"

She released a much-needed laugh before replying. "I'm not sure I could handle that on a daily basis. I was sure the guard would toss me over his shoulder and carry me out."

"You riled Barry up enough that he's making stupid mistakes. His first call was to Jax. We're working on getting an exact location for him now, then one of my team members will pay him a visit."

"You don't believe Elle is with Jax either, do you?" Tanya asked the question, but she didn't exactly want an answer. The trepidation he'd confirm her worst fears overwhelmed her coping skills.

"No, Tanya, I don't believe it at all. But that gives us concrete proof to put more pressure on them both. Even if they don't know where she is, they know more than they're saying. Don't give up hope— we're just getting started. You know Devon won't rest until she's home again."

With Reaper's direction, they left the studio offices and drove straight to the entertainment news station. Within minutes, they'd arranged an exclusive first interview and had a pushy reporter with a crew of cameramen at their disposal. Upon returning to the executive offices, they found the police and the lot guards waiting for them.

"This is perfect," the reporter hungry for the juicy scoop exclaimed. She grabbed the microphone and ordered the cameramen to take their places to get multiple angles.

"Hello, officers. Mary Ellen Gallie with Hollywood Biz News. Can you tell me why you've locked down the offices of Timeless and Classic Entertainment Studios?"

"We had a previous issue with trespassing. The offices are closed to any visitors for the rest of the day." The guard glanced nervously between her and the cameras.

"Is that because executive Barry Jacobson is hiding the truth from the world? Is that why he won't speak with the parents and brothers of Elle Sinclair?" Mary Ellen thrust the microphone into his face and waited for an answer.

"She didn't have an appointment," he stammered.

"Let me get this straight so that I—and all of our viewers watching this live broadcast—understand. This family maintains Elle Sinclair is actually missing, but they can't speak with Barry Jacob-son...because they didn't have an appointment?"

The guard opened his mouth to reply, but he was abruptly interrupted when Barry stepped outside.

"Thank you, officers, for your assistance, but I believe we can take it from here." Barry took a few steps toward the camera and turned on the charm. "Mary Ellen, so good to see you again."

"Barry, I've spoken with Elle Sinclair's family, and they've provided some very damning information that directly contradicts your assertion Elle and Jax ran away together. Your reply?"

"Mary Ellen, I completely understand their concern and need for concrete proof that their beloved daughter is safe and sound. Here at Timeless and Classic Entertainment, we are one big family. When one hurts, we all hurt.

"As soon as I realized their level of concern, and that they haven't heard from Elle yet, I tracked Jax down myself. Mrs. Moore had already left when I spoke with him, but he assured me he'll have Elle contact them as soon as possible. She was indisposed when we spoke, but he promised the call would be made soon."

"Did Jax give you any indication of where they are?"

"No, and I didn't ask. I've tried to respect their privacy, but I couldn't let this loving family continue to suffer." Barry's smile was warm and sincere, but something else burned in his eyes when he met Tanya's gaze.

Conceit. Victory.

Fury. Resentment.

"You are lying, Barry Jacobson. We both know it. Shall we wait together in your office for this make-believe call? So we can all hear my daughter's voice at once? Or better yet, see her beautiful face? Surely, if you reached Jax once today, you can do it again for all of us." Tanya challenged him, meeting his fiery gaze with one of her own.

"I'm afraid I have other commitments I can't break, but I look forward to hearing all about their trip."

With that, Barry turned and walked back into the building, his guards maintaining their position between the Moores and the entrance. Mary Ellen turned to the camera and spoke to her live audience.

"Danny and Tanya Moore, parents of Elle Sinclair, will be with me in the studio for an exclusive interview on the sudden disappearance of one of Hollywood's favorite sweethearts. Tune in tonight to hear why they're adamant foul play cannot be ruled out. If Elle calls to check in, you'll be the first to know."

On the way back to the studio for the interview, Tanya's phone rang, and her heart nearly jumped out of her chest. She'd love to be wrong about Elle. She prayed she was wrong—but she knew her daughter better than anyone. Jax Hart held no position in Elle's heart. She'd reserved that spot for Devon Kane years ago. Even over the past year when Tanya encouraged her to date and get over him, Elle's reply was always the same.

No one else will ever compare to Devon Kane.

Elle's elation at being cast opposite Jax turned to ire after the first day on the set with him. Her frequent conversations with Tanya revealed growing tensions between them. Tanya talked her off the proverbial ledge many times when Elle threatened to quit the film. In the end, her strong work ethic and loyalty to her fans won, and she endured "just one more day with Jax Hart."

Tanya's heart sank when she saw the number on the caller ID. It wasn't Elle calling to confirm Barry's story.

"Nice move with the live feed. We're helping Barry along with the promise to hear from Elle. He has people in the sound booth now creating a recorded message from her. The clips will be spliced together to make her say what they want her to say. Let him hang himself with it. We'll send you the unedited version to air on Mary Ellen's show immediately after his."

"How do you know all this, Reaper?"

"We're all Special Forces—it's our job to know. My men are the best at what they do. Barry won't be able to take all the pressure we'll put on him. Just remember—no mention of Devon. We can't call attention to him. If you even hint she has another love interest, they'll demand you produce him. And they'll want to know why he hasn't stepped forward before now. For both Elle's and Devon's safety, don't forget that."

Tanya silently questioned if Reaper could read her mind, since that was the exact thought she had before he called. "You're right. I don't know what Devon is doing, but he stressed to Jeff it's a matter of life or death to leave him out of the conversation. That's not an exaggeration, is it?"

"No, Tanya. It's actually an understatement. You don't want to know what could happen to them if anything is accidentally leaked."

They disconnected, and Tanya relayed the conversation to Danny and her sons. With a new understanding of what was at stake and how far the studio was willing to go to hide their involvement, the family of four silently reflected on the dangerous situation they were in. And how much worse that danger was for Elle and Devon.

"Mary Ellen Gallie will love this scoop," Mark chortled when he envisioned her reaction. "You know this could backfire on us. Every major news outlet in the world will run the edited versus unedited versions day and night. The internet will break from people on social media. What if exposing their lies just makes them mad?"

"Son, I've considered that too, and I've decided I'd rather lose her knowing I did everything I could to fight for her than lose her because I just rolled over and let them run over me," Danny replied solemnly. "Your mother and I talked about this very scenario all night. Beth's family agreed. We'd all rather do anything than nothing at all."

They remained silent for the remainder of the ride, each fortifying the resolve needed to see the plan through. Trusting that Devon and his friends knew what they were doing and wouldn't advise them wrong. Brokenhearted over the fate of one of their own and livid they couldn't do more, the feeling of helplessness that saturated the interior of their car was stifling.

ELLE WOKE WITH A START BUT COULDN'T FORCE HER EYES TO REMAIN open. Throwing the covers back, she swung her legs off the side of the bed, her vision blurry, but the panic of being late to the set controlled her movements. If the sun was already peeking over the horizon, she was already late for work. Apparently so was Beth since she hadn't pounced on Elle yet.

"Beth!"

The memories came rushing back to her. The strange house. The terrifying man who stopped her escape. The elegant mansion that was her prison. The spray that rendered her unconscious—twice—with merely a misting.

And Beth, her best friend, was nowhere to be seen when Elle left the sound stage late that night she was abducted. Terror filled her chest at the thought they didn't take Beth also but did something far worse to her. Elle had to force her body to comply with her will to move. Finding Beth was her first order of business. They would escape together—two heads were better than one.

She padded barefoot across the ornate wood floor toward the door. While holding a deep breath, she slowly turned the knob and was both relieved and surprised to find it wasn't locked from the other side. The soft squeak of the hinge made her freeze in place and actively listen for her captors.

Without opening the door wider, she slid through the narrow opening into the hallway. She decided to check each room behind the closed doors in the long corridor. If they put her in one, maybe Beth still slept in another. The first few rooms were empty, but set up nearly identical to the one she'd snuck out of. The view waiting behind door number four reduced her to tears.

Tied to the four-poster bed was her best friend and confidante, still deep in slumber and blissfully unaware of their current situation. Elle rushed to her side and began tugging at the ropes to free her. Beth's head lolled to the other side, as if she were simultaneously trying to sleep and wake.

"Beth," Ellie whisper-shouted at her. "Beth, it's me. Wake up. We have to find a way out of here."

Beth's mumbled reply was incoherent, leaving no doubt she'd been drugged. The struggle between leaving without her and bringing help back, or staying with her until the effects wore off enough for Beth to stand was unbearable. Elle kept working at untying the knots while she weighed the pros and cons of each, hoping Beth would become coherent in the meantime.

When she'd finished with the last figure eight knot, Beth's arm fell limply against the bed. "What have they done to you?" Elle whispered through her tears and pushed the hair out of Beth's face.

"We just helped her sleep. She's quite combative and feisty when she's awake."

Elle jumped and whirled around to find a distinguished older man in a butler's uniform standing in the doorway.

"I assure you, no one has harmed or assaulted her in any way. The ropes were used for her ultimate protection. She has already slapped two of our staff members. Should she assault the wrong man, I cannot guarantee her safety."

"Where are we? Why have you taken us? Just let us both go, and nothing else has to happen. I'm sure my disappearance is all over the news. People everywhere will be looking for me. She's my makeup artist on the set and my best friend from childhood. They'll know something is wrong. You'll never get away with this."

Elle rambled on, not taking a breath between sentences as she tried to convince her captor of the folly of his plan.

He smiled at her, the kind of sneer that confirmed she was wasting her breath by trying to convince him to let her go. She knew then she wasn't the first person they'd abducted, and she likely wouldn't be the last.

"I've been sent to bring you to the media room. There's a documentary of sorts my employer would like for you to watch. If you come quietly and willingly, there will be no need for your own restraints."

"What about Beth?"

"She will be here when the documentary has concluded, likely beginning to awaken by then. You may rejoin her at that time if you wish."

Such a cordial captor, Elle thought as she followed him to the high-tech-equipped media room. The chairs were arranged in theater seating, plush recliners providing clear views of the wall-sized flat-screen TV. The surround sound system added to the theater experience, topping off the opulence and wealth of the state-of-the-art room.

The butler placed a glass of water on the table beside her and moved to the back of the room while her eyes remained glued to the enormous screen. The vibrant colors lit up the screen as Mary Ellen Gallie greeted her viewers.

"Hello, and thank you for joining us tonight. We have a full show, so I'm going to jump straight in without delay. As many of you saw earlier this morning, Elle Sinclair's family has arrived in LA, adamant she and Jax Hart have *not* eloped. They insist something terrible has happened to Elle.

"The family confronted Timeless and Classic Entertainment executive Barry Jacobson, and Hollywood Biz News was there to capture part of it live for you. During that confrontation, Mr. Jacobson claims he spoke to Jax Hart today and that Jax will make sure Elle contacts her family as soon as possible. According to the studio executive, Elle was 'indisposed' at the time he spoke to Jax.

"I'm excited to tell you we have a recorded message from Elle to share with you and with her family. It was emailed to the studio just minutes ago with a note saying the internet service is spotty at their secluded resort, but the local news channel was kind enough to record her message in return for autographs for the staff.

"It's now my pleasure to show you this message from Miss Elle Sinclair. Or should I say, Mrs. Elle Hart? Let's watch."

Elle stared at the screen in sheer disbelief. Before her eyes, an image of herself appeared on the screen, extolling the romance between her and Jax, how they were perfect for each other, and she'd never been happier than she was at that moment.

Words she'd never uttered.

A message she'd never sent.

Lies that sealed her fate.

Complex deceptions that took talent to achieve.

She'd cried too many tears over her circumstances. At that moment, she was absolutely numb. From the moment she saw herself deliver a falsified message to the world, her emotions automatically shut down in a self-preservation and coping mechanism.

"Most people would accept that prerecorded message as the gospel and move on with their lives, allowing Jax and Elle to live and love in peace. However, Elle's parents have maintained from the start that this is all a ruse and a far more sinister agenda is afoot.

"Ladies and gentlemen, our video department received a second file of Elle Sinclair, with an email urging our station to compare the two videos and see for ourselves that the first one is an edited farce. So we did. Industry film editors have reviewed them and formed an expert opinion. Before we hear from them, have a look for yourselves."

The screen cut to a series of press junket interviews with Elle, where a long line of journalists entered the room one at a time and were given fifteen minutes to ask their questions. Her answers, all conveying the excitement and enthusiasm she displayed while speaking of Jax, her fake new love, were projected toward working with him on the movie. Each time one journalist was escorted out of the room, another one was brought in to ask additional questions.

"After reviewing these two videos, all our industry experts agree the first video is a spliced and fake recreation, using clips of the second video. The unanimous decision is there is no possible way the purported message from Elle is valid. This evidence has been sent to local law enforcement to urge them to open a missing person's case for Elle Sinclair, Beth Condra, and Jax Hart. Hollywood Biz News suggests the detectives start with Barry Jacobson as the primary person of interest."

The screen went black before Mary Ellen finished speaking, but Elle caught just a glimpse of her parents and brothers when the camera panned in their direction. Knowing they were close and pushing for the truth gave her an instant swelling of hope. Whatever plan her captors had for her would surely fail.

"Your family is very tenacious. We expected your video message would be enough to satisfy them for a few weeks, giving us time to complete our business deals before they started looking for you.

Make no mistake, Miss Sinclair, this wrinkle temporarily changes our plans but does not cancel them in any way. You will not be returned to your family or to the life you used to have."

Elle stared at the woman, dumbfounded, and shook her head. Her eyes floated between the badge she wore on her belt and her angry eyes. Her words and her attire were direct opposites.

"Oh, I'm so sorry. I know who you are, but I haven't introduced myself. I'm Detective Joanna Gough, and I've just been assigned to your missing person's case. Since they're so closely related, I also volunteered to take Beth Condra's and Jax Hart's cases. Unfortunately, my stellar record for solving cases will take a major hit, but I'll just have to find a way to live with it."

"Why? Why would you do this?" Elle wailed.

"Don't be stupid," Detective Gough replied. "So naïve and stupid. Take her back."

The butler wrapped his hand around her bicep and pulled her to her feet. Once they were out of earshot of the detective, Elle turned to him.

"I don't understand what's happening. What are you going to do with us?"

"Do you want to go to your room or to your friend's room?" His reply was cordial, but his avoidance of her direct question was blatant.

"Take me to Beth."

He opened the door to find Beth pacing back and forth across the bedroom, shouting obscenities and her own terroristic threats. When Beth saw Elle in the doorway, she rushed to her and pulled her into a death-grip hug.

"I thought I dreamed you earlier. You really were here, weren't you?"

The butler pushed them into the room and closed the door again. Elle waited until his footsteps could no longer be heard before she told Beth what had happened. When she finished repeating every word for the third time, Beth paled and quickly sat.

"What? What are you thinking?" Elle had to push her friend to speak her mind for the first time in their friendship.

"They abducted us. Drugged us to bring us to this secret mansion prison. Put us in separate rooms. Concocted this elaborate video of how happy you are with Jax. The detective assigned to our case is in on this scheme. But now they're letting us talk and stay together? Something about that last part doesn't sit well with me. It's the complete opposite of everything else they've done."

Dread settled in Elle's gut.

CHAPTER SEVENTEEN

"Do you know where they're keeping Katrina?" Elle asked.

"No. You think she's here too?" Beth rose from the bed and walked to the window. "It would make sense. Honestly, I haven't been able to think past finding you and getting out of here."

"They don't lock the bedroom doors. Maybe we should go look around. I don't even know how long we've been here, but when I first woke up, I got as far as the front yard. There's a tall brick fence around the property as far as I could see."

Elle told Beth the rest of the details she remembered from that night. Together, they agreed to explore as much of the house as they could before anyone stopped them. Since no one knew where they were, they couldn't wait and chance being rescued. They'd have to be their own heroes in this real-life thriller.

Elle opened the door and stepped into the hall. Something about the dead space gave her a sick feeling each time, as if a monster hid behind one of the doors, waiting to devour her. *That's probably not far off the mark, actually,* she thought as she approached the next closed door. Much like she'd done when she searched for Beth, she inspected the room for any sign of inhabitants and moved to the next one. Beth checked the doors on the opposite side, also holding her breath until a flood of relief washed over her when she realized the coast was clear.

"Katrina?" Beth's voice carried down the hall to Elle.

Elle's gaze snapped to Beth's, waiting to learn the fate of their mutual friend.

Beth stepped inside the room, and Elle heard muffled cries. Without a second thought, she ran to the room and found the two women in a tight embrace. Katrina looked up at Elle and stretched out one of her arms to her. Elle immediately joined in, wrapping her arms around them both and clinging to them in the comfort of shared misery. When Katrina could release them, Elle and Beth stepped back to visually inspect her for wounds.

"I'm okay. No one has hurt me. It's so odd, though. Not that I want them to do anything to me, but I almost feel like we're part of some rich, eccentric guy's collection. A life-size doll collection." Katrina walked to the window and pointed outside. "Look. Do you recognize where we are? I don't see any landmarks I know from around LA."

They joined her at the window and took a minute to memorize the landscape. Knowing the layout of the grounds and what awaited on the other side of the brick wall would be helpful in an escape attempt.

"Wait a minute—that looks so familiar." Elle pointed at a rocky outcrop in the distance.

"Rocks on the Pacific shore look familiar?" Beth asked. "They all look the same to me."

"No, it's the unique shape they make. Mark and I used to laugh about how it's shaped like a breast. I think we're close to my family's vineyard."

"Where no one is looking for us," Beth replied gloomily.

Elle and Beth gave Katrina a condensed version of what they knew, ending with Detective Gough's involvement with their imprisonment while being assigned to find them. Katrina listened carefully, doing her best to keep up with the details while keeping her panic under control.

"Wait—did you just say she's assigned to Jax's disappearance case, too?" Katrina asked.

"Yeah. What are you thinking?" Elle asked.

"It just seems like Jax is a common denominator in this whole sordid mess. Do you think he could be behind it?"

"Even he couldn't afford this place," Elle replied. "But that doesn't mean he's not involved somehow. I just don't know how or why. The movie production will be put on hiatus with me gone—it's too late to replace me, and the sound stage has already been booked for the next movie anyway."

"So it's a coincidence I rejected him just before I was taken?"

"I don't believe in coincidences." Elle turned the facts over in her mind, examining them from various angles. But like a jigsaw puzzle with the picture missing, she couldn't make the pieces fit together and make any sense. Her only hope was she knew her family wouldn't give up until they got to the bottom of her recorded message fiasco.

"Ladies, come with me, please." The butler stood in the doorway eying them, no doubt eavesdropping on their conversation.

"Where are you taking us?" Beth asked defiantly.

"My employer wishes to have a word with you. It's best not to keep him waiting."

The three ladies followed him down the hall, across the foyer, and down the stairs at the back of the kitchen. The narrow staircase opened into a large basement. Bile rose in Elle's throat, and her neck muscles worked to swallow it down. The floor, walls, and ceiling were covered in thick black sheets of plastic. In Elle's mind, there was only one reason why that would be found in a multimillion-dollar mansion.

"Ladies, have a seat, please," the voice behind them instructed. They gasped and turned to see who'd joined them. A handsome older man, distinguished by the strands of gray at his temples and salt-and-pepper smattering throughout, gestured to the four folding chairs. His face was vaguely familiar, though Elle couldn't place where she'd seen him before.

"Carrie? Carrie Snow?" With a slack jaw and wide eyes, Katrina stared at the woman beside him.

He gently pushed Carrie forward as she nodded at Katrina, confirming her identity.

"Have you been here the entire time?" Katrina whispered and walked with her to the brown metal chairs.

"Yes. Is anyone even looking for me anymore?" Tears welled up in Carrie's eyes, and her voice broke on her last word. Katrina didn't have the heart—or the time—to tell her no one suspected foul play in her case. Widespread rumors of her repeat drug and alcohol addiction just weeks before she went missing provided more than enough of a cover story to explain her absence.

The older man began speaking, drawing their attention to him and the empty chair beside him. "Ladies, I've brought you down here to ensure we understand each other. As long as you obey my rules, you are free to roam to any unlocked area of the house. I know you didn't reach your current star status because you played by the rules, so I'm sure at least one of you will try me. In fact, I understand one of you has already tried to escape, so I'll give you a demonstration of what happens when someone pushes me past my limit."

The man dressed in black leather, the one who sprayed Elle's face the night she attempted her escape, stepped into the room. He had another man with him—gagged, bound, and blindfolded. He directed the man's steps to the empty chair, forcefully shoved him down onto the chair, and removed his blindfold.

Still unable to speak, the man's frightened gaze darted around the room, searching for someone to help him. He made direct contact with each woman, using his eyes to plead for help. The black plastic shrouding the room only added to his frantic behavior, and he attempted to stand. The rough man in black halted his movement with a firm hand on his shoulder, pushing him back down.

"This man has been a member of my private parties for many years. I've trusted him enough to allow him into my home. He'd been welcome, until I learned he's been running his mouth to others, boasting about his status with me, and revealing private details he swore to secrecy.

"To show you how seriously I value my personal affairs, you will watch what happens to those I consider to be a traitor. Spider." He nodded to the man in black. "You're up."

The older man stepped out of the way, but he stayed close to the women to ensure they didn't look away. The gagged traitor grunted loudly, obviously trying to beg for his life or explain some misunderstanding. The man's cries had no effect on Spider as he leveled the gun against the traitor's temple.

"Do not look away," the older man reminded sternly.

"Any last words?" Spider asked mockingly. "Oh, that's right. You can't speak. Guess not, then."

The man yelled, his gaze locked on to Elle's, begging for her to intervene on his behalf. Before she could murmur a word, a loud noise rang through the room. In slow motion, she watched matter spray from the opposite side of the man's head while a single stream of blood ran down the entrance side. Spider returned his gun to its holster, an amused sneer covering his face while he watched the man slump to one side, lifeless.

Gasps followed by muffled cries filled the room, each woman afraid to make too much noise and call undue attention to herself. Elle couldn't cry and she couldn't breathe. Her lungs seized in her chest, refusing to cooperate and do their job.

"This is what happens to those who disappoint me. Spider has no problem killing them—in fact, I think he prefers it. If you try to escape in any way, you will be stopped. But one of your silver screen sisters will die in your place while you watch."

That visual prompted Elle's body to inhale sharply, reminding her lungs of their intended function a little too well. Her rapid breaths on top of her racing heart pushed her closer to hyperventilation. The older man walked over to her and placed his hands on her shoulders.

"Calm down, Elle. Take deep breaths and clear your head. As

long as you cooperate, everything will be fine. You'll have nothing to worry about at all."

The butler returned to escort the ladies upstairs, locking the basement door behind him. That was one door Elle didn't mind being forbidden from entering again.

"You may return to your rooms or any other unlocked room. The kitchen is always open and well-stocked with anything you may need. You have nothing and no one to fear if you adhere to the instructions. My employer has strict rules about that, and none of his associates will cross the line."

Elle ushered the others into her room, away from anyone else who may be watching or listening. She stood on the threshold, watching for their captors, and spoke quickly in hushed tones. Her voice quivered and her hands shook, but she knew they only had two alternatives. Have a nervous breakdown and let them win, or pretend they didn't just witness a man get shot in the head in front of them so they could focus on an escape plan.

"Listen. There's no way they'll let us go unharmed. Whatever their plans are for us are obviously bad, or we wouldn't be here at all." Her voice broke, and she pressed the back of her hand against her lips. "When he said we had nothing to fear—that was just to placate us. But I do believe if one of us runs, they'll kill one of the others. So we have to go together. No one gets left behind."

"When? How?" Katrina's eagerness surged through her posture, readying herself to run at that moment. Carrie's apprehension was equally as obvious when she shrank back and wrapped her arms around her midsection. Beth jumped to her feet, prepared to fight the devil and rescue herself.

"As soon as we can safely do it together. We can't wait too long, though. It's time we start checking out the house thoroughly and find anything of use."

~

Shadow spent the first week in his service-station apartment setting up his legal and illegal businesses, letting his beard grow out, and brooding in his anger and hatred toward the ones who took Elle. Through his contacts, he set up a collection of small arms to sell in backroom deals. The sooner his name became established, the sooner Nick could get him inside.

With the service bay door open, he sat on a mechanic's chair, working on a customer's bike Jack had thrown his way. It was a simple job he could do blindfolded—a meaningless task to busy his hands and legitimize his business. He sensed the presence of another person before he lifted his eyes. He'd memorized the faces and names of every major player in the Devil's Dominion motorcycle club. There was no denying who approached him.

Spider Skull—the club secretary. The one who kept the membership list, the bylaws, the club rules, and the appointment book for every club officer. The one who knew the comings and goings of everyone—where they were, who they met with, and why. He had every piece of information and correspondence on the club members —the epitome of a field asset.

But he wasn't the sergeant at arms.

So why is he here?

"I heard this old place was in business again." Spider walked into the garage and looked around, like he belonged there as much as Shadow did.

"Word travels fast, then, since it's only been a week."

"I have friends who keep me updated on things of interest around here."

"A small-engine repair and bike detail shop, with one customer, is interesting to you?" Shadow stood and turned, following his visitor around the room.

"Don't like anyone behind you?"

"No. Prison will do that to a man if life doesn't do it first."

"Where were you?"

"Federal pen. Atlanta."

"Federal charges, huh? What were you convicted of?"

"Drugs and weapons. Fucking undercover DEA agent." He tossed his wrench into the toolbox, the loud clanking emphasizing his disgust.

"Something similar happened to a friend of mine. He wasn't dumb enough to get caught with drugs, though."

"You want to tell me your name first?" Shadow asked, narrowing his eyes.

"First? Before what?"

"Before I kick your ass and have to notify your next of kin."

He burst out laughing. "Name's Spider. Jack's a friend of a friend, and he suggested I drop by here."

"Jack's a good man. Strange I didn't hear your bike pull up. Did you pedal?"

Spider smiled. His sneer sickened Shadow, but he hid his contempt. "Maybe. Or maybe I cut the engine and coasted in to test your reflexes. Took you a minute to realize I was on top of you."

It was Shadow's turn to flash his smug grin. "The hell you say. You cut the engine a block and a half back, just when you passed the fire hydrant. If the car in front of you had turned, you would've lost your element of surprise completely."

"I'm impressed. And I'm not impressed easily. You're Shadow, right?"

"That's right. Something I can do for you, Spider? Or did you just drop by for tea?"

"After Jack told me about you, I did some checking up on you. Seems you already have a lucrative business starting, and not only with your one customer." Spider inclined his head toward the work Shadow had done on the bike. "Some of the items you've acquired could be good for my club. But it would be bad for you if they find out about your extracurricular activities. It could be seen as an act of war against us."

"Interesting perspective, since I'm not part of any club. You don't see any colors on my back. I'm just doing some minor work on motor-cycles for avid riders, restoring classics for rich collectors. What busi-ness are you referring to?"

Spider nodded slowly, mentally sizing Shadow up. With a couple of steps, he sauntered up to Shadow, reached into his vest pocket, and pulled out a business card. "Come by here tomorrow night at eight. I want you to meet the officers of the club, maybe become a pledge if they like you."

"You trying to move in on my turf, Spider?" Nick asked from the doorway.

"Renegade. What are you doing here?"

"Shadow is a friend of mine. I've already arranged a meeting with the prez and VP," Nick replied.

"Strange it's not on my radar since I keep the calendars for both of them."

Nick held up his cell phone and shook it from side to side. "Just hung up with Headbanger. You should get a call any minute now."

Just as Nick finished speaking, Spider's phone began ringing. When he walked off to take the call, Nick and Shadow exchanged knowing glances. Word on the street spread fast when the information was given to the right people.

Spider rejoined them, his suspicious gaze cutting back and forth between Nick and Shadow. "Good thing we all agree how Shadow could be an asset to the club. Of course, that just makes Bonebreaker even more suspicious than he normally is."

"Should make for an interesting meeting, then," Shadow retorted.

The clubhouse was a two-story cinder block building with no windows, painted completely black, sitting on the corner of the block. The long string of buildings attached also belonged to the club and were used for storefront businesses. The long corridor that attached to the clubhouse at the back provided a quick getaway when rival clubs took cheap shots, or when the federal agents arrived for a raid.

Nick and Shadow arrived early, before the rest of the officers returned. Nick showed him around, being careful with his words since the paranoia had escalated and he never knew when extra eyes and ears were around. Headbanger made the food and drink run while he was already out on official club business. Nights when the entire club was required to attend church, their club meeting, the probies and pledges carried all the food and beer in. But they weren't allowed in the officers' area unless specifically called, so Nick and Shadow watched for Headbanger to arrive so they could assist.

The thundering rumble of several motorcycles approaching at once drew Shadow to the door. Angry voices and loud threats streamed through the closed metal door. Shadow opened it and stood face-to-face with Headbanger. Nutcracker and Bonebreaker stood immediately behind him. All six eyes bore into the outsider, anger rolling off them in waves at finding him in the officers' area.

Shadow opened the door wider and stepped out of the way to give them room to pass. The first two stepped by him, and Nick stepped forward to take some of the cases of beer from Headbanger's hands. Bonebreaker stopped directly in front of Shadow and glared at him menacingly. Instant suspicion lit his expression.

"Who the fuck are you? The doorman?"

"That's me. The Devil's Doorman." He knew on one hand he was expected to be respectful to the officers and to every other lifelong member. His place among them was the lowest of the ranks, and they enjoyed reminding newbies of their place. On the other hand, it would take minimal effort for him to snap Bonebreaker's neck and be done with him, so taking insults from him asked too much of Shadow's patience.

A stare down between the two brutes ensued, with neither man showing an ounce of weakness. Headbanger began laughing loudly, his booming voice filling the room and drawing their attention. "Looks like you have a new nickname, Shadow. You're the Doorman now. Renegade told me all about you. Then you hit Spider's radar, and he had our PI check you out immediately. Seems you've made quite an impression on our little club."

"All the more reason to suspect him," Bonebreaker grumbled.

"I told you to cut that shit out. I've known him for years. You're doubting and disrespecting me when you question him. Why don't you try questioning my loyalty to my face and see what happens?" Nick changed into his role of Renegade flawlessly, issuing his dare as a threat rather than a question. His glare taunted Bonebreaker to try him. His muscles tensed, and his hands curled into fists.

"Fine. You're responsible for him, then." Bonebreaker stomped away, conceding to Renegade. Shadow noted to ask Nick about it later. There was obviously bad blood somewhere in their history.

Nutcrusher, the VP, called for several of the sheep they kept at the clubhouse. "Get this food and beer ready for us," he barked at the women when they entered the room. "We're hungry and thirsty, so don't take all damn day."

Shadow's blood boiled over at how the girls were treated. They took women who'd already had a hard life and used them in any and every way. Some of them admittedly volunteered for the position, feeling like they were part of a larger family and protected by the nature of the club. The members could abuse them, but no one else could.

The thought of the same men having their hands on Elle made Shadow the most lethal man in the world. He couldn't find her soon enough. Every minute that passed added another vision of horrible acts Elle had to endure.

When the women finished with the food, they delivered heaping plates and chilled beer to the table. Headbanger told everyone to take their seats and gave Shadow the rare opportunity to join them.

"You're here because you obviously built quite a network before you were sent off. You trusted the wrong person. Bone did the same once. Now he trusts no one."

"It only takes one mistake for the house of cards to fall." Shadow's cryptic reply had a purpose. Showing his distrust of others gave him and Bone something in common. "What is it you're looking to acquire?"

"We have a list of things." Bone sat back in his chair and continued. "Are you not good enough to get more than one piece?"

"I'm good enough to get whatever I set my sights on."

"All right, boys. Enough." Headbanger's brows furrowed when he slammed his fist on the table. "We'll meet your contact and decide if he's good enough ourselves."

"Then there's no reason for us to continue this conversation. My contact is just that—mine. He deals with me. If you don't want to work through me, find your own supply chain." Shadow crumpled his napkin and threw it on his plate of half-eaten food. "Thanks for lunch. You can send me a bill for it. You know where to find me."

He stood, pushing his chair back with the force of his movement, and turned to leave.

"You're right, Renegade. He is a stubborn one." Headbanger chuckled, his laughter reaching his eyes and mixing with the malice. The combination only revealed the madness he hid underneath his calm exterior. "Sit down, Doorman. We're extending an honorary life-long member position to you. We've never done this before, but you bring an advantage we need at the moment. You'll still have to go through our initiation process."

"I can take whatever you dish out." *If it means I'll get Elle back.*

Headbanger motioned to the chair. "Sit down. Let's discuss the specifics before we arrange your initiation tonight. You may not be able to speak for a while after we're done with you."

Spider burst through the door, breathing heavily from running. He was late to an officers' meeting, and that didn't go without punish-ment in their paramilitary rank and order. "Sorry about that, Head-banger. Had to take care of an issue at the country club, and it took longer than I thought."

"Everyone okay up there?"

"Yeah. Except I had to move one to the old clubhouse. Bitch was a troublemaker, so she had to be reminded who's in charge. Now she knows not to fuck with me."

"Did you leave a mark on her face?" Headbanger put his palms on the table, ready to push up and lunge at Spider.

"No, boss. Didn't have to do that. She slept the whole trip down."

"You'd better have a good excuse for taking a risk like that this late in the game. The pressure hasn't let up at all. Everyone is still talking about it. You said you had that under control, too."

"I'm working on a new plan to draw attention away."

"Your schemes and excuses will get you in a lot of trouble one day, Spider."

Under the table, Shadow's knuckles turned white from curling his fists so tight. His facial expression remained passive, indifferent. Too much interest in anything other than why they'd brought him in would get both Elle and him killed. Spider's comments had sealed his fate, though. He'd be the first to die. Painfully. The moment Elle was safe. Shadow had already made that decision.

CHAPTER EIGHTEEN

"Everyone knows what to do, right?" Elle whispered, her lips barely moving, as if she were a ventriloquist.

"Yes," came three hushed replies, their voices shaky.

Every day for a week, each one had a specific area of the house to roam, to check for information, to find a way out. Something—anything—that wasn't locked down and could be used to fight back. The kitchen was open to them, but every knife was in a locked drawer. The drinking glasses were plastic—and not very effective for self-defense.

All exterior doors were locked and guarded by the hired thugs. The inside rooms were monitored by a recording system. Elle had seen the monitors once when the butler opened the door. She'd gone back to her bedroom and searched high and low for a camera in there, but she didn't find one. She wanted inside that room to see where the camera blind spots were or where there were no guards. The need to have access to the one room with a view to the whole house kept her awake at night.

She'd seen him go into the room earlier and decided she and the other ladies had officially outstayed their welcome. It was time for the four of them to get out together. True to his word, their captor had ensured their stay was comfortable and none of them had been harmed. As much as she hated to admit it, that was the very thing that worried her the most. The ladies were being kept in pristine condition for a very specific reason—and she knew that reason would be worse than death.

Elle had tried to explain her fear in depth to the others. While Katrina and Beth were visibly upset and afraid, they appeared to grasp the urgency of their escape better than Carrie. After witnessing what their captor was capable of doing, Carrie was even more afraid of escaping than remaining in his custody. Keeping him placated. Elle was concerned what continued captivity would do to Carrie. She'd already been there the longest—alone for many weeks.

Though Elle was taking a big gamble with their lives, Carrie's mental status was the exact reason why Elle chose her for their elaborate scheme. It gave Carrie a specific task, something to focus on that would help her friends as much as it would help herself. To remind her she had a say in what others could do to her, and she had a right to a happy life.

"Carrie, remember what we agreed to do. Just like we practiced. Okay?" Elle grasped Carrie's arm and squeezed it gently. The terrified glint in Carrie's gaze cleared enough to seal their sisterly bond.

"Okay," she agreed, nodding her head. "I can do this."

"That's right—because you're a damn good actress. This will work."

Using every trick and tactic she'd learning in acting classes, Elle drew in a deep breath, stood tall, and showed Carrie her most confident stance. "We are all getting out of here together—and as soon as possible."

"Let's do this. We're in this together, and we're getting out of this together. Places, everyone. This may be our only chance to pull this off," Carrie replied.

Beth waited in her bedroom, and Elle walked past the door to the monitors to wait in the kitchen. She'd sat on the barstool every day staring out the window to establish a pattern no one would question when they were ready to make their move. When they heard the lock on the door turn, Carrie and Katrina rose from their seats and hurried across the room, banking on the fact that he had his back turned to the monitors.

Elle rose from her place in the kitchen and prepared to rush to the door before it closed behind him. Timing was everything. One second too late could mean certain death for one or all of them. On Carrie's cue, Elle sprinted down the short hall between the kitchen and the monitoring room.

"Help! Oh, my God, someone help us! She's dying!" Carrie shrieked. Her voice held genuine fear, though not for Katrina's fake condition. "Help us!"

The butler flew out of the room, leaving the door standing open in his haste. "What the hell happened? What did you do?"

"I only handed her some crackers. She ate one and said she felt funny. So I was taking her back to her room. She just collapsed."

"Why do I smell peanut butter?"

"I had some with my crackers. What does that matter? Help her!"

"I'm trying to," he growled. "She has a severe peanut allergy. If you just ate it and didn't wash your hands, you've now put her into anaphylactic shock."

Elle quickly checked each monitor, identifying where all the cameras and guards were located. She kept one monitor on the scene outside the door, her gaze returning to it every few seconds to ensure the situation was still under control. With a few clicks on the computer, she found a way to scroll through all the views quickly. Her heart raced and tears of joy sprang to her eyes when she found their way out.

Just as quickly, her heart stopped and she felt as if she'd been punched in the gut when a familiar face filled the screen.

The scary, evil man in St. Lucia who smiled at her and made her skin crawl.

The one she was certain Devon knew.

The one who didn't belong there.

The one watching them when the man died right in front of her, when she thought she'd seen Devon stab the back of the dead man's neck.

There was no way his presence at her palatial prison was a coincidence.

"Does this mean Devon is involved?" She shook her head from side to side, disbelieving how far her thoughts had strayed from the possible and probable. "But, still…"

"She's coming to—look!" Carrie yelled loud enough for Elle to hear her through the door had she not seen the cue on the screen. "Katrina, are you okay?"

"What? What happened?" Her eyes fluttered open and darted between the two people hovering over her.

"You fainted—passed out cold. I thought you were dying." Carrie wiped tears from her cheeks and sniffled. "You scared me to death. Don't ever do that to me again."

"My blood sugar must've dropped too low. It does that sometimes and I get the shakes, but I've only passed out once before. I didn't recognize the signs this time."

They helped Katrina sit up, the butler watching her closely for signs of any other problems. Katrina glanced over his shoulder and saw Elle watching them. Relief washed over her with the knowledge they'd given her enough time to get out of the room without being seen.

"Katrina, what can I do? What can I get you?" Elle asked, joining the commotion.

"Some orange juice would be great. Thank you, Elle."

"Are you sure you're okay? Do you need the doctor?" the butler asked, genuine concern filling his tone.

We're under his watch, and apparently, he'll be held responsible if anything happens, Elle thought as she poured the juice. *Interesting.*

"I'm sure," Katrina replied, taking the plastic cup from Elle. She sipped the juice, giving an Oscar-worthy performance and holding his full attention with the most mundane scene ever written. "I feel better already. Maybe I'll just relax on the couch in here for a few minutes."

He helped her onto the couch and went out of his way to make her comfortable. Pillows, a blanket, and more juice as a precaution. "I'll be back to check on you in a few minutes. I thought for sure you'd been exposed to peanuts."

"No, nothing like that. I wouldn't be breathing if I had. No need to worry about me now."

"We'll stay with her for a while." Carrie sat beside her, still playing the guilt-ridden, despondent friend.

"Was it worth it?" Katrina whispered when he'd left them alone.

"Definitely," Elle replied. "We have a plan."

Elle and Carrie helped Katrina up to take her back to her room. Elle glanced over at the room she'd just left and saw the door had been shut. The narrow window of opportunity she'd been given wasn't lost on her, nor was the slim chance of success they'd have to escape. But she'd take that chance and make it count for all it was worth. If she died trying, at least her death would be for a noble reason. Rolling over and being a good little doormat was never her style anyway.

Beth joined them in Katrina's room, anxious to hear what Elle had found. "Great performances, ladies. That's why you make the big bucks and I do your makeup. Let's hear it, Elle. How do we get out of here?"

"We have to go through the basement."

"No." Carrie's stern tone mixed with her clenched fists, and she shook her head in vehement rejection.

"I don't want to go back down there either, but it's our best option. There are no active cameras in that room—only in the stairwell down and outside the outer door. They must specifically activate the cameras down there. And with us up here, there's no reason to. Plus, I may have taken them offline completely while I was in there.

"That door leads to a separate driveway on the back of the house. There's a smaller gate at the back of the brick fence. We can climb it and get out. We'll have to run like hell once we get out the door. I say we do it at night when we won't be seen as easily."

"Yes. Let's go tonight. We're pushing our luck more and more the longer we stay here," Katrina agreed.

"I'm in. Tonight, it is. I'm ready to get home," Beth added.

All eyes turned to Carrie and waited for her assent. "Okay, I can do this."

When the house was silent late that night, they each left their rooms at different times in case anyone was watching the monitors. They made their way to the kitchen and listened for anyone else stirring. When Elle was satisfied they hadn't been seen, she led the group down the back stairs to the basement door.

"How do we get past the door without making noise and alerting the entire house what we're doing?" Beth asked.

Elle pulled a key from her pocket. "I stole this from their control room." She slid the key into the lock and said a silent prayer. The tumblers disengaged, and the knob turned in her hand. Like a shot in the dark, the foursome sprinted across the basement, now void of all the eerie black plastic that covered it before.

The door leading outside was easily unlocked from the inside; the owner obviously didn't consider his captives would make it that far. Elle threw the door open, and they dashed across the lush, green grass behind the house. Their adrenaline was at an all-time high—the gate to freedom was in view, glowing like a beacon in the pale moonlight, illuminating their path.

Freedom was almost within their reach when the yard was lit up by floodlights that seemed to come from everywhere. Angry male voices shouted orders and four-wheelers skidded to a halt between them and the gate. Men jumped off and rushed at them, much like a linebacker targets a quarterback to stop the play. The four women scattered, running in different directions to draw attention and give the others a chance to escape. If only one got free, the rest would be saved.

Screams filled the night, echoing on the breeze as they were corralled and caught one by one. All four were brought together by a host of clean-cut guards in uniforms mixed with scary men dressed all in black, wearing leather vests, and sporting long beards and shaggy hair. The thugs' presence was a direct contradiction to their palatial prison, exactly how the man in St. Lucia appeared to be out of his element at the überposh resort.

As they were forced to their knees with their hands behind their backs, their reactions were as varied as the women themselves. Carrie bowed her head and cried, knowing one of them had to die for their actions. Katrina was terrified of the dozens of men leering at her. Beth's gaze kept returning to the gate as she calculated the odds of actually making it to it and over it without getting caught.

Elle spoke first when the owner arrived in the middle of the scene. "It was my idea. The only reason they're out here is because I coerced them. Put all the punishment on me. Just don't hurt them."

The distinguished-looking man regarded her, contemplating her words for a moment. The tension around the ladies was thick and heady, feeding his controlling nature. "Take the other three back inside and leave your gun with me."

"No!" Beth screamed as one man lifted her to her feet. She fought against him, struggling in vain against his strength. "No, Elle! Leave her alone!"

They were forcefully taken back to the house while Elle remained kneeling on the ground alone. Just as they stepped into the basement, a gunshot rang out in the night, followed by the screaming wails of the three who still lived.

"Move—or I'll make you move," the man behind Beth threatened.

With tears streaming down her face and sobs racking her body, she forced her feet to move, following the others back up the staircase and down the hall to her room. The door was slammed and locked behind her. Resigned to her fate, she fell onto the bed and cried herself into a restless, fitful sleep.

Elle remained motionless in a heap on the ground outside while the two men stood over her. "Spider, she has to go first thing in the morning. The rest can stay here for now, but we need to arrange to transfer them soon."

"You got it." Spider picked up Elle and slung her over his shoulder. "Guesthouse for tonight?"

"That's fine. Just make sure she's gone by the time I leave for work."

"Don't worry. I got you covered, Uncle B."

Spider walked off toward the guesthouse, his brother-in-colors, Axle, falling into step at his side. "She's hot, isn't she? We could fuck every hole she has twice tonight, and she wouldn't know it. I gave her an extra spray of our sleeping juice for good measure."

"No way, man," Axle replied. "You know I wouldn't normally give a shit what you do to some sheep, but this one brings a special price. Your dick isn't going to rob me of my retirement fund."

"Just as well, I guess. I do prefer them to be conscious when they suck my dick. Can't get enough of those girls who can suck better than a Hoover." Spider laughed and opened the door to the guesthouse. He dropped her on the bed and shook his head. "Shit. I don't want to sleep in the fucking guesthouse to babysit her all night."

"Head on back to the main house. I'll stay. This place is nicer than my shitty apartment."

After Spider left, Axle moved into the living room, leaving the bedroom door open so he could see her, and dropped down on the couch. He raked his hands over his face before removing his phone from his pocket. "Hey. Yeah. I got eyes on her now. It's just a matter of time."

Deception seems to be the name of the game with these guys, Elle thought. *I can play that game, too*

After she'd been caught and they'd taken the others inside, Spider sprayed the sleeping serum in her face. When she slumped on the ground, her captor fired his gun into the air as a scare tactic to keep the others in line. She'd prepared herself by holding her breath to avoid inhaling the spray when she saw Spider moving toward her. With one eye barely open, she saw the older man lift his arm above his head and knew what would come next. She kept perfectly still, not giving away her advantage or her subterfuge.

She waited for Axle to fall asleep in front of the television, hoping the noise would mask her movements. When his breaths became even and he didn't move for an extended time, she silently rolled off the bed and tiptoed to the door. With her hand on the knob, she began to turn it.

"If you open that door, every alarm in this place will go off. You'll be sorry this time, trust me. You've already tried twice. Third time will be lights-out for you."

She gasped and jumped at the same time, turning to look at him. He remained on the couch in the same position he was in when she'd thought he was asleep.

"Best just to go on back to bed and wait until tomorrow. You'll be moved from here. They won't let you escape. Even if you get away this time, they won't let you live. They can't take the chance you'll talk."

"So I'm just supposed to take it? To let them do what they want with me?" Fire lit in her eyes, and her lips formed a thin line. Rage built up inside her, pushing her to the limit.

"You don't have much choice. You're in this now, so you'll just have to ride it out till the end. Whatever that may be."

"Why are you here? I remember seeing you in St. Lucia. Were you following me then? Helping them to kidnap me?"

"Nope."

She waited for him to continue, to elaborate on his single-word answer, but he didn't. "That's helpful. Thanks for the detailed explanation."

He chuckled and sat up, his gaze finally meeting hers. "Go to bed. You're safe in here with me. I won't let Spider back in until morning when we move you. Might want to remember that handy trick you used earlier when you see us coming for you, though."

"Why are you helping me?"

"Because I'm selfish."

She rolled her eyes, huffed, and spun on her heel, heading back to the bedroom. She stopped in the doorway, the question she wanted to ask searing her mind. It was there, on the tip of her tongue, and she desperately wanted to know. Almost as much as she didn't want to know at all.

"Don't ask, Elle. Just try to get some sleep. You'll need it for tomorrow."

Dread filled her heart, then her feisty anger took control. She wasn't giving up without a fight. She refused to bow down to them. Though she didn't trust Axle, he had spared her more than once in a short time. Crawling back on the bed felt a lot like defeat, making it difficult for her to rest and sleep as he prompted.

She heard the door open and recognized Spider's voice before he saw she was already awake. She waited for the two men to enter her room, sensing they were close, before opening her eyes. They were closing in on her, leaning down toward her in a surprise attack.

"Hey!" she yelled in mock surprise.

Spider sprayed three short bursts of liquid into her face, and her body went limp. "Works every time," he boasted. "I love this shit. Used it on this one slut the other night, and she didn't remember anything."

"Man, you know if Headbanger gets wind of you flaunting that, he'll cut your balls off and mount them on his handlebars as a warning to the rest of us." Axle released a harsh huff toward Spider and snaked his arms under Elle's back. "Grab her feet. I've got her head."

They carried her out to the waiting van and put her in the back. Spider climbed on his motorcycle and pitched the keys to the van to Axle. "Drive her to the old clubhouse. I'll meet you there to help get her inside. Headbanger will have my head on a platter because I'll be late for our officers' meeting by the time we're done."

Axle slid behind the wheel and followed Spider off the property. "Just stay down and pretend to be asleep. He'll be gone soon enough. The club takes the officers' meetings seriously. He's already on thin ice with the prez, so he won't risk being too late."

"You can just let me go, you know?" She had to try—he was looking out for her well-being for a reason.

"Ah, you know I can't do that. And if you know what's good for you, don't act like I'm your friend. None of us are good guys, sweetheart. You wouldn't want to be our friend."

"You're not as good of an actor as you like to think you are, Axle."

She barely heard his laugh over the roar of the road. "I guess I'd better go back to acting classes, then. Evidently, I won't win one of those little gold statues anytime soon. Or maybe I will. Maybe I've completely played you to get you to cooperate."

"Maybe," she conceded. "You wouldn't be the first. Hopefully, you won't be the last either."

At the former clubhouse, a wide metal door opened for the van to pull completely inside, fully hidden from the outside. Once the door was shut, the blackness covered everything. "Pretend you're still asleep. He's coming now," Axle whispered.

The back door of the van swung open, and Spider grabbed her ankles, dragging her roughly toward the edge. "Grab her head. I've got to get going. I'm so fucking late."

Axle grabbed Elle under the arms and helped carry her inside. The musty, mildewed smell of the interior was a stark difference to the opulent mansion she'd been expelled from the night before. Dust and dirt covered everything, infiltrating her nose and threatening to make her sneeze. She held her breath until Spider dumped her on an old, filthy mattress thrown on the floor in the corner of the room.

"Want me to send someone by with food and beer?" Spider asked on his way out.

"Nah. I'll call one of the probies and put him to work. Get to your meeting before you get kicked out of the officers' club."

When she heard the rumble of Spider's motorcycle and the loud metal clank of the roll-up door, she bolted up from the mattress and searched her new cell. The lights barely cast dim rays around the windowless room. The interior doors were thick steel, designed for maximum security. The rooms with working lightbulbs were near mirror images of the first room.

"You must be hungry. Come in here and choose what you want. I'll order takeout," Axle called from the other room.

"Is this what I needed my rest for?" She held out her arms and gestured to the dilapidated furnishings.

He cut his gaze to her, and his lips lifted on one side in amusement. But something closer to remorse shone in his dark eyes. "No, sweetheart. Not hardly."

~

THE MIDDAY SUN IN SOUTHERN CALIFORNIA WAS HOT. IN THE REMOTE, arid hangout of the Devil's Dominion initiation grounds, the heat was nearly unbearable. But the members of the club didn't mind, because the Doorman's induction into the group was cause for celebration. And for beating up the new guy.

"Gather 'round," Headbanger yelled over the roar of the crowd. A hush immediately fell over the group as they did as he commanded. "Some of you have met our newest member. He had a nickname before he came to us, but we've changed it. He's now known as the Doorman. Tonight is his official induction into the club. Some of you will be pissed to know he's entering the ranks higher than any of you pussies did because he's of better use to me than you are. What do you think of that?"

A loud rumble of discord and outright threats floated over the crowd of angry bikers. "What the hell? What the fuck's so special about him?"

"He has contacts we need to complete our next weapons ship-ment. AR-16s, fully auto, locked and loaded. We're keeping a few dozen for ourselves and selling the rest. Military-grade aerosol canis-ters, gas masks, and whatever else we need. He's our man." Head-banger smiled broader the more the men grumbled and groaned.

He loved riling them up before an initiation. The extra surge of testosterone and adrenaline produced much more creative conse-quences for the new recruit. It also kept the men sharp, ready to dole out pain for pleasure. As long as no one killed or permanently inca-pacitated the new member, nothing else was off-limits.

"All right, boys. Make the Doorman feel at home." Headbanger stepped back, his snide sneer in place.

A group of twenty handpicked men closed in on Shadow, taunting him with insults as they shuffled around him. He braced himself, knowing the first hit would be a sucker punch meant to disorient before the brood jumped on him at once.

The biker tried to be nonchalant, but Shadow saw the punch

coming and turned his head away from it slightly, softening the blow. The others immediately jumped at the chance, fists flying, flesh smacking against flesh. He ducked and shielded his head with his thick arms as much as he could. Several banded together and pushed him to the ground, where they commenced kicking and punching him repeatedly.

He heard Headbanger's laughter roar over the angry mob surrounding him.

From between his arms, he saw the crowd part to allow another man a wide berth to pass. He could barely make out the outline of what the guy carried in his hand, but the glowing red end left no room for mistaking it. They were getting ready to hold him down and brand him.

Elle's face flashed in his mind. Amid the kicks to the back and legs, the punches to his jaws and ribs, he focused on her safety as a reminder of why he allowed the beating to occur in the first place. His revenge would be swift and terrible as soon as she was out of harm's way. It was the feel of her embrace and smell of her smooth skin that prevented him from screaming out in pain when the skin on his back sizzled from the searing hot branding iron.

"Enough." One word from Headbanger halted all action. "Get up, Doorman. Greet your brothers."

Shadow stood and faced the man holding the branding iron. His mocking laugh was met by the cold, fierce stare of a man who tortured people for a living to gain intel from them. For that dick-head, Shadow decided he'd do it for free.

With his lightning reflexes, Shadow snatched the brand from the biker's hand and had him flat on his back before anyone knew what had happened. With his heavy boot across the guy's neck holding him in place, Shadow twirled the hot iron in his fingers, watching the fear fill his victim's eyes. The angry mob stood stock-still, shocked at the sudden turn of events and unsure of how they should react.

"We're brothers now, right?" Shadow asked, taunting his mocker. "We need matching tattoos, then."

On a downward twirl, Shadow pushed the brand into his chest.

The biker screamed in pain, his arms flailing as he tried to hit Shadow's leg, the brand—anything he could reach that would stop the pain. Shadow lifted the brand and inspected the angry, burnt skin in the middle of the biker's chest.

"That's better." Shadow released him and spat on the ground, barely missing his shocked face. He threw the branding iron, making several of his new brothers jump out of the way. He turned his sights on the men who had so brutally inducted him, ready to return the favor tenfold. The first one within reach was the unlucky poster boy for the others. Shadow held him with one hand and repeatedly punched him with the other.

When the rest of the initiators attempted to stop him, he released his victim and let his fists fly. When they thought they had him contained, he outwitted and outmaneuvered them, while hurling insults about their inability to overpower him, even with twenty men to one. Every word and every blow only added to his determination. At the end of the case, he would be surprised if a single Devil was still standing.

"Stop." Headbanger moved into the crowd and surveyed Shadow from top to bottom. Then he turned to do the same to the men he'd picked to induct Shadow. "You're beat to shit—your face, arms, everywhere. But you give as good as you get. These boys look like they've been through a meat grinder."

"And I was only getting warmed up."

Headbanger laughed at his response, but Shadow wasn't joking.

"You're part of the Devil's Dominion now. But you have to complete a couple of tasks to get your rocker panels and patch. You ready?"

"Absolutely."

He pulled a picture from his vest pocket and handed it to Shadow. Nick moved around the crowd so he was in a direct line of sight behind Headbanger, reading Shadow's expression. "Find her. Take her. Don't get caught or be seen by anyone."

"Take her where? Who is she?"

"To the country club. Spider can fill you in. And who she is doesn't matter. Complete this, and you get the bottom rocker and the club patch."

"And the top rocker?"

"You are ambitious." Headbanger smiled, knowing Shadow wasn't the type to do anything half-assed. "Someone has been a thorn in my side. You can take care of that for me, right?"

"Of course." Shadow shrugged, as if a request to kill someone was an everyday occurrence. "Who?"

"The girl first. Then the top rocker. One step at a time."

Shadow shifted his eyes slightly over Headbanger's shoulder and connected with Nick's. An imperceptible nod was all it took to confirm his suspicions.

"Spider, take the Doorman to the old clubhouse with you. Explain our process to him. Take Axle and Renegade with you, too."

"Axle is already there, babysitting our company."

"Even better. You head on over to the old clubhouse and keep him company, then. Renegade and Doorman can handle this one on their own. Can't you, boys?"

"Piece of cake," Shadow replied.

"Renegade, come talk to me before you leave," Headbanger called over his shoulder when he walked away.

CHAPTER NINETEEN

Silas Steele, Noah's brother, pulled up to the gate and pressed the call button, holding it an extra few seconds longer than necessary.

"Can I help you?" the female voice asked.

"Yeah. You can open the gate and let me in. I need to talk to Jason Hartman immediately—it's urgent."

"What is your name? Do you have an appointment for today?" she asked, hesitant to let him in or send him away.

"My name is Silas Steele, and I'm a federal agent. Tell Jason he can either willingly talk to me now, or I can come back with the SWAT team and a warrant for his arrest. Either way, this gate will open for me." Silas removed his badge and held it in front of the camera. The automatic gate began to swing open, giving him access to drive in. "Good call."

When Silas reached the secluded house in the woods, Jason Hartman, also known as Jax Hart, stepped out of the house with his private security detail surrounding him. Even though he stood between three men who could double as club bouncers, Jax wore a leery expression. His gaze roamed over the cab of Silas's truck, trying to see through the blacked-out windows.

With a glance, Silas knew Jax Hart wasn't involved in the kidnapping scheme, but he definitely knew something about it. He took his time exiting the truck, letting Jax make all the wrong assumptions before Silas even asked the first question.

"Are you alone?" Jax asked as Silas rounded the front of his truck.

"Yes, I'm alone."

The three security guards chuckled to themselves, confident they'd have the upper hand on him. Silas smirked to himself, stifling a laugh at their expense. *It's not about size, guys. It's about who's meaner.*

"What do you want?" one of the bodyguards asked.

"I have questions for Jason." Silas intentionally used his given name and inclined his head toward Jax. "He can refuse to answer them, but then he'd be refusing to cooperate in a federal investigation and he'd be under arrest. Is that what you want? I can haul his ass in right now, then."

Silas produced a set of handcuffs, held them in position to slap them on Jax's wrists, and advanced on him.

"Whoa, whoa, whoa!" Jax shouted, backing up. "I didn't say I wouldn't cooperate. What's this about?"

"We need to speak inside," Silas stated, looking past the security detail and directly at Jax. "I believe you know what it's about."

Fear and acceptance flashed across his face. He was hiding in a remote location and the press had been fed lies about his true whereabouts, but he had to face the truth sometime. With a gloomy nod, he commanded his security team to stand down. "Come on in. Let's get it over with as soon as possible."

Silas followed him into the sprawling log cabin. The family room covered half of the entry level. The entire back wall was made of folding glass patio doors to give an unobstructed view of the mountains and lake surrounding the property. Jax motioned for Silas to have a seat.

"Nice house. Knowing your Hollywood persona, I wouldn't have pegged you as the outdoorsy type. But then, you were probably banking on the true facts of your background remaining hidden when you chose to hide here."

Even Hollywood's leading man couldn't hide his shock after that statement. "Guess what the conspiracy theorists say is true. We have no secrets from Big Brother."

"It's actually worse than they think. Do you want to be called Jason or Jax?"

"Jason is fine. No more pretending, at least while we're here."

"Fair enough. Jason, tell me why you're hiding in Idaho at your aunt and uncle's vacation home."

"Getting right to the point, huh? Okay." He released a harsh breath. "I'm here because I'm scared for my life. Literally. And I get that makes me a complete shit because Elle and Beth are missing, so they're even more afraid than I am."

He shook his head and dropped his face into his hands, shame and guilt consuming him. "The night they disappeared, they left the sound stage before me. When I walked out, I rounded the corner and expected my driver to be waiting for me. But he wasn't. Two rough-looking men dressed in black, with leather motorcycle vests, were putting Elle in the back of a van—the kind of long cargo van they use for deliveries and stuff. No windows on the side panels."

"Did you get a good look at the insignia on their vests?"

"Yeah, I saw it plain as day. It said Devil's Dominion."

"When you saw them put Elle in the van, was she conscious at the time?"

"No. She was completely limp. Honestly, I didn't even know if she was alive at first. It was only after everything was over when I realized I'd seen her chest rising and falling when they put her down. After they closed the doors, they turned, and that's when they saw me standing there. One of them used his finger and thumb to make the sign like a gun and 'shot' me. Then he laughed, like he thought it was so damn funny, and climbed in the van. They drove off, didn't even stop at the guard station to the lot, and left me standing there."

Silas watched Jason's face as he relived the scene from that night, giving him time to remember any other details he'd tried to forget. Jason was visibly shaken by the entire incident and believed they'd kill him, and he was correct. They would, without a second thought.

They had no use for him—they were after the women. When Jason appeared to have checked out of the conversation, Silas drew him back in.

"What did you do next?"

"I tucked my tail between my legs and ran back inside the sound stage. When I found Vince Rossi, the director, I told him to call the police. Then I explained everything, just like I told you. He told me to go home and he'd take care of it."

"Did he take care of it?"

"At the time, I honestly thought he did. He grabbed his cell and began barking orders, yelling he needed the police right away. When he realized I was still there, he called my driver and basically pushed me into the car. On the way home, my agent called and said they were putting the publicity tour on hold, but they'd finish editing the movie so we'd be ready to go when it was time. I told him I didn't care about that—what about Elle and Beth? He said the police were there, and the studio was handling it. They didn't want me involved in the case because it would hurt more than it would help."

"Hurt what?"

"My career—because I didn't rush to stop them, like the hero I play in my movies. Elle's career—because our onscreen relationship wouldn't be believable after people realized I allowed her to be taken. The movie itself—since it would get bad reviews and no one would go see it. Everything from our reputations to being cast in future movies would be destroyed. That's how he sold it to me anyway, and I went along with it."

"When the van left the lot, you said it didn't stop at the guard station. Does your driver always stop to check out with the guard?"

"Yes. Always. They're supposed to check everyone in and out of the lot."

"Did your driver stop that night?" Silas asked.

Jason's brows drew down and he stared straight ahead, his eyes slightly downcast while he tried to remember. "You know, I was so shaken up by the time I got in the car, I didn't even think about it. I just wanted to get home, as far away from there as I could get. But, no, we didn't check out." His eyes jerked up to meet Silas's. "What does that mean? They're all in on it?"

"I can't comment on an open investigation," Silas replied. "Which way did the van turn when they left the lot?"

"Right. Why are you not taking any notes?"

"I don't need notes to remember. Were you aware that Vince Rossi left LA this morning for an undetermined length of time?"

Jason blanched and sat back against the couch. "No, I didn't know. Why did he leave?"

"The official statement said there was a medical emergency, and he was returning home to be with his family." Silas studied Jason, watching for clues to confirm he honestly didn't know about the director's abrupt departure from the studio.

"*Returned home?* Where—all the way to Orange? That's where his family lives."

"Yes, I'm aware. I found it interesting too." Silas stood and walked to the large bank of patio doors. "Jason, there's something I want you to do. They're planning to do something terrible to the ladies they've kidnapped. We must force their hand so we can stop this before it's too late."

"What do you want me to do?"

"Call Mary Ellen Gallie and tell her you're not with Elle. You don't have to give any details of that night, simply confirm you left LA for an extended vacation off the grid before the promotional tour started. Then you were hit with all this nonsense about you and Elle running away to get married. So you wanted to set the record straight, because if she's in danger, law enforcement needs to do something about it.

"The video they sent of her talking about how happy you two are has already been proven a fake. The people need to hear it from you now, so your fans will demand action on your behalf, and hers."

"Of course. I'll do whatever you need me to do."

Silas checked his watch and nodded to the phone. "Her show is about to come on now. Perfect time to set the public straight on the facts." Jason grabbed his phone, scrolled through his contacts, and dialed the line dedicated to celebrities. Silas listened while Jason donned his Jax personality. Without giving details of that night, he answered questions from the host and call-in viewers. By the end of the hour-long show, word had spread across the waves. Calls and emails flooded law enforcement offices across the state. From the governor to the mayor to the chief of police, concerned fans demanded immediate action and questioned the effectiveness of assigning only Detective Gough to such a complex case.

"Stay here with around-the-clock security until this is over. When Elle is home safely, you'll know you can return to LA." Silas stepped out the front door and turned back to Jason. "You should know, Jason, there's no shame in what you did. If you'd tried to stop them, they *would've* killed you and still left with Elle and Beth. These are not the kind of men the average person tangles with, and you have no reason to be ashamed. What you did today will do more to help save them than you know. Thanks for your help."

"Thank you, Agent Steele. I can't tell you how much I appreciate you saying that."

Once Silas was back in the truck, he called his brother. "Jax Hart handled that very well. Turned on the charm and rallied his troops. That should help with the message Elle's and Beth's parents are pushing daily."

"His message was perfect. Did he say anything that could help?"

"Nothing we don't already know." Silas repeated the conversation for Reaper, who also wasn't surprised to hear the director appeared to be involved.

"Sounds like we need to pay a visit to his sick family member in Orange. We know who to look at, but we haven't figured out why they're doing this yet. Have you heard anything from your analyst with the agency?"

"Coded messages sent to a buyer in Hong Kong were intercepted. Nick Tucker has been trying to identify the name on an offshore account. My analyst is helping unravel that a little faster. We should have the details soon. Nick is a little more by-the-book than I am," Silas chuckled.

"Most everyone is more by-the-book than you are, Silas. Other than Shadow. Must be part of the training manual for all spies to break the rules as much as possible," Reaper retorted. "Speaking of, have you heard anything about our boy? Even through unofficial channels?"

"Not yet. I've got his analyst, Steadman, and my analyst, Chris, watching him on satellite as much as possible. He put himself and Nick at more risk by going in as quickly as he did. I'm concerned it'll backfire, and they won't be able to handle the backlash from it."

"Agreed. Are you on your way here now?"

"I'm heading to the airport now and will be in LA County soon."

"What did Headbanger want to talk to you about?" Shadow asked as Nick climbed into the van, sparing no time.

Nick rubbed the back of his neck, trying to ease the tension and stress accumulating in his muscles. "Your initiation—he was impressed with how you handled yourself, so he wants to replace Spider with you as an officer."

"How's Spider going to take that news?" Shadow chuckled.

"He won't. That's the other news he sprang on me. The way you'll earn your top rocker is to kill Spider, the thorn in his side."

"What's the problem? I can take him out easily."

"Seriously? What is wrong with you spooks? You can't just kill everyone." Nick openly gaped at Shadow, incredulous at his blasé attitude toward taking another man's life.

"I most certainly can. I'm a trained soldier. I protect our country every day, from all kinds of threats. Sometimes I *have* to be the bigger threat to get the job done. Spider is a dangerous man who takes lives indiscriminately—innocent people, defenseless women—and he does it for pleasure. The more he gets away with it, the worse he'll be. Taking him out of the game is a public service."

"I'm genuinely concerned you're missing the entire point of this conversation," Nick deadpanned. "You do remember I've been undercover for two fucking years, right? I'd like to actually arrest someone for all my trouble."

Shadow glanced over his shoulder at Nick, understanding his angst. "Undercover life is hard. I know. Truly, I get it. You want to see someone pay for all the time you've given up of your own life. You want the satisfaction of putting them behind bars for a very long time, knowing it was your dedication to your job and country, and that time has been repaid.

"I hate to be the bearer of bad news, but you'll be sorely disappointed with the due process. The lawyers, the trials, the delays, the deals. Years of your life already spent collecting irrefutable proof, only to have your every past mistake paraded through court to discredit you. The slap on the wrist they get for being 'brainwashed and coerced' into being part of this gang. You'll wish you'd killed him yourself when it's all over."

"It's a good thing we only have to kidnap another Hollywood starlet in the meantime," Nick replied dully.

"Do we have a plan for this abduction? Shall we surprise her, or give her a heads-up before we grab her off the sidewalk and pitch her in the back of our Chester Molester van?"

"Does the CIA require regular brain CT scans? Check for changes or anomalies? Seriously, Shadow."

He threw his head back and released a deep belly laugh. "Man, it feels good to laugh again. It's been a long time. I'm joking about the kidnapping. While you were chatting with Headbanger, I made some calls on my secure cell to make the arrangements. She's being briefed and convinced to cooperate as we speak."

"Who's prepping her?"

"Bull and Rebel—they're demonstrating how the GPS injected in her arm works regardless of where she is, assuring her that the two big, scary guys sweeping her off her feet are both undercover agents who will take care of her, and we'll return her home, safe and sound, as soon as possible. Reaper went to pick up Silas at the airport."

"We can't possibly guarantee she's safe while we're not around. We have no idea what they're doing to them," Nick protested.

The temperature in the van dropped instantly when Shadow turned his gaze to Nick. Or maybe it was from the chills running up Nick's spine when he recognized the dark, lethal expression on Shadow's face.

"Shadow, I'm sorry, man. I didn't even think... Besides, I don't think they'd hurt them. They're planning something else for them, I can feel it. They want more money. Manufacturing meth, selling for the cartels, and running guns isn't making them enough for some reason."

Before Shadow could reply, his secure cell began vibrating in his pocket. "Talk to me, Bull."

"Lori Hensley is ready for her chauffeured ride," Bull replied. "She's been tagged and is ready for an extra special surprise visit."

"She does understand what's really happening, right? You didn't trick her into thinking she's going on a blind date or anything?"

Bull chuckled. "I'm giving you the one-finger salute right now, in case you're wondering. I know how to do my damn job. Just come kidnap the girl. We're waiting on the lot, just outside the sound stage door. Let me know when you pull up. I'll step back inside."

"Copy that. See you soon, princess."

"Bite me."

Shadow and Nick turned into the lot and were waved on by the guard. Checking the side mirror, Shadow noted the guard immediately left his station and pointed it out to Nick. He circled slowly around the buildings until he found the perfect spot to avoid detection. If they'd been followed, he didn't want to take any chances that would blow their cover.

Lori walked across the drive toward the area where her driver should have been waiting and stopped, looking around for her ride. Shadow and Nick jumped out of the van and walked up stealthily behind her. Nick tapped on her shoulder, raised his hand up to her face, and squeezed the spray twice in quick sequence. She slumped in Shadow's arms, and he placed her in the back of the van.

"I hated to knock her out, but we can't take the chance of anyone else realizing she's not asleep. We can't make the slightest move out of character now."

"It's not a big deal, man. I would've done the same in your place."

Nick's cell began ringing, and he exchanged a leery glance with Shadow. "Renegade."

"Change of plans. When you get the girl, take her to the old clubhouse instead of the country club."

"We just got her, in fact. They must have wrapped up early today. Her driver hadn't even arrived to pick her up yet."

"Good work, Renegade. I'm glad to hear that. We're moving up the schedule, so it only makes sense to take her to the old clubhouse rather than risk moving her again."

Nick relayed the message to Shadow then directed him to the old building. Bonebreaker waited in the garage with the large metal door rolled up so they could pull straight into the covered area. While Bone closed the door, Shadow and Nick circled to the back of the van to pick up Lori. Shadow snaked his arms underneath her and pulled her to his chest. He hauled her body weight over his shoulder with ease and carried her inside.

"Where does this one go?" he asked, looking around the dingy room.

"Throw her in there," Bone replied, pointing to the closed door.

Shadow swung the door open with one hand, flipped the light on, and turned his head when Bone issued a warning. "Be careful of the other one in there. She's mouthy and gets on my fucking nerves."

Shadow turned back to the bedroom, stepped inside, and deposited Lori on the grungy bed. His skin tingled, and the air sparked with electricity.

She's here.

When he turned, Elle stood rooted to her spot behind the door. Shock and anguish crushed her spirit. Devastation rocked her foundation, driving her down to her knees.

"No," she breathed, defeat overtaking her. "*No.*"

20

***

CHAPTER TWENTY

"You've been there every day for the last three days, and she hasn't even made eye contact with you. You're going to draw attention to us that we don't need." Nick ran his fingers through his hair and stomped across the floor of his ratty apartment.

"I know how to operate an undercover investigation, Nick."

"But you're not running one, are you? You're only here to get your girlfriend. Fuck my case. Fuck the last two years of my life. Fuck my career. As long as you get what you want."

"I can't leave her there any longer and risk something happening to her."

"You're not thinking clearly. You will get her killed by pulling her out now. You'll get both of us killed. Who will be there to protect her, then? You're too close. You need to get out."

"What you're really asking is if you need to push me out," Shadow countered. "The hell you will. I'm not leaving *without* Elle."

"And you're not leaving *with* her yet. I need more information—like exactly who is behind this and why."

"You know who—Barry Jacobson and Vince Rossi. Who else do you need?"

"The DEA requires this little thing called evidence. We can't prosecute someone and stop them unless we have everything on them—and more. If you bothered to check the rules, you'd know that.

"Look, I let you come in on this case as a favor. Not so you'd blow it all to hell. You've seen her. You know she's okay. She's fed well, she's taken care of, no one has hurt her. They're moving the other girls there with her soon. We're tracing the money, unraveling the tangled web of fake companies to get to the offshore account. We know something's going down—likely this week. Just be patient so I don't have to shoot you myself."

"I'm going over there to relieve Bone. He said you have an officers' meeting this morning." Shadow slid his fingers into his leather gloves and picked up his keys. "I'm sure I'll see you after the meeting."

"Expect a phone call from Headbanger as soon as the meeting is over. Spider has been fucking up more over the last couple of days. He's on his way out. Oh, and Shadow?"

"Yeah?"

"Don't do anything stupid while I'm gone."

Shadow grinned, the mischief playing in his eyes once again. "Cross my heart."

Nick glared at Shadow's back as he walked out. As if he didn't have enough to manage with all the fast-paced, confusing pieces of the case, his old friend added more stress to an already unbearable situation. He was doing all his thinking with the head between his legs instead of the one between his shoulders. But Nick had to get his own head in the game at play that day instead of worrying about Shadow doing something crazy.

Shadow strode into the old clubhouse and found Bone in the large common room. The bedroom doors that lined the long wall were all closed, leaving Shadow to question which one Elle used to hide from him that visit.

"Fuck, I'm glad you're here. I'll never complain about our new clubhouse again. This building is a fucking dump. The last rat that ran by was as big as a fucking gopher. Damn thing may carry me off in my sleep." Bone paced back and forth, speaking fast, and his eyes darted aimlessly around the room.

Great—he's as high as a fucking kite, Shadow thought.

"Yeah, well, I'm here to cover for you while you're at the officers' meeting. Whenever you're ready to take off is fine."

"I'm ready now. Have fun, man. They're both in that room." Bone motioned to the room farthest from the kitchen area, at the end of the long room. "We have an unspoken agreement to stay away from each other. The mouthy one pisses me off, and I don't want the prez taking my head off over her."

Shadow stood in the same spot, staring at the closed door, when he heard Bone's Harley fire up. The familiar thump, thump, thump of the engine rattled the metal door in the garage when he rode away. The metal grinding against metal sound of the door closing drew his attention. He moved quickly through the room toward the kitchen until he reached the door leading out to the garage to see who had joined him.

And why.

The door swung open, and Axle stepped into the room. He had a knack for seeing everything while remaining in the background. Extra-cautious and suspicious of everyone, Axle had every classic sign of a man who'd served hard time in a maximum-security prison —and didn't want to go back.

"Wasn't expecting to see you here." Shadow tried to keep the disappointment out of this tone. He wanted time alone with Elle more than anything.

Axle narrowed his eyes and tilted his head slightly. "I'll just bet you didn't. What are you up to, Doorman?"

"Nothing. Just entertaining our guests in Bone's absence."

"Uh-huh," Axle replied. "You can go if you want. I got it."

"I just got here. Maybe I'll hang out for a while."

"Suit yourself." Axle shrugged and opened the drawer to go through the delivery menus. "Hungry?"

Shadow chuckled. "Always."

"I'll ask the ladies what they want." Axle walked to the last bedroom door and knocked lightly. The door barely cracked open at first, then opened wide when they realized who stood on the other side.

Lori and Elle walked out into the main room, their postures at ease and small smiles lighting their faces. They weren't afraid of Axle in the least, despite his rough appearance and outlaw gang ties. Shadow's heart leapt up into his throat watching Elle, knowing he couldn't tell her the truth but dying to pull her into his arms.

After he'd dropped Lori off and Elle had seen him in the act, he knew the crushed expression she wore was because she believed his act. Why wouldn't she? He looked and dressed the part. Elle had been abducted by the very men he openly called brothers. Then she watched him put an unconscious Lori on the bed.

After Elle's momentary breakdown, she found her strength and her anger flared. When she stood, she beat her fists against Shadow's chest and let her rage flow. "How could you help them do this to me? To her? Did she think you loved her too?" Though her heart was broken, her defiance was strong. She wanted to cause him as much physical pain as he'd caused her emotionally.

As much as Shadow wanted to tell her the truth, he already knew what Nick had scolded him over that morning. She couldn't know the truth and risk giving them away. Lori didn't know which men had nabbed her—she couldn't have identified either man if she'd had to. If he'd told Elle, she would've reacted differently toward him and raised everyone's suspicions.

So he turned his back on her and left, leaving her to think the worst about him. Without telling her he'd walked away from his life to save hers. Without her knowing about the beating he'd taken— and given—to join the club. He'd kept the branding mark hidden while it healed. The scar would require plastic surgery to correct. The faded black-ink prison tattoos he'd had strategically placed were a special ink developed by the CIA. The removal would be painful, but if it meant she was safe, he'd gladly endure it. And more.

Three days later, she still refused to make eye contact or acknowledge his presence. But she seemed to enjoy Axle's company. A small part of him was thankful she'd found someone who could comfort her in the middle of the worst time of her life. But a bigger part of him was angry with himself for not being the man she needed. The war playing out between his head and his heart was unrelenting.

She walked with Lori into the kitchen, keeping her distance from him. Lori cast furtive glances in his direction, apprehension and fear rolling off her in waves. His size was intimidating. His intense glare exposed his deadly inclinations. People naturally moved out of his way when they saw him coming. Her reaction to him was typical, even if it stung strangely.

He opened his mouth to speak to Elle, but his phone rang and stopped him just in time. "Yeah," he snapped. He listened wordlessly to the instructions from the other end for a moment. "Understood."

He turned to Axle and pocketed his phone. "Never mind my order. I have to go. I'll see you later."

SPIDER SAUNTERED THROUGH THE HALL OF THE MANSION THEY CALLED the country club. He'd already rendered Beth unconscious and moved her to the van. He whistled as he made his way to Katrina's room to collect her. Then to Carrie's room. With the three women sleeping in the back of the van, Spider started his trek to move them to the old clubhouse, reuniting them with Elle.

When he strolled in with Beth thrown over his shoulder, Elle visibly withdrew away from him, toward Axle, until she realized who he carried. She watched silently as he brought them in, one by one.

"What's happening? Why are you bringing them here? What are you doing with us?" she demanded sharply.

"Nothing at all, sweetheart," Spider replied with a smirk. He stepped outside and called Headbanger. "It's done, boss. All the girls are here. You can make the call for the sale now."

"That's good news. I'll get the ball rolling. Head back over here to the clubhouse so we can make our final arrangements with your uncle." Headbanger disconnected and turned to Bone. "Go get his uncle."

"You got it."

Once Bone left, Headbanger turned on the television to catch the promised news update on the search for Elle Sinclair and her makeup artist, Beth Condra. He'd been following the updates religiously, waiting for any clue the authorities were closing in on them. He'd agreed to include Detective Gough in their scheme as a precaution, someone who had the inside track to cover their asses while putting her own on the line.

He turned up the volume when the ticker at the bottom of the screen showed the district attorney's name.

"Thank you, Mayor Porter. As the district attorney, I'm here to assure you the chief of police and I are working together to ensure the missing entertainment industry professionals are found and returned, safe and sound. I can't go into details about the steps we're taking, but know that we've heard your concerns loud and clear. We're taking this situation very seriously and have had agreements from all the major studios to increase their security presence. We encourage everyone involved with the industry, regardless of job title, to be diligent about their surroundings and to move around the lots in groups, never alone."

The governor, mayor, DA, and chief of police all stood shoulder-to-shoulder on the stage, showing their solidarity. To the side of the stage stood Detective Gough, her shoulders held back in her staunch military stance, her back rod straight, and her face expressionless.

"One of the city's best detectives has been assigned to the case. She has the highest percentage of cases successfully solved and is one of our most decorated officers. We will update you as we can without jeopardizing the case."

The DA closed the press conference by saying she wouldn't accept any questions, and they filed off the stage and into the justice building behind them. Headbanger watched Detective Gough's body language when she walked away. He didn't trust anyone for a reason —most everyone had disappointed or double-crossed him at some point. The club was his family, a proven brotherhood of men who had his back and proved water was thicker than blood.

He put all of his trust in his brothers, making any act of betrayal acutely devastating to him. Like a wild animal when it's wounded, he became more dangerous when he was hurt. After he discovered he'd been fooled, his trust had been thrown back in his face, he was wounded. A wounded wild animal. That kind of betrayal couldn't be forgiven and forgotten. It was premeditated, well planned-out, and overtly deliberate. They wanted to make him look like a fool, to play him—but they'd be the ones played when he was finished with them.

He moved to the back room and began setting up his interrogation tools. One way or another, he'd get the answers he needed. And when he was finished, his ferocity would never be doubted again.

"Hey, Prez," Spider said when he entered the club.

Headbanger glanced up at him. "Everything go okay?"

"Smooth as glass."

"Good. Take a load off." Headbanger gestured to the open chair. "Just watching a little TV, waiting for Bone to get back."

"Want a beer?"

"Sure. I'll take one."

When Bone arrived, he forced their guest into the clubhouse and locked the door behind them. "Look who I found," Bone announced when they entered the club's media room.

Spider looked up and saw his uncle, who was beaten and battered and wore a terrified expression, compliments of the gun held to his back. "What the fuck? Uncle Barry? What's going on?" Spider stood and met Bone's hard stare with one of his own. "What the fuck have you done to my uncle?"

"He did what I told him to do," Headbanger replied from behind him. "We need to talk."

They led Spider and Barry into the interrogation room. All color drained from Spider's face as realization of what was to come set in. Bone shoved them both into the waiting chairs and strapped them down.

"I have a few questions you're going to answer. Some I already know the answers to, some I don't. So I dare you to lie to me." Headbanger reared his fist back and smashed it into Spider's face amid his protests to wait, to explain what was wrong. But he didn't stop. Spider's pleas didn't register through his rage.

"Stop!" Barry bellowed. His tone, a mixture of terror and alarm, caught Headbanger's attention.

"Did you think I forgot about you?"

"You haven't even asked anything yet. You haven't told us what's wrong."

"You're absolutely right," he replied, leaning down to stare directly into Barry's eyes. "Where the fuck is my money?"

"What money? What are you talking about?"

He grabbed Spider's mangled face and turned it toward Barry. "Tell him, Spider. Tell your uncle why he's about to die with you."

"Boss, wait. It's not what you think."

"Let's go over the facts. Renegade is the treasurer and you're the secretary. At first, I did question Renegade's loyalty, so I had an outside contact comb through everything from my companies all the way to my offshore account. You did a good job of covering your tracks and making me suspect someone else. But you also did a good job of keeping club records.

"Money started disappearing from my account immediately before Renegade became the treasurer, so it couldn't have been him. The timing was close, but no dice. You've mastered signing my signature. The outside auditor noticed the change in it over time to more closely match my real signature.

"So you set up a new account in my name and transferred money from my actual account a little at a time. When the amounts started adding up, you covered up my account balance by showing me the fake account instead. Renegade wouldn't have had any reason to suspect a second account, thanks to your club records."

One of Spider's eyes had already swollen shut, but his one good eye was open wide and filled with fear. "No, boss. I was just trying to protect you and your money. It's still in your name. It's yours. This is how money is laundered, small amounts transferred to different accounts over time."

"You know what, Spider? I could almost believe that—if you

hadn't booked a one-way flight to the Bahamas leaving one week from today. You almost made it, didn't you? You almost pulled off a great heist. But not quite. I trust no one implicitly, I double-check everything. Surely you know that about me if you know nothing else."

"No, boss. You've got it all wrong."

"You know I hate a liar. The more I have to spend time proving I know this beyond a shadow of a doubt, the worse it'll be for you."

He motioned to Bone, and they pushed Spider over onto his side. Bone grabbed Spider's wallet from his back pocket and stepped back, his disgusted glare firmly set on his victim. Bone dug through the wallet, removing Spider's license along with the fake identification he'd had made.

Spider's whole body sagged in defeat as his prez read the name on the fake license. "Bobby Blalock. Is that your name, Spider?"

He shook his head from side to side.

"Whose name is it?"

"Yours."

"Spider, what have you done?" Barry asked, surprise and dread equally infused in his whisper.

"I'm sorry, boss. I was just trying to protect you."

"It's a good thing I don't need your protection, isn't it?" He nodded to Bone, who stepped out of the room and got Shadow.

When Shadow walked in and realized who sat beside Spider, his skin pricked, knowing the case was unraveling quickly.

"Doorman, take Spider out and get rid of him. I have other plans for Uncle Barry." Headbanger mocked Barry, emphasizing his name with a blatant sneer.

Bone slid a pair of zip-tie handcuffs over Spider's wrists and tied a gag around his mouth. Shadow drew Spider to his feet and shoved him through the door with Spider's grunts begging for his uncle's safety.

"Now, Barry, how much do you think the studio will pay for your safe return? Bet they'd pay a pretty penny if we return all their talent at once, wouldn't they?"

Shadow couldn't delay his departure any longer without drawing attention to himself. Once outside, he put Spider in the club's truck and slid behind the wheel. Spider glanced over at Shadow and grunted when he tried to speak. Shadow shook his head and sighed loudly. He should be in that room, preventing them from killing the studio executive, but he was with Spider instead.

"Barry Jacobson is your uncle?" Shadow verified.

Spider nodded, grief covering his features.

"You screwed over your uncle, didn't you?"

Spider nodded.

"And it never occurred to you they'd suspect he was in on it after you disappeared? Or that they'd take it out on him because he's your uncle?"

Spider shook his head, understanding of what he'd done beginning to sink in.

Shadow dialed Nick to give him the news. After he'd explained what had happened and what he was doing, Nick advised him to take Spider to Jack's place.

"He's been tracing the fake companies and offshore account. He'd just uncovered the discrepancies in the accounts today. What Headbanger doesn't know yet is there's a third account. The full balance of both accounts under Bobby Blalock's name is scheduled to transfer to the third account one week from today."

"Whose name is that one in?"

"Barry Jacobson."

Shadow looked over at Spider. "You don't say."

"Yeah. Great family, huh? I'm heading to the clubhouse now to try to keep them from killing Barry. If they find out Barry has double-crossed them all, there'll be a long line of people who want to kill him."

Shadow parked at Jack's apartment and marched Spider inside, where two DEA agents waited to take him into custody. With fake blood and a staged scene, Shadow took pictures of Spider's "dead" body as proof for Headbanger.

"You're undercover DEA?" Spider finally asked, still dumbfounded with the turn of events.

"No, I'm not DEA at all. But I did just save your life," Shadow replied. "So, you're going to tell me everything."

Over the next hour, Shadow questioned Spider and listened to his rendition of the kidnapping scheme.

"It was my uncle's idea. He's a big-time executive, but he'd spent too much of the money that was earmarked to go to movie production on himself. He couldn't finalize the movie without being found out, so he wanted us to take the girls until he fixed his money problems. Once he got more funding, we were supposed to let them go, and he'd pay us for grabbing them.

"But it took a lot longer than he thought it would, and another movie was wrapping up before he had the money to finish. Then another. It just kept adding up on him, so Boss decided to sell the girls. The cartels gave us the spray to knock them out, and they got it from a guy in Hong Kong. They arranged a deal for us, with the cartel getting a cut, of course. The girls are supposed to be moved through Mexico to the port in the next few days. That's why I moved them from Barry's house."

"Selling them to whom?"

"The cartel's contact in Hong Kong."

Shadow cut his gaze to the DEA agents. One spoke up. "We'll cast a wide net across the border—land and sea. They won't leave the States."

Shadow nodded and stood to leave. Spider had lost all his bravado when he searched Shadow's face. "Are you going to save my uncle's life too?"

"I'll try," he replied after a few seconds. "No promises. I have no idea what those two are doing to him since we left." He turned to leave when Spider stopped him again.

"Bone suspects you, ya know? He told Boss this morning. He thinks there's something up with you and that actress. He swears he heard the two of you talking the night you brought the new girl in.

But when he moved to the door to listen, she'd quit talking. Since then, she's avoided you. He wants to off both of you."

"Thanks for the heads-up." He nodded to Spider and left, calling Nick as soon as he got into the truck. "Tell me you saved Jacobson."

"Oh, he's alive, Guess you haven't seen the news over the last hour."

"No. What now?"

"Now we're into extortion via ransom demands. Headbanger sent a video showing Jacobson tied up and beaten, and he demanded the studio pay for the release of their executive and actresses. The money is supposed to be wired to his offshore account."

"The same one that's about to be drained dry?"

Nick chuckled at the irony. "The same. Karma can be such a bitch."

"What's his exchange plan?"

"When the money transfer is confirmed, he'll leave them all at one location and send the address when he's long gone."

"Because those schemes always work exactly as planned."

"Don't underestimate him. He's likely to have another plan in mind but not tell any of us. We need eyes on him at all times."

Shadow told Nick the last words Spider said to him. "Don't let them hurt my girl, Nick. I swear to you, I will mow every one of those bastards down if she's harmed."

"I hear you, man."

CHAPTER TWENTY-ONE

Brianna, Chaise, Heather, and Liz entered the enormous suite that had become the temporary headquarters of Steele Security. The Moore and Condra families had been moved to the same floor for their own safety, traveling to interviews under the watchful eye of Reaper, Bull, or Rebel.

"We're here. You can all take a break now. We've got this," Liz exclaimed upon her entrance.

"Case is closed, boys. Liz is here. We can all go home," Rebel teased as he rose to greet Heather. He enjoyed seeing Liz's feathers ruffled.

"You think you're better at this than me? As far as I can tell, you only started solving cases after I showed up to help you."

Bull snorted, then coughed exaggeratedly to hide his gaffe. "We were just saying we couldn't wait until you got here. We've missed you, Liz."

Liz beamed with pride as every other eye in the room bore through Bull's skin with a burning intensity.

"Yes, that's exactly what we were just saying," Reaper added, his tone rife with sarcasm and humor.

"Never fear, my boys. Mama Liz is here to protect you."

"When did you become Mama Liz?" Heather asked as she wrapped her arms around Rebel, happy to be in her husband's arms again.

"Since I started my own day care with just Steele Security kids. Have any of you figured out what causes repeat pregnancies yet?" Liz moved through the expansive adjoining suites, checking every bedroom before claiming hers. "I'm glad you reserved several suites on this floor. We'll need one just for my headquarters."

Reaper had learned not to argue with Liz more than absolutely necessary. Over the years with her as their nanny and friend, she'd trapped him by his own words one time too many. He rushed to Brianna and scooped her up in his arms. "Hey, baby. I'm so glad you're here."

"Me, too. Your parents and my parents argued over who would babysit while I'm here with you." She laughed then kissed him. "I gave them each a week, so you need to wrap up this case and take me away for some adult time."

"Oh, lord. Another Steele baby coming right up," Liz groaned.

Reaper and Brianna chuckled while they continued their kiss hello.

Chaise melted into Bull's arms, and their lips fused together. "Hello, gorgeous," he said against her lips. "'Bout time you showed up."

"Got here as soon as I could. Your parents and my parents are taking turns with the kids, too. I agree with Bri—we all need an adults-only vacation once this is over," Chaise replied.

"What can we do to help?" Brianna asked.

"Elle's and Beth's parents have had a hard time with this. We've tried to calm them as much as possible without giving them much information on Shadow."

"Where is my man?" Liz asked, reappearing in the living room decked out in black leather pants, a long-sleeve black Henley shirt, and a black leather vest. The matching black leather hat and finger-less gloves completed her biker look. "I'm his ride-or-die chick. Gotta support my man no matter which road he chooses."

"Uh, Liz," Rebel began, wiping the smile off his face with his big hand. "Your man is deep undercover. In an outlaw motorcycle gang. We can't just insert you undercover with him. It'll get him killed. Besides, I'm not sure your slip-on Skechers are approved by the Devil's Dominion."

"What's wrong with them? They're comfortable and easy to get on and off my feet when they swell."

"Maybe we should let her loose on the gang. She'd probably take them down single-handedly," Bull quipped.

"Damn straight. Let me at 'em." Liz stood in front of the entry mirror and adjusted her hat. "Did anyone bring me a gun?"

"No!" came the unified reply from all three men.

Liz turned slowly and glared at each man. "Wait a minute. Where's Silas?"

Reaper buried his face in Brianna's neck, his body shaking so hard with laughter he couldn't speak to respond to her question.

"Silas is working a different angle of the case, Liz. He's protecting Jax Hart and working through his CIA contact to help Shadow. I'm sure we'll see him soon."

"Not when he finds out Liz is here," Reaper whispered to Brianna. She immediately shushed him.

Liz narrowed her eyes at Brianna and Reaper. "Noah Steele. Silas taught me how to be a spy. I know everything he knows. Call him right now—in front of me and on speaker—and tell him to get over here. Jax Hart can stay here with the others and be just fine. Silas needs backup, though."

"You'll have to lose your biker chick outfit. He's not in the gang. In fact, if they find out he's here, they'll kill him. He infiltrated the gang years ago and was 'sent to prison' to get out of it. But he's sure his cover was blown in the process," Rebel countered.

"Like I said, I'm Shadow's ride-or-die girl, so the leather stays. If anyone sees me with Silas, I can vouch for him as a real biker chick." Liz lowered her gaze to Reaper's phone pointedly and raised her eyebrows.

With a resigned sigh, he picked up his phone and pressed the button for Silas. When the call connected, he smiled and hit the speaker button. "Hey, big brother, you're on speaker. There's someone here who wants to see you."

A few seconds of pregnant silence filled the line before Silas replied. "Oh, yeah? Who's that?"

"You know damn well who it is, Silas Steele," Liz called. "You lied to me. You said you couldn't bring me with you as a matter of national security."

"It is a matter of national security, Liz. The nation is not secure when you're on the loose as a rogue quadruple agent. You missed the whole point of a double agent."

"There's no reason why I should be limited to just double. I can play many sides against each other. Just because I'm more talented and flexible than you are is no reason to let envy keep me from helping you."

Another punctuated silence stalled the conversation.

"Silas?"

"Yes, Liz?"

"Come on over to the hotel and bring this Jax person. He can stay here while we wrap up this case and bring Shadow home."

Silas dropped his head backward and stared at the ceiling, ceding to Liz's demand before disconnecting. "Fine. We'll be there later tonight."

Silas turned to Jax and smiled a devious smile. "I know I just moved you here from your Idaho mountain hideout, but Liz actually does have a valid point for once. I'm moving you to another location tonight. It's secure and under armed protection. Elle's and Beth's families are also staying there."

"Okay. But why the creepy smile?"

"You're going to help me with Liz."

"Who's Liz?"

"You'll see." Silas laughed out loud. "You'll see."

When darkness began to fall over LA, Silas had Jax put on his disguise so they could leave the building without him being recognized. They reached the hotel and stepped off the elevators to find Liz waiting impatiently with her foot tapping.

"It's about time." She crossed her arms over her chest and huffed loudly. "Do you know how much time we've already wasted?"

"Patience, Liz. Let's get Jason set up in his room."

She looked at Jason suspiciously. "I thought your name was Jax."

"Jax is his spy name. To everyone else, he's Jason." Silas made his statement so matter-of-factly, so nonchalantly, knowing Liz's interest in Jason would double.

"Hold up. You're a spy?"

"Of course. He's in disguise right now. What's really interesting is he used to be a special-effects makeup artist here in LA. He has mad skills with a makeup brush and a little putty." Silas pulled out the big guns early, hoping his distraction was enough to entice Liz.

"Well. We'll just see about his mad skills, won't we?" Liz challenged.

Hook, line, and sinker, Silas thought as he smiled to himself.

"Let's practice on Silas before he and I go out to help Shadow tonight," Liz continued, effectively bursting his happy bubble.

"What? Who's Shadow?" Jason asked, looking at Silas for help.

"Never mind. You don't need to know anything about him. Now, my outfit is already perfect to join a motorcycle club, but I need more of a kick to my makeup. A good disguise to protect my real identity," Liz decided.

Jason started with the leather cap on her head and worked his way down to her white slip-on Skechers. He jerked his head up and opened his mouth to object when Silas stopped him.

"That's a great idea, Liz. Why don't the two of you work on your makeup while I go check in with Noah."

"All right, Silas. But you know what happens if you sneak off without me," Liz warned.

He rolled his eyes, knowing full well what Liz would do. He'd made that mistake once before on a far less important grocery store run on a group trip. When he awoke that night, Liz stood over him with her bright pink nail polish in hand. Not only had she painted his nails, but also his lips. To date, he still hadn't figured out how she'd pulled that off, and she refused to divulge her own trade secrets.

But removing her as his self-proclaimed spy partner was worth the painted lips and nails he'd endure later. For the time being, his focus had to be on getting Shadow and the others out of the Devil's clutches. Events had been escalating in severity, ramping up the danger Shadow and Nick faced if their covers were blown and increasing the probability someone would be killed before the sting was finished.

"Noah," he called out when they entered the suite.

"Back here," Reaper answered.

Liz escorted Jason to another room so they could begin work on her disguise. Silas breathed a sigh of relief when he joined the other men in their temporary command center.

"I just got here, and she's already threatening me."

The others laughed at his misfortune. "We're just glad she's taken a liking to you, Silas," Reaper replied.

"Noah, you're my brother. You're supposed to have my back."

"Brother, you know I'd take a bullet for you. But when it comes to Liz, we've all agreed it's every man for himself," Reaper replied.

"Bastards," Silas mumbled under his breath.

"What have you found out, Silas?" Rebel asked.

Silas filled them in on his entire conversation with Jason and what he'd seen. Noah, in turn, brought Silas up to speed on the events of the day. "Jack, Nick's handler, called and gave us the rundown of Shadow's interrogation of Spider. He was singing like a songbird, hoping Shadow could save his uncle after he'd double-crossed his club and his family. He has no idea his uncle planned to double-cross him in the end, though."

Silas listened intently, following the explanation of the first account feeding the second, until both were to be transferred to the third account held by the studio executive Barry Jacobson. It was a good scheme, he had to give Barry that. Mismanage funds, run out of production money, have the girls kidnapped by his nephew's gang until he could secure more investors or recover money from somewhere else, all while the studio covered for him because losing their insurance policy would shut them down forever.

Barry never considered Shadow's commitment to Elle, though.

SHADOW RETURNED TO THE OLD CLUBHOUSE, PER NICK'S REQUEST. Since he hadn't been invited to take Spider's place as an officer, his presence around the officers' area would be suspicious. Nick tried to keep Shadow's interactions with Headbanger and Bone to a minimum. The wrong word uttered regarding Elle would result in all-out war, something Nick wasn't prepared to initiate just yet. They'd had another disagreement over the phone.

"You have all the info you need on the bank accounts. You said that's what you were waiting for—to find out who was behind this. Now we know the funds came from the club's drug and weapons money funneling into the offshore account through shell corporations, and Jacobson is behind the abductions on the lot. There's no reason to continue this charade. We need to get them out of that clubhouse before Headbanger kills them all out of spite." Shadow had argued his points until he was blue in the face, but Nick wouldn't back down.

"I have orders from my superiors. Since Headbanger is openly taunting the police and the feds, they want to tack on extra charges and make sure he never sees the outside of the prison walls again. This isn't over until we have the all-clear and our teams are in place to ensure everyone's safety," Nick shot back.

"While you follow orders and your superiors look to add one more charge to a list already a mile long, those civilians' lives are in mortal danger. That should be your first priority—not an extra star for the agency. Is there something else you're not telling me?"

"No. It'll be over soon. Don't jump the gun."

"You'd better hope Headbanger and Bone don't jump the gun." Shadow hung up on Nick, angry and frustrated his friend wouldn't listen to reason.

Shadow killed the engine outside the old clubhouse and sat on his bike, fighting the urge to storm into the old clubhouse and ride off into the sunset with Elle on the back. With an impatient growl, he climbed off and sauntered up the steps to the door. He stepped inside and came face-to-face with Elle.

At least she's looking at me, Shadow thought.

"Didn't expect to see you," Axle said, throwing Shadow's words back at him.

Shadow grinned knowingly. "I like to keep you guessing."

Elle huffed and walked out of the room, carrying her meal with her and leaving the others at the table. Shadow glanced over at them, hoping Beth wouldn't give him away. The expression on her face matched the hatred in her eyes. She wanted to relieve him of his head. When her lips parted and she prepared to speak, he moved quickly out of the kitchen and in the direction Elle had gone.

He heard a chair scrape against the floor, followed by Axle's command. "Sit down and eat." The distant sound of the chair sliding across the floor confirmed she'd obeyed.

With one person in mind, his feet carried him straight to her. She sat with her back to him when he approached. The closer he got, the more he realized she wasn't simply sitting on the couch to eat. Her shoulders shook softly at first, but the shaking grew more intense with his every step. Her quiet sobs and muffled wails reached his chest before his ears, causing a tightening he could only describe as a vise around him. Her face was mashed into a pillow, giving her the only private place she had to completely melt down.

He wasn't sure which was worse—seeing her like that and not being able to comfort her, allowing her to believe he'd helped put her in that predicament, or walking away to give her the privacy she needed and deserved.

His hand hovered over her head, waiting to stroke her hair.

His arms ached to lift her from the couch and cradle her against his chest until her tears dried.

His lips craved to claim hers, to kiss away the pain she felt until she remembered the love they shared.

His ego strained against his loyalty, wanting to defy Nick and burn the case down around them when he freed the girls and kidnapped Elle for himself.

Instead, he backed away from her. And decided that was definitely the worst-case scenario.

"How could you? I loved you. I thought you loved me." She whispered each sentiment to herself between gasps for air.

I was so wrong, he thought. *I've never been so wrong. Letting her think I'm behind any of this is definitely the worst.*

CHAPTER TWENTY-TWO

"Are you and your boys a bunch of ignorant, inbred assholes?" Detective Gough barged into the officers' area of the Devil's Dominion clubhouse. "I mean, I've busted some dumbass criminals before, but you and your boys take the fucking cake."

Headbanger leaned back in his chair and leveled his death-glare at her. "Either you were dropped on your head repeatedly as a child, or you've lost your bitch mind."

"Is that right?" She pinned him with her own pissed-off stare. "Well, I haven't lost my bitch mind enough to let a fucking undercover federal agent join my outlaw motorcycle club and not even fucking know it."

Headbanger's face turned beet red. "What the fuck did you just say?"

"You heard me. Shit rolls downhill, you know? After all your fuck-ups with a simple snatch and grab of a couple of actresses, I really shouldn't be surprised. But you've effectively fucked us both. Your boys grabbed Elle Sinclair and her makeup artist in front of Jax Hart. Jax went to the media with it. Do you have any clue how much pressure gets put on us to quickly solve anything to do with our stars?

"The governor called the mayor. The mayor called the DA. The DA called the chief of police. The chief chewed my ass up one side and down the other. Somewhere in the chain of command, they demanded to let the FBI take over, but the DEA confirmed there's already an undercover agent in your club. So they have jurisdiction to protect their asset."

"How the fuck can you not tell one of your men is a federal agent? That's why you and your boys are stupid, inbred assholes. That undercover agent has already made me, I can guarantee that. He just hasn't been debriefed to rat me out yet."

"Get the fuck out of here. You ever come at me with one ounce of disrespect again, I'll put a bullet between your fucking eyes and feed your goddamn body to the sharks." He stood and rounded his desk, charging toward her like an out-of-control bull. When she didn't move fast enough, he grabbed her with one hand, opened the door with the other hand, and shoved her outside. Before she could speak, he slammed the door shut in her face.

"Bone," he bellowed. "Get in here."

Within seconds, his sergeant at arms stood in his office awaiting orders. "Yes, sir?"

"Take Nutcrusher, and you two put a bullet in Gough's, Doorman's, and Renegade's skulls. Then rip the patches and rockers off their vests and bring them back to me, soaked in their blood."

Shock crossed Bone's face before he nodded. "Renegade? He betrayed us?"

"That fucking detective just said we have an undercover agent in our club. Doorman is the first man I suspected. The way he got up and fought back after his initiation should've tipped me off, but I ignored it. If he's an agent, Renegade must be too. Either way, he endorsed a fed, and he has to go."

"I fucking knew it. Renegade was behind my brother getting busted at that bar, I'm sure of it. I'll gladly take care of them both."

Bone went into the armory and took four Glock 9mm pistols and extra clips, two for him and two for Nutcrusher. One bullet to each of their skulls wouldn't be enough. He walked through the clubhouse, calling for his friend, when a door opened suddenly and a half-dressed Nutcrusher rushed out.

"What? Where's the fucking fire?" He buttoned his pants and pulled up the zipper. The girl he was with sat up on the bed, wide-eyed while she watched him.

"We have orders." Bone handed him two of the handguns, effectively conveying the rest of the message.

"Who?" Nutcrusher asked, tucking the guns into the back of his pants.

"Renegade and the fucking Doorman. But first, Gough."

"What? Why?"

"They're undercover feds, and that bitch detective rubbed the prez the wrong way."

The two men left in the truck, heading toward the detective's apartment. Bone couldn't help but hear what Headbanger threatened Gough with—and he knew his boss didn't make idle threats. She'd die exactly as he'd described, and when she saw them approaching, she'd know exactly why.

Nutcrusher knocked on her door while Bone flattened his back against the wall and waited. The peephole darkened as she peeked through it, but Nutcrusher left his expression neutral. He sensed her hesitancy and considered kicking the door in just before the deadbolt turned.

"What do you want?" Her bravado was fake, but he had to give her credit for trying.

Bone swung around, his gun drawn, and ordered her out of the apartment. Her eyes cut to the side, and Nutcrusher knew she planned to run. He grabbed her arm and jerked her toward him. She lost her balance and fell against his chest. With a gun pressed into her spine, they walked her to the truck and forced her into the cab between them.

"What's going on? Where are you taking me?"

"Detective Gough, we thought you were smart," Bone taunted.

"You fucked up royally, sweetheart," Nutcrusher added, knowing she hated that endearment. "Not only did you threaten the prez, you disrespected him and failed to identify a fed in our midst before he'd gained too much intel on us. You're supposed to be our police protection. You suck at your job."

The false bravado she had just moments before was nowhere to be found. Realization dawned, and she understood how dire her situation was. "Guys, come on. We can fix this. I'll help you find him, and we'll take him out of play. I have a lot riding on him being out of the picture too."

"Not anymore, sweetheart. You're out completely. No sense in worrying about your job anymore. Remember how Headbanger said you'd die? One custom-made death package coming up." Bone loved his club and was loyal to his boss. If he'd learned one valuable lesson in life, that lesson was loyalty was most important.

They drove to an abandoned mall and marched her inside, with Detective Gough pleading for her life the entire way. With every word, they mocked her, repeating her pleas in abnormally high-pitched voices. Nutcrusher pushed her down on her knees while Bone chambered a round. He lowered the top of the barrel to her forehead, lining it up directly between her eyes, and smiled when he pulled the trigger, despite her flowing tears and frantic requests.

"Well, that was easy." Bone smirked and spread out the plastic tarp. "Grab her feet and put her on this. We'll drive up toward the country club and dump her into the ocean."

They rolled her up and carried her back to the truck, throwing her in the back with no regard. Nutcrusher slid across the driver's seat, fired up the truck, and drove north out of the city until they reached an isolated area along the coast. From the top of the cliff overlooking the rocky shore, they unwrapped her from the tarp and tossed her lifeless body over the side. The waves crashed against the rocks, and the foamy plumes leapt into the air from the force and claimed her as part of the sea.

"Goodbye, sweetheart." Nutcracker watched the ebb and flow of the waves pull her out into the deeper water until she was no longer visible. "The current and the fishes have her now," he heckled.

"Let's go kill those undercover pigs now," Bone replied.

"You really think it's them? She didn't say two agents. She said she'd help us find *him*. What if we kill two brothers, and they're not undercover agents?"

"It's them, all right. My gut has told me it was Renegade from the start. The Doorman made his way into the group all too easy with his weapons and endorsement from Renegade."

"Spider wanted him too."

"And where is Spider now?"

"Same place these two will be. I say we make them talk first. Find out what they know and who they've told. May be useful info to have in the near future. We may be able to avoid a federal raid—or at least laugh at them while they look in the wrong place."

"Good idea. Maybe we'll cut their fingers off one knuckle at a time —whether they talk or not. My castration shears have been feeling unappreciated lately."

By the time Bone and Nutcrusher reached the old clubhouse, night had settled in and darkness permeated the dimly lit rooms. The tension between Shadow and Nick had subsided, but neither had been overly talkative. Shadow watched the two bikers stroll through the house, nonchalantly checking each bedroom and demanding they all come out to the main room. The feeling something major was going down grew with each step they took.

Their demeanor was off. The more they tried to act natural, the more obvious it was they were anything but natural.

The longer they delayed their intentions, the more they showed their hand.

They thought they were smooth and stealthy, when they were transparent as glass and nervous.

Shadow caught Nick's attention and slid his left index finger along the right side of his nose. An innocuous move to signal his friend to get ready—they would have to fight their way out of the clubhouse at any minute. Shadow's gaze traveled over their outlines and quickly spotted the two guns each man carried. They came more prepared than they normally were.

"What's going on?" Nick asked and leaned against the doorframe. His stance hid his right arm, which was bent behind his back so he could reach his gun in a split second.

"Headbanger sent us. Seems there's a new development and a change in plans for the girls," Bone replied. "The deal is off, so we can do what we want with them before we put a bullet in their brains."

"Prez didn't tell us about any change of plans." Nick's fingers firmly gripped the butt of his gun.

"I'm telling you now. He doesn't have to tell you when I can do it for him." Bone walked toward Katrina. "Maybe I'll start with this one." He ran his callused fingers along her cheek, his sneer conveying the images conjured by his imagination.

"You're not doing anything to any of these girls unless I hear it directly from the prez. He didn't give me the okay, so I sure as fuck don't take your word for anything. These girls have a specific purpose, and I won't be the one to fuck that up for him."

"No, you won't be the one to fuck anything up. I'll be the one who fucks you up if you talk to me like that again. Call him yourself. While you wait to talk to him, this one will be sucking me off. Come back later," Nutcrusher replied and wrapped his fingers around Elle's wrist.

Shadow flinched, an uncharacteristic reaction for him after what years of training and work had drilled into him, but the man in him responded before the spy did when another man touched her or even thought about enjoying any part of her body. Though she still believed the worst about him, he'd protect her with his life. He had to make her believe he was part of the scheme so she wouldn't give them a reason to suspect or kill her. But there was no way in hell he'd allow Nutcrusher to do anything to her.

"Get your hand off her." Shadow stepped forward—threatening him openly. "Unless you want to lose that hand for good."

Nutcrusher looked over at Shadow, a small smile playing on his lips. "You know, Bone always said you were sweet on this one. You wanna watch? See how good she is before you give her a try?"

"You only get one warning. I'm counting down. When I get to zero, I'll snap that hand off and shove it up your ass. Three, two, one." Shadow stomped across the floor, his face dark with malicious intent.

Nutcrusher released her wrist, turned to face Shadow, and took a couple of steps backward. When Shadow had moved in front of Elle, effectively blocking her from Nutcrusher's view with his sheer size, he stopped abruptly. "Just in time. Maybe you're not as stupid as your nickname suggests. To be clear, the countdown doesn't start over if you touch her again."

The room became eerily quiet with the only sounds coming from the ladies' rapid breathing. Tension filled every square inch as time ticked by slowly. Shadow stood motionless, daring Nutcrusher to say or do the wrong thing one more time. Shadow arched one eyebrow, lifting it slowly as he wordlessly questioned the other man's intelligence.

"Fine. She's all yours," Nutcrusher ceded. "It is strange, though, how protective you are over a girl you don't even know."

"I'm protective over this entire play we're making. You screw it up, you screw me over. Any man who screws me over ends up without a fucking head."

"You two can't take a joke for shit," Bone chimed in. His easy laugh was meant to lighten the mood in the room. But the nervous edge to it contradicted his intent.

"We can take a joke just fine. None of this was fucking funny, though." Nick adjusted his stance but kept his gun arm hidden.

Nutcrusher moved away from Shadow and Elle, back toward Bone. Shadow sensed they were refortifying their positions, moving back into attack mode by aligning their combined force. Bone pulled his hands from his front pockets, giving Shadow a quick glimpse of something in his hand. He began walking toward Nick, palming something suspicious.

Nick's keen eyes homed in on Bone's movements. His fingers gripped his gun, and he mentally prepared for a shootout. The problem was his conscience got in the way. He made a note of where every woman stood and the likelihood she'd be hit in the cross fire. Bone and Nutcrusher wouldn't care about collateral damage. Nick's gaze drifted to Shadow, and he caught the tail end of a secret signal.

Shadow slid two fingers across his throat.

Their cover was blown.

Though Nick saw it coming, he remained in place and let Bone think he had the upper hand in his surprise attack. Bone lifted his hand to Nick's face and pumped the sprayer several times in quick succession. Nick threw his hand up, forcefully knocking Bone backward while wiping his face with his other arm. Bone, shocked Nick wasn't unconscious on the floor, was temporarily confused and didn't see Nick's right hook until it was too late. His head jerked violently to the side, his feet stumbled under his shaky legs, and he went down to the ground. Nick drew his gun and held it on Bone.

Shadow corralled the ladies and rushed them into the kitchen area, toward the door to the garage, and out of the line of fire. He turned in the doorway, ready to fight to the death. With his gun in his hand, he faced Bone and Nutcrusher, resisting the urge to shoot them both in the head, take Elle home, and be done with the entire farce.

"What the fuck was that, Bone?" Nick roared, testing whether their covers were truly blown.

Bone pushed up to stand and glared at Nick, his face hard and angry. "We all know what you are, pig. You and your friend here. At least one of you is undercover. I don't really care which one of you is the rotten pig and which one isn't—or if you both are. Our orders are to kill you both, and that's exactly what we're going to do."

"You two think you can take us?" Shadow asked, the first genuine smile in weeks covering his face. "By all means, let's see what you've got."

"Everyone just calm the fuck down. Why would you accuse me of being undercover? I've ridden beside you for the last two years, had your back countless times, and you've repeatedly insulted me. What the fuck have I ever done to you?"

"You're the one who put my little brother away. You are an undercover cop, and you had him arrested at that bar almost two years ago. We never had one problem until you joined." Bone's face turned beet red, anger and hatred welling up inside him.

"It wasn't him," Axle said, entering the room behind Bone. "It was me."

"You?" Bone whirled around, his jaw slack and his eyes wide. "You've been with us for years."

"And I have so much shit on you, I could put you away tomorrow and you'd never see the light of day again."

Bone roared with thunderous rage. He moved with lightning speed and drew his gun on Axle. In an instant, Axle's gun was out, and he fired at Bone first. Bone dropped to the floor, narrowly missing the bullet that passed by his head. Nutcrusher pulled his gun and began shooting, the adrenaline flowing out of control, making his hands shake and the bullets fly indiscriminately.

"Get out of here, wait in the garage," Shadow yelled to the ladies.

Once they were out of harm's way, Shadow moved beside Nick, behind cover. "We can't let them shoot Axle, man. We have to take them out."

Nick nodded. Uncertainty clouded his eyes, but his sense of right and wrong won. If that meant revealing his true identity, he could live with that easier than knowing he'd let a fellow agent die in his place.

What seemed to take hours had literally only been seconds. The events escalated so quickly, Shadow lost count of the number of shots that had been exchanged. He raised up from behind the overturned table and aimed his gun at Axle. When Nutcrusher saw Shadow's movement, a broad smile of victory covered his face. Shadow knew Axle had taken all suspicion off Nick and him.

When Nutcrusher turned his gaze back in Axle's direction, Shadow adjusted his arm and his cross hairs. Directly on Nutcrusher's temple. He centered and squeezed the trigger, incapacitating him instantly.

"You want Bone, or want me to take him?" Shadow whispered to Nick while Axle and Bone continued to exchange fire. Screams of terror emanated from the garage, echoing off the high ceiling with every shot.

"I'll take him. I've hated that guy for two fucking years."

Nick eased around the table and crouched behind a chair, lining his sights up with Bone's head. While Axle had him occupied, Nick pulled the trigger. Just as the bullet left the barrel, Bone dropped his extra clip and bent to grab it. The shot whizzed by, obviously coming from a different direction. Bone jerked his head up, his eyes met Nick's, and the disgusted expression on his face confirmed he knew Axle wasn't the only undercover officer. Nick's choice was gone—he couldn't let Bone live and expose them to the other 300 chapter members.

Axle sprinted to a new position and squeezed off another shot. The bullet hit Bone's shoulder. He spun around and fell to the floor with a howl of pain. Axle moved closer and fired another shot just as Bone rolled behind the door. Silence filled the clubhouse one heartbeat too long.

"Bone! You can't hide from me for long. Come out here and face me like a man, you pussy!" Axle yelled.

"Move to that side and check. I'll take the other. Let's get this motherfucker." Shadow took a covering position beside the door, and Nick joined him on the opposite side. With precision and determination, Shadow slowly pushed the door open to give Nick a better view inside. Not seeing Bone in his field of view, Nick moved farther into the room, his gun drawn and his senses heightened.

"He's gone!" Nick yelled. "He's fucking gone. There's a hidden hallway behind this fucking room!"

Shadow bolted toward the garage, where he'd left Elle waiting. Where he thought she'd be safest. Where she was now a sitting duck for an evil man who would kill her simply out of spite. He jerked the door open and flew into the open room, seeing the ladies huddled together in terror. All he could see was Elle—he had to get to her and protect her from Bone's wrath. An arm extended toward Elle. A finger slid across the trigger. A second passed while Bone focused his aim.

A shot rang out, the noise amplified by the echoes, quickly

followed by a second shot. The first one tore through Shadow's upper side, and the second bullet hit his upper chest. Shadow stumbled as he turned, using his body as a shield for Elle. He raised his gun, seeing Bone was injured worse than he originally thought, and fired six shots into his body—the final shot hitting his head.

The white-hot pain seared his torso, making it hard to breathe. The room began to spin, and his vision began to fade as he turned to Elle. Every move he made took tremendous effort and used up what little strength he had left.

"Elle," he choked out then coughed. He looked down and saw blood on his hand.

Her eyes were wide, filled with fear, and her face was wet with rivers of tears. She wanted to run to him, to comfort him, but she was frozen in place by the growing bloodstains on his shirt. The two enormous spots were quickly becoming one. Her gaze traveled up his body to meet his eyes, and she snapped out of her haze instantly. The sparkle in his eyes that made him unique, that enhanced his entire personality, was fading.

He collapsed to the floor as Nick emerged from the hidden hallway, and Axle appeared in the doorway from the kitchen. "Call an ambulance!" Nick yelled and ran toward Shadow.

Elle lurched from where she'd knelt on the floor and sprinted to his side. "Devon," she cried repeatedly while stroking his face and hair. "Talk to me, Devon. Stay with me."

Sirens rang out from many blocks away, but Elle only heard her own wails when Nick yelled into his phone.

"Tell them to hurry! He has no pulse—I've lost him! He's dead! Man down, we have a man down!" Nick dropped his phone and began doing chest compressions, yelling at his friend to hold on with each push. "Don't you dare die on me now."

Axle opened the roll-up door and flagged down the ambulance. The paramedics rushed to his side and took over CPR from Nick. Elle watched in shock and anguish while they attempted to revive him. Chest compressions continued once they had him loaded into the back of the ambulance.

"I've got no pulse, no respirations. Pupils are nonreactive to light. Patient is nonresponsive to pain stimulation. We're running emergency with lights and sirens. Have the trauma team on standby for our arrival," the paramedic relayed through his radio. The back doors of the ambulance were closed, and they sped away.

CHAPTER TWENTY-THREE

Elle and Beth rushed into the emergency room, frantically searching for Devon. The agents who'd swarmed the old clubhouse told her she couldn't leave. The cops who showed up after the federal agents forbade her from leaving before they'd completed their paperwork. Axle had been her saving grace in that moment. When everyone else told her to wait, he told her to go —before it was too late.

"Where is Devon Kane?" she shrieked at the triage nurse.

"We don't have anyone here by that name," the nurse stammered. "When was he brought in?"

"About thirty minutes ago, by ambulance. Gunshot wound."

"Okay, I know which patient you're talking about now. Are you family?"

"She's his wife," Beth interjected. "She'd like to see her husband."

The nurse looked at her computer screen and back up at Elle. "He's in surgery. They took him straight to the operating room when they got here—didn't stop in the emergency room at all. Go up to the fifth-floor surgical waiting room. The surgeon will come out and talk to you when they're finished."

Elle and Beth made their way to the waiting room, expecting to be the only ones there, but they found a room full of sad, anxious faces instead. They found two seats and sat quietly, holding hands and waiting for an update from the doctor. Elle's eyes stayed glued to the door, willing the surgeon to magically appear, though she could feel eyes on her. She waited for the moment cell phones emerged to snap pictures of her to sell to the paparazzi or for someone to tip off the media where she was.

But she didn't care. She needed answers. She needed to understand what had happened. She needed an explanation that made sense of the chaotic state her emotions lived in.

How can he be part of this?

All the time we spent together, was it all a lie?

No, it couldn't have been. But then, why did he do this?

Is he in trouble? Was he forced to help them?

Doesn't he care about me at all anymore?

Has this been his life all along? Is this why he never let me be part of his life? Why he said it was too dangerous?

Some of the federal agents who'd rushed in after Devon was shot walked into the waiting room. At first, she thought they'd tracked her down, but they moved past her and sat against the wall. Their expressionless faces gave nothing away of their intentions, but Elle assumed they wanted to question Devon almost as much as she did.

"Beth, we have to call our families and Devon's. I've been so crazy, I didn't even think about them until right this second."

"That makes two of us. When I saw him get shot, and all that blood, I think my brain just shut down. I'll go call them right now. You can wait here."

Elle was lost in her thoughts when she heard familiar voices from the hallway. She looked up to see her parents and brothers enter. She rushed into her parents' open arms, feeling safe for the first time in weeks. With hugs and kisses and tears all around, they had a family reunion in the hospital waiting room. She couldn't answer their questions about anything regarding her time held captive by the gang. There were too many aspects of it she needed to understand first.

Her father wrapped his arm around her shoulders and led her

back to the chairs. Beth stepped in front of her and knelt. "Elle, my parents are taking me to the station to answer their questions, then we're going to the apartment. I'll grab some clothes for you. Do you need anything else?"

"No. Thank you, though." She touched Beth's face, thankful to have such a loyal friend.

Beth squeezed her hand and smiled through her tears. "You and I will need therapy after this. You know that, right?"

"Without a doubt."

Beth kissed her cheek before leaving, then lingered in the doorway when second thoughts clouded her mind. She gave Elle a questioning look, but Elle waved her on. It had been quite an ordeal, and Elle understood her need for normalcy, or a semblance of it.

Elle watched Beth disappear around the corner, then kept her vigil over the door while waiting on any news about Devon. Time seemed to stand still and fly by at the same time. She was desperate to know. When a tall doctor's frame darkened the doorway, she decided she was definitely not ready to hear.

"Kane family?" he called into the room.

Elle and her family stood to greet the doctor, and she was startled when eight others quickly stood and gathered around her. She glanced at the men and women around her, not recognizing the first face. She met the doctor's surprised gaze when he asked, "You're all here for Devon Kane?"

"Yes," came the simultaneous reply.

"Okay, looks like we have the room to ourselves. Please have a seat." He waited until everyone sat before he began. "I'm sorry to tell you all Devon died during the surgery. We did everything we could to stabilize him, but the damage from the two bullets was just too much. We couldn't repair it fast enough to stop the internal bleeding. I'm very sorry."

"No! God, please, no!" Elle began screaming. The emotional toll of the past few weeks suddenly took a back seat to the pain rippling through her entire body. "Don't tell me that. Tell me you got him back. He can't be gone. It can't end this way."

Elle's father pulled her close to him, and she sobbed into his chest.

"I'm really very sorry. We did everything we could," the doctor consoled.

"Thank you, Doctor. We're sure you did. It's just a hard pill to swallow," her father replied.

Cries filled the room as the news sank in. He was gone, and they'd never get him back. After everything they'd been through, losing him had never been a thought. It wasn't ever an option. Facing one of their worst fears collectively but separately was their only bond. Everyone in that room loved Devon and felt the loss in their own way. That feeling of profound bereavement covered Elle like a heavy blanket, threatening to crush her and steal the air from her lungs. The pain was becoming unbearable and only increased with each tick of the clock.

"Can we see him?" someone in the room asked.

"I'm sorry. The federal officers have already taken custody of his body as part of their investigation. They're collecting evidence and taking pictures of the gunshot wounds. When they finish, I'm sure we can arrange for you to see him."

"Take me home," Elle whispered to her father. "Please get me out of here. I can't take it anymore." The walls began closing in on her, and she felt as if she were in a shrinking box. If she didn't leave immediately, the whole world would witness her complete and total breakdown. She needed the privacy of her bedroom to process her feelings and work through them one at a time. For as long as it took.

Sympathetic faces watched her stand and walk toward the door, but she couldn't stop to address anyone. All her energy and focus were spent on simply putting one foot in front of the other. One step at a time away from the nightmare. One step at a time in a desperate attempt to flee from the pain and heartbreak. One step at time toward a life that would never be the same again.

THE DAY OF THE FUNERAL WAS HARDER THAN THE DAY HE DIED. ELLE thought the pain couldn't get any worse, until the morning she opened her eyes and realized that was the last day she would ever see him. Every night before she fell asleep, she prayed she'd wake up and all the events would fade away, like a bad dream long forgotten. But her prayer hadn't been answered, and on that day, she had to say goodbye forever.

Goodbye to the only man she'd ever loved.

Goodbye to all the hopes and dreams of their future.

Goodbye to all the lingering questions and doubts that nagged her.

Goodbye to her heart—he'd had it in one way or another since she was a little kid. It was his as much as it was hers, only she didn't want it anymore.

Tracey, Devon's mother, had visited Elle at her apartment since Elle refused to leave home. Their conversation replayed through her mind, further driving her aversion to the memorial service.

"Elle, sweetheart, how are you doing?" Tracey sat on the edge of the bed and studied Elle's appearance and demeanor.

"I should be asking you that, Tracey. This has to be your worst nightmare come true." Elle covered Tracey's hand with hers, their bond of mourning sealed.

"It's our worst nightmare, love. We'll get through it together." Tracey smoothed her hair down. "Devon really loved you, ya know?"

"I thought he did," she replied sadly. "He never said he did, until the day he left me."

Tracey drew back and furrowed her brow. "Of course he did, Elle. He never brought dates around us. Only you. He never went on vacation with anyone else. Every break he had on his job was spent right here with you. Every decision he made was with you in mind—what you needed, what you wanted, what was best for you. He showed you he loved you with everything he did."

"And helping my kidnappers? Was that out of love too?"

"There's actually no greater love than what he did," Tracey replied with tears streaming down her cheeks. "Which brings me to the other reason

why I'm here. This is so hard to say, but I have to. Devon's wish was to be cremated."

"I remember him saying that."

"So, we'll have an open casket viewing for one hour only. That's the longest we can do it…since he won't be embalmed. They'll take him away for cremation after that, but we'll still have the chapel. Do you want to stand up and say a few words?"

"Tracey, I'm sorry to let you down, but I can't speak at his funeral. I can barely make it from here to the shower without becoming hysterical. I'm not even sure how I'll make it through the service at all."

"It's okay." Tracey hushed her when the oncoming panic attack became obvious. "You don't have to. I can't do it either, but I didn't want to take that opportunity away from you. Our pastor is coming to preside over it."

Elle forced herself out of bed and into the shower. She moved through the motions of getting dressed—hair, makeup, dress, shoes. But every task only brought her closer to what she didn't want to do.

"Elle, it's time to go, honey," Beth said from her doorway.

Elle's eyes focused, and she realized she'd been staring at herself in the full-length mirror without even really seeing anything. "Okay."

"Your mom came by last night. You were asleep. She left this and wanted you to take it before we leave." Beth held her hand out and offered the small blue pill.

"What is it?"

"It's for anxiety, to help you get through the day."

She stared at the medication while making up her mind. Did she want to feel everything? Or did she want to simply move through the motions and get it all over with? She snatched the pill from Beth's hand and swallowed it quickly. *I've felt enough,* she thought. *I can't handle more feelings.*

By the time they reached the funeral home, the effects had set in and rendered Elle next to numb. Devon's casket sat at the other end of the room, amid all the flowers. A large US flag was draped over him, the corner of it attached to the inside of the casket lid so it flowed over him in memorium. His picture while on active duty in the Army was displayed on an easel at his feet. She walked on unsteady heels toward him, *for the last time* on repeat in her mind. The closer she got, the slower she walked, until she could no longer deny the truth.

Devon Kane lay in wake in the casket in front of her.

Her knees buckled, and she crumpled to the floor before anyone could grab her. She felt strong arms snake under hers and lift her off the floor then place her in the pew. She looked up and recognized the face of one of the men from the hospital waiting room.

"Thank you," she mumbled.

"You're welcome, my dear," he replied and went back to his seat.

The pastor was talking to Devon's parents when he moved behind the pulpit. Her stomach dropped, knowing his memorial service was actually about to begin. It was all real. Every last horrible detail of it. Everything seemed to happen in slow motion, as if she watched from outside her own body.

"Shadow!" An older woman bellowing drew her out of her misery for a moment. "Get up out of that casket right now!"

"Liz, this is not the time," one of the women hissed at her. Elle continued watching the scene play out, feeling detached from reality.

"It's the perfect time. I'm not falling for his trickery. We all know he's not really dead. This is just to throw everyone off his trail. Shadow, this is your last warning!"

One of the women jumped up and rushed to Liz, trying to stop her. But Liz was obviously a spry little old lady because she evaded capture and rushed the casket. While attempting to climb on top of it, she yelled, "I'm coming to collect my kiss, Shadow. And I'm going to use the tongue. You'd better jump up out of there unless you want *le tongue* in *le French kiss*."

Two of the big, burly men jumped up and ran to her, picking her up off the casket just before she reached his face. She struggled against them, craning her neck in an attempt to reach him.

"For the love of God and all things holy, get off Shadow's casket, Liz!"

"Wait a minute," Liz replied solemnly. "Then Shadow's really gone?"

"Yes, Liz. Shadow is really gone." He pulled her into his arms and consoled her while they made their way back to the pew. Elle knew exactly how Liz felt, even though she didn't know Liz at all.

"I'm so sorry, everyone. Shadow and I always teased and played jokes on each other. I meant no disrespect," Liz announced.

"We know, Liz. Devon told us all about you." Tracey smiled through her tears. "It's okay."

Several men entered the room and took Devon away, wheeling the casket out of the room and away from them. The pastor cleared his throat, choking back emotion, and began the eulogy.

"We're here to celebrate the life of a man who lived his life shrouded in darkness so others may enjoy the freedom of living in the light. His selfless sacrifices didn't lessen the impact he had on others' lives, as we can see from simply looking around the room. His many friends and family are here to pay last respects to a man who rushed into situations everyone else ran away from.

"His wish was to be cremated, but I don't know if most of you were aware of the stipulations he made. He asked that his ashes not be put into an urn. There will be no remains or plaque to visit. He wanted his ashes to be made into a white gold ring that bears his fingerprint. The inscription will read, 'You're my girl—forever,' and it's for someone very special to him."

Elle's gaze snapped up to the pastor's in shock. Tears ran down her cheeks though she paid no attention to them. The pastor smiled sadly at her before he continued. "Miss Elle Moore, his mother told me just this morning the ring will be delivered to you in about four weeks. He loved you very much and wanted you to be happy above all else."

The rest of the eulogy was lost to Elle. Once the tears started, they wouldn't stop. Once the tidal wave of feelings hit her, she drowned in them—every single one. The onslaught was terrible, but the memories they evoked also brought the many happy times, and that comforted her. By the end of the service, she was completely spent.

The four weeks following the funeral were hell on earth for Elle. The first week, everyone stayed to help tie up loose ends. And all of them hovered over her as if she would shatter into a million pieces at any time, putting more pressure on her to be "okay" all the time.

But she wasn't okay and never would be again. That was a given. The brief reprieve from sympathetic eyes came from the demands of the government agencies identified with an initial that demanded to speak with her regarding her ordeal. She'd delayed it as long as she could. Reliving the moment Devon was shot brought it all rushing back to her mercilessly, but she maintained her composure long enough to give them the info they needed. She only hoped it was enough to put those sons of bitches away forever.

Week two brought a different kind of suffering because everyone returned to their regularly scheduled lives, leaving Elle feeling as if she were drifting aimlessly through life. There was no one around to watch her every move except Beth, who was busy looking for a new job. Elle envied her friend in a way. A new job would bring a new start, a clean slate to put all the ghosts of their abduction ordeal behind her. While Elle felt a little bit stronger every day, her heart wasn't in returning to the fake life of a Hollywood starlet.

With the newfound free time she had, her thoughts kept returning to that moment when Devon was shot. She began to remember details that didn't stand out to her at first. Fear had gripped her so tightly while she was in the middle of the chaos, she didn't realize she'd blocked the memory of Bone leveling his gun at her. The panicked expression on Devon's face when he'd entered the garage. The way he'd sprinted across the floor and stopped when he was directly in front of her.

"Did he do that to save me?" she asked herself, pacing back and forth across the room.

"Elle?" Beth asked softly. Elle looked up at her concerned eyes. "Why don't you come with me to therapy? I wasn't kidding when I said we needed it."

"I know. But I'm not ready. I'm just remembering the sequence of events and trying to make sense of everything."

"Okay. Did you hear about the studio?"

"No, I haven't heard anything about anything. What's going on?"

"The studio is closing the lot and filing for bankruptcy." Elle's brows drew downward, her eyes narrowed, and her lips parted. Beth understood Elle's confusion was because she'd cut herself off from the outside world. "Okay, from the beginning. The person behind our abduction was actually a studio executive. He mismanaged investor funds and tried to hide it by delaying movie releases. Anyway, once the gang took him hostage because he double-crossed them, the investors figured out what happened and they withdrew all funding, so the studio has no capital to operate with. They're closing the doors for good."

"What about the movie we just finished? It's scrapped too?"

"Maybe not. Another studio is asking about buying it. There's also talk about a group of investors producing it independently," Beth replied.

"I like option number two better."

Week three post-funeral, Elle started watching the news and began entering the world of the living again. The television was safer than going out in public—not because she was afraid but because she'd become indifferent to everything. For the sake of her own career, should she ever go back to it, she had to maintain appearances. At that moment, she recognized she simply didn't care about anything.

Then the images of the Devil's Dominion club officers flashed across the screen, and she turned the volume up to catch every word the news anchor said.

"These high-ranking members of the Devil's Dominion motorcycle club, one of the infamous one-percenter gangs, have been arrested and denied bail because of their flight risk. Their charges include human trafficking, kidnapping, murder, extortion, and drug trafficking. Federal agencies say they expect to file more charges soon, including organized crime and money laundering.

"Two weeks ago, Detective Joanna Gough's body washed ashore. The gang has been linked to her murder. You'll remember she was the detective in charge of the kidnapping investigation involving Elle Sinclair, Beth

Condra, Katrina Fox, Carrie Snow, and Lori Hensley. Director Vince Rossi and agent Ray Burke have also been indicted on conspiracy charges."

Fueled by rage over what they'd stolen from her, Elle flew up from her seat and moved into action. Just the sight of their faces was enough to turn her stomach, but more than that, she was ashamed of what she'd allowed them to reduce her to.

"No more," she decided. "No more living my life behind closed doors. Devon would've wanted more for me. I want more for me."

CHAPTER TWENTY-FOUR

"I'm so glad you started coming to therapy with me. In group, there are so many people who've decided to speak out because you had to courage to do it. You've changed already from just a week ago. I was honestly getting worried about you." Beth threw her arm around Elle as they strolled on the beach, enjoying the warmth of the sun and the sand beneath their toes.

"Me, too. It's been very helpful. And I'm glad my big mouth helps others when I give them a chance to speak."

"Yeah, you have to take a breath every now and then," Beth teased. "Man, it feels good to laugh and joke again."

They had lunch at an outdoor oceanside café, carefully avoiding certain topics so they wouldn't step back into melancholy, but still enjoying each other's company. "I think it's time we stop tiptoeing around each other and get back to saying what's on our minds like we used to. The more we act normal, the faster we'll feel normal," Elle said between bites.

"Agreed. So, I'm glad you're showering again. That made a nice change to the smell coming from your room."

"Bitch," Elle laughed and threw a piece of her bread at Beth.

With the tension finally broken, she found a new spring in her step and could breathe easier. One step at a time, she was beginning to feel better. She was actually beginning to feel anything again.

Later that evening, Elle and Beth were watching a movie together in Beth's bedroom when the doorbell rang. "I'll get it," Beth announced. "Elle, it's a package for you. Come sign for it," she called from the door.

Elle froze in place, suddenly remembering the date. Four weeks to the day since his funeral. The ring with his fingerprint made partly from his ashes. The last piece of Devon Kane waited for her.

She padded across the apartment toward the front door and grabbed the knob while she steeled her nerves. Anything remotely related to Devon was still a trigger for her, but she was learning to embrace the memories of their good times. She swung the door open with her best face forward, even though it put her acting skills to the ultimate test.

"Elle Moore, this is the only confirmed fingerprint of Devon Kane. Every other print has been expunged from every file accessible anywhere as a safety precaution to national security. I want you to wear it, as part of your bridal set, as a constant reminder of my promise that I'll never leave you again."

She couldn't move. She couldn't breathe. She couldn't speak.

Devon Kane was kneeling down on one knee outside her apartment door. There was only one explanation for that—she'd had a complete break with reality.

"Elle, will you marry me?" Devon extended the ring to her.

To test her sanity, she reached out, took it from him, and slid it onto her finger. It fit perfectly. She admired the unique lines and grooves his fingerprint created.

"Elle?" He stood slowly and slid his hand across her cheek until his fingers threaded through her hair. "Darlin', talk to me. You're scaring me."

She leaned into the warmth of his hand and closed her eyes, lost in her fantasy. Then her eyes flew open when she realized she could feel this daydream. She reached up and touched his face, several days of stubble covering his jaws.

"Devon? Are you real?" she whispered, scared she'd interrupt the best dream she'd ever had if she spoke too loud.

"I'm real, darlin'. It's me, Elle. I know I have a lot to explain, but believe me when I say you'll understand everything when I'm done. I love you, Elle. And I want to spend my life with you as my wife."

Her hands flew to her mouth, covering it after a loud gasp. Her eyes grew big and locked wide open, staring at him and shaking her head from side to side.

"You died. I saw you get shot twice. The ambulance. The surgeon said... The funeral. I went to your funeral!"

"Just listen, okay?" He spoke softly, calmly and approached her cautiously. "I know it was all hell on you. It was on me, too. I've been in the hospital recovering. At my funeral, I was in a medically induced coma, with a special medication to slow my breathing. I knew nothing that happened. That's why my casket was only open for an hour, so they tell me. They had to get me back to the hospital.

"From the beginning, here it is. After I left the Army, I joined the CIA's clandestine black ops team. I've spent most of my life under-cover and pretending to be someone else. That's why I was part of the motorcycle gang. I went in undercover to save you. I would never do anything to hurt you or put you in any kind of jeopardy. Letting you think I was actually part of all that killed me, but I couldn't risk telling you the truth and letting it get out. We'd both have been killed. The best I could do was stay close to you and protect you, so that's what I did."

He explained how Nick, Axle, and Jack were all working together as part of a joint task force to bring the club down. With Nick under-cover DEA, Axle undercover CIA and working through Silas, and Jack being Nick's handler, they had her and the other ladies well covered.

"You brought another actress in." Her statement was disguised as a question, hoping he had a valid answer.

"The actress you saw me bring in the old clubhouse that night was one of their targets, but she participated willingly. She was prepped by trained agents and knew we were coming to get her, but she didn't know which of the gang members were undercover agents. She never saw our faces so she couldn't give us away."

"She never told me."

"She was strongly warned not to say anything. Her life depended on it too. She had a tracking device inserted into her arm just in case." He stepped toward her, tentative in his approach, afraid she would bolt away from him forever. "The past eight years, the only reason I've left your side was because I was on a case. In between working assignments, I was with you. If I was in town on assignment, I checked on you and watched you from a distance, like an obsessed fan. But only because I've hated every second I've been away from you.

"You once asked me who Ava is. She's my little sister, but she was taken from us when she was only five. Kidnapped by a monster. My parents had just bought me a new bicycle for my birthday, and at nine years old, I was preoccupied with tricking out my ride. I took my eyes off her for too long. They must have driven by and snatched her out of the front yard.

"Remember the man who died while we were in St. Lucia? He was a party to her disappearance, and he was there to coordinate the movement of more abducted children. Since I was completely off the grid while we were away, Axle showed up to deliver my orders in person. It was a sanctioned hit, but I gladly killed the man who took my sister away from us. I've blamed myself for what happened all my life, and I've dedicated my every move to protecting innocents as best as I could.

"So many times, I've wanted to lay all my cards out on the table for you to know all about me. I've said repeatedly the only way to leave the CIA is to die. Shadow was my nickname, the only name most people have ever known me as. Shadow died on his last operation and is finally released from the CIA. Devon now stands in front of you, asking for, I believe, the third time—will you marry me?"

"I'm sorry," she replied and watched his face fall. "I'm still trying to catch up to you actually being alive and deciding if I should be mad at how much anguish you've put me through. When I opened the door and saw you there, I actually thought, if I was hallucinating because I'd had a mental breakdown, I didn't want to be put back together. So now I know I'm not crazy, you are real, and you've been a spy and an undercover agent the entire time we've been together. It's...a lot to take in.

"Plus, as I recall, you left me a year ago and haven't been back."

"I've been back many times," he replied quietly. "But I can understand how you're hurt over the secrets and the month since my funeral. To be fair, I've been in the hospital all that time, but you didn't know that. It is a lot to accept and forgive. So I'll go and give you the time to think about everything that's happened. Mull it over. Decide what you want."

He turned to leave, and she noticed his grimace when he moved, the slow pace of his steps, and his hand on the wall for support. The pallor of his skin struck her hard, as did the noticeable weight loss.

"I never said I didn't know what I want, Devon."

He stopped in his tracks, but he didn't turn to face her. "And that is?"

"You. All I've ever wanted is you. All I'll ever want is you. Had you asked me to leave the glamour and glitz of modeling and movies to join the undercover world in the shadows, I wouldn't have thought twice about it as I packed my bags. My first choice has always been you."

She slipped under his arm on his injured side and wrapped her arm around him, gripping the other side tightly. He looked down at her, his eyes overflowing with love. "Let me help you into my apartment. You need to lie down before you fall down."

"You're just trying to get me into your bed."

"Damn straight." She smirked.

His thumb and index finger found the ring on her finger and tilted it slightly from side to side. "Does this mean yes?"

"It means yes. With all of my heart, body, mind, and soul—yes."

She walked him toward her bedroom, and her steps faltered only when she saw Jeff standing in Beth's bedroom doorway with his hand firmly over Beth's mouth.

"It's the only way I could keep her from blabbing." Jeff shrugged and winked, clearly enjoying his role in the game. "I'll be on my way now." He nodded to Devon, his eyes conveying the sincere gratitude he felt inside.

Elle smiled at her brother and continued assisting Devon to her room, then watched with tears brimming in her eyes as he struggled to crawl into the bed. Tears for so many reasons—elation, sadness, concern, and relief. Euphoria topped the list of feelings overwhelming her senses, though. Completely grateful for everything she'd gone through because it only made her that much more thankful to have him back in her life.

"When did you get out of the hospital?"

"About thirty minutes before I rang your doorbell."

She slid into the bed beside him, his back to her front, and gently draped her arm over his side. "Does that hurt?"

"No." He wrapped his hand around hers and pulled her closer to him. "You feel like heaven."

"I have so many questions to ask you."

"Ask away."

"I don't even know where to start," she laughed.

"We have the rest of our lives, darlin'."

She raised up on one elbow and put her chin on his shoulder. "So, black ops. Does that mean you know how to torture people for information?"

He slowly turned his head until he could see her. "That's the first thing you want to know? Out of everything you could possibly ask?"

"It was the first question that popped up in my mind," she giggled.

"Fuck, I've missed you so much."

"Can I see your scars?"

One corner of his mouth lifted slightly, then he grabbed the hem of his shirt and began pulling it up. She sat up on the bed behind him and helped. She expected to see raised lines of red, angry skin from the bullet holes and surgeries, but the wounds barely had a pink tinge. The outer edges already matched his normal skin tone. She ran her fingers over the barely visible scars.

"I can't believe the wounds are completely healing without leaving a scar," she marveled.

"The agency called in the best doctors. I was lucky to be in LA and have immediate access to the best plastic surgeons in the world."

She continued her examination of his wounds, letting her hands roam freely over his back and side. When she reached his lower back, she stopped and examined the raised white skin. There were two larger letters on top—DD—and three smaller letters curved underneath it—KSD. "What is this?"

"Nothing you need to worry about, darlin'."

"Devon, no more secrets. Please."

He raked his hand down his face and exhaled slowly. "It's not a secret, Elle. You can see what it says. *Devil's Dominion. Kill, Steal, and Destroy.* The same wording as on their patches. They branded me as part of the initiation."

Elle dropped her chin to her chest, closed her eyes, and quieted the frantic thoughts running through her mind. The ordeal was over, and the memories couldn't hurt her. She inhaled deeply, a peaceful calm enveloping her as specific memories returned to her and reality dawned.

I prayed he'd return to me, and he's here.

"You're my girl—forever."

"I love you and only you, all my life."

He was undercover to save me.

He risked his life multiple times for me.

"That's not all they did to you, is it?"

"During initiation? No. But I'm okay, Elle. You don't need to worry about me. I'm a big boy. I can take care of myself."

She crawled over him, careful of his healing wounds, and lay facing him. "You can, there's no doubt about that. But you don't have to do it alone, in the darkness of the wicked shadows anymore. You've protected me so I can walk freely in the light. Now it's time for us to walk together."

"Every day, Elle, for the rest of your life. Just try to get rid of me. I'm your shadow now."

He slid his hand to the back of her neck and pulled her face to his. When their lips touched, the intense yearning consumed them, burning with a new intensity. The year apart hadn't extinguished the flames of their desire. The gentle peck quickly became a passionate embrace. Hands desperate to touch. Skin demanding to be caressed. Bodies hungry for more of anything and everything they could get.

Gentle hands slid her shirt off, revealing the smooth, creamy skin beneath. Deft fingers unhooked her bra before he rolled her to her back. His lips trailed down her jaw, to her neck, over the hollow space at her collarbone, continuing until he reached her bare breast. The warmth of his mouth covered the hardened tip of her nipple, sending electricity zinging along every nerve ending in her body. The sensation shot directly between her legs, igniting the craving for what only he could give her.

Devon took his time, ignoring her no-so-subtle cues to rush him. He'd thought about this moment so often, planning every move he'd make in his mind. He ravished her body in his designed sequence with no conscious effort. Every second was committed to memory. Every sound she made. The scent of her skin. The weight of her breast in his hand. The aroma of her arousal that grew with his ministrations. The sharp intake of breath when he slid lower down her body. The way her fingers gripped his hair when his tongue laved her abdomen. Her enthusiasm and eagerness to remove the rest of their clothes.

He shifted lower, anchoring his body between her legs, spreading them to make enough room to carry out his mission. He changed positions gingerly, ignoring the lingering pains and focusing on the incredible pleasure that awaited him. He lowered his head, lightly brushed his face against her sex, and inhaled her unique bouquet before covering her clit with his lips. He looped his tongue around it, his forcefulness increasing with each circle.

Her hips bucked under his grip as the intensity grew. He flicked her sensitive nub with his tongue, her moans spurring him to take what belonged to him. At that moment, her ultimate pleasure was what he wanted most. To hear his name fall from her lips in the culmination of her gratification. He licked up her slit, lapping up the proof of her desire, until he reached her swollen core. His teeth grazed across her clit when he pulled it into his mouth, sucking harder on it before teasing her entrance with his finger, gliding up and down until her essence coated his fingertip.

Hungry for more, he slid his finger inside her wet channel, easy at first then with more vigor when her body naturally adapted to accept the carnal invasion. She lifted her hips higher, giving him full access and wordlessly asking for more. Her fingers dug into his shoulders, her nails biting into his skin while her inner muscles contracted around his finger. His lips, his tongue, his teeth, his hands—they all claimed her, wanted to own her, needed to possess her.

When his name rang out through the room, carried on the sweetest music he'd ever heard, he made a decision he'd never thought possible. He surrendered, willingly. Deliberately. Purposely. He acknowledged his feelings ran deeper than the usual declaration of love. Only she awakened the part of him that wanted a normal life. Only she matched him in every way, complemented his flaws with her perfection, and propelled him to forsake everything he'd worked toward in exchange for a new life goal.

"Devon." Her voice was breathy, still reeling from her carnal high. "Let me help you out of your clothes. You've spent enough energy. It's time for you to lie on your back and enjoy the view for a while."

His cock twitched from the visual her offer inspired. After he stood, she scooted to the edge of the bed and began removing his jeans. She unconsciously licked her lips when her eyes landed on the bulge in his boxer briefs. She looked up at him from under her lashes, emboldened by how desire had darkened his eyes to almost black, and smiled seductively.

"I thought you were always commando."

"Now that I'm out of the hospital and never leaving your side, you'll be lucky to get me in pants again, much less briefs. You can keep these as a souvenir—the last pair I'll ever wear."

She kept her gaze locked on his while she slid them down his legs. His cock sprang free and stood at attention against his abdomen. Her soft hand flowed up his shaft, gripping tightly as she teased and tormented him in the most delicious manner. Her fingers clutched the hem of his shirt and carefully pulled it over his head. With his clothes shed and his body bared, she motioned for him to take his place on the bed.

Propped up on pillows, he watched with hooded eyes as she placed open-mouthed kisses across his chest. Her tongue darted out, leaving a wet trail of affection on his skin. Across his ripped abdominal muscles, she licked and tasted every ridge and dip. Her fingers glided over his body until they touched the tip of his cock. The bead of moisture drew her attention downward, and she hungrily took him into her mouth, as far as she could until he hit the back of her throat. She relaxed the muscles, taking him deeper, and he groaned in ecstasy.

While working her mouth and hand in tandem up and down him, she focused on giving him as much pleasure as he'd given her. When she went down, she held the tip at the back of her throat and intentionally mimicked swallowing, forcing her neck muscles to contract around his head like a soft, velvety clamp. His hands gripped her hair, and he called her name with a throaty grunt. Sensing he was close to the edge, she pumped and sucked until the overload of pleasure left him no choice but to abandon his control and succumb to his release.

He tugged on her arm and guided her to lie next to him, securely tucked into his side, wrapped in his arms, and enveloped by his love. The roller coaster of emotions she'd lived on came to a crashing halt after she relaxed, melting into him. The tears she was sure had dried came back with a renewed vengeance. She couldn't hold them back. The hot, salty tracks covered her face and soaked his chest. He lifted his hand to her face, cradled her wet cheek in his palm, and gently raised her head to look at him.

"Talk to me, darlin'. Don't try to hold it all in."

She smiled through her tears, a bright, happy smile that lit up her whole face. "For the first time in a long time, I am so happy." She emphasized each word, amazement prevalent in her voice. "You're here with me—alive, on the mend, but otherwise healthy—and you proposed to me."

"And you said yes. That means you've agreed to be my sex slave for the rest of your life. This is a binding legal agreement with no exit clause. You belong to me and only me for all time."

"Like any of that is a surprise to me," she joked, her giggles filling the air with joy and love. "But the best part is you belong to me for all time."

"Yes, I do, darlin'. Always have—always will. I'd walk into hell and slay the devil for you."

"I believe you. You already have."

Despite her protests that he hadn't healed enough, he rolled her over onto her back and covered her body with his. His hard cock rested between her legs at the entrance to her wet core. She was ready for him with a single touch. Her body craved his, but she'd been too concerned with his injuries to encourage him. Who was she to deny him when he was so insistent, though? Her body hummed with need, waiting for him to finish what he'd started.

His arms framed her face, and his expression conveyed his profound love. He sank into her one inch at a time until he was fully seated inside, giving her body a moment to accept and adapt to his size. Her muscles quivered around him, gripping him tightly and urging him to keep moving. With slow, deliberate strokes, he surged into her repeatedly until his sweat mixed with hers during an erotic dance built for two. All their emotions poured out of them as promises of a forever love fell from their lips. The crescendo of their encounter built to an unbelievable high that ended in their mutual climax.

"You are my world, Elle. The last year has shown me I'm dead without you. You are the breath that sustains me. You bring me to life, make me feel, and give me hope for a normal life. I wouldn't even be here now it if weren't for you. Thoughts of seeing you, talking to you, and loving you are what pulled me through the darkest days in the hospital. I couldn't die with you thinking I'd done anything but protected you with my last breath."

"I should've known. Maybe a part of me did. None of it made sense to me. I couldn't reconcile the Devon I knew with the Doorman I met. But I have no doubts now—you've always been my Devon."

The next morning over breakfast, Elle cast furtive glances toward him. A few times, she started to ask another question but stopped herself before she started. Devon finally set his fork down and rested his elbows on the table.

"If you don't ask me whatever it is you want to know, I'm going to hold you down and use my torture techniques to make you talk." The mischievous gleam in his eyes was back, the signature twinkle a little brighter.

"Who knew you weren't really dead?"

He knew that question would come, and he braced himself for her reaction. "Besides the agency, only my parents and the guys at Steele Security."

"They knew, but no one could tell me for a whole month? I could've been at the hospital with you. I could've helped you, and knowing you were alive would sure as hell have helped me. Do you have any idea how miserable and depressed I've been?" The more she thought about it, the angrier she became. "That was really shitty, Devon."

"Can I explain?"

"That would be best."

"Easy there, tiger. My condition was touch and go there at first. If I didn't pull through, there was no reason to put you through that again. My parents were my beneficiaries and had medical power of attorney, so they had to be there to make decisions for my care. The guys have a high enough security clearance to be read in on the plan. While evidence was gathered and charges brought against the gang, my condition had to be kept secret for my safety. When I was coherent enough to make my own decisions, I planned my return to the living and my marriage proposal. Though, I did see it all going very differently in my mind."

"Oh, yeah? How?"

"You know...you falling at my feet, grasping my leg, thanking God for my safe return." He smiled and winked, instantly defusing her anger over his deception.

"If you ever fake your death again without telling me first, I'll kill you."

"Fair enough. You'll be the first to know next time."

She threw her wadded-up napkin at him while laughing. She couldn't be mad if she tried—she was simply too happy and blessed to let anything from the past impact her bright future.

"Oh, and, darlin'? Can you clear your schedule next week?"

"What do you have in mind?"

"There are four other women in Miami I have to go face and take my lashes. I want you to go with me and meet everyone. They're dying to meet you."

"I'd love to meet them, and my schedule happens to be wide open for the foreseeable future."

"Good. I have plans for you every single day. Forever."

CHAPTER TWENTY-FIVE

"You're moving around so much better than you were last week." Elle watched Devon get out of the bed and walk to the bathroom. The light pink scars had faded to his natural skin color even more. Her eyes drifted to the brand seared into his skin. *Funny how the memory of what happened doesn't bother me as much as it did last week,* she thought. *My scars are fading too.*

"I can feel your eyes on my ass." He smirked at her over his shoulder. "Don't be shy. You can look all you want."

"Yeah, I know I can. As fine as it is, that's not actually where my eyes landed this time."

"You're staring at my brand again. Does it bother you that much? Do you want me to have it removed?" He turned to face her, sincerely interested in her reply. Then he shook his head and chuckled when her eyes dropped to his package. "Hey. My eyes are up here."

"It's your fault for going commando and pantless." She met his amused gaze and continued. "The brand doesn't bother me. And no, I don't want you to have it removed because that would mean more surgery and pain for you. A month ago, it may have freaked me out, but I can't honestly say. It already feels like a lifetime ago. I'm just thankful everything worked out the way it did in the end."

"Okay. If you're sure."

"I'm positive."

"Now get your fine ass out of bed so we don't miss our flight to Miami. I'm taking you home to meet the family of Steele."

Packed and ready to leave, they climbed into the taxi and Devon gave the address. Elle looked at him, her eyebrows raised in question. "Private airport. I have a little surprise for you."

When they reached the small airport, Elle stepped out of the car, and the private Steele Security jet on the tarmac immediately caught her attention. She helped Devon get their bags since he was still under strict orders not to lift anything heavy, and she'd packed her entire wardrobe for the trip.

"I've never been on a private jet before. This is exciting."

"You really need to use your star status more effectively. There's no reason why you shouldn't have already had a private flight. Unless it means you fly privately with some other guy. In which case, you fly coach."

"No one else will ever compare to Devon Kane," she replied automatically.

"What?" He stopped walking and waited for an explanation. "You said that so offhandedly, like you've said it a thousand times."

"I have—at least that many times. Whenever anyone encouraged me to move on, date someone else, tried to convince me there are other fish in the sea, that was my standard response. You have no reason to worry or be jealous of anyone. No other man has ever compared to you—and no other man ever will."

"Just when I think there's no way I could love you more, you prove me wrong again." He bent his head and kissed her sweetly. "I love you."

"I love you too." She beamed.

Devon took his seat while Elle examined every square inch of the private Steele Security jet. "Oh, my God—there's a bedroom back here!"

Devon laughed at her excitement, thrilled he was experiencing it with her. Unable to sit still, he joined her at the back of the plane.

"There is a bedroom. And it has a bed." He leaned against the door and watched her, his libido kicking into overdrive.

"I know that look. You can stop devouring me with your eyes right now, mister. The flight attendant will know exactly what we're doing back here. No, Devon." She tried to sound stern, serious. But even she wasn't that good of an actress.

"Elle, you worry way too much about what others think. What's the worst that would happen if she heard us? She'd tell the rag magazines, they'd run an article saying you're part of the mile-high club, and every man in the world would know it was with me. I don't see the downside. But the upside is we get to have sex and join the mile-high club." He closed the door behind him and advanced on her like a tiger stalking its prey.

Four hours later, they emerged from the bedroom in time to prepare for landing. Devon couldn't hide his amusement over Elle's red face every time the flight attendant approached them. "She knows what we were doing back there," Elle hissed at him. "I'm so embarrassed."

The ride from the airport to Noah's secluded mansion passed quickly. Before she knew it, they'd turned into the driveway and the driver pressed the call button on the state-of-the-art security system. The gate slid open, giving them access to the grounds with no questions asked. Elle watched intently as the estate came into view.

"Devon, what's going on? What are they doing?" She pointed to the odd scene on the ornate front lawn. In the middle of the expertly manicured and professionally landscaped setting stood four women, four men...and five large doghouses.

"Is it too late to pretend our flight was delayed?" Devon deadpanned.

"Yes, considering they can see us, and they're already motioning for us to come to them."

He sighed, resigned to accept his punishment like a man, and opened the door. "Here we go. Oh, before we get out, I'm sorry now for whatever Liz does or says."

"Liz?"

"Shadow, get out of that car right this second." Liz stood a few feet away with her hands on her hips, her lips in a tight, firm line, and her eyes on fire with anger.

"That's Liz," he replied to Elle. "Liz, sweetheart, how are you?"

"Don't try to sweet-talk me. It didn't work for these four, and it won't work for you either."

Elle watched as men emerged from the house and took their luggage inside the stately mansion. A quick glance in Devon's direction told her to relax, as their actions must be commonplace. He laced his fingers with hers and walked toward the waiting hosts. The closer they got, the more confused Elle became.

She recognized the men from Devon's funeral, though she didn't know their names. Except Liz. But then, everyone in the chapel knew her name that day.

"Elle, this is Noah 'Reaper' Steele and his wife, Brianna."

"Hello, nice to meet you," she said to Brianna first and shook her hand.

"Elle, we wanted to approach you in the hospital waiting room, but it just didn't seem like the right time. You'd been through so much already, and we didn't want to appear to be insensitive fans. I'm so glad to meet you now."

"Thank you. I wasn't in the best frame of mind, so keeping your distance was probably best," Elle chuckled.

Her gaze drifted up to Noah's, and she reacted before she could stop herself. Her eyes grew wide and her lips parted—but no words would come out. "Umm," she stammered. "It's nice to meet you."

Noah offered his hand, and Elle hesitated briefly before accepting it. From the corner of her eye, she saw Devon cover the smile that split his face in two. "Very nice to meet you, Elle."

"You're the one who picked me up off the floor and set me in the pew," she said while staring a little too long at his lips. "Thank you so much for doing that. I would've stayed on the floor had you not."

"It was the least I could do for you."

Devon snickered beside her and tried to hide it with a fake cough.

"Something to say, Shadow?" Reaper asked, lifting one eyebrow in challenge.

"Nope. Not a thing. Elle, this is Colton 'Bull' Lanier and his wife, Chaise. Noah and Chaise are brother and sister."

Elle found herself in the same predicament when she greeted Bull and Chaise. And Devon didn't help when he unsuccessfully tried to hide his laughter. After Bull cordially addressed Elle, he threatened Devon with, "I'm kicking your ass as soon as you're healed. Fucker."

Devon wore a huge, shit-eating grin when he steered Elle away from Bull and to the next couple. "This is Braxton 'Rebel' Reed and his wife, Heather."

"Elle, it's great to meet you. My condolences to you on what will happen to Shadow the second he's healed enough to take his beating."

She had no idea what they meant, but she couldn't take her eyes off Rebel's lips or his fingernails.

"Don't pay any attention to Rebel, Elle. The heat down here fries his brain sometimes," Devon explained. "This is Silas Steele, Noah and Chaise's older brother."

"Elle, I'm so glad everything turned out well for you after your ordeal. You should probably purchase big-and-tall-sized diapers for Shadow as soon as possible. He'll need them for a while after we get through with him."

"You too, Silas? That hurts," Devon lied through his smiling teeth. "And, my love, this is Liz."

"I knew you were faking it at the funeral. Hello, sweet girl. How are you? You didn't fool me for one minute, Shadow. I'm so sorry you have to witness this, Elle, but it's best for us all. What you did is just unforgivable and inexcusable, Shadow. Did you have a nice flight, dear? Now that you're here, it's time for you to face the music."

Elle attempted to keep up with Liz's conversation. She was terrifying and angry when she addressed Devon, then loving and grandmotherly when she spoke to Elle. Liz had carried on two entire conversations, in two distinctly different tones, without taking a single breath.

Liz picked up a small black makeup bag and retrieved two vials of fingernail polish. Her keen eyes snapped up to Devon's and held an inherent threat. The other men smiled broadly.

Reaper's pink leopard-print-colored lips spread across his face. Bull's lips were white with pink, blue, and green dots covering them. Rebel's lips had been painted with a bright, sparkling blue polish. Silas's appeared to be black stripes on a bright orange background, until he closed his lips. Then the word "TRAITOR" could be read clearly. Their fingernails matched the colors used on their lips. And apparently, Devon was her next target.

"What's the story behind the nail polish?" Elle finally asked.

"It goes with the doghouses. Each man out here has one. We even painted names on their specific homes. They lied to us, let us believe Shadow was dead instead of letting us in on the ruse. They didn't trust us enough, so they had to be punished," Liz explained. "Did you know?"

"No, I knew even less than you did. And I was mad at him for about a second, but then I remembered how hard I'd prayed to wake up from that nightmare and have him back with me. Being left out of the loop when his life was in danger didn't seem like a big deal then. Though, I did threaten him if he ever pulls that on me again."

"Oh." Liz dropped the polish back into the bag, her voice flat and her eyes downcast. "I didn't think of it that way. Maybe I should've talked to you before I painted these guys. You're right. His life is more important, and we were all so thrilled to learn he was okay."

Four large and angry men began shouting and pointing at once.

"Do you know how long we've been wearing this shit?"

"I actually slept all night in the fucking doghouse!"

"No way does he get out of his punishment! I'll hold him down and paint him myself!"

"I took my punishment like a man! Now he will too!"

Liz kept talking to Elle as if a brawl weren't about to break out in front of them. "If you're not upset, then I'm not either. Besides, I knew it was all fake. Tracey told me before the funeral."

All the yelling stopped cold.

"You knew?" Silas asked.

"Of course. Took you long enough to get me off the casket. I thought I'd actually get that kiss I've been hankering for."

Silas glared at her, the ability to connect letters into those things they made had escaped him.

"What? What's the problem?" Liz prompted him.

"We all took our punishment...but you knew."

"Did you hide it from us?"

"Yes, but—"

"No buts. You knew. You hid it. You got punished. Now, imagine what I would've done if I hadn't known the truth. Chew on that for a while."

Devon leaned down and kissed Liz's cheek, then winked. "Thanks for always having my back."

"My pleasure, my boy. Now it's time for us to get to know this pretty little lady." Liz took Elle's hand in hers and led her to the house, leaving everyone else standing on the front lawn, by their assigned doghouses, in shock. Devon watched them walk together, then realized he'd been left alone with the angry mob. He sprang into action, holding his side while he took long strides to reach Elle's side and Liz's protection.

Later that evening, after the men had scrubbed all of the skin off their lips and removed the polish from their nails, they sat on the back deck. Steaks, chicken, and seafood cooked on the grill. The team was all together, laughing and sharing stories again as if nothing had happened. Elle felt welcomed with open arms and became instant best friends with the ladies.

Devon leaned over and placed a chaste kiss on her cheek while she talked with Brianna. She turned and looked at him thoughtfully. "What was that for?"

"Because I love you. Because I'm so glad you never gave up on me all the years I was such an idiot. Because I can't imagine ever being happy again if I lost you. Because I finally understand why these guys can't function without their better halves and why they'd move hell and earth to reach their loves, and God help anyone who gets in their way. Because if I had to choose between having decades to live alone undercover, or only one night, but it was with you, I'd choose you every time."

Elle kissed his lips, lingering and savoring the moment. "We'll never have to be apart again, my love. There's never been a remote possibility of you losing me. No matter what happened, I've always loved you. And I'll always love you, no matter what happens."

"I'm so happy for you two," Brianna gushed. "Have you decided on a wedding date yet?"

"No, we haven't even talked about it yet. Devon has been healing and getting stronger. I haven't decided what I'm going to do now that the studio closed and my movie hasn't released yet. I don't even know if it will release now. Nothing in my life is definite except this man beside me."

"We're getting married as soon as possible, and I'm keeping her chained to the bed the entire first year," Shadow added.

The group laughed, but they didn't doubt he'd actually try to do what he'd threatened. Silas leaned forward and steepled his fingers. "Actually, I wanted to talk to you both about that."

"About chaining my woman to the bed? Do you have a death wish?" Shadow fired back.

"No and no," Silas replied sardonically. "I mean talk about what you're going to do next. Steele Security is here. The studio lots are in LA. Are you moving to California? Is Elle moving to Miami? Have you thought about what you're going to do next, Shadow?"

"Not really. I'm waiting for inspiration to hit me. Or for Elle to demand I move in with her. Or for Elle to demand to move in with me. Or for Elle to demand we move to Kansas and commute to work."

"That's what I thought. So I have an early wedding present for you." Silas pulled a business card out of his wallet. "The offshore account the gang used to launder money, courtesy of the CIA for your years of valuable service to your country. You were grievously injured in the line of duty during a join CIA-DEA-ATF-FBI investigation, so you've been awarded hazard pay, too."

Silas handed the card to Elle. "Since Shadow died during the investigation, the funds go to his beneficiary. As of today, that's you. Don't spend it all in one place."

Elle narrowed her eyes at Silas, unsure if he was joking, before inspecting the card. "Holy shit! The motorcycle club made that much money?"

"Yes, and more, but they made it for you when they kidnapped you and killed my friend. Payback is a bitch."

"Thank you, Silas. I don't even know what else to say. This is incredible." Elle showed the card to Devon and turned to him, bouncing in her seat with excitement. "Babe, I have an idea. This is perfect."

"Let's hear it. I'm all ears."

"What if we split this with the other ladies, and we all executive produce the movie on our own? Buying it from the bankruptcy court will cost a lot less than trying to buy it from the studio. The royalties we'll make on it will pay out for years."

"That's a great plan," Silas interjected. "Except, each of the ladies has their own account. Not as hefty as yours, but enough."

"Perfect. What do you think, Devon?"

"I'm with you, sugar momma." He leaned over and kissed her.

"Do you need more executive producers?" Reaper asked and turned to Brianna with a smile.

"You have something in mind, Reap?" Shadow asked.

"Yeah. We've all discussed what would happen when we decided we're coming out of the firefight and into suburban life. I see an excellent opportunity for us to get out of the security field and into the movie industry. If we buy in now, we'll start on the ground floor with a major A-lister movie for a fraction of the cost."

"You want to close Steele Security?" Bull asked.

"If all of you are in on this, yes. This can be our new business, and we won't have to worry about making it home to our wives and kids in one piece," Reaper replied.

"We're in," Rebel replied, hugging Heather to him. "Come on, Bull—you know it's time to hang up your camouflage hat and ghillie suit."

Bull turned to Chaise, silently asking her opinion. "Let's do it, babe. A brand-new adventure for the crew."

"All right, then. We're in too," Bull replied. "Let's own this bitch and take Hollywood by storm."

"Silas?" Reaper asked.

"I'll be a silent partner. You can't put my name on anything, but I'll buy in."

"Look what you did, darlin'," Shadow teased Elle. "You just got me fired."

EPILOGUE

Fall at the winery was the perfect time of year for an outdoor wedding. The sycamore trees lining the driveway from the main road to the house were in full spectacular color. The bright yellows, oranges, and reds in the surrounding oak and aspen grove mixed with the changing grapevines and provided the perfect backdrop against the still lush green grass.

Devon stood with the pastor under the canopy, waiting for Elle to make her grand entrance. While he waited, he soaked in the features around him so he wouldn't forget a single detail. The garden area was beautifully decorated with a variety of fall-colored planters and flowers. The October air was crisp and invigorating, the slight breeze gentle enough to be comfortable in the setting sun.

The path Elle would take to him was adorned with thick grass, manicured hedges, and white marble statues. The walking bridge over the reflection pool was what sealed the deal for Elle, but the reception area was a close second. Pergolas over linen-covered tables with hanging paper lanterns and candles in glass jars on the tables completed the ambiance. Knee-high hurricane candles were staggered along the pathway and around the pool. The guest chairs were draped in matching linens, completing her dream wedding theme.

Beth, Brianna, Chaise, and Heather emerged first, escorted by Jeff, Reaper, Bull, and Rebel. When the music changed to the wedding march, Shadow craned his neck to see Elle. She'd insisted on keeping her wedding gown a secret from him and had spent the night at her parents' house, away from him, the night before. One night away from her was more than enough. Over the past year while they'd worked the movie junkets and planned their wedding, he hadn't spent more than a few hours apart from her. The sudden change was not welcomed or appreciated.

Then she stepped into view, escorted by her father, and he forgot every other detail. All he could see was the most beautiful woman in the world walking to him. To stand by his side. For better or for worse. Through sickness and health. Till death claimed them both, for real this time.

She wore a floor-length gown, the train extending behind her only slightly. The top was sheer, with lace appliques strategically placed to give the illusion of much less fabric. The waist tapered in to show off her figure and elegance. Her hair was curled and piled high on her head in a perfectly messy heap. Small flowers and baby's breath were secured inside the ringlets, giving her a graceful and carefree effect.

When she reached the last row of guest chairs, she smiled at him, and pride swelled in his chest. The moment he'd always said would never happen couldn't happen soon enough. He was marrying the love of his life. He was giving her his name. She moved closer to him, her eyes sparkling with unshed tears of happiness.

Her father passed her hand to Devon, and she gripped his tightly. Her lifeline, her rock, her love—her everything. The demons of the past no longer plagued her because the life she'd built with Devon drove out all the wicked shadows. They lived every moment in the light, grateful for one more day together, thankful for every night in each other's arms.

The pastor went through the usual verbiage found in a wedding, but they'd written their own vows to each other.

"Elle, I promise you will never regret agreeing to be my wife. My sole purpose in life is simultaneously to make you happy, give you more love than you've ever known, and fill our home with light and laughter. I promise to be the best husband, friend, confidant, and partner I can be. Your needs will come first, always. All I ask in return is that you're my girl—forever."

He slid the wedding band onto her finger and raised it to his lips.

"Devon, since the day I met you, you've owned my heart in one way or another. As a little kid, you were my hero. When I was a young adult, you were my love. Our love and relationship progressed, and you became so much more. My champion, my cheerleader, my savior, my best friend, my partner, my very heart. I promise I will be all these things and more for you. I promise to love you until my dying breath, and then take that love to the afterlife with me, where I'll wait for you to join me again. I promise to be there when you wake in the morning and when you go to sleep at night, giving you whatever you need or want. I promise to love you and only you unconditionally for all time."

She slid the wedding band onto his finger.

With a long, lingering kiss, they sealed their union in front of their family and friends. The bond had always been there—tried, tested, and true.

After the reception dinner, Mark turned on the lights around the dance floor and had the DJ fire up the sound system. Devon and Elle took the floor alone for their first dance as husband and wife. She melted into his arms, still eager for his embrace after having him at her beck and call for more than a solid year. She accepted and embraced she'd never grow tired of him. She'd never not want him with her.

The night she spent alone was proof of that. She awoke several times and picked up her phone, nearly calling him to her each time. She was amazed she'd been strong enough to resist.

"I missed you last night," she admitted.

"Darlin', I missed you too. I almost drove up here to climb in your window. I don't know how I ever slept without you."

"Same. I got no sleep last night."

"You won't get any sleep tonight either."

"I don't want to sleep tonight. I want you."

"You have me—all night, every night, forever."

"It's a good thing we're already packed for our honeymoon then, isn't it?"

"Yes, ma'am. I'm so looking forward to our two weeks in St. Lucia. Back to our spot. Our room. Our happy place."

"I've found my happy place. It's wherever you are."

"That's all I want. Because I'll be wherever you are. You're my girl —forever."

And they lived...*happily ever after.*

~

Keep reading! A FREE sample of Her Dom and Fine Line are included in this ebook. You'll also find Shadow and Nick Tucker in the Dominic Powers duet.

~

FINE LINE

A Terrible Idea
Nick

"FOR THE RECORD, THIS IS A TERRIBLE IDEA."

My director, Calvin Montgomery, locks his angry eyes on me while speaking to the handler who will be assigned to me—if Calvin approves the operation, that is.

"Sir, Special Agent Nick Tucker has repeatedly proved what a valuable asset he is in the field. He's one of our best. He has outscored most of his peers in both field and psychological profile tests—even those who have previous undercover experience. We can't deny the man has the skills we need on this assignment. He deserves this chance."

"Yes, I can read the reports as well as you can, Jack. But Nick doesn't have any true undercover experience—not even on short-term cases, and the others do. Maybe they didn't score as well on the psych tests because they're already accustomed to living among the criminal element and acting as one of them. Did that ever occur to you? We both know how hard this life is even for a few months, but the case you're asking me to put Nick on is potentially a multiyear mission."

Calvin turns his penetrating gaze to me, constantly assessing my every reaction, looking for a weakness and a reason to deny my involvement. I've been in hectic firefights before and kept my cool, though. My time in the military, working for Steele Security, and providing private security for billionaire Dominic Powers before joining the DEA prepared me for most every perilous situation they can throw at me. Drawing on my inner strength, I keep my expression passive, my breathing regular, and my instinct to remind him he's driven a desk for too many years to remember what working in the field is actually like under wraps.

"You'll be cut off from everyone you know, Nick. You'll essentially divorce your entire life—for years. Your friends, your family, wife, girlfriend, boyfriend. *Everyone.* You hear me? And that's the easy part of the job. Even contact with Jack will be sparse, especially due to the group you'll infiltrate, so you'll be making decisions on the fly. Any outside affiliation will be scrutinized—and these guys won't ask questions first. They'll shoot you in the head and replace you with the next guy in line. I'm not convinced you truly understand what you'll have to do to be one of them."

"I can assure you, I do understand."

"Is that right? This UC op has been issued special permission to break the very laws you've sworn to uphold. Your psych profile shows a strong sense of duty and a penchant for following the rules to the letter. So, you'd be fine if they order you to force some young kid to sell drugs on the street corner and bring you every penny of the money he made? Then rough him up if he doesn't bring you enough?"

The visual that pops into my brain before I can stop it makes my heart rate increase instantly, the artery in my neck jerking and giving away my reaction.

"Or maybe it's not a him. Maybe it's a her. You'd willingly force a young woman into prostitution, selling her to any Joe Blow off the street, who'll do whatever the fuck he wants to do to her? You can make them believe you don't care about her at all, just how much money she brings in for getting her John's rocks off? What if that means her customer gets to beat the shit out of her just because he has mommy issues? I mean, as long as he doesn't kill her and she can perform for her next trick, what the fuck does it matter, right?"

My stomach churns with disgust, and the room around me turns red with my rage. But I tamp down those feelings inside my chest until they form a mangled ball full of drive and determination to see this through to the end.

"I'll do whatever the fuck I have to do to stop these bastards. The longer we sit here repeatedly arguing the same points and imagining hypothetical situations, the more time they have to commit those very crimes. Sir."

"I'm sure I don't have to remind you we're after the major charges to shut them down for good. Small-time hoods are a dime a dozen. We want the source—their suppliers. Local reports say this group is using a prescription drug that hasn't even cleared the FDA yet. It's highly effective and lethal in the wrong hands. That's in addition to the influx of opioids and other controlled substances from their

Mexican drug cartel affiliation. We can't blow the entire operation because you feel the need to feed your savior complex over every sob story you hear. Most of those women asked for it anyway—they probably even enjoy it."

"I'm well aware of what we're after and how to do my job." Inside, I'm seething; outside, I display a calm demeanor.

He's testing me, that much I know. His last comment was to gauge my knee-jerk reaction because that's exactly how this gang thinks. If Calvin approves my request for undercover work, the group I'll join will say and do a lot worse to me than my director has ever even thought about. If I can't handle my boss yanking my chain inside the comfort of his office in our secure, air-conditioned building, I have no business being an undercover agent where anything and everything can go wrong.

Will go wrong.

Something always does.

To stay alive, I have to think fast on my feet, improvise, and give an award-winning performance.

No time like the present to start earning a few of those golden statuettes.

"Sir, I can handle anything they throw at me. I've been in intense situations in my career, starting in the Army, through private details, and in my time with the DEA. I'm ready to take my career to the next level, and I need undercover experience to do that. This wasn't Jack's idea—I requested to be assigned to this case."

The muscles around Calvin's eyes contract, crinkling the skin until only small slits remain. He draws a slow circle around his mouth with his thumb and forefinger before resting his chin on his hand. With my gaze locked on to his, I wait for him to make his decision. The first one to blink will be Calvin, because I am all in.

"All right, Special Agent Tucker, you've convinced me to give you a chance. On one condition."

"What condition is that?"

"If at any time you suspect your cover is blown, or your gut warns you that something is off and they've turned on you, get out of there.

To hell with the case and the charges. Call Jack, get to the safe house, do whatever it takes to extract yourself from the situation."

"I appreciate your concern, sir, but it won't come to that. I'll see this through till the end."

"All right. We'll get your name, background, and criminal history established. Congratulations, Nick. You have the distinct honor of pledging to one of the most notorious motorcycle gangs in the world. The Devil's Dominion rules their LA territory with an iron fist. I only hope they don't turn that fist on you."

"Thank you, sir. I won't let you down."

~

Six Months Later

"Are you sure you're ready to approach them, Nick? No need to rush things." Jack paces in his kitchen while I sit at the table and finish my coffee.

Jack Collins fits the bill for a retired biker. He is a handler, but he's curated his entire life around the motorcycle club lifestyle to avoid arousing any suspicions. He hasn't pledged to any outfit, but he is known by enough bikers that no one questions his presence, and no one crosses him. He has the don't-fuck-with-me air down pat.

His long black and gray hair is pulled back in a low ponytail. His sun-weathered skin bears the ravages of years on the open road—the deep-set wrinkles, the sunspots, the year-round dark tan. His brown eyes are keen, assessing a man and his intentions with a quick glance. The skin on his hands matches his face, but his grip is as strong as a man half his age. The long span of his career gives him advantages others could only hope to attain one day.

"It's time, Jack. You're my handler, you know I'm ready, and you know that shit is escalating out there. My hair has grown out, along with my beard. All my ink is finished—nothing overly distinguish-able but still believable. My criminal background is airtight, and my stints in San Quentin and Pelican Bay legitimize my badass felon status."

"You can't use words like *legitimize* around these guys, Nick." Jack scrubs his hand down his face.

"I can talk real dumb too, Jack. Like I ain't got no schooling or nothing."

"Make fun of this all you want, Nick. But I'm telling you, these guys have a grittiness about them, a certain way they talk, a language all their own. It's a combination of the motorcycle gang lingo and prison slang."

"Trust me, I got this. I've mastered how they speak, the motorcycle gang terms, and the prison slang. I've memorized my background and rehearsed how I became a badass ex-convict, looking to join the baddest MC club around. One point that is pure genius on your part is showing I was part of a Tijuana-based gang before I was sent to prison. Thanks for that."

"Anything I can do to keep you from having to murder someone as part of your initiation. Because that's what they usually require—and could still order you to do it. But we'll cross that bridge when we have to. If you can patch in, you won't have to do the lowly probie bullshit. That'll at least give you a leg up in earning their trust and working your way up the chain faster than most.

"If you have to improvise and add anything to your history, don't forget to tell me immediately. We can build your experience around whatever you need, but it could take a little time to get it on paper. And don't say gang. You know how one-percenters feel about that word."

"Striking the word gang from my vocabulary now. And I'll try to keep the improvisation to a minimum, but I'm sure it'll come up. My documented history is solid, but that doesn't account for the things I never got caught doing. If you happen to have any former gang members in your back pocket, that would be useful too."

"I'll see what I can do. You never know, this old dog may still have a few tricks you don't know about."

One thing about Jack Collins, he always has another trick up his sleeve no one else knows about. How he stayed one step ahead of the agents under his charge when he went weeks without hearing from them is a mystery in our world. He takes his job home with him every night, and the safety of his agents is his first priority. I know I am in good hands.

"Thanks for the coffee. I'm heading back to my dinky little apartment to get into character. They're having a party at their clubhouse tomorrow night, so I'll use that opportunity to make my presence known."

"Good luck, kid. Don't die."

"That's the nicest thing you've ever said to me, Jack." I smile over my shoulder as I leave his bachelor pad and climb onto my bike.

My new life waits for me, in the gritty, dirty underbelly of the criminal world. Getting the approval for this level of undercover work is a boost to my ego and a rush to my senses. The heightened danger, constantly surveilling my surroundings, and testing my ability to decipher friend from foe within a matter of seconds will take my career to the next level.

I feel as if I've found my purpose in life. Finally.

～

Major Mistakes
Savannah

THE WOMAN STARING AT ME LOOKS FAMILIAR, BUT I DON'T KNOW HER. Not anymore anyway. Her red hair is longer than when she was younger. Her deep green eyes hold so many secrets, ones she'll never tell. She's also much thinner than she used to be—a telltale sign of stress and depression settling in over the long haul. The sad fact is, I used to know her very well. But now she's only the outer shell of the vibrant, bubbly personality I remember from just a couple of years ago. The light in her eyes is dim now, barely perceptible even when I'm searching for it.

"When did this happen, exactly? How did I become *this* woman?"

I stare into the hollow green eyes reflected in the mirror, talking to myself. Again.

A loud bang on my apartment door abruptly ends my one-sided conversation. My heart drops, and a groan escapes from my throat. Dread covers me like a lead blanket. There's only one person that can be...the one person I really don't want to see, much less spend the evening around. But I don't have a choice. I'm trapped, like a frightened, timid animal in a cage.

After removing the door chain and unlocking the multiple bolts I had installed, the door swings open before I can even grab the knob.

"Why the fuck do you have the door locked like that? Who are you hiding in here?" Butch pushes past me, moving from one room to the next through my apartment as he searches for the invisible man.

"There's no one here except me. Just like last time. And the time before that. You know I always keep all the door locks in place when I'm here alone."

It's a phobia I have—an intense fear that drives me to check the locks several times before going to bed every night. He knows this about me, because he's complained about it every time he's stayed at my apartment. Thankfully, that hasn't happened in a very long time.

He stomps toward me in his heavy leather boots, the ones he wears every day because they best protect his feet and ankles while he's riding his motorcycle. It's strange how what I initially thought was intriguing, dangerous, and sexy about him when we met are the very traits that make me want to run away and start a new life somewhere else today.

I just haven't figured out how to get away from him yet.

"Pack all your shit. We're leaving."

"What?" I whirl around on my heel and stare at him, completely dumbfounded.

"We're moving. Prez is sending me and a couple of other guys to DC to induct a smaller club into ours. We have to try them out, see if they're worthy enough to wear the Devil's Dominion colors. This is my chance to show him I'm officer material and get on the voting ballot to move up in the club. I've been waiting years for this day."

The only thought in my mind is that my opportunity to get away from him is finally here. The day I've been waiting to come for far too long. There's no way I can move from LA to DC—they're at completely opposite ends of the country. Literally from one coast to the other. My entire life is here in LA, including my job and the few friends I had before I started seeing Butch.

Maybe my friends will take me back when I get rid of him.

"That's great news for you, Butch. I'm glad the president finally sees your potential in the club, and I hope they make you an officer soon. But I can't just up and move across country with you. My job is here—my entire career I've worked years to establish. I also have a lease on this apartment I can't just break."

I'm listing every logical reason I can think of, no matter how lame it will inevitably sound to him. He doesn't care about excuses—he only cares about results. More specifically, he only cares about the results he wants to see.

"Wouldn't that just fucking thrill you? Wouldn't you just love for me to go across the fucking country for the next six months and leave you here alone so you can fuck every swinging dick that crosses your path? Of course you're going with me, you stupid bitch. Who the fuck do you think is gonna drive the truck behind us and haul our shit across the country? All our stuff won't fit on our fucking bikes, you moron. Now, pack your shit like I said."

With his final command, he shoves me and slams my head into the wall, catching the edge of the doorframe with the full blunt force of the impact. Even with my eyes closed, I can feel the room spinning. Nausea settles into my gut and the bile churns, threatening to work its way up my throat. The pain in my skull makes me whimper. His only reply is a disgusted huff.

"Now, rent the fucking moving truck, pack your shit, and let's go to DC before I'm too old to ride my damn bike anymore."

After I hear the door open, he hurls one last threat at me. "If you even think of trying to get out of this, I'll kill every single person you love. All your fucking friends from the hospital. Your mom. Your sister. Try me, bitch. I dare you."

He stomps out, the chains on his boots and belt clinking with every step, growing fainter until I hear the engine of his bike roar to life. Funny, or not funny, how it reminds me so much of his own terrible roar. After he rides away, I open my eyes and gingerly move off the wall where he left me.

The door to my apartment is standing wide open.

He knows my paralyzing fear of leaving the door unlocked. Irrational or not, it's still there.

I want to rush to lock every bolt, but the first step in that direction reminds me of my head injury. The disorientation, nausea, and I are not new friends. With slow movements, I lift my hand to feel the goose egg forming behind my ear. I'm not even surprised to find blood on my fingers when I lower my arm again.

My walk to the door is slow as I calculate each step and how much farther I have to go. My chest is heaving from the building anxiety. When the door is finally locked—every bolt is secured and every chain is in place, my pounding heart slows enough so I can breathe normally again.

After I put a cold compress on the back of my head, I slide onto the couch and carefully lie back on the throw pillows. I waste a few minutes daydreaming about never leaving my apartment again, never unlocking the door again, while waiting for the throbbing in my head to subside. As often as I dream about this, I should've already found the master plan for leaving Butch in my dust.

Since nothing else I've tried so far has worked, I pick up my laptop and rent the moving van as the asshole commanded. A one-way trip to Washington, DC coming up, sans the excitement a cross-country trip should elicit. The only way I can describe how I feel about what I just did is I'm positive I've just signed my own death certificate.

In fact, the longer I'm around Butch, the more I realize that outcome is inevitable—it's only a matter of time. The odds there will come a day when it's him or me increase with our every encounter. I let my eyes drift up to the ceiling, staring at nothing in particular while thinking about my situation. My job as an emergency room nurse is stressful and adrenaline-filled, but it pales in comparison to a single interaction with Butch. In an ironic twist, I would be required by law to report potential domestic abuse if one of my patients presented with the same signs I bear.

He wasn't always like this. When I first met him, the tall, muscular, brooding man was much sexier. His brown hair was longer than other men I'd dated before, but it gave him an edgier appearance. Eyes so brown they're almost black sparkled with playfulness and teasing. But it was all a charade—he was pretending to be someone he wasn't. And he was so good at it for so long—long enough to ensure I fell for him. Long enough to ensure I was caught in his trap. When I look at him now, all I see is the ugliness inside. Any desire that once burned for him has long been doused.

Thankfully, those nights with him have dwindled to an occasional visit—and only when he needs me to do something for him. He disappeared for a couple of weeks one time, and I thought he'd found someone else to prey upon. Selfishly, I hoped he had—but then I immediately felt bad for wishing him on anyone else. Unfortunately, one day, he simply walked back into my apartment as if he'd been here all along. No explanation. No questions.

His visits have been sporadic since that day. Usually when he's drunk and looking for somewhere to crash after a night out with his friends. He passes out in my bed, and I sleep on the couch, unable to stand being in the same room with him any longer than absolutely necessary. His insane jealousy makes no sense to me whatsoever. We are not a couple and haven't been for a very long time, yet he calls me every name in the book when he accuses me of seeing other men.

Not that I'm the least bit interested in even trying to date. I still can't get rid of the last mistake I made.

Now he shows up and demands I move across the country with him. I'm having a hard time wrapping my head around this one. It's not like either of us wants to be with the other. That much is clear. But I believe he'll make good on his threat to kill everyone I love. In fact, I have no doubt he will.

One problem at a time, though. Before we even reach the East

Coast, I have to survive the actual 3,000-mile trip with him and his buddies. That should be fun—waiting for them to pass out on the bed from the abundance of drugs and alcohol so I can grab the extra linens and sleep on the nasty floor. But I prefer the floor over touching any of them. Maybe I'll sleep in the truck...with the doors locked...under the guise of protecting our belongings.

A few hours later when I walk into the hospital for the night shift, my heart is heavy, and all my feelings show on my face. My coworker takes one look at me, and her face falls.

"What has Butch done now?" Stella puts her hands on her hips and draws in a deep breath. She already knows she won't like the answer.

After explaining the series of events and the commandment Butch issued, I watch her face for the disappointment I know will come. On one hand, I completely understand it, and I was even the same way...before I became the abused and battered victim. Life is now divided into two sections: BB and AB. Before Butch and After Butch.

Before Butch, I said no man would ever lay a hand on me and live to tell about it.

No man would ever abuse me in any way—physically, mentally, or verbally. I would leave him in a heartbeat.

No man would replace my job, my dreams, or my friends—the sacred relationships I'd always held so dear.

After Butch, I withdrew from my friends.

My dreams took a back seat.

Self-esteem was what others had, but not me.

I miss the Before Butch version of myself. But now I feel as if I'm in too deep and can't claw my way out. One thing I've realized after looking back over the past eighteen months is none of this happened suddenly. He chipped away at the very core of me little by little, bit by bit, day by day. Until the very spark that made me *me* disappeared. And I allowed him to do it.

It's my fault.

If I'd been stronger, smarter, faster...maybe I would've seen the warning signs for what they really were.

Huge signs that flashed "Bridge Out Ahead."

But his apologies were so sincere at first. So heartfelt. He was remorseful and promised those bad things would never happen again.

He'd drunk too much. He always liked to fight when he drank. Such a man's man.

He was under too much stress. Work was a constant sore spot. His coworkers or his boss never liked him. They always made up a reason to get rid of him.

Of course, that was before I found out the truth about him. Before I understood what being in a one-percenter motorcycle club really meant. When I made the mistake of calling his club a gang during a heated argument, I saw stars after he backhanded me for disrespecting his brothers.

That was the day the apologies stopped and the real threats began. Old ladies didn't leave bona fide club members. Ever. It wasn't the woman's decision whether to stay or go. She just did what she was told and lived with what she got. He warned me to be glad I wasn't a sheep—one of the women they pass around to each other indiscriminately, using at will for any hedonistic pleasure they wanted to indulge in at the moment.

Ignoring the pleas and concern in Stella's eyes, I continue updating her on my plans. "I'm turning in my two-week notice tonight. That date was the earliest I could get a moving truck big enough for my stuff plus theirs anyway. I'm so glad it has a towing hitch for my car too."

I leave Stella, disappointed expression and all, to start my rounds and focus on the emergency cases. I wish I could stop time so my shift would never end. But working in busy emergency rooms always makes the time go by faster than the slower pace, comparatively, on the medical-surgical floors. Before I know it, the sun rises and a new day dawns, and I have to face the unpleasantness of packing all my belongings.

Two weeks will pass in the blink of an eye.

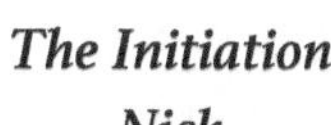

The Initiation
Nick

"YOU READY FOR TONIGHT?" JACK'S SERIOUS EXPRESSION GIVES AWAY HIS thoughts. Unusual for him after the years of handling undercover officers.

"I'm as ready as I'll ever be." I slide my arm into my cut and complete the persona of Renegade.

Turns out, the idea to convince them I was part of a Tijuana-based club was a stroke of genius on Jack's part. The Devils' ties to the Mexican cartel are already in place, but with my joining them, the full backing of the cartel is implied, giving them more muscle than they already have. An ATF agent has been working a few members of that gang over the last several years, so interagency cooperation kicked in, and my alibi was instantly airtight. With my background in prison and ties to the Mexican cartel-sanctioned motorcycle club firmly in place, I approached the Devils with an offer they couldn't refuse.

The Devils' already long reach just increased with no effort on their part. At least as far as their reputation with rival clubs is concerned. Keeping those other clubs at arm's length while the Devils conduct business is vital to maintaining their dominance in the territory. When the club president realized the possibilities I could bring, the dollar signs in his eyes were so bright, they rivaled the neon signs of the Vegas strip.

Headbanger, also known as Bobby Blalock, is the club president. He has a rap sheet longer than my leg, along with countless other crimes he's never been charged with committing. Or ordering. His officers and many other members are all too eager to carry out plans on his behalf. They're brothers in colors, but they're also all vying for the attention of one man. The one who can make or break them in the club.

Tonight is initiation for a few new prospects who are on their way to becoming full patch members. The ceremony to patch in is a big deal to these guys—it seals their identity and their place in the family.

I've been riding with the Devils for the past two weeks. Hanging out with them in the clubhouse provides a completely unique perspective on the inner workings of a notorious outlaw gang. Some of the guys have done hard time, and it's a miracle most aren't still in prison. I've had to bite my tongue way too many times already—something my director knew about me before he approved the assignment.

My moral compass always points due north. Always.

Their skewed sense of right and wrong doesn't mesh well with me. In fact, we're like oil and water at the very core. The only peace I have is when we're on the open road, the wind whipping around me, and the road rushing by under my wheels. The sense of freedom on a motorcycle is the sole only thing I have in common with these guys. It's the only time we're even remotely on the same page.

The long ride to the initiation grounds in the hot, arid desert of Southern California gives me time to get myself back into character. Jack stressed over and over how I have to be part of the group to avoid suspicion. Because of the high stakes, I've been given special clearance to break the laws I've sworn to uphold. But there are oaths I've taken, and I have no intention of reneging on them.

There are lines I refuse to cross.

There are rules I refuse to break—even for the greater good and the thrill of closing the case.

But I have to act like there are no lines I won't cross. To be convincing, I have to put Nick Tucker away and be Renegade to the bone. In my mind, I have to think of Renegade as a completely different person. It's the only way I can pull this off.

He's an ex-con, fresh out of a maximum-security prison, and that has to be my persona. As a convicted felon on parole, I can't legally cross the border to ride with my old club because the pigs will nab Renegade immediately. I can't exactly drive my motorcycle through the underground tunnels to cross the border. Of course, as Renegade, I have the contacts, so I could find an illegal way, like a fake passport or hidden in a caravan. But I'd take that risk only for a golden opportunity, a sure thing.

Renegade has talked a good game in his two weeks with the Devils. Tonight, Prez will present me with the final piece of my colors —the top rocker panel for my cut—because I scored the largest shipment of meth and negotiated the best deal for the club he's ever seen. Compliments of my DEA and ATF friends.

When I finally roll up to their private hideaway in the desert, my Renegade character is in full swing. After grabbing a couple of beers from the cooler, I stroll over to where the officers are hanging out with a few of the lifers—the men who have been part of the club for so long, they aren't required to attend all church meetings and outings anymore, but they're every bit a part of the club as any other member. They can come and go as they please, though most stay more than they leave. This is the only life they know.

"Good of you to bring me a beer, Renegade." Axle reaches for one of the longneck bottles I'm carrying, so I hand it over without a fuss. He's one of the most respected lifers in the group. His experience combined with his naturally level head makes for a powerful ally in a group of trigger-happy thugs. Despite Axle's advanced age and lack of officer status, no man in this group wants to tangle with him.

"You know I always got your back, Ax."

"Back atcha, kid." He takes a long pull from the bottle but keeps his eyes locked on mine. "Heard about that big score you got for us. I'm impressed—and I don't impress easily. Good job."

"Appreciate it, man. Just glad I could help out."

"Well, well, look who's coming our way. The new prospects are here, and they brought their offerings to the Devils with them." Nutcrusher, the club vice president, stands and rubs his hands together, eager to get down to business.

When I glance over my shoulder at the approaching prospects, my stomach drops to my knees and my empty hand curls into a tight fist.

Their "offerings" are new sheep, women being shoved into the midst of the already rowdy scene. The three prospects are each forcing a woman to walk in front of them. The women alternate from stumbling ahead a few steps to digging their heels in to try to stop, only to be shoved from behind and start the process all over again. Their eyes are wide and full of fear. Their faces are tear-stained and their hair is disheveled—and not from the ride here since they arrived in the club van.

I'm positive these three women have already been used as offerings before the new patches ever brought them to meet the brothers. Before I consciously realize I'm moving, my feet develop a mind of their own and take a step forward. Then I feel a hand on my shoulder, holding me back.

"What you see tonight will test your mettle, boy. You've never been around anything like this, I can already tell. But I guarantee, if you blow your cover now, you'll never see anything at all, ever again."

Shocked by his words, I whip my head around and meet Axle's knowing gaze.

"Use it, kid. Use everything you have to see and do as a member to take them down. As shitty as it sounds, you can't save these women and do what you came here to do at the same time. Keep your eyes on the end goal, son, and make them pay for their crimes when it's all said and done."

"What are you talking about, Axle?" He knows. We both know he knows. But I'll be damned if I'll blow my own cover.

"I'm CIA, Nick Tucker from the DEA family. I've been on this case for a long time, waiting for my foreign target to make his move so I can take him down. I told you, I got your back."

"The CIA can't operate on US soil, Ax. Everyone knows that."

His grin resembles one connected to an inside joke. Everyone else is clueless, and one person holds all the aces in his hand. "Sure we don't. I'm on loan to whichever agency wants to take the credit for the bust when it goes down. If you're still here when it happens, maybe that'll be the DEA."

Before I can reply, the shrill shriek of a woman's scream combined with ripping fabric fills the air, making my guts churn with disgust. Any man who would lay a hand on a woman in anger or abuse is no man at all. He's a pussy who knows he couldn't stand toe-to-toe with a real man.

The crowd that gathers around the three women—to watch, to encourage, or to participate—are the worst of the underworld. Preying on the defenseless and taking advantage of those who are hanging on by a thread as it is.

"Come with me, Renegade. This is as good as this scene gets. It's all downhill from here, and I don't think you can stop yourself from intervening yet." Axle guides me away from the ruckus.

I can still hear their pleas to stop. Their screams that echo through the desert air. Their cries for someone to please help them... to make it stop.

But I do nothing.

What kind of man does that make me?

"When they finish with the girls, they'll take them back to the clubhouse, and the club doctor will patch them up. They'll use them as sheep, or they'll cycle them into the prostitution ring and run them on the streets. They're not easy on them, but they don't permanently damage them either. Headbanger has a strict rule on that part since it affects his cash flow."

"Axle, your explanation doesn't help me one fucking bit. Do you even hear yourself? Of course they're permanently damaged now. Maybe not in the way you meant, but they still are." He nods in understanding, and he knows he can't say much more to justify what we've witnessed. "Where did they get those girls? Did they kidnap them?"

"No. They pick up hitchhikers or strays. Bring them into the family. Give them food, a place to sleep, and the protection of a notorious motorcycle club. But they expect the girls to earn their keep one way or another. This may be the first time you've ever seen this, but it won't be the last. It won't even be the worst thing you've seen by the time your undercover operation ends."

The silence between us only seems to amplify the mixture of screams and catcalls behind us.

"Talk to me, Axle. Tell me about life in the CIA. Were you in the service? Anything, man. Talk about the fucking weather. I don't care."

"This gets easier, kid. You'll learn to compartmentalize shit like this. Picture those assholes in prison orange, enduring the same fate they're subjecting those girls to right now at the hands of a big, angry brute in their cell, where they have nowhere else to run. Then make that your end goal and sole mission in life. Find what gets you through the rough spots one day at a time. Your assignment will be over before you know it. Then you can put all this bullshit behind you."

I don't see that happening.

READ THE REST OF FINE LINE NOW!

You'll also find Nick Tucker in the Dominic Powers duet. Keep reading for a free sneak peek of Her Dom!

BLURRED LINE & HARD LINE ARE NOW AVAILABLE! SPEND MORE TIME WITH NICK, SILAS, AND ROMAN!

HER DOM

HER
Dom
DOMINIC POWERS SERIES BOOK ONE
USA Today Bestselling Author
A.D. JUSTICE

CHAPTER ONE

Today has been the day from hell. There's no other way to describe it but as the shittiest day in history. Well, in my history anyway. I am the Chief Executive Officer of my company, Dominic Powers Software, also known as DPS. We develop the software programs that run most of the other *Fortune 500* companies. The software engineers that are the backbone of my company are the best in the world. Recruiting globally from the top universities, we bring the talent to the office here in Dallas, Texas.

My problem is that I'm hiring a Personal Assistant and, so far, not *one* person has been qualified enough to even wipe my ass, much less be my right hand. My assistant must be able to make executive decisions when I'm not available, know what my expectations are, and have the gumption to carry out my orders with employees at all levels of my company. After endless interviews and countless yawns, I'm almost convinced the ideal candidate doesn't exist.

There are department leads for each of the major divisions. We also have a Vice President, Darren Hardy, but his main focus is being our Chief Financial Officer. He has no interest in making decisions that don't require number crunching. His recent revelation is the reason behind my current search through an endlessly disappointing applicant pool. My phone buzzes as my secretary, Dana, calls from her desk outside my office.

"Not another one, Dana. I can't deal with one more Ivy League graduate with no damn common sense," I say as a greeting.

"Mr. Powers, your four o'clock appointment is waiting to speak with you. Her name is Sophia Vasco," she responds professionally. However, since I know her so well, I can hear the motherly admonition in her voice. She won't allow me to be rude and brush off the last interview of the day and I love her for it. She's saved me from myself more than once.

"Do I *really* want to talk to this one, Dana?" I ask, genuinely interested in her opinion.

"I do believe so, sir," she replies and I can hear the smile in her voice.

"Give me five minutes then send her in, Dana. Thank you," I instruct before hanging up.

I rise and walk toward the fully stocked bar at the other end of my executive office. After pouring a tumbler of bourbon, I quickly down the amber liquid, enjoying the sweet burn as it flows down my throat. One more quick shot and I'm ready for the last interview of the day. This candidate better be good because I'm quickly losing faith in being able to find a good match.

The familiar, three-rap knock alerts me that Dana is at the door and I call for her to enter. Dana walks into my office and gives me a knowing smile. She's been with me since the very first day I was able to afford a secretary. In her later fifties, she is old enough to be my mother, but young enough to understand what I'm looking for in an assistant.

Her smile tells me she approves of this candidate. I straighten my stance and walk across my office toward her. Approaching them, my feet halt in mid-stride when the latest applicant steps out from behind Dana. Beautiful doesn't even *begin* to describe the lady standing before me. There's an unmistakable air of innocence about her, combined with a determination and steeliness that's evident in her perfectly straight stance.

She's unlike any woman I've ever seen before, especially in this cutthroat business. I've never been caught up in a woman to the point where I forget my own name, or what my purpose is, but she has me completely and utterly enthralled. Her long, reddish brown hair cascades over her shoulders with wavy curls scattered throughout. She's petite but her high heels provide just the right amount of lift to make her perfectly fit my six-foot height. As she looks down at the floor, her black eyelashes are fanned out across her cheeks. When she looks up at me from under her lashes, her deep brown eyes are full of both anticipation and trepidation.

When her eyes meet mine, my breath catches in my chest and I have to consciously keep from audibly gasping. My need for control kicks in and I feel my blood pressure returning to normal. There's something about this one that Dana obviously identified—she knows me all too well. Resuming my trek toward them, I remind myself of why she's here to see me. This is an interview for a job in my company, as my right hand, not as my paramour.

I strive to be the consummate professional at all times and somewhere my psyche chastises me for my momentary lapse. By appearances, she is young, inexperienced, and innocent. None of these are traits that I hold in high regard in any woman. Her beauty had momentarily stunned me, but now that I'm thinking with my business head, I know what needs to be done. Time to put her through the grueling interview process every employee of DPS has to face. We hire only the best and brightest here.

"Mr. Powers, this is Sophia Vasco. Miss Vasco," Dana says, emphasizing the *Miss* as a message to me, "this is the owner and CEO of DPS, Mr. Dominic Powers."

Sophia extends her hand while maintaining eye contact with me. Her boldness gives me an unexpected thrill and the front of my dress pants begins to become uncomfortable. I take her proffered hand and instantly feel the sizzle from the connection. Her handshake is firm, but her hands are soft, and my mind wanders to imagine how they would feel on me.

"It's nice to meet you, Mr. Powers. I've heard great things about DPS and I'm anxious to learn even more," she politely says.

I hear her words but I can't completely focus on them at the moment. The pitch of her voice is like silk and crushed velvet across my skin, simultaneously soothing my nerves and exciting my body. I'm still holding her hand, slowly moving in the normal handshake manner, but nothing seems normal about this meeting.

"Thank you for coming, Miss Vasco," I say, intentionally choosing my words just to observe her reaction. The timbre of my voice mirrors the one I use in more intimate settings. She doesn't disappoint me—the flush of pink in her neck quickly crawls up her cheeks as she lowers her eyes. A shy smile spreads across her face as she takes a moment to regain her composure.

Very interesting, indeed.

"Thank you for seeing me today, Mr. Powers. It's my pleasure to be here," she responds with a genuine smile that reaches her eyes. They sparkle with a hint of mischief and playfulness. I release her hand and have a sudden urge to grab it again.

There's something about her that causes my thoughts to stray from the task at hand. My momentary reclamation of my senses has passed, and I am once again thinking of the various things I would love to do to her. Things I'm positive she's never experienced before. At one point in my life, I would've been more than happy to teach her. In more recent times, I've been more than hesitant to even consider it.

"Thank you, Dana," I say, finally recognizing that my secretary is still present with us. She smiles that familiar smile–the one that tells me she thinks she knows exactly what I'm thinking but offers no input. I can say with all certainty that she has *no idea* what thoughts are really flying through my mind.

"Can I get you something to drink, Miss Vasco?" I ask after Dana has closed the door behind her.

"Please, call me Sophia. Just a glass of water, thank you."

"Very well, Sophia. Please have a seat and I will be right with you."

Walking back to the fully stocked bar, I feel her eyes watching me, sizing me up and trying to read me. I know she hasn't taken her seat yet because her back would be to me and I wouldn't feel her eyes on me, burning through me and creating a physical presence on my skin. She obviously thinks she has time to take me in before I finish making her drink. I'm letting her believe she can stare at me without getting caught, just to gauge her true reaction. Merely envisioning the imminent busted look on her face makes me smile.

Turning quickly, our eyes lock and her face heats to bright red after I catch her brazenly ogling me. "Do you want that water on the rocks, Sophia?"

The tone of my voice doesn't give away my delight but there is no doubt that my eyes betray me. The truth is I attract women most everywhere I go but I'm used to it by now. I am in no way conceited, but I know I'm a handsome man and I work hard to maintain my physical fitness. My personal trainer puts me through a grueling workout every morning, alternating weights and calisthenics, but it's paid off in ways most people have never considered.

"Um, whatever is easiest for you, Mr. Powers," she answers before she quickly takes her seat as I previously instructed. Her answer pleases me in ways that have nothing to do with business deals. That's the part that concerns me, however. I need someone who can be as ruthless in business as I am, who can represent me when I am otherwise engaged, and who can make the best decisions for my company.

I muse over this as I drop a few ice cubes into a tumbler and fill it with bottled water. My mind questions if she has enough backbone to stand up to the many executives I meet with on a daily basis. Executives of other *Fortune 500* companies who are accustomed to getting their way and having others jump at their command. Right or wrong, this is still very much a man's business world. Many business deals are brokered over a game of golf and a few stiff drinks. This tradition doesn't normally include women unless the executives specifically request to bring their wives along.

If she's trainable, she could be a formidable asset, though. They wouldn't see it coming from her and she would knock them off their game. Any weakness of theirs gives us the advantage in a negotiation. It's time for me to test her strengths and weaknesses by suddenly thrusting her into an uncomfortable and stressful situation. My interview process is unconventional in ways but effective as the company retention rate is excellent.

I watch the movement of Sophia's shoulders as her chest rises and falls with each breath. She's practicing a calming technique and preparing herself mentally for the difficult questions she knows are coming. Intently focused on her meditation, she doesn't hear me walk up behind her. Reaching over her to place the tumbler on my desk directly in front of her chair, I keep my voice low as I say, "Here's your water, Sophie."

She jumps slightly as my proximity startles her. Her eyes fly open and she inhales sharply—our faces are inches apart and her eyes flit to my mouth. She watches with baited breath as I intentionally lick my lips, her eyes tracking the movement of my tongue across my lips. Willingly or not, she can't deny that I affect her—the desire is there and I have but to ask and she would be mine.

Keeping my movements fluid, I quickly retreat from her space and walk around my desk. She clears her throat and takes a quick sip of water. "Sophia," she responds.

"Sorry?" I quiz, knowing exactly what she means. This is the first test. Is she too polite to correct a basic misunderstanding? Will she subjugate herself and give someone else the upper hand in her attempt to be nice, to not offend the other person? Or will she stand up for herself and tell me that I've misstated her name?

"My name is Sophia. I believe you said Sophie. I just wanted to make sure you knew so that you don't give the job to the wrong person," she explains amiably but pointedly. Score one point for *Sophia*.

"So it is, Sophia," I reply as I take my seat. "Easy question first. Tell me about yourself," I request as I lean back in my chair. This is actually a very telling question even though it's one of the least structured of the interview questions. The information this applicant chooses to disclose tells me where her true intentions lie. If she replies with personal information, it tells me that my business is not her main priority. If she replies with her business accomplishments, I know she's attuned to the needs of my business.

"I graduated from the University of Texas—double majoring in International Business and Management. Since graduation, I have worked in the software development field in increasingly responsible positions over the two years. My latest position was as a manager of a small team of software engineers. I was responsible for overseeing every aspect of a ten million dollar project with a *very* tight timeframe for completion and a high probability of failure. Under my leadership, the project was completed ahead of schedule, resulting in a bonus for the company *and* my team.

"While I have been successful in my current role, it is time that I expand my horizon, learn more and apply more of my skills and expertise. My current employer doesn't offer that opportunity and when I saw this position, I wanted to interview with you to determine if this is the right place for me."

Her enthusiasm and genuineness are obvious in the way she speaks, the tone and inflection of her voice, and in her mannerisms. But she doesn't show the desperation that so many applicants demonstrate. This question sets the tone for the entire interview and she hit the mark dead center. She focused on her education, her accomplishments, and the reason why she is interested in making a job change without automatically assuming that this job is a perfect fit for her. She understands that she is interviewing me just as much as I am interviewing her.

Impressive.

Throughout the rest of the interview, I learn so much more about Sophia and what makes her tick, what she likes, and her sense of humor. Even during a formal interview for a very high level position, she has managed to infuse her humor into it in a professional and genial way. I can't recall the last time I actually laughed during a formal interview or enjoyed it so much. My mind goes to the everyday tasks and plays through how the scenarios would change if I add her to the mix. The only downside I've been able to determine is that being in such close proximity to her for prolonged periods of time will be hell on my libido.

"As you know, this position works directly with me. If chosen, you would be my go-to person—that includes making business decisions when I'm not here, acting on my behalf, and taking responsibility for major interactions. I expect each task to be carried out to my strict instructions and I expect you to make the decisions *I* would make. That requires you to spend an extraordinary amount of time with me, learning my methods, vision, and long-term goals for the company. I have to be able to trust you *implicitly*. Do you foresee any problems with any of that?" I ask, holding her gaze with a burning intensity in my eyes and giving no room for her to break our eye contact.

"No, I have no problem with any part of those duties. I want to do the best I can possibly do for the company, for you and for myself. I would be honored to spend time with you, learning from you and perfecting my skills. I know there's a great deal I can learn under your guidance," she finishes and I'm glad my desk hides the lower half of my body from her view.

"If chosen, when can you start?"

"After a two-week notice. I wouldn't leave without giving them time to replace me, even if that's only on an interim basis."

I regard her for a moment, watching her as she waits for me to reply to her last statement. The truth is, I can't control my racing thoughts about late nights, early mornings, and out of town trips with the splendid beauty sitting across from me. None of my thoughts are what anyone would consider wholesome and I can't help but feel that I will ultimately lead her into temptation. I see myself as the serpent and I'm tempting her with the fruit of knowledge—knowledge of a life of which she has no clue. This life could very well be her unraveling, destroying her delicate nature and shattering her innocence.

The intense pull is too much for me to resist, even with my great arsenal of self-control techniques. The devil on my shoulder whispers to me, telling me to teach her everything she wants to learn. He says to let her be the guide and reassures me that Sophia will tell me when it gets too intense for her. He lies to me frequently and I can usually ignore him, but I have to admit to myself that this time I don't *want* to ignore him. I want to take him at his word and bring her neck deep into my world.

Giving her my best smile, the one that always works on the ladies, I watch the pink creep up her face again. I know she likes what she sees and it spurs me on in my plans for her. "I'm glad to hear that, Sophia. You're hired. Report here in two weeks at nine o'clock on Monday morning. Dana will get you set up with all the paperwork and then we will begin your training," I explain and finish my sentence in my head, *in more ways than one*.

Sophia stands, grasps my hand in hers, and says, "Thank you so much, Mr. Powers. I am very much looking forward to working with you and learning everything you want to teach me."

Score one point for Mr. Powers.

ABOUT THE AUTHOR

A.D. Justice is the USA Today bestselling author of the Steele Security Series (Wicked Games, Wicked Ties, Wicked Nights, Wicked Intentions, Wicked Shadows), the Crazy Series (Crazy Maybe, Crazy Baby), the Dominic Powers series (Her Dom, Her Dom's Lesson), the Immortal Obsessions series (Immortal Envy) and a few stand—alone romance novels, such as Saving Grace, Completely Captivated, Just One Summer, Envy, and Intent.

When she's not writing, she's spending time with her own alpha male character in their North Georgia mountain home. She is also an avid reader of romance novels, a master at procrastination, a chocolate sommelier, a twister of words, and speaks fluent sarcasm. An avid animal lover, A.D. Justice has two horses, three cats, and two very spoiled dogs.

While the primary focus of her books has been romantic suspense, she has expanded into different sub—genres of romance. Stay tuned to read what she has in store for you!

Connect with her online!

Newsletter
Facebook Reader Group
Website

facebook.com/adjusticeauthor

instagram.com/authoradjustice

bookbub.com/authors/a-d-justice

amazon.com/author/adjustice

pinterest.com/adjusticeauthor

BOOKS BY A.D. JUSTICE

Steele Security Series

Wicked Games (Book 1)

Wicked Ties (Book 2)

Wicked Nights (Book 3)

Wicked Intentions (Book 4)

Wicked Shadows (Book 5)

Crossing Lines Series

Fine Line

Blurred Line

Hard Line

The Vault Series

Warning Part One

Warning Part Two

Warning Part Three

The Crazy Series

Crazy Maybe (Book 1)

Crazy Baby (Book 2)

Crazy Love (Book 3, Free Short Story)

Dominic Powers Series

Her Dom (Book 1)

Her Dom's Lesson (Book 2)

Stand—alone Novels

Saving Grace

Completely Captivated

Intent

Mistletoe Not Required

Immortal Envy

Just One Summer

ACKNOWLEDGMENTS

Special thanks goes to –

Tabitha – my PA, you stand your ground and argue with me endlessly. I love that about you—I never doubt your true thoughts and feelings. Thank you for always being there for me!

Lisa Hollett, with Silently Correcting Your Grammar – my editor and my friend, thank you for all your help, the messages at all times of the day or night, and the margin notes that never fail to make me laugh.

Michelle Dare – you have been my truest friend and I appreciate you more than you'll never know. I love you, my friend!

My beta team – I want to thank each and every one of you for taking the time to read and provide your feedback, and for waiting oh-so-impatiently for Shadow's book. **Beth & Dana,** special thanks to you for urging me to kill off a main character!!!

Bloggers – I know how much work goes into what you do for free, to support others, to share the word of new releases and books you love. I just want you to know I appreciate you so much!

Readers – I am so grateful for each and every single one of you! Without your constant support and willingness to shout from the rooftops about your favorite books, none of these characters would have a chance to live, even for a moment, in this fictional world we love so much. From the bottom of my heart, thank you for everything!